W9-CAY-723

IMPOSSIBLE! A PLEISTOCENE PREDATOR ON THE LOOSE TODAY?

Band by band, the image began to appear on the laptop's small, grainy screen. He stared at it. Nothing but brush, part of his shoe. This one was from before he'd fully raised the camera.

He loaded the next.

What was that?

Through the obscuring screen of a thicket, he could clearly make out a clawed, scaly foot. Perfectly, he could see three toes. *And those claws.* The rest was just brush and palmetto.

He scrolled to the next. A mishmash of vegetation.

The next. Similar.

And then the fifth. He stared. This couldn't be. This was not possible.

"A dinosaur," he whispered. "*Jurassic Park,* for real."

"What Bob accomplishes here is to persuasively steep the reader in the mind-set of a pack animal's culture, ecology, and pecking order amid life-altering conflict and crisis, and he does so with straight-forward, yet always imaginative, efficiency. It's the unwavering intelligence, insight, and empathy for the feral intelligence and ferocity of his predatory creatures that places *The Flock* amid my fave reads of 2007. I read a lot of fiction, little of it sticking to the mental ribs, but *The Flock* delivered and will be one of those I revisit down the road, for sure. Give it a try, you won't be sorry!"

—Steve Bissette

Books by James Robert Smith

The Flock
The Clan (coming in 2011)

Published by Tom Doherty Associates

THE
FLOCK

JAMES ROBERT SMITH

A Tom Doherty Associates Book

New York

This is a work of fiction. All of the characters, organizations, and events portrayed in this novel are either products of the author's imagination or are used fictitiously.

THE FLOCK

Copyright © 2006 by James Robert Smith

The Flock was previously published in a hardcover edition by Five Star.

All rights reserved.

A Forge Book
Published by Tom Doherty Associates, LLC
175 Fifth Avenue
New York, NY 10010

www.tor-forge.com

Forge® is a registered trademark of Tom Doherty Associates, LLC.

ISBN 978-0-7653-2801-4

First Forge Trade Paperback Edition: November 2010

Printed in the United States of America

0 9 8 7 6 5 4 3 2 1

For my sister, Nancy S. Kirk, for support

ACKNOWLEDGEMENTS

Professor Jon A. Baskin of Texas A&M University for information regarding the possible existence of *Titanis walleri* in more recent years of the Pleistocene.

I would also like to point out that when I wrote this novel, the Ivory-Billed Woodpecker was still listed as extinct and its survival was merely wishful thinking on the parts of wild-life enthusiasts.

CHAPTER
ONE

May 23, 1946

The Flock was out in the Sun. It had been a long time since they had moved in daylight. But this occasion required such a measure. They could not fail. Scattering in the tall grass, flashing between the longleaf pines, the Flock hunted.

Torelli had lost the wireless somewhere along the way. He wasn't sure of the exact location, but he suspected it had been when they had crossed the small creek about half a mile behind. He hadn't noticed, because that was where Bauman had been standing when one of those things had exploded from the brush. And before any of them could aim and fire, Bauman had gone down in a shower of blood.

The whole company had scattered after that, and Torelli had found himself afraid of being hit by the odd burp of one of the other soldiers' automatics. His men were firing blind, shooting into the brush and into the trees and at one another. He was certain that Rainey had cut down Wilson out of pure fear, in his crazy panic to just get the hell away from whatever it was that was chasing them.

What were they?

Finally, Torelli found himself alone. It had been almost half an hour since he'd seen anyone. After Bauman had gone down, he'd caught a glimpse of Hopkins, the colored guy who had been added to the company the week before. Hopkins had been screaming; firing his weapon at every bush he passed as he ran like a crazy man. Torelli would have been hit by one of Hopkins' bursts if he hadn't seen where the guy was aiming and eaten dust. Soon after, he had gotten up and run again, racing across those weird grasslands with the palmettos and Spanish bayonet sticking up here and there among the pines. That had been Torelli's last contact with his company. He was sure those final screams had been Hopkins.

It had been a brief sound.

Now, he was more worried than when the company had first encountered those things. If there weren't anyone else to chase, they'd be after him, now. Torelli had glimpsed them. He'd never seen anything so big—not outside of a zoo. The largest ones were half again as tall as he was. And they were so *fast*. Jesus, he'd never imagined *any*thing could move like that. Ralph Weiss, who'd just been made corporal, had been a sprinter at the University of Tennessee, and he'd been run down and *stepped on* as if he were sitting still. Torelli had watched, frozen, as the thing had stooped, its upper body vanishing in the grass, and had raised its bloodstained head holding a good portion of Ralph's torso.

Stopping, peering at the tall prairie grass that shivered in the slight, Florida wind, Torelli was very afraid. He crouched, thinking that perhaps they hunted by movement and if he was out of sight, they couldn't find him, for a while, at least. But there were so many of them. When the company had first started retreating, the things had spread out, like a well-trained platoon, cutting his squad into commander-less sections that could be taken down one by one. They were smart; that was certain.

Torelli got hold of his panic. He was a lieutenant in the United States Army. He was *not* going to let some kind of *animal* outsmart him. His men had panicked. They hadn't *listened* to him. They'd been undisciplined. It was all Jenkins' fault. If that idiot had listened to him, had stayed away from that bit of red in the brush . . .

Torelli hadn't seen what Jenkins had seen, but he felt certain it had been one of their babies, several, perhaps. Because Jenkins had shot at whatever it was, and after that the madness had cut loose. The woods had *swarmed* with them. You wouldn't think so many animals *that big* could have been all around them like that. Not and remained unseen. But they had.

He crouched down a little closer to the ground and tried to organize his thoughts. The teams were supposed to cross to the north side of the base and rendezvous with the D Company. He'd had the maps, and knew what route they were going to take. They'd been advised to steer east of the savanna that lay between the starting point and the rendezvous. Captain Stevens didn't know that part of the base that well (*nobody did, apparently*), and he didn't want anyone under his command slogging through unmapped swampy terrain. They'd lost some men in the swamps on the south side of the base the year before and they didn't want that happening again. Now Torelli wondered if it had been just the swamp that had swallowed those men up.

The sun burned down on Torelli's head, baking his jet-black hair. He rubbed his hand over his close-shaven scalp. *Damn.* He hadn't even realized he'd lost his helmet. He pulled his gun tight to his bosom. *That* he still had, and he didn't plan on losing it. He wasn't going to panic like the others. When they came at him, he was going to fire steady, cold. He reached down with his left hand and made sure his

11

spare clips were handy. They'd eat his rounds before he'd let them kill him.

Mosquitoes hummed at his ears, and gnats made their maddening song at the corners of his eyes. Florida was for shit, he decided. If he could just get out of here, he wasn't ever coming back. He'd put in for a transfer to Alaska, by God. He'd go anywhere but bug-infested, hotbox, Florida.

And who would have bet on *monsters?* He had to stifle a laugh. He was cracking up. He had to be strong.

Torelli tried to remember where he was. He looked up, and figured he'd come about a mile west of the point where the company had come apart. If that was true, he was close to Aiken Creek, which emptied into Aiken Lake, which usually had half a dozen off-duty soldiers fishing out there or just lying around dozing with no sergeant to bother them. If he was careful, he could follow the creek down to the lake and yell for help, or commandeer a jeep if someone was there. He'd *swim,* if he had to, even though they'd all been briefed on the alligators that lived in the water on the base. The base was one of the few places left where you could see a gator; they'd been hunted out everywhere else.

He wondered who knew about these *things.* Someone *had* to know. Maybe they'd been sent out to *test* them, see how a couple of fire teams could stand up to them. If so, the things had passed with an almost perfect score: eleven men dead to none for them, unless Jenkins had killed a baby one. But *he* was still there. Anthony Torelli's boy was still kicking, and he was damned if some *animal* was going to take him down without a fight.

Well, he'd rested enough. It was time to move out. Aiken Creek couldn't be but a quarter mile or so away. That wasn't far. He could do that, easy. All he had to do was look and listen, and watch where he stepped. That was all. *Piece of cake.*

Slowly, Torelli stood.

He was in the middle of a grassy plain. The young man, born and raised in a Philadelphia row house neighborhood, didn't know that he was standing in the last upland longleaf savanna in Florida; all the rest of it had been cut down and plowed under and either planted in slash pines or had been paved over. This was the last, and it was a very strange thing to look at: primal. On a purely instinctive level, in something that tickled at some dim and faded racial memory, Torelli knew there was danger lurking out there, out in the tall grass.

Carefully, he took a step. Looked behind. Was intensely aware of what he picked up in his peripheral vision. He breathed slowly. Fear was in him, like a smoldering fire that threatened to flare into panic. He controlled it. Torelli took another step. From his right, he heard something. He tensed, bringing his gun up. Saw a gently sliding movement on the ground, in the grass. He breathed out a sigh as a long, brown water snake moved swiftly by like a living band of liquid. If the snake felt safe enough to move, maybe *Torelli* was safe.

He took another step.

But that snake had certainly been in a hurry. Torelli froze. He pivoted slowly, looking. The wind blew the tops of the grass so that it made patterns like breaking waves in the acres and acres around him. He was not alone. He felt it. If he was going to live, if he was ever going to make it to the lake, to the barracks, to a day when he would see his mom and dad and that Philadelphia neighborhood again, he was going to have to move and move *fast.*

Torelli broke into a run. The creek couldn't be more

than a quarter mile away. He could do that, easy. Just go. Don't think about Hopkins (*he'd screamed*) or Bauman (*his arms had been bitten right off*) or Jenkins (*run down like a rabbit*) or the others (*they were all dead*). Torelli bit his tongue and refused to scream. He bit down hard and tasted blood in his mouth. Someone was screaming; he heard it, but it wasn't him, it couldn't be him. It *was*, though. Torelli was running, screaming.

And something was behind him. It was going to catch him. It was going to *eat* him. He stopped, skidding in the sandy soil, drawing his gun to his shoulder, and he fired a long burst into whatever it was that pursued.

Into thin air.

Nothing was there.

The Italian kid stood in this ancient, forgotten land and gasped and moaned. Alone, he cried. And, crying, he turned back along his path and trotted toward the creek, not looking back again.

So he did not see them as they rose up from the tall grass where they'd been crouching. He did not see them lift their huge heads high above, their long legs taking them swiftly over and through the sea of grass. Only at the end, at the very end, as three adults struck at him with heads as large as those of a horse, did he suspect what was coming. The sensation was intense and painful, and mercifully brief.

The Flock consumed the men. They left nothing. Bodies were sliced into small pieces and swallowed up. Clothing, too. The guns and other metal bits were gathered together. Yellow and Brown and Egg Mother lifted up the men's metal things and carried them to the water where they let them sink. In time, the current would take the metal things down to the lake, into the swamp. There was nothing left but vague red stains in the grass and the brush. And Walks Backward took care of even these minor signs, as was his task.

Soon, there was only the grass again. There were only the things that *belonged* in the grass and in the trees and at the verge of the great pine and oak forest. There was only the Flock and all with whom they lived.

The danger of the men was gone.

The Flock would bed down for a few days and watch the young ones. It was good to watch the young ones. It felt *right* to see the future.

CHAPTER
TWO

May 10, 1999

Ron Riggs turned off the radio and rolled down the window of the new Ford pickup. The Department of the Interior had seen fit to purchase a whole fleet of these white trucks for their valiant Florida employees, and damned if they hadn't given Ron the one without air-conditioning. That was going to be *tres* wonderful when summer kicked in. He could imagine it now, the cab of that truck like so many cubic feet of hot, soggy cotton. This morning was cool, though, by mid-state standards. It had hit sixty-five degrees just before sunup and now it was closing in on eighty-two. And it wasn't even noon. So went another Florida late spring day.

He checked his side view mirror, and caught only the top of his head, sandy-brown hair running amok in the high-speed wind whipping in as he cruised down the interstate highway. He glanced for a second into his own eyes, and thought he could catch just the barest glimpse of his last full-blooded Seminole ancestor, three times removed.

Driving one-handed, he readjusted the mirror until he could spy the other cars dogging his ass. He'd lay money that half of the cars behind him were rentals, tourists running off to Universal or Disney World or Berg Brothers Studios of Florida. He shuddered, eyeing the piney woods whipping past, each tree a dark stick against the grass-and-palmetto backdrop that the Board of Tourism loved to promote.

It was partly because of one of those theme parks that he was out and about that moment. The Brothers Berg had basked for long enough in the popularity and wealth brought in by their family oriented films and their family oriented amusement park. Now they had gone and bought a big chunk of undeveloped land and had built what they were calling "the perfect American township." *Ooo la la and hokahey.* Ron couldn't wait to get there. He'd heard about it, but hadn't had the opportunity to cruise past and see what obscenity the Brethren were up to.

He sighed, looked again in the side view mirror and once more caught a glimpse of his sun-browned face, which quickly scowled at him as he realized the mirror had shifted out of position again. The damned thing was *brand new.* Oh. Great. He nudged the mirror with his left hand and made a mental note to tighten it up later.

A huge green sign ahead informed him that he was two miles from exit 117, which would take him to that perfect American village built from the ground up by Berg Brothers Studios of Florida. Its very name brought saccharine images to mind. His stomach did little flips at the very idea. It wasn't so much that Ron hated schmaltzy movies and false fronts; it was that he had grown to love his adopted state. When he'd come to Florida as a kid, there were still plenty of wide open spaces around. You could drive for miles down sandy roads and never see a soul. Just you and the birds and an occasional white-tailed deer. But now it seemed as if there was a shopping center cropping up every quarter mile or so, and all of those miles of piney woodlands were now subdivisions stretching off into infinity. He sighed.

He made the long, slow turn off the interstate and came to a halt at the top of the exit ramp. *Five miles to Salutations,* it read.

"Salutations," Ron muttered. And then, recalling the old children's book, "Saaaaaaaaaal-yew-taaaaaaaaay-shunz." In a high, keening voice. Such as that made by a tiny, friendly spider.

Looking both directions, the way his driving instructor had taught him back in high school, he made a right turn down the state road that shot like God's yardstick into the pines. This had been one of the last unspoiled tracts of land left in Florida, Ron knew. For decades it had been locked up within the borders of Edmunds Military Base and Bombing Range. He had to chuckle. While he and his pals had been complaining about Uncle Sam and his free enterprise cohorts raping the environment, the arbitrary lines that marked the edges of Edmunds had protected this important chunk of real estate. There had been rumors there were even some Ivory-Billed Woodpeckers out there. But he didn't believe it. The EPA had been in there, searching, and had found nothing out of the ordinary.

Most of the land was still untouched. Berg Brothers had bought only a fraction of it, so far. Enough to get their perfect little town off and running. But the rest of it was tied up in legal limbo—about 450,000 acres—partly because some environmental groups were lobbying against any further sales, and partly because of Vance Holcomb, a crazy billionaire who wanted to buy up the rest for himself. No one knew exactly why, but Ron sure would like to ask the rich eccentric.

Ahead, down that straight-as-an-arrow road, he watched

as a large animal appeared out of the forest, paused at the verge, and then leaped across the asphalt. *Deer*, Ron noted. Big one, too. Antler-less buck. By the time he got to where it had crossed, it was long gone and all he saw was the green pressing in all around him.

The singing mud tires of his new Ford pickup quickly gobbled the five miles up, and he slowed again and made a left into the entrance of Salutations, USA. Not Salutations, Florida. No. This was USA! He chuckled and keened out, "Saaaaaal-yew-TAY-shuuuuuuuuunz."

Stopping at the gate, he was surprised to hear the not too distant yelp of a dog. A dog that was obviously in a great deal of either pain, or panic. The Berg Brothers engineers built up the road on a tall berm, a wise move, for this part of the country could get plenty soggy. Each side of the four lanes had a wide, solid-looking shoulder covered with a manicured coat of Bermuda grass. Taking his foot off the accelerator, Ron coasted to a stop on the right, where a bike-and-foot path crossed the ditch on that side.

Over the idling of the motor he heard the dog yelping again. And then he could hear a human voice, joining in with that of the dog. There was cursing: a man's voice. Ron switched the motor off and climbed out.

He stood beside the truck, glanced once at the *U.S. Fish & Wildlife Service* painted on the door, and walked briskly around the back of the vehicle and started down the paved pathway. This was the outer edge of Salutations, what the company propaganda was calling "a natural greenway surrounding this pristine community." He'd read their spiel and had some detailed maps of the area in his truck. It seemed they were having trouble with prior residents, and that's what had brought him there. He took a few strides down the pathway, noticing as he did some of the vegetation around him. Even a cursory glance told him that several threatened plant species grew here. There was no way these bike paths should have been allowed.

The dog yelped again, and once more he heard a man cursing.

"Dammit! Hold *still,* dammit!"

Ron looked to his left, where the patch curved down toward an arm of the waterway that meandered into the forest. There were lily pads floating on the still surface, mirroring the action just beyond the pool.

"Hold *still!*" A paunchy man who appeared to be in his mid-fifties, dressed in white shorts, white short-sleeved shirt, white socks drawn almost up to his knees, and a pair of even whiter Nikes, seemed to flail madly at a silvery poodle that was bounding even more madly around his feet. The fellow's white porkpie hat was sitting at an odd slant on his balding scalp, and he was trying vainly to land a blow with his polished walking stick: solid oak, Ron realized. Attached to the dog's left foreleg was an impressive snake struggling vigorously against all odds.

Before Ron could announce his presence, the man finally landed a blow on the snake's thick body, a blow which was little more than a glancing thump that bounced off. Even if the strike had been aimed a little better, Ron knew it wouldn't have had much effect. This snake was a constrictor and heavily muscled. A healthy specimen, too, he noted—six feet, at least.

"Hey," Ron yelled. "Hey, there! You! Stop that."

The older man looked Ron's way, bringing his right hand up and knocking off the precariously perched hat. And Ron saw that the dog was tethered; the leash twisted around the man's left forearm and looped around the fellow's left ankle. He probably thought he was going to be bitten, too. A couple of long strides brought Ron up to the man and his frightened doggie.

"Hold still," Ron told him.

The man had drawn his walking stick back again, but held it there. "What are you going to do?" he asked, puffing out the words.

"Just hold still," Ron told him again, kneeling quickly and grasping the dog firmly by the nape of its neck. He reached around with his right hand and gripped the black snake tightly at the base of its jaws, applying a lot of pressure there. Quickly, the snake's jaws opened wide and Ron extricated the reptile's needlepoint teeth from the dog's flesh. The teeth were so fine that he spotted no blood as he pulled the snake free.

Standing, he let the snake loop itself around his right arm, and he chuckled in admiration at the strength the reptile displayed as it constricted, doing what it was born to do.

The man knelt and retrieved both dog and hat. The dog had begun to bark in anger at the black snake. "Prissy. Are you okay, girl? Is Prissy okay?" The man stared at Ron and his cold-blooded cargo. "Is it poisonous? Will she die?"

Ron smiled reassuringly at the transplanted Yankee. "No, sir. This is just a common black snake. They're pretty darned harmless, actually, unless you're a rat or a rabbit or something small."

"*Harmless?* I'd hardly call it harmless!" He pulled the twenty-pound poodle to his face and rubbed his nose in its neck. "Poor Prissy," he muttered.

"These guys are fine animals. An important part of the forest ecology around here." He indicated the pine and oak forest around them. "Their population fluctuates with that of the small game they hunt," he began, but noticed that the dog owner was scowling at him.

"I don't care about it. Are you going to kill it, now?"

"No, sir. Absolutely not. I'm going to release it." He took a couple of steps off the asphalt trail and into the woods, setting the snake down between a couple of palmetto bushes. It uncoiled from his arm and raced off into the underbrush. In a couple of seconds it was just another silent shadow in the trees.

He turned to see the man gaping at him. "Why didn't you kill it? I can't believe you did that! You let it *go*."

"They're completely harmless."

"You said that. Try to tell that to Prissy." He held the poodle out to Ron.

"They're harmless, Prissy," he said.

The man, his face red with either too much sun or the excitement of the day, gaped again. "You're a crazy man," he said.

"No, sir. Just with the Fish and Wildlife Service." And he turned and went back down the trail to his truck. Once there, he paused and looked back, seeing nothing but the now empty path and the forest. "By the way," he yelled. "You're *welcome*."

CHAPTER
THREE

As Ron continued on he was impressed with the beauty of the surrounding forests. It seemed ironic that this place, having been within the confines of the Edmunds Army Base and Bombing Range, had been spared the commercial exploitation of so much of the rest of the state. Certainly the military had been unkind to some of the property, but largely the forests and streams and wetlands had remained completely pristine. He thought again of the rumors that Ivory-Billed Woodpeckers were there, tucked away in the lower bottomlands. He personally doubted it, had passed it off as wishful thinking from some of the environmental activists who were trying to save the place.

But seeing another deer posing by the road, and spying the ever-present raccoons poking at the verge of the roadside waterway, he was ready to believe the improbable. The pines were thick and tall, the oaks sturdy and old, the cypress trees green and ancient. One never could tell, he supposed.

And then there was Salutations proper. He passed another of the old warning signs from the military days, before the recent round of base closings, and saw the garish yellow-on-white sign proclaiming Salutations, USA. Beneath those six-foot letters, somewhat smaller: Another Berg Brothers Production. Cartoon characters cavorted along the base of the sign, which formed a bridge over the roadway twenty feet overhead. He did an approximation of the voice of Sid the Squirrel. "Welcome Home, Everybody!"

There was a pair of guardhouses, yet another remnant of the base days. But, while they had been repainted and refitted with the latest in air-conditioning, there was no one manning either of the stations. Since this place was still what amounted to a gated community, he was surprised to find no one there, at least to hand out propaganda on what a wonderful and perfect place this was to live.

Salutations was spread before him, what there was of it, so far. He had to admit that if one was into the middle class ideal, this was certainly the place to be. The town was quite impressive. The Corporation engineers had laid the town out pretty much along the lines of the existing streets and structures of the old military base. Everything was there in almost perfect grids. Everywhere there were patches of grass and manicured shrubs. Even old-fashioned village greens right up front, a great white pagoda standing in the middle of that brilliant grass almost glowing in its limed and fertilized glory.

Off to the right was what was serving as a police station. The building was a sprawling, single story structure done up in red brick and white trim, pale shutters bordering the kind of windows one would expect to see on a house, rather than a police station. In fact, it was a private security firm, owned and operated by Berg Brothers Studios, that gave the citizens their sense of safety from the outside world. There was some debate already about how and when *real* police were going to be integrated into Salutations. Currently, the place didn't even have elected officials, but that was coming soon, since no other town was near enough to have incorporated these lands into its borders.

He drove on, passing the already thriving retail and entertainment district. The place looked busy with people, mainly young mothers, children in tow, and older women with silver hair and no one to fret over. He noticed a pair of competing groceries, the superstore types, and a small indoor mall took up most of a block. There was a sign for a cinema that was showing the latest films, including the newest Berg Brothers bomb that had ceased to show everywhere else save for the odd dollar cinema here and there. Ron admired the particularly long and tanned legs of a mom holding hands with her little blonde tyke, her short shorts giving a truly traffic-stopping view. He almost did run the next intersection and his tires barked quickly as he came to a stop. Even so, he watched the woman until she vanished into some kind of curio shop on the opposite corner. An older lady scowled at him from the parking lot of one of the groceries, and Ron felt a bit guilty. He would have tipped his hat at her if he'd been wearing one.

Taking a moment to refer to his street map, he looked at it, frowning at the parade of cartoon characters along the borders who smiled and pointed at various sights. "Harmony Way," he muttered. "Give me a break." He noted the address again: 100 West Harmony Way, and continued on, pressing the brightly colored map into the folds in the seat.

At the next intersection, he took a right. And there he was, right in front of Town Administration. The company men were keeping it neat and orderly until such time as the town voted to form their own government. He was sure they were looking forward to that. At least there was plenty of parking. He found a space well away from the building and got out. The temperature had already climbed another degree or two, and he paused just long enough to lower the windows a couple of inches on both sides of the cab. Once again he made a mental note to requisition a truck with air-conditioning.

The parking lot was busy with tourists, he noticed. It had seemed the way in was a road to nowhere, and he had seen no other vehicles coming in or going out along the way. But here they all were, Florida's combined curse and blessing: the tourists from points north. Everyone was a Yankee to a native Floridian. Overweight parents and their hamburger fatted broods went this way and that, going toward the curio shops and the enclosed mall and the theaters and the restaurants. Ron reckoned Salutations didn't really *need* any citizens to make this place work. The green oil from the tourists would probably lubricate the money machine just fine, thanks.

As he approached the red brick steps leading up to great, wide, whitewashed pine walls, the door opened and a tall, carefully groomed man in a neat suit came out. A wide face capped by a blond buzz cut beamed down. Although he was only standing two steps above, the fellow seemed to loom there, like a giant. Ron quickly decided the man stood at about six and a half feet, considerably taller than Ron. The big man's appropriately big hand shot out as Riggs came up the stairs.

"You must be Mr. Riggs from Fish and Wildlife." He took Ron's hand and squeezed it. Ron squeezed back.

"Yes, sir. And you're Andrew Dorkin?" Dorkin was the company executive who had first called the Service, touching base with those who could be either the company's friend or adversary, depending on the circumstances.

The big man smiled, a perfect grin in a tanned face, crow's-feet webbing out upon skin that had spent considerable time in the sun. "Oh, nonono. I'm Bill Tatum," he said, giving Ron's hand a final athletic squeeze and then releasing it. "I'm in charge of security here at Salutations. Have been since the studio broke ground two years ago." He smiled even more broadly and gazed around them. "This place was just the old base going to weed when I got here."

"I see," Ron said. "Well, I just assumed I'd be talking with Mr. Dorkin, since he's the one who's been speaking with the boys down at the office."

"Mr. Dorkin is very busy. I usually take up the slack in minor situations like this." He breathed in, seeming to enjoy the intake. In fact, the air was sweet, scented by the forest and wetlands that lay all about the town like a carefully painted picture.

Tatum was staring hard at something in the parking lot behind them, his smile fading ever so slightly, and Ron turned to see what it was. The expression on Tatum's face was that severe.

A smallish man was coming their way. He was dressed in rumpled khaki, a new digital camera hanging from his neck. Ron almost smiled at the way the man bounced their way, until he realized that his odd up and down gait was probably due to some old serious injury or, perhaps, a moderate birth defect. The guy was very thin, a dark brown beard artfully covering what was a generally chinless face. Coke bottle lenses expanded a pair of friendly eyes above a beak of a nose. And the whole picture was capped by what had to be one of the thickest and curliest heads of hair Ron had ever seen. Three pens of various types jutted out of that hair like a tribal decoration on some ancient Neanderthal. Once again Ron wanted to chuckle, but quickly noted that all vestige of Tatum's friendly demeanor had vanished as the goofball came their way.

Tatum spoke first. "Mr. Dodd. We keep telling you

there's no story here. And we can do without your kind of publicity."

The Dodd fellow came up the steps, and Ron had in mind that the three of them looked to be a mismatched set of progressively smaller figures. "Hello," he said, and extended his hand to Ron. Ron took it. "I'm Tim Dodd, with the *National Inquirer*. Down here to get the story on what's going on in paradise." He smiled a lopsided grin.

"Ron Riggs," Ron told him. "U.S. Fish and Wildlife Service."

Tatum cleared his throat and seemed to glare a message at Ron. Ron got the message, but lying to the press wasn't part of his job. At least not this one.

"Yes. I saw your truck," the reporter said. "What exactly is the problem around here, Mr. Riggs?"

"There *isn't* a *problem*," Tatum said. "Due to the outstanding status of most of the property surrounding Salutations USA, we are obliged by law to confer with various governmental and environmental agencies whenever the company wishes to make any kind of decision involving construction or modifications of almost any type."

"Modifications, eh? Is that what you call a hunting party to exterminate the local wildlife?"

Whatever of friendliness remained in Tatum's face vanished and was instantly replaced with something quite darker. "Mr. Dodd. I've warned you once. You can't *find* a story here, so you're just trying to *create* one."

"What story?" Ron asked.

"Don't you read the *Inquirer*? My column, 'In Dodd We Trust'?" Dodd looked indignant.

"Afraid not," Riggs told him, a grin cracking his face.

Dodd raised his thin arms in the air, as if asking the gods for a reason. "You're a deprived individual, Mr. Riggs.

28

Which is better than being depraved, eh Tatum?"

"This *is* private property, Dodd." Tatum ground out the words.

"Yes, it is, Mr. Tatum. But you don't really need or want the negative publicity of having me tossed out of here, do you? I know you've already discussed it in your various board meetings. So I'm just going to hang out until I dig up the truth. What do you say, Riggs? Want to cough it all up for me?"

Ron finally smiled at the little man. "I'm just here on minor business, actually. I'm going to scout the area here and see what kinds of populations the local forest currently serves as home. Nothing sinister or dramatic, I promise."

"What *kinds* of creatures, Mr. Riggs? Giant snakes, maybe?" Dodd stepped back and lifted the camera to his face. Before either of the other men could complain, he had at least two shots of them there in front of the security building.

"Stop that, Dodd. I mean it." Tatum was pointing at the reporter and was rewarded with having a shot taken of his menacing posture.

"You can't stop the Press, Tatum. You know that."

Tatum was at the end of his patience. He put his hand on Ron's shoulder and nudged him toward the door. "Let's go inside, shall we? Where we'll have some privacy."

Dodd called out to them as they went in. "Riggs. I'm at the Executive, down the street. Give me a ring or leave a message with the front desk. I'd like to talk to you."

And then Riggs and Tatum were inside, walking down a neat, pale yellow corridor with doors on each side leading into offices from which young secretaries and junior clerks emerged and vanished as the two men went toward an elevator at the end of the hall. Once in the elevator, Tatum breathed in, held it, then released, calming himself.

"Do you know what they've been calling Salutations in that rag he writes for?"

"Um. No. I have to say I don't read that paper."

"*Jurassic Park.* They're calling us *Jurassic Park.*"

Ron, in spite of himself, laughed. He looked guiltily up at Tatum. "I'm sorry. But you have to admit that it's funny."

"We have some trouble with alligators, a couple of people are snakebit. Next thing we see, the *National Inquirer* is calling us *Jurassic-freaking-Park* and claiming we've got a monster living in the forest around the town." Tatum squinted his eyes, an expression of exasperation, then seemed to recover a bit. "Sorry. But that guy gets on my nerves."

"No offense. I can see where you're coming from." Still, if Dodd was writing that stuff, he at least had a good sense of humor.

They came to the third floor. "This way," Tatum indicated with a wave of his arm. "The office up here has a truly impressive view of the area. You'll see." They went through a door at the end of the short hallway, and Ron noted that the third floor was much smaller than the two below it. He hadn't noticed from the parking lot.

As Tatum had promised, the office did afford an impressive view of the town and its environs through the wide window set in the north wall. The town's roads led into a residential area a few blocks north, then vanished at the forest that stood like a frozen green wave. Off in the distance, Ron could make out what looked to be a patch of longleaf pine savanna, a truly rare environment in America. To the left, and west of the town, he noticed a series of buildings that looked completely out of place, almost what appeared to be a fort of some kind, although a modern one.

"What is *that?*" Ron asked, pointing at those odd buildings.

Without turning to look, Tatum answered. "*That* is what we've taken to calling the Eyesore."

"Eyesore?" It did look terribly out of place, and was not characteristic of the rest of this carefully planned community.

"Holcomb's place. Vance Holcomb."

"Ah. I'd heard about the . . . *situation* with Holcomb."

"You'd think a man with a few billion dollars could find something better to do than sit out here and cause problems for this company. Pointless problems, too, I might add. Salutations USA is as concerned with protecting the environment as any other American organization. We've done our utmost to minimize the impact of modern living on the natural world around us." Tatum moved behind the big desk that sat facing away from the view. He indicated a padded leather chair for Riggs.

Both seated, Tatum continued.

"You know the drill," Tatum said, this time with a bit of coldness in his voice. "We've had several more dogs vanish. Mainly in Phase Three, eh," he turned and shrugged toward the houses that bled into the forest to the north, "over there."

"Has anyone seen anything?" Riggs stood and went to the window to look out at that neighborhood. Most of the forest was that same pine-oak mix. But there was that savanna area beyond it and past that he could see some truly impressive cypress trees rising up in wetlands beyond.

"Nothing. No one has even heard a dog struggling with anything. No yelps or barks. Dog there one minute, gone the next."

"I doubt it's a gator," Riggs said.

"Why do you say that?" Still seated, Tatum was looking in the same direction as Riggs.

"That area is too high and dry. No streams, no swampy area there. And you said some of the dogs vanished from fenced yards. Gators can dig like nobody's business, but you'd see the sign, of course. And that neighborhood's elevated, too. I'd almost call it a hill. What passes for a hill in this area. An alligator would have to be terribly hungry to go up there, and from what I can tell from looking around, and from the environmental impact statements I've read, there's plenty of food in the gator habitat to keep a sizable population well fed and in place. I think we can rule out alligators. So no need to call in one of our licensed trappers, just yet."

"Well, that's a relief. I'd hate to see Dodd take that one to town. Can you imagine what he'd write? And the last thing I'd want to see is a photo of some trapper hauling off another one of those big alligators in the bed of his truck. Christ. That last one was a fifteen-footer. Damned dinosaur was what it was. Ate *two* dogs, that one." He sighed, pinched the bridge of his nose. "What else, then?"

"Well. I won't know for sure until I check. One of the impact statements I read mentioned a panther track."

"Panther?"

"Florida panther. *Felis concolor floridanus*. Mountain lion. Cougar."

"Oh, Jesus."

"But I don't think so."

"Why not?"

"We're too far north, for one thing. There aren't but fifty or so of them left, and most of them live in or near the Everglades. Every once in a while one strays north, especially

32

since the Department began seeding the area with transplanted panthers from Texas, to beef up the bloodlines
because of inbreeding. But I don't think it's a panther.
They're very afraid of dogs. More likely to run from one
than eat one. Still, they do weigh over a hundred pounds,
and killing a dog wouldn't be that difficult for a healthy
panther.

"But, no. I think someone would have heard something.
At least one of the dogs in the neighborhood would have
caught wind of a panther. And there's been no sign of
struggle or of blood. I can't see a panther operating like
that. Nope. Doubt it's a panther."

"Then what?"

"Could be bear, I guess. But I'd rule that out for many
of the same reasons, although I *know* these woods have a
healthy bear population. A bear coming in to eat a dog
would just make more of a fuss, I think." Ron gazed off into
those woods, peering even beyond the longleaf savanna.

"Then there's coyotes. They've been known to lure dogs
out into the bush and then ambush them and eat them. But
I haven't seen any credible evidence that there are any coyotes in this part of the state.

"So . . . barring the dogs just wandering off into that wilderness and getting lost . . ."

"Yes?"

"I'd have to say a snake."

Tatum stood and took a few steps away from his desk.
"A *snake?* You mean, like Dodd is writing about? A giant
snake? Are you crazy?"

"Well, look at it this way. The dogs don't even raise an
alarm. They're in the yard one hour, gone the next. No one
sees anything or hears anything. No blood. No tracks. In
the past, people here in Florida have either lost large pet

snakes, or released them when they got too big to handle. Pythons, usually, but there are a couple of Anacondas on record as having been recaptured around the state. One near Big Springs State Park was a twenty-footer. It had been chowing down on the local dogs when it couldn't find enough raccoons to eat."

"Twenty feet? You're serious?"

"Yes, I am. I've read the reports about that one. They found it under a lady's house when her poodle started barking at something under there. A snake that big could eat a child, you know."

"Jesus." Tatum strode back to the desk and picked up the phone, then put it back down. "I guess we leave this up to you guys, then? Endangered or threatened species, right?"

"Actually, if it's an escaped large constrictor, we don't want it roaming free. It's a non-native species and not officially welcome here. But, yes, I'd like to take a look around, and we can recommend a specialist to trap it if we decide that's what the problem is."

"Well, that's a relief." The smile returned to Tatum's face. "So. When can you get started?"

CHAPTER
FOUR

Walks Backward laid his head in the cool shadows, sighed. The Scarlet had gone rogue and the rest of the Flock was in danger because of it.

Nearby, Egg Mother and Egg Father murmured to the young brood, telling the great stories of their ancestors. He raised his head a small distance and peered toward them. They were so well concealed that even he could not spot them. Quickly, though, he looked back the way they had come, the direction in which he lay, the way he always did, as was his task.

It was also his task to worry. For years he had worried about the Scarlet. It was not good that its coat was so different from the others. They lived in concealment and in safety because they could blend so well with the land in which they roamed. But not the Scarlet. His coloring did not allow him to vanish so completely as the rest of the Flock. But he had been born directly of the Egg Mother, and so it was not the place of Walks Backward to eliminate the threat by eating the Scarlet while he was still a hatchling. Not his place to act, only to worry.

But now the Scarlet was grown. And *how* he had grown. The Scarlet was much larger than any other member of the Flock. Larger even than Egg Father, heavier even than Walks Backward himself, who was heavier than all the others. Until now.

The Scarlet was not right, did not do things as they were to be done. In times past, this one should have made his move to take his place as foremost of the Flock. He should have learned to lead and to hide and to hunt, and to take a mate and be a father. But he did none of these things.

Instead, he had left the Flock, coming back only from time to time to stand and watch them from a distance. Walks Backward had spotted him a number of times, so easy to see, that ridiculous red mark revealed against the forest and field. Walks Backward suspected that the rogue was plotting to try to cull some of the females from the Flock, to form a new group. This would not do. There was not room here for two Flocks: they all, each of them, knew this fact.

The Man had left them this one place to live. Whether by design or by accident, none among them knew. But it was theirs, almost untouched for the life spans of two pairs of Egg Fathers. The humans sometimes had ventured in, and once, when Walks Backward had been a hatchling, the Flock had killed and eaten humans. But that was the only time they had met, Flock and Man. Man was everywhere beyond this place; in packs too numerous to comprehend. The Flock could not make a practice of competing with Man. This was common knowledge taught to the youngest hatchling. Everyone obeyed this rule and so the Flock bedded down in the Sun, hid well; only at night did they emerge to run and to hunt. This was the way things were supposed to be.

Except for the Scarlet. The rogue among them. He no longer acknowledged the first rules that had meant life for the Flock when so many in their stories became only that: stories. The rogue among them endangered all, and they were at a loss for a solution.

Walks Backward knew what should be done. The Scarlet should be hunted down, at night, and killed. It was the only way, but it was not his place to decide such. The Egg Father and Egg Mother only could decide an act of that magnitude. He sighed again and raised his head from the ground and peered, seeing with a perfect sight still strong after so much time. He was older than any other member of the Flock. He could recall things that were now only stories memorized in the songs of the others. But he had lived them. He had been so small when the men had attacked the nests, when the Flock had been forced to defend itself by tracking the men and killing them all. The Flock had had a most wise leader, then. One who had never made an error in judgment such as that made by this Egg Father. He trilled a note of discontent, and the hatchlings' lesson was interrupted. Without checking, he knew that Egg Father and Mother were looking his way, although he doubted they could find him.

He sighed again and peered out at the forest that had sustained them. Somewhere in the trees or at the lake or perhaps even in the open grasses, the Scarlet was moving, ignoring the ancient rules that had preserved the Flock for so long. Or maybe the mad one was even scouting at the edge of the forest where Man had built its crazy home, where numbers of them had invaded and taken a prime hunting area from the Flock. He hoped not. He hoped that even the stupid rogue would not make such an error.

But he had learned that to hope did no good at all.

CHAPTER
FIVE

Being an official with Fish & Wildlife, Riggs had the right to cross almost any boundary, public or private. But when Tatum put out the word that Riggs had the run of the town, it made things a bit easier. He didn't have to worry about some pesky security man with a private badge asking him what he was doing poking around a pump house or a sub-station.

He had spent that first day just driving around Salutations, getting the lay of the land. He had a knack for remembering something the first time he saw it, recalling locations and making the transition from map to the real thing, and back. In college he had almost always won the orienteering competitions he'd entered. *Ronny-on-the-spot,* they had called him.

Before getting the nod at the office for this assignment, Ron hadn't given this area much thought. He'd read the newspaper concerning the legal battle being waged between competing camps, each armed with their own lawyers trying to fight off the other. But now that he'd had a chance to look at the place, he could fully understand why so many people were willing to go to the mat for this land.

Except for the road leading in to what had been the Edmunds Military Base, the 400,000 acres here was one of the largest roadless areas in the state. It was probably only second to the Everglades National Park in that respect. As military bases went, the construction had been minimal. Most of the area had been used as a bombing range, and even since the 60s, most of the bombing had been done either with dummy ordnance or had merely been bombing runs with no real armaments used. The U.S. Armed Forces had inadvertently created a vast wilderness area.

Of course the wilderness aspect of the former base was now what was in contention among the varied parties. When it had been decommissioned and evacuated, the land had gone on the public auction block. The Berg Brothers group had stepped in and had snapped up the area that had been housing and ops for the base. Since it had already been inhabited, there was no need for environmental impact statements, and they had begun almost immediately with construction of Salutations, to quite a bit of fanfare. Ron had to admit that they had done a wonderful job in building their ideal fantasy town. There were already over five hundred families living there, and more houses were under construction.

The studio boys had even managed to lock down first refusal rights on an additional 50,000 acres, pending environmental impact statements. And that was when the proverbial shit had hit the fan.

It had taken only a few weeks before several environmental groups had taken to the courts and filed suits that were serving as staying actions on any further development beyond the couple of thousand or so acres the studio had bought outright. But they were not well funded, being environmental groups, and the big company was having no major problems in outflanking those suits.

The true monkey wrenches had come from two unexpected sources.

First and foremost, one Vance Holcomb was found to

have legal right to a one hundred-acre tract of land abutting that of the Salutations town limits. Concurrent with the groundbreaking of the town, he had begun construction of what the billionaire was calling a "research park," to be the nexus of a school for the study of the pristine environment of the land. With all of those dollars in assets to back him up, Holcomb was proving to be a greater bother than almost any other group vying for the status of the acreage.

The second cog breaker had been the appearance in court of Colonel Winston Grisham, U.S. Marines, retired. He was best known as a right wing extremist with widely publicized racist views, what amounted to a private army, and friends in the Florida legislature. He also owned a one thousand acre farm, which also lay cheek by jowl with projected expansion for Salutations. While a wealthy man, he was not in Vance Holcomb's money class, and his legal strengths had so far lay in the good ol' boys he chummed with in the state government. He'd become something of a thorn in the side of plans to expand Salutations. But he was also a thorn in the side of those who wanted to preserve the acreage as wilderness.

And that was the extent of Ron's knowledge of the current legal status of the almost half a million acres of roadless wilderness he now stood beside and peered into.

The sun was up and startlingly yellow in a clear blue sky about as dark and cloudless as any. Florida skies were the equal of any he'd seen, from the East Coast to Alaska. They rivaled those of the Big Sky country where he'd spent a year as an intern with the Park Service when he was just out of college. Rainy days scoured the air and the prevailing winds from the Atlantic or the Gulf brought in clean breezes. He enjoyed the skies here, most definitely.

He had parked his truck on the south end of Salutations,

near an unobtrusive electrical substation that was surrounded by a red brick wall eight feet tall capped with a cast
iron row of ornamental spikes. The station had been built
on a bed of crushed river rock, he'd noted, hauled in from
out of state. That was a very expensive setup for a small
substation. But the place reeked of money. He supposed the
average price of a home here was about $400,000.

Riggs looked back, down the street, as someone in a
Mercedes sedan drove by. A kid in the back seat waved at
him, and he waved a return greeting. He walked around the
side of the substation and followed a small path through the
grass that led off into the tall pines. There were sedges
growing here and there, brown in all of that greenery, and
the path took him through a field of a type of grass he
couldn't identify. But botany wasn't his strong suit. He
bent and tugged on a tuft and put the stuff in a plastic
baggy he drew out of his pocket. He'd let one of the guys
back in town have a look at it. Might be endangered or
threatened. Wouldn't hurt to check.

Stuffing the sealed bag back into his pocket, he continued down the path. It was possible humans made the
path, but he suspected it was more likely a deer trail. Apparently some of the deer were coming into the new neighborhoods and eating the shrubbery and whatever garden
vegetables some of the housewives and retirees were
planting. Tatum had admitted that a couple of the residents
had shot at deer, once successfully. Ron told him that he
wouldn't call the game warden, but asked that Tatum in-
form the shooter that the act was illegal.

The sun was tilting up toward its high point in the sky.
He looked back through the grasses and through the trees.
There was no sign of anything not put down by Mother
Nature. Just trees and palmettos. He calculated he'd hoofed

half a mile, maybe a shade more. The vegetation and the breezes swallowed up even the sounds of any passing cars. Some quail called off to his right. He smiled.

Ron supposed that a big snake might follow a path such as this one. He had touched up his knowledge concerning big constrictors and knew that they would cruise game trails looking for a place to waylay their victims. Deer were a bit out of their league, but other animals could use a deer trail, too. He suspected that raccoons and opossum were probably the main prey of any introduced python or anaconda. But considering the size of some snakes, there weren't many animals out of the question for their menu.

Soon he was two miles out from where he'd parked the truck. He'd seen a Pileated Woodpecker on a tall, dead pine ten yards to the left of the deer trail. Ron knew that bird watchers sometimes made the mistake of identifying the Pileated as one of the extinct Ivory-Bills. Hopeful thinking on the part of novice bird lovers, he suspected. Every so often he heard tales that there might still be a pocket of Ivory-Billed Woodpeckers living here or there, but he knew it was just hopes and wishes. He was convinced they were all gone. It was a good thing that the dead snags and dying trees here were left to stand and fall on their own. Some birds preferred to feed on the insects that lived in such trees, refusing to dine on the trunk if it was on the ground. If ever there was a place to find a lost Ivory-Bill, he supposed this was it.

The trail had branched a couple of times, but Ron had kept to the main one, which led southward. A dog might use such a trail to snoop around, checking out the nearby forests. Dogs would be quite edible where a big snake was concerned. Alligators loved them, and that was for certain. Ron had lost count of the number of dogs that were taken by gators every year; it was a common occurrence, and he knew that a resident construction worker had lost at least a pair of dogs to a gator before the place had opened to the public. Apparently, that had pretty much started Dodd's Jurassic Park articles. Ron hadn't seen the reporter since that brief meeting on the steps of the administrative building, and he wondered if the man had gone back to home base.

He was about two and a half miles out when he came to the longleaf savanna he'd spotted from Tatum's office. There was a line of mixed oaks and pines, and suddenly he was out on a wide plain interspersed with longleaf pines, a species mostly gone from Florida, pushed out by the planting of slash pines and other more commercial types. He'd read about such environments, but had never seen one this large. This one was almost a mile square and he was tempted to hike across, just to see what it was like. The trail led out a ways, and just vanished in all of the low grasses and Spanish bayonet. This was a type of forest and grassland that had once dominated vast areas of the Gulf and low country of the East Coast. But now it was reduced to small pockets here and there.

Standing in it, viewing the wide, open country, the pines tall and strong amidst the fields, he understood why groups would vie to own or protect it all. Despite the fact that he was supposed to remain officially neutral about these things, he found himself hoping that no one would be allowed to harm this area in any way.

He smiled. At one time, this kind of country would have been prime hunting area for a large constrictor. This would be perfect habitat for such an animal. Which threw his thoughts back to the job he was there to do.

The only thing that was bothering Ron about the possibility of a python being the culprit of the missing dogs was the time between the disappearances. In the past ten days, four dogs had vanished. Having spoken to owners of the missing dogs, he was aware that only one of the pets had weighed less than twenty pounds. One had been a full-grown Airedale terrier. That dog alone would be enough food mass for even a big snake to sleep off for several weeks.

So why would it take four dogs? The probability that there were more than two large snakes here wasn't even worth considering. Of course, he supposed, stranger things had happened.

Taking his small daypack off, he laid it at the base of a big pine tree and sat down, his back against the tall trunk. He looked up, watched the needles undulating in the breeze. Despite the warmth of the day, he felt comfortable out there, and the wind had chased away whatever biting bugs were about. The thought of taking out the camera and snapping a few shots occurred to him, but he decided it would be better to eat a sandwich and get back to Salutations to start scouting around. After all, if there really were a snake, he'd be better off looking under someone's house than off in the wilderness. He reached into the pack and began to rummage for the roast beef on sourdough he had prepared. The thought of tangy deli mustard had him salivating.

Almost, he didn't catch the rustle of moving grass over the small noises his hand was making in the recesses of his little backpack. Ron froze.

Holding his breath, he looked around. Overhead, a Snail Kite streaked across the sky. Even alert as he was, he made a mental note to mention that one to the boys back at home base. Snail Kites were definitely an endangered species. He stared across the savanna, trying to pinpoint the location of the sound. There was only wind whispering through pine needles.

And then it came again.

Whatever it was, it was out in the savanna, maybe a hundred feet away, and it seemed to be coming toward him. He stared, squinting, and finally saw a movement out in the sedges. A tall figure was moving his way, almost a beeline right toward him. He held silent until he could identify it.

It stopped. All he could see was something light colored standing behind a tuft of bear grass. And then it was moving toward him again. Suddenly, it appeared from out of the tall grasses.

"Hello," she called in a husky voice.

Ron breathed out, relieved and wondering why he had been so tense. There really wasn't anything out there likely to be a danger to him. He felt relatively certain he could outrun a big snake. He laughed nervously, low in his chest, before he stood.

"Hey," he replied. The girl was moving his way quickly. She, too, had a small daypack on her back. She was wearing khaki cotton pants and a long-sleeved shirt of similar color, a kerchief of muted green around her neck. She had short brown hair, and she was very tall.

And she was quite pretty, he noticed as she walked up to greet him, her own hand outstretched to take his. Her grip was strong, stronger than he had expected. He had to look up to meet her eyes: she was six feet tall, at least.

"So. You're with Fish and Wildlife." Her gaze was on the patch on his right shoulder.

"Yes," he needlessly replied. "Out here scouting around today."

"You guys thinking of updating those preliminary impact reports you did? Those really sucked, you know. I almost thought you fellows were working for the studio." She was shedding her own pack, revealing a great dark stain down her back. Ron realized she had been out on the savanna for some time, and he wondered how she had spotted him.

"No. I'm not here for anything like that. That's not my gig. They have other boys at the office for that type of thing. I'm more of a Jack-of-all-trades with the department. PR, informational talks, that kind of thing." He indicated his tree. "Have a seat. Plenty of room. Name's Ron, by the way. Ron Riggs."

"Sure. I think I will have a seat. Lunchtime, anyway. Thanks." She tossed her pack next to his and sat, her long legs extending out before her, back against the tree much as Ron had been sitting before she'd arrived. "My name's Kate Kwitney. I was hoping your bunch'd do another impact statement. As I said . . ."

"The last one sucked," he finished. She smiled at him. "Yeah, I read it, too. I thought it was somewhat superficial to say the least. Hell. I just saw a Snail Kite zipping across the sky here. There was no mention, at all, of Snail Kites in the report." He was sitting next to her, getting his sandwich and searching for his water bottle.

"Christ. You have no idea," she told him as she retrieved a bag of dried fruit. "Why, we've identified ninety-three threatened or endangered species living within three miles of here. And that's just birds, mammals, and reptiles. We're not even talking plant species, amphibians, or fish. Botany and ichthyology aren't my line, mind you, but I know a bit. We have a couple guys working on those."

"*We?* Who are you with?" Ron sat there, his sandwich poised.

"Oh. Sorry," she told him, working the words around a mouthful of dried apples and apricots. "I work for Holcomb. Vance Holcomb. You know who he is, right?"

"Yes. Yes, I do. He's fighting Berg Brothers tooth and nail over this old bombing range. How's that going, by the way?"

She stopped chewing, and Ron looked at her as she stared off into the savanna. Her blue-green eyes were terribly pretty, he thought. So was the rest of her. "Well, you know Vance is an extremely wealthy man. A billionaire. His fortune is certainly hefty enough to give anyone pause. However, even he can't successfully fight a corporation like Berg Brothers. Them and their damned town." She scowled at something he couldn't see, but could imagine.

"Saaaaaaaal-yew-taaaaaaaaaaay-shunz," Ron squeaked.

Kate looked at him, and she laughed, showing a lot of straight, white teeth. He laughed along with her.

"What are you doing?" she asked him. "I mean, after lunch." She reached into her bag and came out with another handful of fruit.

"Just heading back to my truck. Why?"

"Would you like to come back to the compound?"

"Compound?"

"Holcomb's place. The research center."

"The Eyesore!"

She laughed again, and Ron found himself liking her.

"Yes. The Eyesore. We hear that one a lot. You'd be surprised at the glares I get when I go into the market in Salutations and someone recognizes me as one of Holcomb's people." She sighed. "But I'm used to that from way back. Anyway . . . you want to come back with me? Vance might want to talk to you."

Ron finally took a bite of his sandwich and chewed, thinking. "Hell. Why not? I've never met a billionaire."

"Billion and a half," she corrected.

"Wow. I'm impressed. Sure. I'll come."

As Ron sat and ate his lunch, Kate began to run down her list of ninety-three endangered and threatened species living in the area. He listened, giving her his undivided attention.

And they were not aware of a brief flash of scarlet that glimmered behind them, off in the trees, and then was gone.

CHAPTER
SIX

Damn it, he was lost.

Tim Dodd was a pretty good reporter. The editors had really liked his work covering the lost doggies and the snakebite victims and the alligator problems at Salutations. So he had figured he'd find something else to crow about if he followed the officer who had been sent over by Fish & Wildlife. There was nothing to it, really. Just park a quarter mile away and wait until the guy walked off into the woods. And then get out and follow him. At worst, he'd be good for a few photos and some Q & A.

Dodd had been pretty sure the guy had gone down a foot trail that led off into the woods. In fact, he had watched him take the trail past that brick enclosure with all of the electrical doodads inside of it. Following at a discreet distance was something he did well, so he faded back a bit and plunged down the path, thinking he would come upon the other man sooner or later.

But sooner had certainly turned into later, and he still had not caught up to the wildlife officer. *Riggs his name was.* Well, he would be happy to see Riggs, if he could just find him. Unfortunately, all Tim Dodd had seen since he'd gone down the trail were trees and bushes. The air was alive with the sound of insects. Things whined and buzzed and chirped all around him, but he was ignorant of the source of each sound. It all was like a bothersome noise to him, and he wondered how anyone who lived out here could concentrate long enough to form a coherent thought. The constant chirping was maddening, he thought. Thank God for air-conditioning, else he would have had to listen to that crap through an opened window whenever he had to use his laptop or steal a few hours sleep at The Executive.

He paused to take in the land for a moment and make certain Riggs wasn't standing nearby laughing at him. He peered around. Pines and other trees stretched off and off. Bees and wasps made patterns in the air. Butterflies floated here and there, some of them quite pretty he thought. And then a deerfly took a nip at the base of his neck and he swatted it and cursed. "Dammit." Examining the palm of his hand, he saw the crushed insect and a smear of blood. The little bastards weren't hard to kill. Not like the pesky mosquitoes he'd encountered around the area. Those buggers defied almost all of his attempts to crush them, and they chose hard-to-reach places on which they stopped to feast. The town was okay, Dodd figured, but all of this wilderness crap was for the birds.

The constant chirp of a hundred thousand cicadas whirred and was really getting on his nerves. If he didn't find Riggs soon, or spot where the man might be moving, he was just going to turn around and head back. How far had he gone, anyway? Tim Dodd was also not good at judging such matters. Maybe on an Atlanta street, but not out here in the woods. He might be half a mile from his car, or five. He didn't know.

In fact, the reporter was two miles down the trail. But unlike Riggs, who had stayed on the straightway, following the main path the local deer had carved through the bush, Dodd had veered off to the left, ending up on a secondary trail. He hadn't even realized he had missed the main artery. Soon he was climbing what amounted to a low ridge of bedrock, what geologists have termed oolitic limestone. The rise was so gradual, he had not acknowledged it, and hadn't even really noted that the local flora had changed as he walked, going from bottomland trees to a kind of field and slash pine environment. Looking ahead, the trail all but ended in tufts of hardy grasses and clumps of palmettos, and suddenly there was exposed rock making for rough walking. Sharp edges gouged into his shoes and he almost stumbled a time or two, catching his balance with the vinyl hiking staff he had bought in a store in Salutations. This wasn't like anywhere he had ever seen in Florida. Where was the sand? Where were the palms?

He stopped next to a big slash pine that had toppled in a recent thunderstorm. The roots, locked tight in the limestone, had held fast to clumps of the rock, and the base of the fallen tree was like a big, rough tombstone standing pale and hot in the afternoon sun. Dodd put his hand on the rock and leaned there, panting. His ever-present camera dangled around his neck, chafing the skin where the strap was digging in. *Gad, he was thirsty*. And he'd thought to bring a two-quart water bottle on a nifty strap that attached to his belt. He snapped it loose and undid the cap, taking a long slug. Half the contents vanished in a couple of gulps before he recapped it.

He looked around.

And that was when he realized that he was no longer on the trail. In fact, he couldn't even see where the trail had been. It had just petered out in the low shrubs and grasses here on this long, low ridge. Everywhere he looked all he could see were pines interspersed by thickets that seemed poised to claw at him with spikes of broken limbs and an array of thorns. Something croaked nearby; his heart leaped painfully in his chest.

Dodd gasped and stumbled back as a black form shot out of a nearby clump of vegetation. *A bird.* He sighed in relief. It croaked again as it vanished low against the horizon. *What kind of bird was that?* It had looked like a crow. The reporter walked over to the fallen trunk and leaned against it, in a half-sitting posture. A corn snake slithered away from his left foot, sliding over his right one before vanishing into the shadows, out of the hot sunlight. Tim Dodd yelled, his voice echoing through the pines as he danced away from the dead tree, finally stumbling and falling to the stony ground, where he gouged a healthy chunk of skin off the heels of both hands as he braced to keep from hitting his head.

There was blood, and his hands were singing a song of complaint. "Ow. Goddamit," he muttered. And then, "Damn," much louder.

Off at the far end of the low ridge, where the oolitic limestone dipped down to the low country again, the Scarlet paused as it heard the sound of the man's pain. And it breathed in, scenting for something in the warm air.

In a moment, carried on a slow, hot breeze, there it was. The few, interspersed molecules floated on the currents and he breathed them into the great nasal canals where he savored the tantalizing clue: blood. A part of it, something learned long ago, a lesson drummed time and again into its psyche, said *not hunt.* The Egg Father taught that it was not good to hunt this creature. The Egg Mother had taught that one must not move in the Sun, that one must not hunt in the Sun, that to do so would be to invite death.

Egg Mother and Egg Father were wrong. The Scarlet

had hunted much in the Sun. It was good to run through the yellow light and chase down the deer while they lay waiting for cool dark, for the stars. He had learned other things that were good, that meant some of the lessons he had been taught were so wrong. He sniffed again. The red scent was drawn in, down the sensitive nasal passages, into his throat, across his tongue. His gigantic mouth opened wide, trapping the smell there where he could savor it for a moment. *Why was it dangerous to hunt the Man?* They walked like the Flock. But they were slow and clumsy. He had seen them so often, from the time of his hatching, and onward. They were almost blind and deaf, stumbling around the Flock and never seeing them.

Why not hunt the Man?

The Scarlet turned his great head, as large as that of a big horse, in the direction from which the sounds and the smells were coming. It lowered that heavy head and made a soundless move toward the source. Scaled feet took quiet steps, leathery skin molding over the edges of sharp stone. Holding its forearms close to its powerful chest, it unfolded the claws there, then tucked them back in close to the body. Quietly, it worked its way toward the man.

Slowly, Dodd got to his feet and examined his hands. It wasn't as bad as it felt, he discovered. He had merely knocked a healthy chunk of skin off of each palm, but the wounds were superficial, though painful. Even the bloodflow wasn't heavy, with just a trickle or three inching down his wrist. He reached into his back pocket and pulled out the blue towel he always carried there. Lori, his ex-wife, had given him a number of the cloths when they'd parted company. She was a nurse and used to bring them home almost daily from the hospital where she worked. Well, his time with her had been good for *something*, it seemed. The bitter thought passed quickly as he recalled her smile in earlier, happier times. He dabbed at the wounds until the bleeding stopped. If nothing else, the fall was a good reason to turn around and find his way back to the car.

But where was the car? He'd have to find the trail before he could find his way back to the auto. Well, it couldn't be *that* difficult. All he had to do was retrace his way. He turned.

Once again, he felt his heart hammer at his breastbone. His breath froze in his lungs. *What had that been?*

Something very big had moved, very fast, just beyond the next thicket as he had turned around. There had been a flash of red. And . . . *what was that* . . . had that been a clawed foot? A leg? He blinked. There was nothing there. Not even any of the bugs were flying around.

The insects had shut the hell up. For the first time since he had begun the hike, he noticed that the bugs had stopped their constant whining. *Why had they done that?* The silence seemed total.

Dodd swallowed hard and put his back to the big, limestone-encrusted base of the dead pine tree. At least he had his rear protected. He looked around, squinting into the trees, into the brush, into the sun and the bright blue sky. He was certain something was out here with him. Bugs always went quiet when something big walked around. He'd read that somewhere.

"Riggs? Ron Riggs? Is that you?" His eyes were wide, fearful. "Mr. Riggs! You here, Mr. Riggs?" There was no answer.

Behind him, something hard scratched against the bedrock. He had the upturned root system at his spine, and he was afraid to ease out and take a look. He was frozen in place, trying to work up the courage to turn and see.

In the periphery of his vision, off to his right, there was that flash of red again. Something tall—*he saw it*—just past the next tuft of brambles, zipped along at an unbelievable clip. It was moving his way, fast. *It was coming at him.* And whatever it was, it was very, very large.

Without thinking about what he was doing, Dodd fumbled for the camera. He brought it to his face, and unable to carefully aim it he began to snap off shot after shot. The thing was about to burst out of the trees, out of the brush. It was going to come out of there like a locomotive bearing down on him.

Dodd screamed at the top of his lungs and bolted.

His odd, bounding gait moved him clumsily away from the downed pine. He almost fell, found his footing and pushed forward, dropped his walking stick. He fell into a nearby thicket, feeling thorns tearing at his face, at his hands and arms, and even through the tough fabric of his pants. But he ignored the pain and pushed on, screaming. Behind, he could actually feel the thump of footsteps as something of considerable mass bore down on him. He wanted to turn and look, but knew that if he did it would catch him. Dodd burst through the thicket, tearing his way out of the thorny stuff, leaving an ounce or so of his forearms and calves on thorns and brambles. But he was out in the open again, moving toward a clump of palmettos. He was going to go right through them, right past the fronds. Dodd reached out to push the green stuff out of his way.

And something met him running the opposite direction. Something grasped him by the arms and twisted his body effortlessly, tossing him to the ground again. Dodd screeched like a woman and waited to die.

"Jesus Christ! Are you a girl or a man?"

The figure standing over him was dressed in military camouflage issue. There was a rifle suddenly in the man's hands, but it was held tight against his lean body and was not aimed at Dodd. The reporter had no idea what kind of gun, but he gazed at it with mixed emotion. At least the barrel was pointed toward the sky. Dodd was drawing in a breath for another scream even though he realized he was looking at a man and not some predator there to eat him.

"Can you talk, boy? You got a tongue in your head? Huh? I asked you a question, son. Speak up when I talk to you." The face peering down at him did not seem so much angry as puzzled. Dodd almost yelped a laugh, thinking of the old radio character, Senator Claghorn. The man's accent and inflections almost mirrored that of the old comedy routine. *That's a joke, son*, Dodd thought.

Finally, Dodd found his voice. "I. Back there. Something was chasing me." He clipped the words off between gasps of air.

The man looked off in the direction from which Dodd had come. He still looked puzzled. "I don't see a damned thing, boy. What are you talking about? There's nothing around here that wants to chase you. Unless it's a man wants to chase you off his private property."

"Eh?" Dodd was on his hands and knees, trying to stand. His chest felt as if it would burst at any second.

"You are on *private property*, boy. You understand me? I *own* this land. Not you. Not Berg Brothers Studios. Not the damned Wilderness Society. Me. Winston Grisham."

By then, Dodd had found his feet. "Colonel Grisham. Yes. I know who you are." Dodd extended his wounded right hand. Grisham eyed the bloodied paw, and reluctantly took it.

"My daddy taught me never to refuse another man's

hand, boy." He quickly released it, checking his own skin for contamination. "You wouldn't be queer, now, would you?"

"Uh. No." Dodd got a good look at Grisham. The other man was not much taller than he was, but wider, more compact and muscular. It was obvious he was in exceptionally good condition for a man of his years. "I'm lost."

"You sure are. Didn't you see my *no trespassing* notices?"

"No, sir."

"Damn, boy. I've got them posted every ten yards all along my eastern boundary. You'd have to be a blind bat to miss them." He eyed Dodd suspiciously. "Who are you, anyway? I've shot at men for trespassing here." He wasn't lying.

"I'm Tim Dodd. I'm a reporter."

Grisham shouldered his rifle. "Reporter? Stinking liberal reporter, are you? Here to help out those tree-hugging wimps trying to tell private property owners what they can and can't do with their land? You one of those?"

"No, sir. I try to stay neutral on such matters. I've been covering the difficulties Salutations has been having lately."

Grisham's lined face cracked, showing a mouthful of perfect white teeth. "You're that guy that's been calling that blight *Jurassic Park*, aren't you? You're that guy writes for the *Inquirer*."

"That's me," Dodd admitted, smiling, too. "You enjoy those?"

"Anything that keeps those jerks one step behind my lawyers. That's all I care about. And anything that'll keep a few more damned Yankees out of the area." Grisham sighed. "Damn, but I hate Yankees. You know . . . I bought this place so I could retire here and not have a bunch of Northerners around. I thought I'd be sharing this place with my cattle and my family and a few screaming jets now and again.

"Damned Democrats and their military downsizing. Screw that. Now not only do I have to deal with damned environmentalists poking around looking for endangered species, but there's a town full of damned Yankees being built on my doorstep." Grisham turned and began to walk away.

"Um. Sir?" Dodd took a step toward him, following, looking back to see if anything was coming. Grisham must have scared it off, he figured.

"What?"

"Can you help me find my way back to my car?"

Grisham stopped, looked back at the bloodied, disheveled reporter. "Shit. An old soldier's work is never done." He shook his head. "Just follow me, son. I'll get you out of here. Come on."

Dodd had an awful time keeping up.

CHAPTER
SEVEN

Riggs followed Kate for some time, admiring her rear end. She had glanced back a couple of times and had noticed where Ron's gaze was centered. She'd merely smiled. *Men. God love 'em.*

The two were moving gradually south by southwest through the savanna. "We'll come to Carson Stream pretty soon," Ron said.

"You've been here?" Kate asked.

"No. But I know my maps, and if we keep going this way we'll hit that stream. It drains into a large wetland, right? We'll have a hard time crossing there without getting pretty soggy." Ron spotted a small copperhead coiled and resting in the shade of a palmetto, but saw no reason to mention it. They were completely harmless unless you stepped on one. Most people didn't know that the last thing a pit viper generally wanted to do was waste its poison on a creature far too large for it to eat. But he found himself wishing he had brought along a walking staff. They were going to be in cottonmouth habitat pretty soon, and those snakes were a lot more aggressive than copperheads or rattlers. This area of Florida should have every type of poisonous snake native to North America. But it had been years since Ron had so much as glimpsed a coral snake—they seemed to be just about gone in most places.

"Ever see any coral snakes around here?" he asked.

Kate had stopped to look around. The area really was quite attractive. "Yeah. Sure. They're almost common in the higher areas, away from the streams and swamps."

"No kidding?"

"No kidding."

Ron had come up next to Kate, sneaking a glance or two at her while she fumbled at the water bottle on her belt. She really was quite pretty, he thought. But she was indeed a tall woman. His first approximation had been off the mark, a bit. She was six foot-two inches tall, at least. Maybe even six-three.

"I'm six-three," she said.

Riggs was so stunned that he said nothing. He swallowed hard enough for her to hear.

"I'm used to it," she said. "Guys are always trying to figure out how tall I am. Especially when I'm at least— what?—five inches taller than you?"

"Uh. Yeah," Ron said. She had stunned him. He didn't know what to say.

Her water bottle in her left hand, she pointed with her right and made a clockwise movement with it, indicating the pine savanna around them. "You know, Richard Leakey says the human mind is accustomed to this kind of terrain. That we seek it out and find it soothing, somehow. Because our ancestors came out of terrain like this in Africa. Out of the grasslands and the open vistas." She took a swallow of water. "You agree?"

"I've read that, yes. I can't say I completely agree. I think he just has an affinity for this kind of place because he grew up around it. Totally subjective thinking on that point. Myself, I like deep woodland. Uplands, preferably." He looked across the wide patch of open grasses; tall, thin pines interspersed every ten yards or so like some gigantic subtropical garden.

"You might be right," she said. "You know . . . this land we're on. It's a little higher than the surrounding area. Just underneath the soil here, we have limestone."

"Oolitic limestone, yes."

Again, Kate smiled. "Nice to meet someone who knows his stuff," she said. "At any rate, this is what the boys all want."

"Pardon?" He was thinking of wanting something, but he wasn't quite sure what she meant.

"You know, this is the best terrain for building in the entire Florida peninsula. This stuff runs in bands in different areas of Florida, and wherever it is the boys love to build on it. It doesn't sink. It doesn't give. Wonderful place to slap up houses and shopping centers and all kinds of buildings."

"I know what you mean." Ron followed her gaze out across the savanna. It truly was unique.

"You know, there are about eighty thousand acres of this here."

"*What?* You're joking."

"Nope. Vance has mapped out at least eight thousand acres of longleaf pine savanna. Biggest untouched plots anywhere in North America. Used to be common all along the low country on the Atlantic and Gulf coastal plains. Almost all gone, now." She looked at Ron. "This is why this place is so important. This is why it should be preserved. And as a whole, not in parcels.

"Vance has some plans. Some grand plans." She replaced the water bottle on its holder and started off. "Come on. We're going to cross Carson Stream and get back to the compound." Ron fell in behind her. "And stop staring at my ass," she said.

★ ★ ★ ★ ★

True to her word, the crossing was made without even getting their feet wet. A big tupelo gum at the edge of the stream had fallen, creating a natural bridge across the creek. It had been a moderately old tree, so they hadn't even had to do a balancing act as they went over it. Downstream, Ron had spotted an alligator, a six-footer, and had pointed it out to Kate. "Seen 'im," she had said, not even bothering to look.

Within an hour they had come to Vance Holcomb's compound, angling at it from the east, through a stand of particularly impressive live oaks, Spanish moss draping down in heavy ropes and tendrils all around them. Under the shadows there, Kate had stopped Ron with a gentle touch, pointing to the ground a few feet away. "A gopher tortoise," she told him, aiming with a long index finger at the shelled reptile. "Now *that's* worth looking at. You don't see many of them anymore."

They watched the tortoise who looked back at them, perfectly still, and calmly sizing them up. And then they headed toward the compound, which really did look like a fortress. There was an eight-foot privacy fence made of dark stained pine, and beyond that was a ten-foot chain link fence with gleaming razor wire coiled along the top. "So this is the Eyesore," Ron muttered.

"We like to call it Fort Apache." Kate stopped at the first fence and fumbled with a rather large and formidable padlock, trying to insert a key from a ring she had pulled from her pocket. "Damn thing always gives me fits," she told him. Ron stepped up and held it for her while she worked the key in and turned it. "Ah." It clicked open.

As they entered the enclosure a short, dark man who was walking just inside the chain link fence, a box on his shoulder, greeted them. The man waved and hollered, "Hey, good looking." Kate waved back to him as he passed and went about his business.

"That's Billy," Kate told him, this time having no trouble with the lock on the inner gate. Soon they were inside it. "He's a Native American."

"Seminole?" Ron watched the retreating figure.

"Yes. He is, actually." She led him toward the first building; long, low walls of tabby construction, flat roofed with wide, narrow windows inset with dark glass through which Ron could not see. He suspected there were people in there looking at them, though. It was something he could feel.

"I'm one quarter Seminole. My grandmother was full blooded, she always said. She never taught me a lick of the native language, though. I can't speak a bit of it, either dialect." Ron always felt guilty about that, even though he couldn't think of a good reason why he should feel so. His father was of Irish descent, and he never felt guilty about not being able to speak Gaelic. He thought of Mary Niccols, her dark, beautiful face, and realized the source of his guilt.

"Why not?" Kate was looking at him in a new way. He always got that when he told people he had Seminole blood in his background. So many people thought it was *cool*, or they thought he had some kind of inner sight for being of Indian ancestry. Both reactions were condescending and annoying.

"I was just never exposed to the culture. I almost applied for the tribal rolls, once. Went down there to see about it, but I never said a word to them. Down there at Miccosukee." He remembered that, just a few years back, after his father had died and when he had first found the job with Fish & Wildlife. Ron had driven down with every intention of talking to someone about his lost heritage, but he hadn't done it, had ended up just looking around like he was merely another tourist.

"Why didn't you talk to them?" Kate had opened the door at the front of the building, holding it for Ron. He could feel cool air inviting them in.

"I don't know," he admitted. "I just didn't feel like I belonged there, I guess." He shrugged. "Heck. I don't know." He shrugged again. "There was someone once, who encouraged me to look into it, into signing on and learning the culture. But, well, it just didn't work out." Mary's name was on his mind, but he decided not to mention her.

Kate ushered him in. "Oh well, then. Welcome to Fort Apache."

They were in a large, pale, brightly lit foyer. The floor was white tile against stark white walls. The overhead lights were all fluorescent, and there were panes of frosted glass covering skylights that let in muted sunlight. "We use a lot of solar energy here. Half the light is powered with solar, and all the water is heated with solar. About one fourth the cooling is done with solar, through evaporation actually, but Vance has guys working to beef that up."

"I'll be damned."

Kate pointed down the left side of the hallway. "You go that way. You'll see a room. First door on your left. Go in there and look around or have a seat. I've got to go see someone. There's a fridge in there and you'll find something cold and refreshing to drink. Make yourself at home and I'll be right with you." She patted him once on the shoulder and quickly strode off, her long legs taking her down the hall and around the corner. She was gone.

Ron went to the door she had indicated. It seemed to be

a lab of some sort. There were the classic lab tables, much like those he had used in college science courses, complete with natural-gas fixtures, sinks, and work areas. A smock-wearing fellow was busy puttering around with something on one of the tabletops, up to his elbows in a plastic tub.

"Hello," Ron said.

The man looked over his shoulder as Ron came in. "Hello," he answered. He squinted his eyes, focusing on the patch on Ron's shirt. "Fish and Wildlife." It wasn't a question. "Sorry I can't offer you my hand, but it's covered in bloody goo, so I assume you wouldn't like that."

"You assume right," Ron told him.

"You want a cold drank?" The guy had lapsed into an exaggerated southern accent. "Git you won out dat dere oss bahx. Might have a RC Cola in thar."

Ron opened the refrigerator and saw an array of beverages. He chose a bottle of distilled water. "Thanks. This one looks good. I think I'll pass on the RC. You guys don't have any Moon Pies, do you?"

"Slap outta them. I et 'em all."

Ron eased over to where the other man was working, looking to see what he was doing. "Well, in lieu of a proper southern greeting, I'm Ron Riggs. You already know who I work for."

"I'm Adam Levin. Formerly with the University of Florida. *At* Gainesville. Now a much higher paid employee of one Mr. Vance Holcomb, all around jillionaire and crusading environmentalist."

"Who's the environmentalist? You or Holcomb?" Ron had all but emptied the water bottle.

"Both of us, actually."

Ron had moved up close, and finally had a view of the contents of the vinyl tub. It looked to be a pile of guts. "Intestinal tract," Riggs noted. "What was it?"

"Turkey buzzard. We've found several dead within the area, and I've been dissecting them to figure out what's going on. We suspect poison. This is the first chance I've had to go through the stomachs. Got three more in the cooler over there." He indicated a waist-high refrigeration unit against the far wall.

"Who would poison a buzzard?"

"Well, someone likely poisoned something else. Something the buzzard subsequently ate. Used to see this kind of crap all the time when I worked out in Arizona. Stupid, short-sighted ranchers would poison the coyote, other stuff would scavenge the dead coyote, and then they'd die, too." He shook his head. "Damned ranchers. Those spoiled brats got away with everything they did. And those jerks grazing their stock on government property practically for free. Makes me sick to even think about it."

Ron said nothing. At times, he felt helpless and ineffective in the face of the turning of events. So he had trained himself to be impassive when it came to something over which he had no control. Why put yourself in anguish when you had no influence to change such things? "Should the stomach be that color?"

"Yeah. That's nothing unusual. Been in the cooler for some days, now. That's the way it goes, you know." Levin was using a small scalpel to open the top of the stomach cavity. Even cooled the smell that oozed out was noxious. It was only then that Ron noticed the scented jelly on Levin's bare upper lip. Unprepared for the stench, Ron backed away.

"Ever come up on a vulture sitting on its eggs? They'll cough up the contents of their stomach at you, hoping the stench will drive you off." Ron was thinking of a black vulture whose nest he had accidentally found while investigating a rocky overhang on a mountain in Georgia.

Levin nodded. "Yeah. Seen it a time or two, myself. And they just lay their eggs right there on the bare ground. No nesting material at all."

"Yep."

Taking a second to glance back at Riggs, Levin spoke again. "So. What brings Fish and Wildlife here to the mighty compound?"

"Kate Kwitney brought me," he said.

"Ooooooooooooh." The biologist nodded knowingly.

"I just met her, actually. Out in one of the savannas a few miles from here." Ron coughed.

"Just met her, you say?" Levin was cutting and squeezing his gory prize.

"Yep. Couple hours ago, is all." He tossed the empty water bottle at the nearest trash bin, but it hit the rim and clattered to the floor. "Oops."

"So, then. You don't . . . *know* her that well."

Ron grunted as he picked up the bottle and tossed it at the bin again. Once more it hit the rim and bounced off and clattered to the floor. "Shoot," he muttered. "Um. Yes. I mean, no. I don't know her well. Just met her, I said." He picked up the bottle and put it in the bin.

"What do you think of Kate?" Levin was sawing and squeezing, looking down at the last meal of a carrion eater.

"Well. She's pretty sharp. Very smart lady. Knows what she's talking about when it comes to the local flora and fauna. Knows more than I do, I'd say. Seems to know more than anyone back at the office, actually. And . . ."

"And?"

"Well, she's good looking. I think she's really pretty."

Levin chuckled. "Air she purdy?"

66

The guy was getting on Ron's nerves. Maybe he was a boyfriend of Kate's. Maybe not. Riggs couldn't ignore him, though. Levin had pushed just a bit too far. "Yeah, I think she's good looking. I'd like to be alone with her and bang her for an hour or two."

"Why, Ron! That's not very nice." It was Kate, of course, having arrived, having watched the exchange from the open doorway.

Adam Levin, whose back was still to the whole scene, his hands full of buzzard guts, let out a full, belly laugh that, for Ron, went on for far too many painful minutes.

CHAPTER
EIGHT

Dodd did his best to keep up with Colonel Grisham, but it wasn't easy to do. He had to practically run just to stay ten feet behind the old soldier. Coupled with the need to take a look behind every quarter mile or so, it was almost going to be impossible to not lose sight of his new companion.

"What the *hell* did you think you saw, anyway, son?"

The reporter almost ran into the retired officer, since his attention had been on the forest they had just traversed rather than where he was headed. "Damn," he blurted before he could stop himself.

"Well . . . I don't know, really." Dodd had decided along the miles they had already walked that he didn't want to tell this frankly scary fellow what he had seen. Especially not if what he had seen was real, and not just part of his panic at being lost and disoriented.

"What do you mean? When you came bustin' out of that thicket it sure looked to me like you knew what you saw. And it didn't seem like it was no cottontail, either." Grisham was set solid, glaring eye to eye at the torn and bloodied Dodd.

Clearing his throat, getting ready to lie (something he did well, on occasion), Dodd's mind danced. "First of all, I got lost. I *thought* I was following a trail that led around the north side of Salutation. But after a while, I knew that wasn't right, because I wasn't coming back to any of the neighborhoods and the roads. I was just getting deeper and deeper into the woods.

"And then, when I came out into that big field-looking place . . ."

"A *savanna*, son. They call that type of habitat a savanna. Got lots of it in Africa, not much of it here." Grisham was rapt, examining his charge.

"Okay. A savanna. Yes. Anyway, I *really* got lost when I was out there. I couldn't tell which way I had come in. I couldn't figure out which way to go to get back to that trail, which I had lost track of before I got out there in the first place." He picked at a thorn mired in the tender flesh in the pad of his thumb. A bright dot of blood welled up where the thorn had been.

"You've got no sense of direction, do you boy?"

"Eh. No. I guess not." He cleared his throat again, afraid to look the retired colonel in the eye. A man like that might be able to spot a lie in a man's eyes. "And so I stopped by this big tree that had fallen over. And while I was standing there, this big blackbird, sounded like a damned foghorn . . . well, it came out of the bushes and scared hell out of me."

Grisham was chuckling, now. That was good, so Dodd continued. He wasn't really lying, yet. "And right after that, I put my foot down and this big brownish and orange snake crawled over my foot and almost scared me to death. I thought I was going to have a heart attack, for sure."

"Corn snake. Just a harmless old corn snake," Grisham told him.

"Well, I didn't know that. I do now, thanks. After that, I walked off from the tree, and then I heard something moving in the bushes. I thought it might be a bear or one of those Florida panthers I've read about. So I started running. And that's when you happened along." He smiled sheepishly and looked away, hoping that Grisham wouldn't mention his camera and ask him if he'd taken any photos.

"And that's when you trespassed, Mr. Dodd. You came across a posted boundary. That's private property."

"I'm sorry. Really, I am. I respect private property. I just didn't see the signs."

"You know, boy. I'm from South Georgia, and where I come from you do *not* dick around with a man's private property. It's sacred ground, another man's land. You don't go where you ain't supposed to be."

"I understand. I truly didn't mean to offend you or violate your rights." Dodd swallowed, was aware of his thirst, which he'd forgotten in all of the excitement. He was really parched.

"Apology accepted. Now, what the heck were you doing out here, anyway? I mean, other than trying to see where that trail went? I've been reading your stuff. Hearing some things. What's this about a giant snake? You guys on the level?"

Dodd looked around, trying to see if there was anything to see other than trees and brush, anything that might look like comfort. Why, this man could kill him out there and no one would ever know. Grisham was certainly no stranger to death. His reputation as a warrior was quite formidable. "To tell you the truth, I'm not sure what's going on in Salutations. They're stonewalling me. I do know that pets are missing. Cats. Some dogs. We think there might be an escaped python or something like that around the town."

Grisham laughed, a big, braying cackle, and slapped his thigh. "You *guys*. You guys are something. You know that? Hell. It's probably just a gator or bobcat killing some pets.

Giant snake. You're a real joker, Dodd. You know that?"

"Yes sir. I try."

Grisham's hand was up in the air, Dodd noticed, as his eyes followed it. And suddenly the woods came alive with men. Formerly invisible figures came out of the trees and up from the earth where they had been waiting. Perhaps they had been following along all the while, or maybe they had been waiting here. He didn't know, and now he was truly, completely afraid.

"Meet some of the boys," Grisham said. He nodded toward the camouflaged soldiers edging toward them, their faces painted in greasy stripes of gray and brown and green. As the group closed in, Grisham stepped up very close to Dodd. "Now. You really *were* out here to do a story about a giant *snake,* right? I mean," and he chuckled, "you weren't here to spy on an old, retired *colonel,* were you?"

Bringing his hands up, palms out, Dodd took half a step back. "No sir. I swear. I was just here to do a story about Salutations. I promise you I wasn't here to spy on you. Swear it."

There was a long period of silence. No one spoke. Dodd could hear his own breath, but oddly could not hear breathing from any of the others, though there were at least ten of them, now. Gnats sang in his ear, but he did not brush them away. His hands remained out, palms up, toward Grisham.

And finally, the old colonel laughed again. It was a cruel laugh, but welcome just the same. "I believe you, son." Grisham turned his head and barked at his fellow militiamen. "Come on, boys. Let's get this citizen back to his car."

As the formerly invisible soldiers marched off, westward, Grisham patted Dodd on the back, his funny *compadre.*

"Let's go, Mr. Dodd. I'll take you to my ranch and drive you to Salutations. Believe it or not, my house ain't but two miles from here. Me and the boys were just doing a little . . . *practice* when you interrupted us." He pointed at one of the men quickly vanishing ahead of them.

"Old Wylie, there. I'll bet you think old Wylie's a nigger. Huh? You think he's a nigger?" Dodd shook his head from side to side, speechless. "He ain't a nigger. He's a Cherokee Indian. God, I swear I purely love our Native Americans. Did you know that Indians make up only one percent of the population, yet they are *eight percent* of our veterans? Did you know that?" Dodd shook his head in the negative again. "Well, it's true. Best damned soldiers you could ask for. God *love* 'em, I say. God love 'em."

True to his word, they soon came out of the woods and began to skirt the edge of a big pasture. There were cattle in the field, and the scent of manure soon came to them. "Beef cattle," Grisham said. "I farm beef here. Florida's great for beef. I've got me a thousand acres out here, and I wish I had more time to farm beef. But, you know, there's more important things to do."

Dodd was quiet. He was going to do his best to keep his mouth shut until he was off this man's property.

"This country is in trouble, you know. Deep trouble."

"I know what you mean," Dodd told him. He was peering around, trying to see if there was a car or truck parked nearby. There didn't seem to be, although he finally spotted a large barn and what might be the edge of a very big farmhouse.

"Take these wilderness types. I'm all for parks. It's good to go out and take in the fresh air and see the sights. But when these *socialists* think they can tell a man what he can

72

and cannot do with his private property, then things are out of hand. You see what I mean?" They were rounding the end of the pasture. The cattle watched them with great, bored, half-lidded stares.

"I know exactly," Dodd agreed. Certainly the man had a truck somewhere.

"These government agencies. They're out of hand. Telling a man dry ground is a *wetland,* for Christ's sake. It's insane. Telling a company they can't build a factory with jobs for people because of a *minnow.*" He breathed in. "A damned *minnow.*

"That's why, you see, we need people like me. Like me, and my friends you just met. We're kind of like a counterbalance to some of that craziness. Something to make some sanity out of it. Make them see the light, so to speak. You understand?"

Dodd nodded his head up and down, his curly hair damp with sweat. "Yes, I do."

"If I ever give you permission to write about me, you remember some of what I've told you. Okay?" Grisham slapped Dodd firmly on the back. Hard enough to clear Dodd's lungs.

Dodd coughed. "Yes. I'll remember it if you think you'd like us to do a piece on you."

"You've probably already heard it on my radio show, anyway."

In fact, Dodd had never heard Grisham's rants on radio. He had actually forgotten the man *did* radio. But it was true. He was carried on a number of AM stations around the country, although mainly he broadcast on shortwave.

As they rounded the pasture, the barn and the house came into full view. Some men were closing the doors of the huge barn, and it was very dark in there, but as it was closed up, Dodd was certain that he had glimpsed an armored personnel carrier parked inside. He stared at the ground and pretended he'd seen nothing. And, anyway, a shiny red Chevrolet truck was parked not a hundred feet away.

"You ready for a ride?"

"A ride?"

"A *ride*. Back to your *car*." Grisham smiled.

"Yes. Yes, thanks. That would be most appreciated, sir."

The two of them headed toward the new red truck and, once there, Grisham emptied the chamber of the gun and released the full clip. He stowed the gun on a rack behind the seat and put the clip and bullet in an ammo box on the floorboard. Dodd eyed the bullets so that he could look them up and figure out what type of guns he'd seen. "Climb on in, son."

As the reporter opened the passenger door and slid in, Grisham produced a key and started up the engine. It purred beautifully and soon the air conditioner was blasting. "One more thing, Dodd."

Dodd looked at him. "Yes?"

"On the way out, don't take any pictures. And don't try to snap one of me when I drop you off. You got that?"

"Got it," Dodd told him.

And each was as good as his word.

CHAPTER
NINE

When Ron was able to turn around with a straight face, Levin's chuckling still going strong, he turned toward Kate Kwitney, the woman he'd just met and who he had already succeeded in alienating. He assumed, at least, that he'd alienated her. And as he turned to give her his most sheepish expression, Ron noticed that someone else had walked in with her. Merely from the way Kate deferred to this new occupant of the room, merely from her body English, Riggs immediately knew that this was Holcomb.

He was a bit younger than Ron would have thought. He'd heard of him for years, had read about some of his exploits since he was a youngster just out of high school. Ron took the hand that was extended to him. "Hello, Mr. Riggs. I'm Vance Holcomb. Call me Vance."

"Hello." He squeezed back and looked into Holcomb's face. In his early fifties, the billionaire had obviously spent a lot of time in the outdoors. His blond hair was still thick, tinged just a bit with gray, and his face was permanently tanned from years spent in the sun. Currently, the darkness of the skin around his eyes and nose was accented, since he had obviously recently shaved off what had been a long held beard. The skin on his chin and around his lips was noticeably lighter, more like the complexion he'd probably sported in younger days. His features were appropriately chiseled for an outdoorsman, Ron thought; he was almost lantern-jawed, but just shy of that. There was a long scar along the left side of his face: pale skin that puckered slightly. Ron wondered how he'd gotten that, and why his millions hadn't bought the plastic surgery to hide it. Perhaps he thought it gave his face character. If he did think that, he was right.

"Kate here tells me she stumbled across you on one of the longleaf savannas." Holcomb took a half step away and put his hands behind his back, as if standing at attention. He was as tall as Kate was.

"Yes. But I'd hardly call it stumbling. Even though I was sitting down, eating my lunch, she picked me right out and headed straight over." Ron looked over at Kate, who was smirking at him. "I don't know how she did that."

"Oh, Kate knows the area, she does. I suspect she would have picked you out even if you'd been half a mile away. Kate's got a sharp eye out there in the forest. She's the best damned field taxonomist I've ever met." Holcomb looked her way and winked.

"Well, I thought I did, too. But I couldn't even tell what she was until she was right up on me." Ron shrugged, still feeling foolish despite Holcomb's manners.

"What do you think of the place, Mr. Riggs?" Holcomb raised his arms to encompass the room.

"I'm impressed. What I've seen of it. You've obviously gone to some great expense." He made eye contact with Kate. There didn't seem to be anything beyond mischief in her eyes. That gave him some relief. "You've got a nice lab here. And you certainly seem to have decent security around the place."

Holcomb shrugged. "Yes. I need the security. You never can tell what kind of problems we might encounter here.

I'm not particularly popular with a lot of powerful folk, just now." He sighed. "But I'm used to it. I'm accustomed to making people angry."

"So I've heard," Ron admitted. Indeed. Ron knew that even a lot of people and organizations *within* the environmental movement did not care for Holcomb. Some said he that he caused more trouble than he was worth. There was his crackpot reputation, for one thing. He'd spent hundreds of thousands of dollars hunting for the Loch Ness Monster. And he'd claimed to have located a herd of Imperial mammoths living isolated and forgotten in Nepal. The claim concerning the mammoths had nearly proved true, but it had turned out to be a population of very large Indian elephants who were genetic throwbacks to another type of extinct species. While they were certainly mutants, they weren't mammoths. And Holcomb had even gone chasing after *Sasquatch* in the wild country of the Northwest.

However, he also could be effective in saving wild places that were worth preserving. The USA was dotted with lands he had bought up and donated to various state governments around the nation. When he was feeling cooperative was when he did the most good. From what Ron had read, he was not feeling cooperative where *this* place was concerned.

"Tell me something, Mr. Riggs. What exactly are you doing here? Why is Fish and Wildlife back here after publishing that *ridiculous* impact statement?" Holcomb had his hand on Riggs' shoulder and was leading him back out into the hallway. Ron allowed himself to be led.

"Actually, I'm just here to look for sign of a large constrictor, Mr. Holcomb."

"Vance. Call me Vance. Please."

"Um. Sure. You see . . . the folk from Salutations gave us a call. Said they were having trouble with pets disappearing. Dogs. A couple cats."

"Cats wander off all the time," Holcomb said. "Wander off and go feral and kill hundreds of birds a year. They're pure *hell* on native birds."

"Eh. Yes, sir. I know."

"Ouch. Sorry, Ron. I get so used to preaching and teaching that I forget myself. Sorry." Holcomb's eyes were downcast. He truly seemed apologetic.

"So, we think it's a python someone released. Maybe even an anaconda. It's not that rare, you know. Maybe one of the soldiers who was stationed here years before this place was decommissioned decided the pet python he'd bought had gotten just a bit too large, and maybe he let it go in the woods, thinking he was doing the right thing. Happens frequently, as you well know." Holcomb had led them down the hallway where Kate had disappeared when they'd come in. The rich man was taking Ron toward an opened doorway at the far end.

"I'm actually surprised they called you on this."

"Matter of fact, the studio seemed rather concerned that they not break any environmental laws. I think they might have handled it themselves if they'd known that there's no Federal protection for an alien species such as a python."

Holcomb threw back his head and laughed. Ron was strangely reminded of Burt Lancaster in his later years. Not so much Holcomb's physical appearance, but his manner-isms. "I can see some lame-brained executive making a dumb move like that. They were probably kicking them-selves after you told them." He pointed at Ron. "You *did* tell them, didn't you?"

"Yes, I did."

Holcomb threw back his head and laughed again. "I like you, Ron. You've got a good sense of humor."

By then, they were at the doorway, and a pale light spilled out of the partially opened threshold. Vance Holcomb pushed it wide. Ron almost fell on his ass.

The room was *huge*. At least, huge for what it was. An office, apparently, but larger than any office in which Ron had ever set foot. A quick guess was that the room was easily three thousand square feet. Twice as big as Ron's own house. It was brightly lit and luxuriously, if sparsely, appointed. If Holcomb liked to do good deeds with his money, he was certainly not averse to lavishing himself with it, either. "This is your office?" Ron's voice was a squeak.

"Yes. Yes, it is. I like a big space where I work," he said. "If I've got to be inside, then I need lots of room to make me feel at ease."

"I see." The place, though huge, was not at all crowded. In fact, for the size of the room there was actually a ridiculously small amount of furnishings.

Seeing the unspoken question on Ron's face, Holcomb addressed it. "I take the Japanese view toward furnishings. Just what is necessary for comfort. Nothing more. Mainly, I just want the space."

"I can understand that," Ron told him, wondering what Holcomb would think of his own cluttered place. Ron followed Holcomb's lead toward a huge desk that was larger than he had thought from across the room, and he had a seat in a big, solid-looking chair that was softly upholstered. Cow leather, he noticed, sitting there. Holcomb was certainly not one of the no-meat, no-furs crowd.

Holcomb took his post on his side of the desk, settling down in a chair that reeked of expense. There were even buttons on one of the great arms, and Ron wondered what the hell they were for. For just a second he thought of the floor opening up beneath him while Holcomb laughed maniacally. He banished the thought.

"What do you plan to do, provided you find evidence of a snake? Or if you actually find the snake, itself? Supposing that there *is* a snake." The rich man found the humidor on the desktop, and he slid the top back along carefully fashioned grooves and took out a pair of cigars. "Do you take a cigar, Ron?" He offered one up.

"Sure," Ron said. "I like a cigar now and again," he lied. He figured if it was a cigar off of the desk of a billionaire, then it had to be expensive and he was willing to see what it was like. Holcomb trimmed both cigars and lit Ron's for him, then his own. The two sat and sampled the flavor. Actually, for a non-smoker, Ron was handling it well. Not bad, he thought. *I could get into this.*

Holcomb chewed his cigar, puffed a great billow of smoke. "Well?"

"Oh. About the snake. Yes." Ron took the cigar out of his mouth and looked at it, looked at Holcomb. "Well, we're obligated to call in someone."

"Someone?" Holcomb's brow went up.

"One of the fellows who contracts with the state to capture problem animals. Usually, it's gators, of course. But sometimes they can come in and take raccoons. And I guess snakes." Ron did not like the look on Holcomb's face. It wasn't anger, exactly, but he didn't look entirely happy.

"They kill those alligators. Correct? And the raccoons? They skin them all out and sell their pelts. All for being crowded out of their habitat by humans."

"Um. Yes, sir. The alligators and the raccoon are sold to markets. Or, rather, their skins are. In the case of the gators, even the meat is sold." Ron spread his hands. "The alligator in Florida is no longer endangered. You know that. It's not a problem to harvest them from time to time anymore."

Vance Holcomb leaned forward and eyed Ron, his demeanor no longer completely friendly. There was now an adversarial feel to their meeting. Maybe it had become a confrontation. "And what will happen to this snake? If it *is* a snake?"

"I'm not entirely sure, if they capture a large snake. I would assume that it would be worth more to a zoo alive than to someone dealing in leather goods."

"But you aren't certain?"

Ron slumped in the chair. He'd been enjoying the day, until then. "No. I honestly can't say. But I don't think it would just be killed outright. We don't do things that way anymore."

Holcomb rolled his eyes and threw his hands up. "*Please*. Spare me that. Of *course* things are still done that way."

"Well . . . *hell*." Ron wilted a bit more.

Holcomb turned his back on the desk, swiveling his chair. Ron saw him depress one of the buttons on the arm of the chair. On the far side of the room, what Ron had assumed was a wall slowly eased back in almost complete silence. If he strained, he could *just* hear the perfect whirring of finely tuned machinery. A gigantic window of truly impressive proportions was slowly revealed. Ron could see the view Holcomb had whenever he wished it. The forest was there, outside the great window, just beyond the chain link fence, no wooden barrier on this side of the compound. The view was impressive: cypress, gum, oaks, pines. Birds were moving across the afternoon sky, heading for roosts: ducks, birds of prey, egrets, cranes, storks. Incredibly, Ron saw a black bear moving at the verge of the forest, its snout testing the winds.

"I'll be damned," Ron said.

"This place *must* be protected, Mr. Riggs. I'm going to

do whatever it takes to save it."

"I don't blame you," he said, the cigar loose in his fingers, his voice feeling like a whisper.

"I think we'll try to locate this snake before you and your animal killer do so. I really don't want the wrong kind of people mucking about around here. Understand?"

"Understood, Mr. Holcomb."

He faced Ron again, his face stern. "Please. Call me Vance."

CHAPTER
TEN

Walks Backward was at his position, as always. Behind him, the Flock was moving ahead, scouting. He surveyed the leavings of the route they had taken, running quickly from one side of the hunting pattern to the other. There: a bit of covering shed by one of last year's youth; he ate it. On a sandy patch of ground: a great three-toed track left by one of the females; he scratched it out with his own great claws, until there was no track to see.

Behind the Flock, he kept his vigil, searching for sign his fellows had left, things for him to collect in his gullet or expunge from existence. They had learned that to continue to live, to continue to survive, all sign of their being must be kept from the Man.

They had lived in this place for a long time, the Flock. Most of their race had vanished, and they were the local remnant of once vast numbers who had hunted here, taking the prey that had come and gone, gift of a fickle sky. The Two, Mother and Father, held the history and told it each day, bit by bit as it came to them in the sunlight moments. Once, there had been other creatures who had lived in this land, other hunters and other prey. Horned antelope, smaller and quicker than the deer on which they now lived, had once danced across these scrubby prairies. Great, hairless mammoths had shared the spaces with them. Huge armored mammals had lumbered across the land. An endless parade of life, less now than in the times faded into history.

And then, almost a hundred generations before, the Man had come. They were tall, although not as tall as a member of the Flock. And they moved on two legs instead of four. The Flock had never seen any other land hunter who moved on two legs rather than four; just like themselves. This Man, this new hunter, was a competitor, perhaps equal to the Flock: the Flock who could race across the grasses as fast as any deer; who were slyer, more cunning than any cat or wolf; who were heavier than any other hunter, even than the bears. The Flock would push out these new things who came in numbers onto the Flock's ground.

But the Flock had been in error. This new creature, this man, could kill like nothing else. They came down from the north in masses, and they could make fire, and could deliver their long teeth from a great distance. The Flocks fell dead for making war on this animal, this Man. Almost; they faded from the land.

An Egg Mother had seen what to do. An Egg Father had followed her. They would hide from this Man. They would hunt at night, when the new creature slept. And they would never again let Man know that the Flock was a part of the land. The first Walks Backward was born, was trained, lived his life, passed his knowledge down the line. The Flock had lived until today, until the now. They had hidden well from Man, who had come in numbers that were impossible for the Flock to reason. Everywhere, the Man had eaten everything, had even eaten the earth itself, pushing up big nests that covered the ground and fouled the water. The Flock had retreated and retreated.

Recalling all of this, Walks Backward did his job.

And the Scarlet rogue was endangering them all. Holding a crimson bit that he'd found, left behind by the rogue, Walks Backward lifted his head high, turned toward the hunting Flock. He wanted to scream it out to them, he wanted to tell them *that the Scarlet must die, must be killed, and must be consumed by the Flock.* He peered at shifting shadows, at youth and adult moving in an agile unit, hunting for food. He turned his snout up, tossed the bit of red into the air and snapped his gigantic mouth shut on it. The Scarlet was a bright taste in his mouth; a taste that brought up his hatred but which did not dull his patience. He was Walks Backward. It was not his place to decide anything. It was only for him to guard the rear, to hide the sign.

To protect the Flock.

Ahead, the Flock fell on the deer that had run from them for a mile, but had finally begun to slow from exhaustion.

Great, clawed feet lifted and dropped, tearing hide and flesh. A razored mouth opened wide and cut into flesh, ripping out a great killing chunk of meat. The Flock fell as a unit on the deer, feasting, calling out silently to one another. Life was good. In moments, they dispersed as a group, vanishing into the black shadows.

Soon, Walks Backward appeared. There was his share. A fine length of shank meat, still warm and wet. He tossed it up, caught it in his maw. Then, scratching the ground, adjusting the brush, he left no sign of their passing. Only someone on hands and knees could find even a spot of blood, a clue that something had killed here.

For now, the Flock was safe and fed.

For now.

CHAPTER
ELEVEN

As he'd promised, the Colonel had taken Dodd back to his car and had left him there, waving as the little reporter got out of the truck. Dodd had waved back. "Goodbye, you crazy fascist bastard," he said, when the man was beyond earshot.

And just as soon as Grisham was out of sight, Dodd had found his key, digging into this pocket and ignoring the pain of his cut and abraded hands. He'd dragged the key out, reopening the wounds and leaving fresh bloody prints on his pants and on the doorhandle as he'd jerked it open. Barely able to contain himself, he had started the engine, pushing the gas down too far and too fast for this idyllic town, peeling off and leaving a great black ribbon on the pavement. He could smell the stench of burning rubber even through the closed windows of the Buick. Tim didn't care. He might not be much of a walker, but he could outdrive most folk.

Keeping one eye peeled for Salutations' ever present security forces, he pushed the limits of the conservative posted speeds through each neighborhood, until he was back at The Executive where his employers had prepaid his room for the next month. Paying little attention to how he parked, he left the rental car canted over two parking spaces and bolted from it. By then, night had fallen and he was running across the lot, Yankee tourists eyeing him suspiciously. He ignored them all, the singles and the families and their raucous kiddies. Pulling the door to the lobby open with all of his strength, he burst in.

The door clacked loudly against the glass panel beside it as he drew it open too wide. But it was shatterproof glass, and so did not crack. But the rude noise brought all attention to Dodd. And for just a second, he realized what a sight he presented to everyone gathered.

There he was, standing at the entrance to the lobby. His clothing was torn, ripped in a dozen places. His hands were lacerated to the point of comedy, blood trickling from fingers and palms. His arms were crisscrossed with nasty scratches, the edges of the wounds black with crusted blood. His pale brown pants were tattered, and likewise stained with his blood. All eyes were on him, and he knew it. "Got lost. Fell down," he said.

And he was *racing* across the lobby. An elevator opened for him, as if on cue. The pair of couples who had been waiting to take it cringed back and let Dodd have it all to himself. "Don't you want to go up?" he asked, pointing a bloody finger at the roof.

One thin, pretty woman replied, "Ugh." The doors closed and she was spared another instant of Dodd's presence.

On the way up, Dodd stood at the door, bouncing, waiting impatiently for the elevator to arrive at the fourth floor, for the door to open. He was wishing he'd taken the stairs. Perhaps that would have been quicker. At the fourth, the door opened and he burst out. A young man who had been waiting for the elevator actually screeched at the ridiculous sight of Dodd propelling himself out of the elevator.

Down the hallways Dodd went, running, his weird,

bouncing gait taking him along in a lopsided manner, head bobbing as he trotted. His normally curly hair was hanging in sweaty tendrils from his scalp, partially obscuring his face. At his room, he again fumbled in his pocket for a key, this time the security card that would open his door. And once again he tore open the dozen little wounds on his fingers as he took the key out and jammed it into the door, waiting crazily for the little green light to illuminate and allow him entrance to 455. The light flashed, the lock clicked open. He fell into the room with a triumphant yell, pulling the key out of the slot as he went past. The door slammed shut behind him.

Taking the digital camera from around his neck, he cast about for the cable necessary to download the photos into his laptop computer. Working with his stinging hands, he had only a little difficulty achieving what he wanted, turning the computer on, and downloading the shots.

Staring, he waited while the information was brought up as a series of files. The little horizontal graph told him when each shot was ready. He had taken six photos before he'd seen the thing in the thicket, and now there were sixteen shots showing. Out of ten, he should have one that would be worth looking at. If he were lucky, he'd have at least a single shot that would prove to him that he had actually seen what he *thought* he'd seen, and had not merely been panicked.

But there couldn't be what he thought he'd seen. There couldn't *truly* be such creatures still living. He waited, standing there like a speedfreak, impatient for the laptop to do what he'd commanded it to do. There was a beep: *Download complete.*

Dodd unhooked the digital camera and tossed it on the bed. Slowly, now that he had it all there waiting on him, he sat and began to scroll down the files with the pointer. He knew that the first six shots were worthless stuff. He'd just been bored and had taken some pictures of the town, one of some kind of turtle plodding across the Salutations village green. He pointed to shot number seven and called it up.

Band by band, the image began to appear on the laptop's small, grainy screen. He stared at it. Nothing but brush, part of his shoe. This one was from before he'd fully raised the camera.

He loaded the next.

What was that?

Through the obscuring screen of a thicket, he could clearly make out a clawed, scaly foot. Perfectly, he could see three toes. *And those claws*. The rest was just brush and palmetto.

He scrolled to the next. A mishmash of vegetation.

The next. Similar.

And then the fifth. He stared. This couldn't *be*. This was not possible.

"A dinosaur," he whispered. "Jurassic Park, for real."

CHAPTER
TWELVE

The sun had set by the time Kate had gotten a truck with which to take Ron back to his own vehicle. Ron had walked with her back to a garage that held no less than a dozen trucks of various makes, each rigged for a particular task, it seemed. And there had been four-wheelers, all terrain vehicles. Ron had made mention of those.

"What's your boss doing with ATVs? I would have thought he'd hate those things, considering they're responsible for tearing up all kinds of habitat."

"Oh, we don't use them very often."

As he climbed into the cab of the pickup, he looked back and remarked once again. "I'm surprised he has them, at all."

"Everything in moderation," she told him, climbing in on the driver's side.

"That doesn't actually sound like your kind of philosophy, Kate." He buckled himself in, admiring the interior of the vehicle. He immediately noticed that it was equipped with some pretty serious hardware.

"Well, that's Vance Holcomb speaking. Not I. And, anyway, he's a man of contradictions. I'm sure you've heard the tales. Even his fellow environmentalists alternately love and hate him, depending on what's cooking in that amazing brain of his." She inserted a key into the ignition and the truck pulled soundlessly out of the garage, the door automatically shutting behind them.

"I'll be damned," Ron said. "This truck has an electric motor?"

"Dual systems."

"What?"

"Electric and propane. We can switch to propane if we want to."

"You're joking." He looked the cab over again, checking out as many details as he could in the cool, green light from the dash. "I've never seen one of these."

"Hey. Vance is a wealthy man. He buys only the best." Kate tooted the horn and Ron saw two fellows appear from the shadows to unlock the gates and let them out. She waved at them and muttered thanks, even though they couldn't hear her through the raised windows. In a moment the compound was a couple of distant lights in the darkness, then gone. They were on a single lane road that was merely a couple of sandy tracks in the wiregrass, a narrow gap that led through the woods, meandering back and forth. "I like driving this little road," she said. "We didn't cut it through here, you know. We just cleared out a couple of loblolly pines and that was all the construction needed. The big trucks that brought in the building materials did most of the work for us, and the forest has even repaired most of that *damage*."

Ron nodded. "He seems sincere about saving this place. I have to say it's an important site. But I don't know if he's going to get what he wants."

Kate glanced his way just as the dirt road met up with one of the paved roads that marked the current boundary of Salutations. "You might be right. But it would hurt my heart to see him fail. You've seen a little of it. This place deserves to be saved, despite shoddy impact statements from the government, high powered lawyers from an entertainment conglomerate, and the slippery good ol' boy politics of a thinly veiled neo-Nazi." There was an edge in her voice. The truck bounced as it climbed up from sand to asphalt.

"I agree with you. It's a big place. Lots of varied habitat."

"Ron, I don't think you have a grasp on this place. Not really. You ought to take a look at it. I mean, a really *good* look. It's one of the largest unprotected roadless areas in the eastern United States. It *has* to be preserved. As is."

In the dark of the cab Ron looked at Kate's face outlined from the bluish glow from the lighted dash. He was finding himself more attracted to her the longer he was with her. "Sorry about what I said today. In Levin's lab, I mean."

There was a moment's silence. "That's okay. Don't mention it."

"I just wanted to apologize. The reason I said it, well, that guy Levin was getting on my nerves. He was baiting me. Maybe he's jealous that I was out hiking around with you, or something." He cleared his throat, feeling nervous again. "Are you two . . . *attached?*"

"Attached? Me and Levin? Heavens, no." She glanced his way. "What was he saying? Did he say something about me?"

"Not in so many words, no. It's hard to describe. He was just giving me a hard time. Making innuendoes. I'm not making any sense, am I?"

"Sure you are. Look, I've known Adam for nine years, and I know exactly what you're talking about. He can be quite irritating." They were going through the center of Salutations. The lights were bright, the quaint mall bustling, people walking down the streets. The place looked very nice. She slowed the truck to a crawl, to avoid hitting any of the kids who might dart into the street. She'd seen kids do that here in the past.

"Apology accepted, then?"

"No need for one, but if you feel like giving one, then sure. Apology accepted." Kate smiled at Ron and accelerated gradually through a green light.

"Then how about going out with me this Friday? I know some nice places to eat. Some nice clubs. I was thinking about driving over to Melbourne. How about it?"

Kate was quiet for several seconds. It seemed like minutes to Ron, and he was beginning to become uncomfortable. She reached over and flipped a switch, letting in cool air. Finally, she spoke. "Look. You don't know me that well. There are some things happening for me right now that are keeping me very busy. But, I'd like to make the time to get to know you."

Ron pressed his lips together. *Okay. A mystery woman.* "I can't imagine what I'd need to know before taking you out. But, okay. Let's talk about it."

For the first time since he'd met her that morning, an expression of something like anger crossed her face. "Not *now*. This isn't the time or the place. We'll talk later. Maybe tomorrow, if you come by the compound. Hell, there's three days before Friday."

Ron reached back and grunted, pulling his wallet free. He opened it, dug around until he found the small bundle of cards he carried there. "Here," he said, handing one to her. "This is a business card. I have to have them for when I'm doing interpretive talks for schools, tourist groups. They have my home phone number. Give me a call and we can make some time. Just to talk."

Without looking at him, Kate reached out and took the card and stuffed it in the breast pocket of her shirt. "Okay." Her eyes were on the road as they left the town center behind and faded into the darkness toward the residential neighborhoods. "Now. Where did you park your truck?"

"North side of town," he told her. "Phase Three, they call it. I parked right next to that substation."

"I know exactly where you're talking about," she said. "I'll have you right there."

She made a couple of right turns, the headlights of the truck spotlighting freshly mown lawns and smart cars parked in pale, concrete driveways, waiting to pull into wide garages. "I hate this place," she said. And then they were there, her bright beams illuminating Ron's truck. "This the place, fella?"

"This is the place," he told her, smiling at her and offering his hand. She took it, gripped it, and released him. "Thanks for the ride, good lookin'."

"Anytime," she said as he slid out. He smiled again, waved, and shut the door.

While Ron walked to the truck and climbed in, she waited until he had started it and was pulling away. Once, when she was younger, she had dropped a friend at a vehicle, a situation similar to this one, and had driven away without waiting; the friend's car had not started and a four-mile hike in the dark had been made to the nearest public phone. She had always felt some guilt over that, and never wanted to repeat that kind of error.

Falling in behind his truck, she followed for a hundred yards or so. Then he turned south, and she had to bear to the right.

CHAPTER
THIRTEEN

Tim Dodd lay in the garden tub and soaked. *Soake*d, he thought. He was thinking of doing that to the *Inquirer*. Sure, he was on their dime, but he'd earned it. They were paying for this fourth floor room, an expensive room at that. They were footing the bill for this hot bath and for the room service, which he had abused for the past two weeks. But they had gotten some good articles from him. Roe Fox, his immediate editor, had admitted that they received a flood of calls and letters concerning his pieces on Salutations. He'd boosted sales considerably in the South, Fox had told him. But the story was starting to flicker out. People had seen enough photographs of trussed up alligators in the back of some gator hunter's pickup truck. And the hospital bed photos he'd gotten of the fat jogger who'd been nailed by the cottonmouth were topflight, certainly. But the paper had run it twice and that kind of stuff was losing its punch.

"Either build up this giant snake thing you've got going, or head on back. You can't run up your expense account like this forever," Fox had told him.

"I'm not making this up, Roe. These people really are losing their pets to some silent predator coming out of the woods. For real."

"Save it for the funny papers, Tim. This is Roe Fox you're talking to. Now, find your giant snake or get your ass back to home base. You've got a week, son."

And that had been four days ago. That's why he had been desperate enough to follow that Riggs fellow into the forest. Riggs. He wondered how much Riggs knew. And Tatum. And that nut, Grisham. *Damnation.* Dodd stretched to his full length in the hot, steaming water, and still his toes could not touch the far end of the tub. He squinted his eyes in pleasure and watched tendrils of vapor steaming up from the soapy water, rising up to condense on the bonewhite tile above. He slid down until his head was submerged, then he surfaced, scrubbing shampoo into his scalp.

"Ouch," he said to himself, his nail coming in contact with a laceration on the top of his head. When he'd calmed down after downloading the contents of the digital camera, he had slowly realized the extent of the scratches and cuts all over his body. And his hair had been home to a couple of ticks that had buried their bloodthirsty little heads near his right ear. Shuddering, he recalled how he had pried one loose from his groin and another from his left armpit. Filthy place, those forests. He had stood under the shower for fifteen minutes, watching the blood and the dirt run down the drain before he had drawn this deep bath.

Taking the bar of scented soap from its place in a clamshaped tray, he swirled it in his small hands, examining the cuts thorns and grass had sliced there. Even now the soap was causing the wounds to sting, but the slight pains had ceased to bother him. A very small price to pay for what he was probably going to get out of all of this. He rubbed soap in his face, lathering his beard, then submerged his head yet again, rinsing himself.

It was time for Tim Dodd to cash in his chips, enjoy a big payday. If he did this right, he could retire. He wasn't really the kind of guy who enjoyed this game. Yes, there were worse ways to earn a living. God knew he'd had some lousy jobs in the past, and compared to them, this gig was a dream. But the fact was that he just didn't care for work of any type. What he wanted to do was make enough to buy a nice condo on a beach somewhere and become a gentleman of leisure. Screw working. Screw being told what to do. For years, he had been searching for the big score, and this, it seemed, was it.

He wondered how much *The Globe* might bid for the story, accompanied by photographs. But he had to plan it right. He couldn't take any chances that some legal technicality might gum up the works. Dodd had to play his cards well, and if he did, then there was a best selling book in it for him, and movie rights, too. Jesus, this was like some throwback story to the early twenties. Nobody discovered things like this in this day and age.

Nobody but Tim Dodd, it seemed.

But he would need some confirmation. Pictures could be faked. They could do *anything* with a computer, now. They could make things come to life on the movie screen so convincingly that it was impossible to say where fantasy stopped and reality began. He'd need someone to back him up. He'd need someone to admit that there was, indeed, at least one dinosaur living in the wilderness around Berg Brothers Studios' dream town.

Or, if it wasn't a dinosaur, then it was certainly something that *looked* like a dinosaur. If not a dinosaur, then what? What else was ten feet tall and walked around on its hind legs and had small, clawed arms and talons on its scaled feet bigger than butcher knives? Dodd had stared for ten minutes at the best image he'd coaxed out of the laptop. Part of the shot had been of the thing's head; a staring black eye focused intently on the viewer.

Thinking of his race with it, he wondered why it had not caught up with him. It had been just behind him toward the end, just before he'd stumbled upon Grisham. Dodd had felt the pounding of its feet; it couldn't have been more than forty or fifty feet behind him, then. Why had it run? Was it scared of men? If it had been, then it wouldn't have chased him.

Maybe Grisham knew about it. But no. Dodd even shook his head, convincing himself of the old soldier's ignorance. If the Colonel had known about the thing, had suspected Dodd had seen it, then at the very least there would have been a much more unpleasant exchange between them. The guy obviously *hated* the crowds of people he was afraid Salutations was going to bring to his island of right wing paradise. And once word of such a creature got out, then the attention this area had gotten so far was going to be *nothing* in comparison. No, Grisham was not the place he would have to go to for confirmation.

Rising from the tub, he pushed the chrome lever and let it drain. Water, cloudy with soap and with dirt began to swirl quickly away, vanishing soundlessly. Soon he was gingerly rubbing himself down with a cream white towel, careful not to rub the fabric too hard upon any of the crisscross of scratches that patterned his arms and legs. He hissed as he drew the towel along the back of his left thigh. Dodd suspected that there might be a thorn or some other foreign object still lodged in the flesh there. He'd have to go to a doctor and have it examined. The thought of someone probing the wound with a needle or some other surgical tool made him shudder. He'd give it a day or two.

There was Holcomb and his bunch out at that ridiculous compound. The more Dodd thought about it, the more sense it made that the billionaire probably knew something about the animal he'd seen. The guy had ruined his own reputation among environmental groups for chasing after nonexistent creatures like the Loch Ness monster and Big Foot. And there had been that episode a few years back when he'd claimed to have discovered a population of mastodons, or some other such extinct elephant. Actually, Dodd had to admit the guy had almost hit the nail on the head with that one. But what he'd thought was some kind of mammoth had turned out to be a mutant form of regular elephants. Someone at the *Inquirer* had gotten a story with legs out of it.

However, the chances of Dodd getting through to Holcomb, to back him up on this, were probably slim and none. First of all, it was obvious to Dodd that the guy was trying to buy up all of this land and stop the studio from getting it so that Holcomb could take the credit for *discovering* these things. And, having "discovered" them, he would have that entire wilderness wrapped up as his private dinosaur habitat. It wasn't a bad idea, and he'd probably try something like that himself if he had the dough and the resources to do it. Nope. He wasn't going to get any help from Holcomb. If there was one thing he'd learned about extremely wealthy men, it was that they were very ambitious and were never happy with what money they had. He suspected guys like that were always trying to figure out how to get it *all*.

And that left Dodd with your friendly neighborhood wildlife officer: Mr. Ron Riggs. It couldn't be coincidence that he had been following Riggs right before he'd encountered the dinosaur. Of course Tim could argue that it couldn't be chance that he had stumbled into a meeting with Colonel Winston Grisham. But he was convinced that the meeting with Grisham had been a fluke, and a lucky one if what he saw in that thing's big eye had been hunger.

Tim finished dabbing himself dry and went out of the bath and into the bedroom. He'd laid his clothes out, a pair of jeans and a dark blue long-sleeved shirt. Room service was going to be bringing up his supper within half an hour, and he didn't want anyone else seeing his arms and legs covered in scratches. Maybe they wouldn't mention it, but word would get around. And right now he didn't want anyone passing along any kind of gossip. The other glory rags had given up on Salutations as a story, and it had been all Tim's for the past few weeks, but one never knew. A rumor or two and he'd have competitors snooping around, trying to scoop him. He couldn't have that, and certainly wanted to do everything in his power to prevent it.

His grand appearance in the lobby that evening hadn't helped though, he thought as he carefully pulled on his pants and drew on the shirt. If the scratches started leaking, he doubted anyone would notice the stains through the dark fabrics he was wearing. Tentatively, he walked around the king-sized bed, taking a couple of exaggerated steps, to test how it all felt. There was just a little irritation, nothing to worry about.

Going into the den area of the suite, he sat on the couch and looked at his laptop. He'd immediately copied the files onto a pair of disks, even the innocuous ones. Dodd didn't want to take any chances with them. They were his only proof right now, and he'd have to go with that if he couldn't find anything more concrete before he got ready to break the story. And that was another problem, he realized.

One of the first things he'd have to do when he got ready to make his move would be to resign from the *Inquirer*. Technically speaking, this was their baby. He was just an employee. This story, these pictures, this whole deal was theirs. He was just a lowly grunt and the articles and whatever came from them was just work for hire. He'd have to time it well, quit his post, wait at least a few days, and then put the whole thing up for auction. Maybe they'd buy their own pictures back. If they bid high enough.

Sitting there, he thought of how close he had come to activating the phone modem and faxing the files straight to the home office. Dodd had even gotten to the point of bringing up the fax program before he'd come to his senses. He ran his injured fingers through his wiry hair, thinking of the big payoff that was going to be his.

With any luck at all, soon he'd have a decent retirement account sitting in the bank, a good money market fund earning a comfortable living, a townhouse (maybe two) with an ocean view. Dodd thought of Seattle; he thought of his time there with Anne, his wife who'd left him. Hell. Maybe he could get whoever bought the pictures to throw Anne in on the deal, too. Despite everything, he still loved her. Who knew? Maybe she'd come back to him when she heard about all of this. Anything was possible, now.

Dodd sat, drying in the cool air, and he waited for room service to bring the steak and lobster dinner he'd ordered.

And a bottle of wine.

CHAPTER
FOURTEEN

Denny Eagleburger got out of his truck and walked around to the rear. The back was a cage, thick wire mesh holding a very big dog. He could hear the Doberman's dull nails clicking and clacking on the steel floorboard every time it took a step. "Howdy, Number One Dog," he said.

The dog huffed and lunged playfully at the cage door. Number One Dog was his favorite of the bunch. This one, despite the paperwork that claimed that Berg Security owned him, was really Eagleburger's animal. He was, in actuality, what was referred to in the old days as a *one-man dog*. They were attached, these two. Eagleburger unlocked the pen and opened the door.

He said nothing, for they needed few words to understand one another. Eagleburger just opened the door and glanced at the ground, and the 170-pound Doberman poured out, a black, glistening arrow of oilstain fur covering a frame of pure, sculpted musclemass. As it hit the ground, it turned its pointed head on a thick neck and nuzzled the man's fingers with its moist nose. If he'd still had a tail, it would have been carried at half-mast, to tell everyone who was the master: Denny Eagleburger. Denny was leader of the pack, and Number One Dog was his first lieutenant. But, since his tail was nothing more than a surgically altered stump, he made do with dipping his head and nuzzling the master's hand. There were other ways to be understood.

"Sit," Eagleburger hissed. And the dog's haunches went down like a hundred-pound bag of stone. Number One Dog didn't make a sound as the man produced a leash and latched it to the dog's collar. There was just a solid, metallic click in the night. "Good," the man said. Dog's big tongue snaked out, but met nothing, and quickly vanished.

Eagleburger looked around, surveying the area. He had parked the truck near the substation. Tatum had given him the report, showing that the guy from the government wildlife agency had parked here. And the reporter who had been giving the company such a hard time had parked nearby also, apparently following the other man—Riggs his name was—into the forest. Both men had been driven back to their vehicles, the reporter first, and then Riggs. And this was the weird part, Tatum had told him: Dodd, the reporter, had come back with Colonel Grisham, whose ranch abutted the town, while the other guy had been driven back by that big chick who worked for Vance Holcomb. "It's all very strange," Tatum had said. He knew, from Tatum's big mouth, that the studio was worried that they might face some kind of united legal front from the folk they were struggling with. This development did not look good to their suspicious eyes.

Well, Denny Eagleburger didn't make the decisions as to what was strange and what was not. He just read the report, which had been written by his boss, and he was out here to do what Tatum had told him to do. "Look around there. Snoop. See what you can find. If Riggs thinks that snake is there, maybe you can find it. Take one of the dogs with you. Find the damned thing." So here he was, with Number One Dog.

The security guard jerked lightly on the dog's chain and began to walk toward the woods. Out here at the edge of Phase Three, there were only a few streetlights, and they were set back nearer the houses. Here, it was dark, and they had only the stars and the moon to light the way. There was a half moon, though, so the forest was not quite so obscured as one would have imagined. And under a clear sky, the moonlight was enough to reveal quite a lot of detail. Eagleburger could make out the waxy leaves of Spanish bayonet, could see clumps of oleander with bundles of flowers blooming in the night. And the tops of the pines made soft forms against the blue-black sky. The security guard liked it out here at night. The air was comfortably warm, the humidity low, and the wind was blowing softly and carrying the sound of a billion insects and ten thousand smells all blended into a great, moist scent that he'd come to identify with home. Everything seemed to be in it: the mud and the sand, the pines and oaks, the Spanish moss hanging in great masses, cattails growing in wet places. He wondered, sometimes, if the bugs, the untold tons of insects that flew and crawled and hid everywhere one looked were also a part of that heavy, earthy scent.

The two, man and dog, moved away from the truck that had brought them. For a moment they followed the road, and then they veered off, taking an almost invisible trail that led over to the asphalt path the bikers and joggers preferred. This path scribed a huge rectangle around the entire town. It hugged the backyards of the four principal planned neighborhoods, and it angled off into the woodlands that surrounded the place. And it crossed the streams that led down into swamps that then emptied out into the Kissimmee River away off in the trackless places into which Salutations was eventually going to spread. Or so the company was fond of saying. A part of Eagleburger hoped it didn't happen quite that way. He found himself hoping some of that roadless wild could be saved.

Number One Dog huffed, not quite a bark. They held up, stopping short. The Doberman was looking ahead, staring toward the trail, which lay just beyond a narrow strip of knee high wiregrass. Denny reached down and patted the big dog's muscular neck, but he said nothing, whispered no words of encouragement. None was needed. This animal had learned to know what Denny was thinking just by the way the man stood, or moved, or breathed.

Number One Dog huffed again, and the hint of a growl was there. Scratch that exhalation with the right scent, and a deep roar might emerge. One could *feel* it just waiting to burst forth.

Denny nudged the dog with his right knee, barely a touch on the canine's heavy ribs, and both moved forward. The pair, part of a larger pack, was roaming their territory. Nothing could stop them from it. God save whatever threat tried to prevent them from claiming their space. Dog moved stiffly, powerfully on, his Leader backing him up.

Something was shadowing them. Something was moving toward the asphalt trail, but coming in from the forest side, testing the edges of where the town had come out to meet the trees.

The Scarlet had not been able to take the man that day. He had wanted to. He had even smelled blood, tasting it on the wind. The blood had not smelled, had not *tasted* so different from that of a deer, or of one of the savage little pigs that rooted about in the recesses of the high grounds around the swamps. He had wondered how the flesh would taste, how it would feel to take the man and eat him. In all likelihood, the meal would be a good one, he surmised. It would be filling and would sustain him as well as any.

But he had been prevented from discovering if he were right. At the last moment other men had appeared. The Scarlet had felt foolish when that had happened. Perhaps Mother and Father were wrong in some ways, but they were right in others. He had forgotten himself, so absorbed had he been in breaking such a primal rule. Even a pig could be dangerous. Even a pig could tear with tusks and several could form a defensive circle when they were hard pressed. Perhaps men could do the same. The Scarlet had peeled away from the chase, moving in a burst of speed that he knew was faster than that of anything that ran in the forest, and it had left the men to do whatever it was that they did. For a while, it had let the ways of men remain a complete mystery to it.

But only for a while.

Under cover of night, the Scarlet had returned to the verge of the forest, where the trees met the places where men pushed up their stony burrows and their ludicrous paths. Spying on them, the Scarlet supposed that men hunted as the Flock hunted, and so made their ranges in such a way that made it easy to run down the deer and the snakes and the other animals on which it was good to feed. Coming close to where men lived in the past, he had seen deer lying dead and broken upon the earth, left there to ripen by the men who had killed them. The Flock had consumed some of this carrion, and had seen that the deer had been shattered within, as by a great killing head strike. The Scarlet had thereafter imagined how a man might do such a thing, with its tiny head that seemed ill equipped for such a use. Still, the world was strange. Perhaps men could do this thing alone. Who was to say?

In a clump of young pines, he came up and stopped, peering out at the two, the man and the dog. The Scarlet enjoyed dogs. He liked the flavor. Despite what Egg Father had taught him, he had discovered that the dogs who lived side by side with Man were easy to kill. For weeks he had been coming to this place, where the men teemed, and had lain back, out of sight of their poor eyes, and had watched how the dogs lived and where they denned. These dogs were stupid creatures. Even a turtle was wiser in the ways of survival than the dogs who lived with Man. The Flock had been deprived of an easy prey by their refusal to come to where men lived and eat the dogs who stayed in such great numbers. There was food waiting to be taken.

The Scarlet hunkered down, making his moves in complete silence. And he watched the man and the dog come closer. When they came within two steps, he would burst out of the cover and run them down. He looked at them, gauged their mass. He was easily twice as heavy as the two of them combined. The dog's tiny mouth, full of teeth though it was, could not harm the Scarlet. He laughed to think of those fangs trying to tear at his tough skin, trying to bite back as his own great maw closed down on the dog. His feet braced beneath his bulk, his legs tensed, ready to sprint, prepared to sprint.

By chance, the wind suddenly changed direction, corkscrewing down like a dust devil and swirling around a copse of oaks, blowing through a patch of young slash pine and oleander on the north side of the trail. On that wind, Number One Dog smelled something that was completely unfamiliar to it. Something *hot*, something whose blood flowed even warmer than Dog's own. Something whose scent was sharp, edged, like that of a hunter.

Number One Dog stopped short, like a rolling sphere of granite that had suddenly lost momentum. He held up and every alarm in his mind sent out warnings. The Doberman went into a mode of perceiving the world that was reserved for preparation, for *protection*. The pack, two though it might currently be, must be defended. The hair all along his back bristled, displaying a creature more massive than he truly was. His legs splayed out, slightly, bracing for a number of options: defense, attack, and flight. He looked forward, toward the source of this strange scent.

Out of his huge throat issued a low growl. Challenge or warning. The noise was flat, but could be altered to be either. For now, though, there was more of warning in it than challenge. He acknowledged the movement of his master as the man reached forward and released the chain that tethered them together. *Permission to attack or defend* was what the action told him.

And though he *felt* that his pack leader wished it, he waited for the command. The man's hand came up, found the place where the leash met with the collar, and there was a tiny click as the dog was released. "Get 'im," said the man. "Go, boy," he was beginning to say, but the Doberman was already gone.

Dog *exploded* away from where he had been. His thick, dull claws gripped the asphalt trail for just a split second, and then he was dashing across it and into the brush. His eyesight was good, even in this dim moonlight. The earth was revealed to him in contrasting shades, perceived in far greater detail than was allowed by the poor eyesight of humans. He could see the trees and branches and obstacles. He could see forms and the layered nature of the forest. He could see from where the strange scent emanated.

Plunging into the underbrush, he barreled through it,

vanishing between the drooping leaves and limbs, clattering across dried sticks and the other detritus of the forest floor. Ahead, there was the mass of vegetation: bear grass and oleander. Something was hiding back there. Something was waiting.

The dog roared a challenge; to spook whatever waited, threatening the pack. He roared, expecting anything there to be spooked by the loud explosion from his throat, fleeing in fear so that the Doberman could run it down and tear it. This is what it supposed must now happen. This is what it *knew* must occur.

One of the last things the dog would have expected was to be suddenly kicked.

The Scarlet had not thought that dog or man could have detected where he was lying in wait. Of course, hunting Man was a new experience, and there was much to learn. But being detected had not been part of the possibilities for which he was prepared.

He was still waiting to attack when the dog was coming through the underbrush. Confusion reigned in him when the big mammal crashed through to where the Scarlet was waiting. And for just an instant, the two were face to face.

But, the Flock had not survived evolution's test by allowing confusion to dim their kind into inaction. The instant passed, and the Scarlet reacted.

He stood.

The dog saw the thing, his own mind full of the need to protect the urge to kill. He, too, hesitated. This was something new. This was something different and completely unexpected.

While he paused, even for that bare moment, the other

creature rose up. The great head went from the ground, where it had been almost resting against the forest loam. And up, and up. Until the head—roughly the size of a man's torso—was raised ten feet up, eyes staring down from the lower limbs of the live oak behind it. There was a hissing sound as the mouth opened wide. The dog could see a stiff tongue jutting out of the razored mouth like a thick, pointed stick. His eyes were locked on that tongue, on that mouth that presented infinite possibilities of death.

And so the dog did not see and was not prepared to be kicked.

The animal's huge, clawed foot lashed out. Fortunately for the Doberman, the claws were not hinged out, since the blow had been from the ground *up*, rather than a downward, slashing strike. Instead of opening his body like an overfilled water balloon, the foot instead struck him like an unimaginably powerful fist. So, rather than falling to the ground as dripping meat, he was kicked like a two hundred-pound football and sent tumbling, airborne.

Denny Eagleburger had had no time to react. He watched his Number One Dog crash through the brush on the far side of the trail. His hand was fumbling for the big, metal flashlight on his right hip, the one that served both as illumination and as a blunt weapon, if the need was there. The guard was still poking at the *on* switch when he heard something—a *hissing,* like a quickly leaking tire—and suddenly.

He was struck in the chest. His dog, his Doberman, his one-man canine hit him like a sack of bricks.

The air whooshed out of Eagleburger's lungs at the impact. Despite the impossibility of it all, he immediately realized what was happening. *Someone has dropped kicked his one hundred and seventy pound Doberman pinscher.* Just like that.

Man and dog tumbled to the ground in a heap, human limbs tangled with hound legs.

As the man caught his breath, sucking in air, he struggled away from the limp form of his animal. Thinking more of trying to see what had attacked the dog than of going for the pistol on his hip, he finally succeeded in firing the light that was still gripped in his right fist. A tight beam of yellow light arced out from his hand, and he shined it at the clump of oleander and bear grass where the action had taken place.

Except for the branches and limbs moving slightly, either from wind or the passing of something more solid, there was nothing. He aimed the beam further into the forest, toward the north where that entire wilderness lay. For just an instant, and he wasn't sure it wasn't just the sparkling of the stars he was seeing from the impact, he caught a brief glance of something red, something *scarlet* vanishing into the trees.

But he wasn't going to give chase. Whatever it had been, if it had been anything at all, was moving as fast as a car on a city street. He put out his hand and touched his dog. Number One whimpered and slowly got to its feet. The Doberman's back was arched, and if it still had any tail to speak of, it would have been firmly tucked between its shivering legs.

"Come on, boy," Eagleburger said. "Let's get the heck out of here." And the two limped back to the truck.

CHAPTER
FIFTEEN

Tatum had been called into the main office in Orlando. And this was not some meeting with his immediate superior. This was Michael Irons, *The Man*. There was no one bigger in the company. His ideas and sense of commercialism had rescued Berg Brothers from two decades of mediocrity and flat profits. He was, in entertainment jargon, a *true genius*. Salutations had been his personal baby, and he had his reputation tied up in it. Every great plan had its rough spots and quirks, but this was starting to get out of hand. You would buy yourself out of most problems, if you could, and the company had deep pockets.

But there was a limit to Irons' patience.

Out in the plush lobby, Tatum had been left to cool, and to wait. His appointment had been at seven a.m., but it was almost eight, and all he'd seen of Irons had been his beautiful secretary's pouty lips whispering sweet nothings into her headset. He assumed she had a direct line to Irons, but Tatum couldn't be sure. You couldn't be sure of anything where that man was concerned. He waited, staring up at the brightly patterned tiles fourteen feet overhead.

The walls were decorated by floor-to-roof paintings of the studio's most famous cartoon characters. "You know who painted these?" he'd once been asked. When he'd been unable to answer, he'd been told. "Karl Tree painted these.

You probably don't even know who Karl Tree *is*, but he created half the characters we animated up until 1965. The guy's a genius. He retired in '68, and lives in a trailer park near Boca Raton. But we got him out here to paint these things five years ago. Old guy's eighty-five, eighty-six years old. *Jesus*, he paints a beautiful picture. Still does, after all this time."

Well, even Tatum, who cared little for such things, had to admit that the toon figures were beautifully crafted. He looked up at Grandpa Duck and Daisy Cow and Sheriff Dog. Every kid had grown up with them, and even Tatum, in all of his hard, buzz-cut glory, was no exception. If he hadn't been so nervous, he would have smiled.

Finally, the secretary looked up at him, her perfect Aryan features glowing just a bit more (if that were possible). "Mr. Irons will see you now," she said, flashing flawless teeth that were about as white as Montana snow. Tatum got up from the plush comfort of the couch, and he marched stiffly across the foyer to a massive door of solid cherry, a hand-carved bas-relief of Sammy Squirrel grinning madly through the stained wood grain. Brass clicked perfectly under his fingers as he turned the knob.

He entered.

Irons' office was gigantic. It took a lot of space to accommodate such an ego. The room was large enough for a Cadillac to navigate a wide U-turn without ever bumping into anything. Tatum had been here before, and the size of the place always intimidated him, as it was intended to do.

The CEO was standing behind his equally gigantic desk, watching Tatum approach across the wide space. He was disconcertingly young for a man who made most of the big decisions for one of the world's largest entertainment businesses. Forty-three years old and ready, willing, and eager to shred anyone who wanted to try to wrest this juicy bone out of his tiger shark grip. He was smiling at Tatum: a full, toothy smile, and the resemblance between himself and a shark were closer than one might have thought, considering the traditional kiddy fare that poured out of the company. In fact, though, there was nothing very amusing about Michael Irons' demeanor. One had only to ask those who had gotten in his way.

Irons extended his right arm, stiffly, palm up. "Have a seat, Mr. Tatum." *So. It wasn't "Bill" today.* "Do have a seat."

Bill Tatum, security chief and company ramrod, did as he was told. He sat, obediently, like a dog. The CEO remained standing for a moment, still with that smile on. It was all Tatum could do not to squirm or wilt beneath that predatory visage. He did himself credit by enduring it stoically.

"Well." At last, Irons sat, his chair not unlike a throne, of course. "Tell me about this latest development. Or develop*ments*, I should say."

Despite not wanting to reveal his nervousness, Tatum swallowed, lubricating his dry mouth before he could speak. "Well, as the reports I e-mailed to you indicate, there might be some kind of contact between a number of the company's adversaries." Irons' stare continued to be icy, unreadable. There might be rage underneath it, there might be calm. Only Irons knew.

"Explain in more detail," he ordered.

"We've been watching Riggs. He's the official sent to us by Fish and Wildlife over our concerns about the, ah, problems some of our residents have experienced over missing pets."

"And how have you administered this espionage, concerning Riggs?" Irons' perfect, manicured fingers lightly caressed the manila folder on the desktop. Tatum knew the files he'd sent had been printed out and were enclosed, and that Irons had read them all.

"A combination of visual contact, and video surveillance. The discreet placement of cameras only allowed limited access to Riggs' movements. He was inspecting an area that's part of Phase Three. We don't have that part of Salutations as well monitored, and I didn't feel comfortable having him tailed this early on. Riggs ended up going far deeper into the forest around the village than we had thought, so we only reported on his actions around the substation where he parked his vehicle."

Irons tented his fingers and stared at Tatum. "*We? We* didn't feel comfortable having him tailed? Since when did I tell you to have your decisions vouched by anyone else?"

"*I* didn't want him to become suspicious. No one else, Mr. Irons. I want to see where he's looking for this damned snake so that I can have it taken care of without any outside publicity. No need to call in his animal control contractor when we can just do it ourselves, no one the wiser."

Irons smiled, said nothing.

"What I did find interesting, and a bit disturbing, was the subsequent arrival of Tim Dodd." Even Tatum noticed that Irons winced at the name. "The reporter had obviously been tailing Riggs and followed his route into the forest. I decided not to pursue him, also, to keep from arousing suspicion in either of them. I assumed that the last thing the studio needs at this point is a suspicious reporter creating another exaggerated headline for his paper."

There was still silence from Irons, and no facial expression that Tatum could decipher. He took it for approval and continued with his verbal report.

"After that, the subjects' vehicles sat undisturbed for some hours. Until after nightfall in the case of Riggs."

"Long walk, eh?" Irons fell silent again, his sarcasm thinly masking anger.

"The disturbing aspect of our observations came when Dodd and Riggs each returned, separately. First, we monitored a truck known to be licensed to Winston Grisham, and this truck arrived at Dodd's rental car and deposited him. There was some verbal exchange between Grisham and Dodd, but we couldn't read it from the distance we were recording. They both seemed rather calm, until Grisham left and Dodd proceeded at a relatively high rate of speed back to The Executive where he's booked.

"What is more telling are the images of Dodd coming into the hotel lobby." Tatum stood and opened the manila folder that sat in his own lap. He extricated a grainy photograph and passed it to Irons who glanced down at it for just a second, for he'd viewed it previously. "As you can see, he's quite ragged looking there and in a state of agitation. Our own people, who were right there with him, concluded that he was covered in a number of minor scrapes and scratches, but not seriously injured."

"A violent run-in with our militant neighbor?" Irons asked, referring to the retired colonel.

"I doubt that. If Grisham had wanted to get a point across, violently, I don't think we'd have seen a mark *on* Dodd. Or Dodd, himself, for that matter. No. I think he just got scraped and cut in the underbrush out there in the woods." Tatum knew Grisham well. In fact, part of his own military career had been spent on the base at which Grisham had ended his long years in the armed forces. He knew the man's reputation as well as any.

"And what did Mr. Dodd do after that? Details, please."

Tatum opened his file again and handed a second photograph to his superior. "This is from his room. The den area, where he set up his laptop. As you can see, he downloaded the images from that digital camera. In subsequent shots we have of him, he seems quite excited over the contents of that camera.

"We don't yet know what he has," Tatum added reluctantly.

Irons frowned. That was an indication of extreme anger, Tatum knew.

"The rest of that night's surveillance is pretty bland. He bathed, he ate, he slept. He made no calls and made no attempt to electronically communicate the files from the camera. We don't know what he has in the way of images."

"That's interesting," Irons said. "I can think of a number of reasons he might be reluctant to have communicated what he has." He didn't elaborate, but seemed pleased, which made Tatum feel a bit more comfortable.

The security chief handed Irons yet another photograph. "And this I personally find even more bothersome." Irons was looking at an image of Ron Riggs standing beside a truck that belonged to that fool, Vance Holcomb. The picture had been taken with a night vision lens. "Riggs obviously met with someone working for Holcomb while he was out there in the forest. And they obviously were, at some time, in the compound over there. Again, we weren't able to eavesdrop very effectively, but the driver was identified at Kate Kwitney, who we know is a longtime employee of Holcomb's."

"I know who she is," Irons said. He eyed the photograph, his poker face as blank as ever.

"Those two did nothing very exciting after the drop. Kwitney drove back to Holcomb's compound, and Riggs returned to his home. We accessed his phone records for all of that day and night, and he made no calls." Tatum placed his own folder on Irons' desk, although he assumed it was largely a duplication of the one he already had. He didn't ask.

"Well." Irons sat and stared, gazing at nothing Tatum could see. "You were right. This is all very disturbing." He smiled his shark's grin. "Some might say we're being paranoid. Eh?" He winked. "But in fact this does not look good to me. Or to you. Am I right?"

"You're right, sir."

"Yes." His eyes ranged around the room as he thought. "The last thing in the world we need just now is for Grisham and Holcomb and some damned government agency combining legal forces to stop our development of Salutations USA." He stood.

"I'd thought we had the government aspect of the thing under control. But as we all know, it only takes one or two of these environmental impact statements to put a halt to any plans any company might have. Believe me. Just getting the first four phases of Salutations underway and seen through were more trouble than I'd care to repeat. And that was under far more friendly circumstances." He sighed.

"Keep an eye on all of these parties," Irons said, touching the files with his fingers spread, like a huge, pink spider.

"It's already done," Tatum said.

"I thought I had this thing in the bag. Currently, we have the fate of about fifteen thousand acres of prime building space, all of the high ground north of Phase Three, awaiting final approval for our purchase and capitalization. God, I have some *great* plans for that area." He felt his blood rising, as it always did when the ambition began to burn in him.

"So. Keep this bunch under your watchful eye, Tatum."

"Yes sir." Irons was quiet, and Tatum stood, ready to leave. He waited to be dismissed.

"And one last thing."

"Yes?"

"I want to see what Dodd had in that camera of his." He stared at Tatum, his face as flat as a dead calm lake. "Get those images for me."

"I'll do it."

He walked around the desk and extended his hand to Tatum. "I'm sure you'll do it." And he gripped the other man's hand to transfer the confidence he felt in his abilities. "Until later, then."

Quickly, Tatum was out of the room, leaving the building. He had his marching orders and did not even stop to take a last look at Irons' beautiful receptionist.

CHAPTER
SIXTEEN

Ron arrived in Salutations early the next morning. He had hoped that Kate would have phoned him, to possibly arrange a meeting, but she had not. Really, she was a strange woman; about as different from any he had ever considered dating. Perhaps it was that strangeness that attracted him. She certainly was the brainiest woman with whom he'd ever wanted to spend time. Along the way from where he had met her until they'd arrived at Holcomb's compound, there hadn't seemed to be a living thing they'd encountered that she wasn't at least passably familiar with. Strange, perhaps. Amazing, definitely.

Very early that morning, he had made a phone call of his own. Not one he'd been particularly looking forward to, though. Mary Niccols' phone number was on a page of his Rolodex that was getting thumbed quite often. With every call about a problem gator, it was time to call Mary. There were a few other trappers out there, but she was the best of the bunch, and the Department had come to depend on her such that she was their first choice in most situations. Of course, it had come to a point where Mary was hard to reach, sometimes.

And there was the problem of their relationship. For a time, they had sparked; they'd had something going for a while. But Ron had put a stop to it. She'd been too persistent about things in general, and about his ancestry in particular. Mary was near full blood Seminole, could even speak a bit of Miccosukee, and she had begun to pressure Ron into "returning to his roots." And that was when Ron had put an end to their budding romance. He told her, and he told himself, that it was that, only that, and not Mary's profession, not her lack of formal education, and not her dark features and fear of his bloodlines that had made him back away.

As their relationship had grown from a playful friendship to a physical love affair, Ron had felt an ugly discomfort rising in his mind. How would he present Mary to his family? His mother had always been so happy that Ron's Indian heritage was so buried in the Caucasian features he'd inherited from his father's side. Indeed, his mother, who was half-Seminole, looked no less Anglo than most of the other women in the neighborhoods where Ron had been raised. He had thought of the expression on his mom's face if he brought Mary home to meet her. He thought of the dark children they would likely produce. Was he some kind of racist? Better not to deal with that issue. Better to end the relationship and never face that particular beast.

And so he had broken it off with her, never telling her and never fully explaining himself. How could he have told her? He wanted to sweep the times with her away, and not be reminded of the shadows that waited in his own thoughts. But due to her reputation as the best trapper on his supervisor's list, Ron was forced to call her more often than he felt comfortable doing.

Ron returned to his spot at the substation. Mary's battered, green truck was already there and she was sitting in it, the driver's side door opened. Niccols was at ease, her legs dangling, boots beating a soft rhythm to some tune that played only in Niccols' head. The lady had a tendency to fidget when she wasn't out hunting; it was just another thing about her that bothered Ron, or something else that he could consider a flaw. He parked his own truck behind the trapper's and climbed out. She came up to meet him, the sun glowing on her. When he was honest with himself, he had to admit that she was a true beauty. Her hair was long and very dark—she wore it over her left shoulder—not quite raven black, but nearly so. The Native American features that were so buried in him were quite evident on her face; prominent cheekbones accented a pair of long-lashed blue eyes that betrayed her own Anglo heritage. She was smiling, flashing those straight, perfect teeth.

"How are you, Mary?" He winced as Niccols gripped his hand, her slim but hard fingers squeezing with powerful ease. There was no bravado in the greeting, but the woman had a natural strength that was hard to control. Ron also felt a familiar jolt of physical excitement when their fingers meshed. But he sublimated that feeling, as he'd taught himself to do.

"Doing fine, Ron," she said, smiling, her sun-darkened face friendly. She would be happy to rekindle their romance, had even told Ron in just those words. But she hadn't been uncomfortably persistent about it. "So. What's this about a snake? Boa? Python? What are we talking here?" She stood no more than five foot five, built lithely, a powerful torso above strong legs, but still very feminine in a muscular way. She was wearing faded jeans and a sleeveless cotton shirt that showed off the physical power of her upper body. He tried his best not to think of her as attractive.

"Well, to tell you the truth, Mary . . . I'm not sure. I'm not even sure there *is* a snake. There have been four dogs that have vanished without a sound and without a trace in the past couple weeks or so."

"Nothing, eh?"

"Nada. Not a peep. Not a drop of blood. Not a blade of grass out of place."

"Cool." Niccols smiled. "I like a challenge."

"This is the part of Salutations where most of the pets vanished. Well, not counting a couple of cats, this is where they've all disappeared. Phase Three, you know."

"Dogs, huh?" She didn't need to mention alligators. Mary knew them as well as anyone, and she knew that if there had been sign of the big reptiles, then Ron would have said something. She had nailed the previous two problem gators in Salutations.

"Yes. Two were small. Maybe twenty pounds. But the other two were big animals. One was an Airedale. I can't imagine any animal making off with something the size of an Airedale without some commotion."

"Unless it was a snake." Mary smiled again, showing her perfect teeth. "I ever tell you about that python I caught over in Frostproof?"

"Frostproof? Hell, no. That's not that far from here. How'd you miss telling me about *that* one?"

"Yeah. Retired doctor had a place on Lake Reedy. Some neighborhood pets had vanished, and the raccoons he was feeding weren't coming around to the slop trough anymore. He told me he and his wife had enjoyed sitting on the deck and watching them come up to eat the scraps every night. I warned him about rabid coons, but he ignored me, of course.

"Anyway, they also had a terrier which they would keep locked up in the bedroom at night when the coons came around. But in the day the dog had the run of the yard. Well, they'd noticed that the coons had stopped showing.

They started leaving all kinds of food for them, but none of them showed up. And they'd noticed that the numbers had been getting thin for a while, less each week. Finally, none of the coons were showing up for supper. He and his wife figured they'd just gone off into the swamps, or something.

"Then, one day they let the terrier out in the yard. This was about a month after the coons had stopped coming around. He said his wife let the dog out, and it started barking at something. But it barked all the time. At anything. So they didn't pay it much mind. But all of the sudden, right in the middle of a barking fit, it stopped. Just shut up. It stopped so sudden-like that they went out to see what was going on." Mary chuckled, a little bit of trapper humor.

"What'd they see?" Ron asked, smiling at Mary's morbidly amused expression.

"What they *saw* was about fifteen foot of python wrapped around their dog. By the time they got out there, the dog was already dead, squeezed about as big around as my wrist. The doc's lady started screaming while that snake unhinged its jaws and made a big snack out of Bowser. After that, it crawled under their house where it had been denning for a few months, apparently, since it had been enjoying a steady supply of baited coon. When the coons were either all eaten or spooked off, the only thing around for it to eat was that dog." The trapper shook her head in disbelief. "Damn, people are stupid."

"Mary! Don't talk about the public that way," Ron chided. "Heck. If it weren't for all of those stupid people, you wouldn't have this career you've got going."

"Yeah, you're right. God bless the stupid buttheads." Mary looked around, taking in the whole of the artificial township that was visible to her. "So. Where do you think this snake might be? Think he's denned up somewhere around?"

Ron turned back to his truck, waving his arm for Mary to follow. "Come over here," he said. "I'll show you this map and maybe you can make some assumptions."

Niccols waited while Ron reached into the truck and produced the map. It was a studio layout, blue line in great detail, which showed each lot and parcel, even naming each individual owner and the size of properties, right down to the inch. Mary looked at the map, quickly picking out the places Ron had highlighted. She pointed with a brown finger at the lot marked # *1*.

"First dog disappeared from here, hey?" She squinted, reading the lines scribbled down in yellow fluorescent ink. "Big dog, too. Biggest of the lot." Mary could see that Ron had written the animal's weight: 60 pounds. Then she pointed again, her index finger etched a bit with dirt and oil. "And the next dog was just a week later? No way. No way does a snake, *any* snake do something like that." She looked at Ron who was still gazing at the map. "I mean, even if it was a twenty footer, it couldn't digest sixty pounds of dog meat that fast and come back for twenty more pounds. Hunh-uh. No way."

Ron sighed, ran his hands through his sweat-damp hair. "Yeah. I know, I know. But there's the way it happens. Each owner tells me the same story. Place is real quiet. Happens in the late afternoons, while the sun is still up. Not night, yet. The dogs have never barked or shown alarm, and then . . . poof . . . they're gone. No tracks. No blood. Nothing."

Mary shrugged. "Hey. Look. I could use the money, hunting for a big snake. Catching it. But this doesn't look like a snake."

"What then?" Ron was folding his Berg Brothers map, carefully bending it the right way.

"Well, hell. I think somebody's taking them."

The paper ruffled in the still air. Ron stopped. "What?"

"Somebody's taking them. Stealing them. Dognaping, they call it."

"Well, I thought of that." He resumed folding the map. "I thought of it, too. But I don't think that's what it is. I'd think of them running away before dognaping would occur to me."

Mary reached out and took the map from Ron. "Give me that thing. You got the names of the folk with missing critters?"

"Yeah, sure," he said, reaching into his shirt pocket for the small notebook he carried there. "Got 'em all right here." Ron began to tear the names and addresses out of the spiral-ringed book. "I've got them at home, and on some paper-work in the glove compartment. You keep these."

Mary closed her fist around the three little squares of paper, Ron's black ink scribblings showing boldly. "Let's talk to some of these people. See what we can figure out. Hell. Maybe there's more than one snake. Maybe there are two."

"Or three," Ron added.

The two of them saw a flash of a shadow in the trees and looked up to see an osprey glide past at treetop level.

"You know," Mary muttered. "There could be a freaking *army* of giant snakes in that wilderness." She indicated the green forest beyond them with a wave of her muscular right arm. "There's no *telling* what's in there."

"No telling," Ron agreed.

"Good idea to take your truck."

"Huh? Why is that?" Ron looked over at Mary, who was

sitting low in the seat, peering at the corner of the mirror on the passenger side of the truck.

"Well, if I had been driving instead of admiring the neighborhood, I think I might have missed the fact that we're being tailed."

Ron glanced in his rearview mirror. "Tailed? Who the hell . . ." He slowed down a bit, almost to a crawl to get a look at the car that was about a block behind them.

"Recognize it? It's a 1999 Buick Grand Regal. Royal blue metal flake paint, with a V-8, loaded. Rental, I'd say. Know who it might be?"

Riggs crossed the next intersection and continued to steal an occasional glance back at the car. The windows were tinted and he couldn't make out the driver. "No. I've never seen it. If it's a rental, it could be anyone. How do you know it's following us, anyway?"

"Believe me. He's following us. Not a very good tail, if you ask me. I've been followed by some guys who were good at it."

"You were?"

"Yeah. Once, back when I was still married, my husband thought I was steppin' out on him and he hired a private detective to follow me. I only found out when he felt guilty about it and told me. He finally coughed up the file he'd built. Pictures and everything. Just added fuel to my desire to divorce him."

"You never told me about that," Ron said, a squint in his eyes that betrayed his surprise.

"Well, as you should recall, you didn't like for me to mention my short-lived marriage when we were dating. It made you jealous."

Ron could think of nothing to say to that.

"Anyway," Mary continued. "I never even knew he was

127

there. That guy was good. This guy," Mary pointed back with her thumb, "ain't worth a darn at it."

"Well, we're going to be pulling over in about five seconds to talk to Mr. and Mrs. Brill who owned that Airedale. If the guy is following us, he'll have to either stop or pass us. Maybe we'll see who it is." Ron squinted, rubbed the sweat off of his brow. "I'll bet it's one of those Salutations security officers."

"I dunno," Mary said. "Why would they be tailing us? Who else wants to know about us?" Mary wiped at her forehead, too. "And tell me something else, Mr. Fish and Wildlife."

"Yeah? What?"

"Why the *hell* did they give you a truck with no airconditioning?"

Before he could answer they had arrived at their destination. He pulled the pickup into the driveway of the Brill residence. The home, a big five-bedroom brick ranch, was built on the highest point of land in the neighborhood. It stood on a rise a full ten feet or so above most of the other homes. In terrain as flat as that around Salutations, the small rise looked impressive. Ron was sure the retired couple had paid a premium for the lot.

"Nice house," Mary said as they climbed out of the truck.

"They're *all* nice," Ron replied.

Both turned to see if the Buick was still following. In fact, it had pulled onto the shoulder of the street half a block away. They still could not see into the car, which sat there, its motor running. "Yep. That guy sucks for someone trying to keep an eye on us," Mary commented.

"To heck with him. Let's get down to business." Ron started up the drive and headed for the door, Mary right behind him. But before they could get to the front stoop, the door opened and out stepped Mr. Brill.

"Hello, son," Brill said, extending his hand. Brill was a retired executive for Exxon. He and his wife had wanted to retire to Florida and had chosen Salutations as the place. They hadn't counted on something eating their dogs, and the couple was pretty upset about it. Brill's pale features were prone to redden either in the sun or whenever he was angry. Just then, the great bush of white eyebrow that made a single line across his forehead accentuated his emotion-ruddied skin.

Ron took Brill's hand and indicated Mary who had come up beside him. "This is Mary Niccols, Mr. Brill. She's an expert on capturing problem animals, and I thought you might want to talk to her and let her take a look around. She has quite a bit more experience in these matters than I do."

Brill grasped Mary's hand, winced at the quick pressure of the gator trapper, and reclaimed his fingers. "Hello, Ms. Niccols. You're more than welcome to look around, if you think it'll help you figure out what's happened. But first, I want to show you two something."

"What is that, Mr. Brill?"

Brill had a finger to his lips. "Shh," he admonished. "Keep it down. I'll show you, but I don't want my wife to see. She was really attached to Sarah. That was our Airedale," he added. "I haven't told her about it, and was really happy when you called this morning. Don't know how long something like this would keep before I'd have to throw it in the freezer, and I sure didn't want to do that."

"What are you talking about?"

Brill had started around the house. Riggs and Niccols were following him through a covered breezeway that connected his garage to his house, and through which one could access his large back yard. Beyond the yard was the forest against which Salutations was waiting to encroach; sixty species of trees waited just beyond Brill's yard, waiting to be left alone, or to be felled.

In the back yard Brill led them over to a very nice brick building almost as large as Mary's own house. It was merely a workroom and storage structure for the retired executive. Both of the wage slaves were growing more impressed by the expression of wealth around them. "I put it back here," Brill told them as he got out his keys and unlocked the door. "I have a little refrigerator in here, where I keep drinks when I'm working here in the shed." They went in, greeted by a rush of cool air.

"Some shed," Mary muttered. The room was large: fourteen feet on a side, a neat one fourth of the building. The trapper wondered what was in the other rooms. This one was full of woodworking equipment. Fine stuff, she noted. Strictly top-of-the-line.

The older man went over to a tabletop attached to the far wall. He opened the door of the dorm-sized refrigerator and reached in, producing a bundle about the same dimensions as a big hardback book. His guests noted that it was a white towel, folded neatly to contain something. Brill laid it on the tabletop as the pair came to him, and he unwrapped it.

"What do you have?" Ron asked, looking.

Brill said nothing. Inside the towel was a plastic bag, which he gingerly opened. He spilled the contents out on the towel.

Unmistakably, what was there was the paw of a large dog, and a section of leash composed of a fine linked chrome chain. The paw had been very neatly sheared off.

The chain, too, appeared to have been cut.

Mary and Ron crowded in close. Without any hesitation, Mary reached out and picked up the portion of the dog's front leg and looked at it. The insects and maggots had been at it, but there was still flesh attached to the bone. The stench, even from such a small piece of matter, was very powerful. Riggs and Brill flinched back. "Ugh," Mary said. Her voice seemed loud in the quiet workroom. "Where did you find this?"

"Well, I was inspecting the back yard after the maintenance crew left when they finished mowing yesterday. And I noticed a line of black ants cutting across the corner of my fence at the very back of the lot. That was where Sarah had been tied up when we last saw her. We had been letting her run on a line back there stretched between two poles . . . like a clothesline. You know the type?" Both nodded at Brill.

"I saw the ants. So many of them. So I crawled through the split rails to see what was there. I could smell something rotting. And in the broom sedge growing over there I found the foot and the bit of chain."

"Find anything else?" Mary asked.

"Nope. That was all. I got a big stick and poked around in there just to make sure. Searched an area roughly fifty feet on a side. Didn't find anything else like that. Didn't see any more ants, either."

Ron had reached over and picked up the chain. There was only about six inches of the leash remaining, and it looked as if it had been cut cleanly with some kind of shear. He held it in the palm of his hand and examined it, looking for patterns where the metal had been cut. "Hunh," he grunted, seeing only a smooth surface.

"Look at this," Mary said, holding the dead animal's

131

paw out to Ron, wrist side up. She pointed at the exposed bone with her left index finger.

"Jesus."

"What is it?" Brill asked. "What did this?"

"Well." Ron stopped. He and Mary exchanged glances.

"*Well*, what," Brill asked again.

"What do *you* make of it, Mary?"

Mary took another long look at the bit of flesh and bone and put it down. "You got somewhere we can wash up back here?"

"Yes. Certainly. Right over there," the homeowner said, indicating a door on the far side of the room. Mary and Ron retreated to it, went into the bathroom, which was far larger than they had thought. They turned on the hot water, got down a bottle of anti-bacterial cleanser they found on a shelf above the big, tub-like sink. And they closed the door, blocking them off from their host.

"What do you say, Ron?"

"Well. We ain't looking for a snake, I'd say."

"What does that to bone?"

"*And* to metal."

Mary stuck her hands into the hot stream of water and lathered them up. Ron stood beside her and soaped up his own hands. They were silent. Ron felt uncomfortable, being this close to her after having ended the physical side of their relationship.

"Some sick bastard killed his dog," Ron finally said.

"Looks that way," Mary admitted. "Looks like I'm out of an assignment."

Ron let the hot water run over his skin, washing off the soap. He immediately poured another dollop of cleanser into his palm and repeated the lathering process. Mary followed his lead, pausing only to sniff at her hands.

"Well, let's not be too hasty. Let's say it is a sick bastard killing the dogs around here. The cops will have to take over. But maybe something else took off that paw. Maybe something bit it off."

"Nothing *I* know of bites clean through like that. You saw it. That paw looks like a surgeon sliced through it with a fine-toothed bone saw. What the hell cuts like that other than a scalpel or some kind of blade?"

"A big cat, maybe? You know some of the reintroduced panthers have wandered north out of the Everglades. Could be a panther. Certainly enough habitat for it around here."

"No, no, no. You know as well as I do that panthers don't hunt down dogs. Especially not a dog like an Airedale. Hell. Those dogs are bred to hunt big cats. No way."

"Looks like Salutations has some kind of slasher loose in it. Maybe one who just does dogs, but still a crazy." Ron doused his hands with water again and reached for a towel hanging from a rack to the left of the sink. He patted his hands dry and passed it to Mary.

"I wonder if the Buick is still parked out there." Mary looked at Ron. For a moment, they were silent. "Let's go talk to Mr. Brill," she said. "And then we can go see if it's still out there. Let's have a talk with whoever's driving it."

Ron thought for a moment, considering the danger of messing around with someone who'd cut up a dog on site. But then he thought of Mary's considerable physical strength and her reputation as a scrapper. "Let's do it," he agreed. They went back into Brill's woodworking shop.

"Can I take this back with me to the lab?" Ron asked, pointing to the grisly bits in the plastic bag.

"Sure. You can wrap it back up in the towel and take it all away." Brill shrugged. "And what did that, anyway? What bites clean through a dog's leg like that?"

"Not an animal, Mr. Brill. Probably some kind of knife." Ron stood back where the paw and chain were, and he gingerly rolled the bagged mess up in the towel.

"A *knife?* You're saying a *man* did this? Why? How?" Brill's face was growing crimson, even in the cool workroom.

"Your guess is as good as mine, sir. I'm going to report this back to Bill Tatum in security. After that, it's his project. He'll probably want to talk to you about it all."

Brill stood there, his hands clenched into fists, his face practically glowing blood red. "Damn. Beth and I moved down here to get *away* from this kind of thing. *Damn.*"

"I'm sorry, Mr. Brill. I really am. But I can't see how anything other than a knife or a saw did this to your dog." Ron blinked, thinking of something else. "This *is* your dog's paw, isn't it?"

Brill looked up, distracted from his rage. "Yes," he said. "It's her, all right. That's her color. We paid extra. She was the only black and gray in the litter."

"Well." Ron was silent. Mary fidgeted. Ron headed toward the door. "We'll be leaving now. I think this clears up a lot for us. Not an animal, I don't think."

This time, it was Brill who followed the other two. They went through the yard, under the breezeway, down the drive to Ron's truck. Riggs stored the towel/bundle in a toolbox in the bed of the pickup. They shook Mr. Brill's hand and climbed into the cab, feeling the blast of heat as they opened their doors.

As the two looked back down the block, they saw that the Buick was still there, its motor running, parked at the verge of an unsold lot, cabbage palms shading the car.

"Goodbye," Brill said to them. "Thank you for stopping by. I assume I'll be hearing from Tatum?"

"I'm sure you will, Mr. Brill. Goodbye." Ron started the truck as Brill retreated and pulled out of the drive as the gentleman vanished into the house.

Ron backed out, pausing in the street when he confirmed that no car was coming from either direction. Just a quiet suburban street in a well-to-do Florida neighborhood. "What's our next move?"

"You just pull up next to that Buick and let me out. I'll knock on the door and see who comes out."

"Just like that?"

Mary shrugged. "What's he gonna do? Plug us in broad daylight with a hundred potential witnesses waiting to come out of their houses? Just drop me off," she reiterated.

"You da *wo*-man," Ron said, driving toward the car.

CHAPTER
SEVENTEEN

The Buick was parked at the front of one of the few vacant lots remaining in Salutations. Like most of the others in Phase Three, it was roughly half an acre in size, new growths of wildflowers and young saplings trying to reclaim the cleared patch of land for Mother Nature. They wouldn't survive long before someone bought the plot and commenced to 'dozing it and plowing the green under. But, for now, the empty lot was a waist-high mass of shrubs and sedges. Insects buzzed and fluttered at the tops of the grasses, while in the thick mat against the ground, who knew what existed.

Ron drove right up to the Buick and parked in front of it, leaving his truck at an angle, so that the car would have to back away to return to the street. He put the truck in park and stopped the engine. Mary was out before he could even get his key from the ignition. And by the time he was climbing out of the cab, Niccols was already rapping a hard knuckle against the driver's side window. "Balls," Ron said.

The Buick's door opened, the motor still running. Ron flinched, but he noticed that Mary hadn't moved at all. He saw a pale hand reach up and grasp the top of the front door. A man rose into view.

"Dodd," Ron said. He couldn't conceal the surprise in his voice.

Dodd nodded a greeting at him. "Who were you expecting?"

"We weren't *expecting* anyone," Mary told him. "But when someone's following me, I like to know who it is."

Dodd smiled. "I can understand that. Me being a newspaper man and all, I understand perfectly." Dodd stuck out his hand, offering it to Mary. "I'm Tim Dodd. I'm a reporter. You've read my stuff. We spoke."

Mary stepped back and pointed one of her sun-browned fingers at the reporter. "I know who you are." Mary glanced at Ron. "This is that guy who took that picture of me with the gators I trapped out of here. He called me and talked to me for an article. I read it. Good article. *Gator Woman!*"

Ron came around to the driver's side of the Buick. "You *would* like that article," he said. "It made you look like some kind of Florida version of an Amazon. Rasslin' gators instead of Hercules."

"Hey," Mary said. "Good publicity never hurts a lady in my position. I picked up some work after that article came out." Mary was smiling, which was good, considering she'd been ready to start punching just seconds before.

Now that he was closer to Dodd, Riggs saw the ragged scratches and cuts all over his face, arms, and hands. "What the hell happened to you, Dodd?" The man did look to have been dragged through glass. "Somebody throw your ass in the briar patch?"

Dodd smiled, stretching some of the healing cuts on his face. "Actually, you're not far off the mark. I hate to admit it, but I got lost in the forest around here."

"Lost?" Mary squinted her dark eyes, taking a good look at Dodd. "How lost did you get? How long were you lost?"

Dodd produced a fake chuckle. "Pretty darned lost. I was lost for most of a day. Tried to hike through some thick brush and got cut up pretty bad. Even my legs. Pants are shredded. Had to toss them."

"Where the hell were you? And what in God's name were you doing out there? I *know* you're aware that there's about half a million acres of wilderness north of Salutations. If you got *really* lost, no one would ever find you. Ever." The word *dumbass* was poised on the tip of Ron's tongue, but there it waited.

"I was just out scouting around. Looking for a snake." He cleared his throat. "You guys looking for a snake?"

Mary and Ron exchanged a quick glance.

Ron spoke up. "I don't think we're ready to say what we're looking for. But, yes, it could be a snake. Might be. We don't know right now."

The three stood in silence for several uncomfortable seconds.

"You never called me," Dodd finally said to Ron.

"Eh?"

"I told you where I was staying when you were talking with Tatum. I thought you'd call, clarify some things for me. But you never did. Which is why I've been following you guys today. I thought we could talk, or set up a meeting. Think we could?"

Ron thought about it for a second. He wasn't particularly fond of Salutations or its corporate owners, or even of Bill Tatum who wanted to keep all negative publicity silent. But that didn't mean that it was his place to spill his guts and talk about the possibility of a disturbed person killing the local dogs. Who knew what a guy like Dodd would do with that kind of information? No. He'd talk to Tatum about it and let things go from there. It wasn't his job to worry about it, nor to fuel the speculations of a reporter who was ready, willing, and able to capitalize off the slightest bit of gossip or hearsay. "Well, to tell you the truth, Dodd . . ."

"Tim. Call me Tim."

"Okay. Tim. But to tell you the truth, Mary and I are kind of busy. I'll have to take a rain check, for now."

"S'right, Ron. In fact, I think we'd better be heading out." Mary was already moving toward the truck. She saluted to Dodd and walked away. "See you 'round," she said. A few steps took her to the truck, and she climbed in.

Ron, halfway back himself, turned as Dodd called out. "Mr. Riggs. Ron. Could I have a word with you? Just for a second?"

Riggs shrugged, gave a quizzical smirk to Mary, and went back to where Dodd was standing. "What is it?" he asked.

"Look." Dodd was whispering, trying to keep his voice down, and he even turned his body sideways to prevent Mary from even reading his lips. "I really, really need to talk to you. I've got something I want to show you."

"What the hell are you talking about?"

"I was going to keep this to myself for at least a few days. But when I was out of my suite today, someone entered and . . . Well, they tampered with my things." Dodd indeed had a concerned expression on his scabby face.

"What do you mean? I'm sure even Salutations has a few larcenous maids."

"No. Not that. Not that, at all. Someone was into my laptop's files. They tried to download some stuff, but I'm pretty good at computer security. Anyway, whoever it was hacked through about three-fourths of my safeguards before I came back to the room. And they must have known I was coming, too."

"What are you saying? Someone's *spying* on you? Why

wouldn't they just steal the computer?"

Dodd reached over and grasped Riggs' arm, squeezing his biceps to punctuate his words. "Listen. I . . . I *saw* something out there. Out there in the forest." He shrugged his head at the mass of green beyond the houses across the street.

"What did you see? Someone out there?"

"Not someone. An animal."

"What? What kind of animal?"

"I was hoping you could tell me. Look. Can you meet me later? Somewhere safe? Not my suite, though. I think it might be bugged, somehow." Dodd blinked, and Ron could see that the little guy was really, truly worried. He looked scared.

"Well . . . sure. If you think it's that bad. Sure. You want to meet me somewhere? Somewhere in town? I mean, outside of Salutations."

"That would be good. How about Orlando? I could get some stuff together and meet you there. How about the Penta Hotel on International Boulevard? I think I'm going to take a look at room availability there, and check in. Get out of Salutations. Today, in fact. How about it?"

"Yeah. That's fine. I'll be done here in a couple of hours, I'm sure. How does seven tonight sound? Rush hour will be over, and I can be there by seven. I'll meet you in the lobby." Ron raised his eyebrows at Dodd; a quirky habit that his friends knew meant that the conversation was over. He turned to leave.

"One more thing," Dodd said. He reached into the front pocket of his pants, a big pocket that zippered up to hold excess paraphernalia. He held out his hand, palm down, and hesitated.

"What?" Ron asked. His voice quavered, Dodd's nervousness infecting him.

"Take this," Dodd told him, whispering. "Take it and put it in your pocket. Quickly. Don't look at it."

"Okay." Ron did as he was asked. He didn't look. Whatever it was, it wasn't very large or very heavy. Some kind of disk, he figured as he dumped it into his own left front pocket. The exchange had been quick, smooth. It would have looked, to the casual observer, like a last handshake.

"Just keep it for me. Until this evening. Just *hold* it, okay?"

Ron shrugged. "Sure. I'm just holding it until this evening. No problem."

"See you around, then." Dodd retreated to his Buick as Riggs turned, finally, and walked off, back to his truck.

Mary gave Ron a questioning look when he climbed into the truck, but said nothing. She generally wasn't the type to pry much into someone's business. If information was forthcoming, so be it. Otherwise, it was none of her affair. But she was curious about the final whispered bit of conversation she'd witnessed. "What was that all about?" she asked. "Anything to do with us going to see Tatum?"

Riggs chuckled, trying to put it into words. "Hell, I don't know. Could just be dramatized grandstanding on Dodd's part. But he says someone's *watching* him and he wants me to meet him in Orlando tonight." He laughed again, trying not to make it look so serious for Mary.

"You gonna do it? Meet him?"

"Hell, I guess so."

"You want some company along? I mean, just to be riding along?"

Ron cleared his throat uncomfortably. He'd never really told Mary of his true reasons for ending their relationship. In fact, he'd never quite admitted it to himself. But however poor and dishonest those reasons, he couldn't bring himself to try to get things going again. "I think I'd just like to go alone. You know. I'm just not in the mood to make a date out of it tonight."

"Okay. Sure," she told him. "Only I wasn't really thinking of it as a date. But that's okay. I understand what you're saying."

Ron hoped she did. He started the truck and backed out into the street, letting Dodd pull out, and he watched as the small man's car headed away from them. He watched until the Buick went down two blocks and hung a left. "Well, we're off to see Bill Tatum, now. Tell him what we've got. What we think happened to the dogs. The ball will be in their court, now."

CHAPTER
EIGHTEEN

Walks Backward was finding it increasingly difficult to obey the First Command. He was certain that the Flock's leaders were wrong in how they were handling this most basic problem. There was something that needed to be uttered, and they were not doing it. The existence of the Flock was in jeopardy. Despite fighting the urges to act, to continue to do the job for which he had been born, he was feeling a deeper need to do the unthinkable.

If something did not happen soon, he was going to have to challenge Egg Father for supremacy of the Flock. And, following that, would be forced to destroy the Flock's Egg Mother and choose a mate.

The signs were there, although at this point only he recognized them in himself. He had already chosen a prospective mate. It was the Third. She was a young, but mature female who corralled the chicks when it looked as if they might stray. She did her job well, and had never lost one of the young to any predator or accident. She would make at least as fine a breeder and nurturer as Egg Mother. Walks Backward had picked her, had chosen her, and would mark her as his mate if something did not soon occur to bar that path.

But, he was willing to wait for just a bit more. The Flock was now in the midst of their range. They knew the wilderness well. Knew this place of no-Man, where only the things that were woven together existed. Before, over all of the lives of all of the living members of the Flock, Man had been present around the edges of the forest and streams and wetlands. But Man had only rarely come into their domain, for purposes it was hard for them to understand. Man did not hunt there. Did not kill there. Only seemed to play strange games among themselves, and send the Screamers overhead. When he was a hatchling, the Egg Mother of his day had given the command to hunt some men who had threatened the Flock's chicks. In the Song of History, it was the first moment in many lifetimes that such a thing had happened, and it had been the last.

This one—who watched the path that his fellows left behind, destroying all trace of their passing—was ready to continue his task in another way. He would cease to be Walks Backward, and would take a new name. He would become Egg Father. The latest Egg Father. So that he would not be the *last* Egg Father.

He thought, that for a small time more, the Flock would be safe. They were north of the new, sprawling nests that Man had begun to build at the verge of their homeland. This was not good, but he (and the others) had thought that they could continue their ways, as long as Man did not venture into the forest and eat it as they ate everything else. There were stories, in abundance, of how Man consumed the world. Walks Backward was acutely aware of the threat.

And, worse, was that *now*, at this time, the one they called the Scarlet would be born. The rogue had appeared to the Flock the previous night. He was singing a song of confusion when he came running along the edge of the track they had made, to hunt one of the pigs that were present in these forests since the second wave of Man had come. The first Man, the ones who had been here for two hundred lifetimes, had been difficult to deal with and had forced the Flock to change its ways of living. But the next Man, the ones who came in such huge numbers only six lifetimes ago—they had brought with them new creatures, while destroying as many as the first men had decimated. If the Man from whom they now hid ever discovered them, Walks Backward knew they would be doomed. Their only hope lay in retaining their effective invisibility. The Scarlet was going to reveal them. He knew this just as surely as he knew that in a few hours the Sun would rise up from its nest in the Earth.

During the previous night, the Scarlet had trailed the Flock for hours. Walks Backward, of course, had spotted him first. Initially they all hoped that he was rejoining them, that he had abandoned his ways and would once more sing with them, hunt with them, *obey the leaders*. But he had not. He had stubbornly nagged at them, trailing behind and making short dashes up to the west and east flanks of the Flock. Tunes of confusion had chirped up from the youngster and the adolescents, as they had not understood. Nor, even, had some of the adults.

However, Walks Backward had understood, seeing in the Scarlet some of the signs of what he was beginning to sense in himself. What the rogue was doing, even if he himself did not quite grasp the fact, was making the false steps that would soon develop into a mating dance. He was going to cull some females from the Flock. He was going to choose young males to act as his supporters. The possibility existed that he might, indeed, challenge Egg Father for supremacy, or else try to form a new Flock.

It was only that the Scarlet was so stupid that had so far spared them either of those particular scenarios. If a challenge did occur, he would be able to destroy the current Egg Father. Of that, Walks Backward was certain. No other in the Flock was nearly as tall, as heavy, as powerfully built. Not even Walks Backward. The Scarlet might be injured in such a battle, but he would certainly kill Egg Father in a struggle. His reach was greater. He could pounce higher and slash with speed, his mass behind each blow. And his gigantic head . . . a single bite could end any confrontation as quickly as one could blink an eye.

Still, even if that unthinkable occurred, Walks Backward was prepared. He would leap in even as the Scarlet sang his victory trill, and he would kill him. He could do it. He *would* do it. If the battle happened.

But there was a better plan, if only the Mother and Father would do it. The Flock could kill the rogue and be done with it. It was only that the problem member had come from one of their own clutches that prevented them from doing it. They could not *quite* bring themselves to destroy one of their own young, hideous and twisted though he was. It was a flaw in their emotions that could spell destruction for the entire Flock.

Walks Backward had decided. He would wait for the Sun to come up from the Earth one more time. If, after that, nothing were done, he would insist that a new tune be sung. And if, after he had given sound to his thoughts, nothing *were* done, he would sing a different song. He would sing a song of death. And if Death would not stalk the Scarlet . . . well, then it would come for Egg Father, or Walks Backward, whomever of them would prove to be weakest.

For now, though, the call to hunt had come. There was no rogue this night running at the edges of their formation, confusing the youngsters and distracting the adults. Tonight, there would be prey and there would be meat. The Flock flowed out of the palmettos and out of the piney woods. And they gave chase.

Life, for now, was still good.

CHAPTER
NINETEEN

They had come into his room!

Tim Dodd could, technically speaking, say that they had broken in. If it was Berg Brothers employees, as it must certainly have been, then they owned the property. But it was still an invasion. The fact that they were so suspicious that the studio would break and enter was amazing. That they were so desperate had frightened him.

The thing that had really gotten to him was the laptop. Tim had installed a wonderful security system on his hard drive. An associate at the *Inquirer* had been one of the top hacks in the underground before he'd grown weary of being chased and had, so to speak, come in out of the cold to a legitimate job with the paper. So Tim had asked him to theft-proof his laptop's hard drive. While the programs his acquaintance had provided could not prevent a truly gifted individual from hacking into it, the attempt would leave a telltale sign behind. The hacker at the office had laid in a set of commands that would bring up an icon on the Windows program—a little screwdriver—if any of the security systems had been breached. At that, all Tim had to do was click on the screwdriver and the system would boot to DOS text and the files that had been tampered with would appear on the screen.

Dodd had hidden the laptop as well as he'd been able

147

when he'd left the room. Of course, before that, he had put the photo files he'd made on disk and had erased them from the hard drive. While a good troubleshooter could unwipe them, he'd first have to crack the security barriers Tim had installed. And that would take time. And, if they ran out of time and had to leave the laptop, Tim would see what had happened as soon as he switched the computer on.

And that was precisely what had occurred.

He had stashed the laptop in the briefcase-sized safety box in the suite. Again, any expert could pick the lock, and someone obviously had. Only this expert had probably had a key and had also been a computer whiz who had worked his way through about half the safeguards the *Inquirer*'s resident hack had put in place. The screwdriver icon had told all. And the experience had frightened Dodd. When he'd unlocked the box to work on the cover letter he was going to be sending out to bidders, his heart had frozen in his chest. *Who's been sitting in my chair?* Who, indeed.

And that was when he had known that he might be into some trouble. Anyone desperate enough to break and enter might also be desperate enough to go another step further. When you were dealing with a mega-billion dollar corporation, the step was most likely going to be a giant one rather than a baby step. Either way, he didn't relish the idea of being stepped on.

So he had decided that he had to get some corroboration. Who else was likely to know of the existence of something that looked like a dinosaur in the forests around Salutations? Who else had suddenly reappeared at the company's *ideal town* shortly before Tim had made his discovery? Who had Dodd been following when he'd stumbled upon the creature? The answer, of course, was Ron Riggs. All Dodd had to do was find the man; that had been painlessly simple. The first pass he'd made in revisiting where he'd parked his car at the substation had revealed the Fish & Wildlife truck with the government naturalist inside. The rest was simple, with only the added problem of an unknown companion becoming a slight difficulty. But he'd sidestepped that one, too.

Immediately after his talk with Riggs, Dodd had returned to the suite. All along the drive back, through the postcard perfect streets with their manicured lawns and past the rows of flawless homes, he had watched suspiciously for anyone tailing him. Cars with gray-haired wives had turned off going to bridge games. Sedans with young professionals on their way to jobs or meetings in town had dogged his bumper so obviously that he had known he'd had nothing to fear from them. All of them, though, had been targets for his rising paranoia.

He'd pulled into the parking lot of the hotel complex alone. There wasn't even a random auto tailing him, and that had made him feel good. As he'd gone into the lobby, though, he had looked up, and for the first time had seen— *really seen*—the video cameras tastefully, but conspicuously placed all around the big, central gathering area. It was to make the tourists feel secure. A chill had gripped him, then. These cameras, he had seen. How many were hidden around the lobby? How many were hidden in the halls? How many were concealed in the rooms? *His rooms?*

As quickly as he could, he had gone back to his suite. But not alone. He'd actually accosted one of the bellboys— a college age youth with short red hair—in the lobby, the only one he'd seen there.

"Excuse me . . . son?"

The boy had looked up at him, gesturing to his own chest with a white-gloved hand. The hotel had the menial laborers decked out in old-fashioned bellboy uniforms, and the doormen looked like decorated soldiers.

"Yes. You," Dodd had told him, waving a twenty he'd drawn out of his wallet. "I need some help getting my luggage."

"Checking out, sir?"

Dodd knew that the boy must certainly be aware that he was checking out, for everyone had buzzed about his mad appearance all scratched and bloodied from two nights before. Still, Dodd supposed, he had his own games to play for a decent tip.

"Yes. Checking out. And I need some help with the bags." In fact, Dodd had only a single suitcase, a clothing bag for his one suit, and the laptop that he was lugging with him even then. He had decided not to let the computer out of his sight again. Not after what had happened. But he did not want to go back to that room without another person with him, even if that person were just a bellboy. There was safety in having a companion. One was less likely to be ambushed with another pair of eyes watching out.

He'd felt much better—*safer*—with the bellboy dogging his heels. Together, in silence, they had taken the elevator up to the fourth. In silence, they had walked the hallway down to his room, only the slight scuff of their shoes to mark the way. All down the hallway, Dodd had looked up at the ceiling, in the corners, at potted plants on pedestals, looking for flaws where a tiny camera might be hidden. He'd seen nothing, though, merely the perfection of the new hotel, solidly built. It did not reassure him.

Finally, as they'd entered the room, the boy had spoken.

"I hope you enjoyed your stay," he said from behind Dodd as they'd gone in.

Dodd had not even had the time to reply. Just as he

heard the door click soundly shut behind them, the door to the bedroom had moved slowly open and two men, men who looked exactly like some stereotype of the northern tourist in sunny Florida appeared before him. They were all decked out in floral prints with white shorts that showed pale legs and ruddy knees. But their faces were expressionless, their eyes hidden by dark shades over fatless cheekbones. They came swiftly in and grabbed for his arms, one on each side. These were certainly no harmless tourists accidentally admitted to the wrong room. They knew where they were and just what they were going to do. The reporter tried to escape, tried to back away.

But the bellboy was behind him, to prevent his retreat.

Of course.

The reporter started to yell for help, and was quickly gagged by the application of a rag held over his face by a strong hand. He gasped, smelling something with a powerful chemical odor, and wondered if this were the legendary chloroform rag. Whatever it was, he blacked out during the second inhalation.

He never felt them take his laptop out of his rubbery, drugged grip. He never heard any of the things they said to one another after the bellboy had asked him if his stay had been a nice one.

And, some hours later, after they'd beaten his story out of him, Dodd never heard anything again. Not ever.

CHAPTER
TWENTY

It was the ringing of his phone that woke Ron. For some reason, even in his sleep, he'd been thinking of the remainder of the previous day. He was thinking of it even as he reached for the receiver.

After he and Mary had informed Tatum of their suspicions, even handing over the severed dog foot, the two had figured their jobs were over, as far as this little problem was concerned. Ron had enjoyed seeing Tatum's expression when he'd unwrapped the towel to reveal the plastic bag with the rotting canine paw inside. Mary had made some comment about eating it there or taking it home.

"Still the joker, Ms. Niccols?" Tatum asked. He had not been amused at her humor.

Ron was a little surprised to see that the security cop and Mary knew one another. "You two have met?"

"My other visits," Mary had told Ron.

Ron was growing certain of one thing—Mary Niccols would be a frequent visitor in the future, as the village quickly expanded to take up more and more of that prime wilderness. Such was life.

And then he had gone to the Eyesore, to try to see if Ms. Kwitney was there. He was growing more and more disappointed that she had not called him, and the prospect that he was just not her type was beginning to bother him. Maybe she just hadn't been as enamored of Ron as he had been of her. If so . . . *oh, well,* he told himself. But, truly, he hoped that was not the case.

He took the single sandy track leading out to the Eyesore. Finding it had proven to be something of a chore. The road was not marked, of course, and it was such an ephemeral avenue that it was nearly invisible in the wall of pines from which it emerged. He'd had to make two passes in his truck before he'd spotted it. Others must have had the same problem, for as he had turned off the paved road and into the forest; he had spotted a small yellow flag of nylon fabric tied to a pine sapling, close to the ground. That was Holcomb's idea of a road sign, he supposed.

Ron kept expecting to encounter someone else along the way. An employee headed out for supplies, or maybe one of Holcomb's people out spotting wildlife. But there had been nothing to encounter except for the ever-present buzz of central Florida's insect population screaming wildly in the yellow sunlight, and an occasional bird flitting from tree to tree. It had really been too hot for anything but the liveliest of Mother Nature's progeny. He'd watched clouds of sandy dust billowing up in his wake as he had driven down the road, perhaps moving just a bit faster than he should have. But it was the thought of talking again to Kate that drove him to push the pedal too close to the metal.

At last he had come out of the woods and into the clearing where Holcomb's compound sprouted out of the ground like a gigantic set of building blocks. Ron had pulled up to the front gate, shut the motor off, and had climbed out. For a minute or two he had stood in the golden light, feeling it press down on the crown of his scalp like a hot, but weightless hand: God caressing the hair of yet another of his children.

Ron had stood there, waiting. He had looked to the gate, expecting to see someone come out of the guardroom, which stared at him with a great, reflective eye of a window. No one came. He expected to see someone moving around, doing work, going from one building to the next, carrying boxes or equipment. He thought that he might see one of the four-wheelers come putt-putting out of the garage, or maybe one of the trucks.

But all was still. All was silent.

After a few minutes, Ron had called out.

"Hello!" Silence. "Anyone here? Anyone home?" Cicadas screamed at one another, yelling out their lust for all to hear. "Mr. Holcomb! Adam Levin?" A pair of Love Bugs floated on a hot current, joined genitally, one to the other, locked in a moment of reproductive passion. "Kate," he had screamed. "Kate! It's Ron Riggs!"

Only the bugs replied.

He'd reached into the cab of the truck, honking the horn once, twice, again. No one called. No one came. No one moved.

Ron had stood there for a moment or two more, thinking that he could feel that he was being watched. He knew that a number of people worked in Vance Holcomb's weird little compound. Ten or fifteen at least, just to keep it going. There were windows looking out at him, gilded filters of golden film making mirrors of them. Ron could see himself reflected in them; he was small and vulnerable as he leaned against his truck. He wondered who might be in there, seeing him, looking at him as if he were a specimen to be studied. Levin, perhaps, laughing at him. Or not laughing.

It was then that a chill had passed down his spine. This was not right. He was not wanted here. Not now, at least.

Shivering away the gooseflesh, he had broken his gaze from the buildings and had climbed back into his truck, finding not a small amount of comfort when the engine fired right up. Perhaps he had turned around a little too quickly, had gunned the engine a tad too much, and had left the place in just an embarrassing bit of a hurry.

The way out was longer than he had thought, driving in. He kept expecting to see the paved blacktop of Salutations around each curve, but met only more of that sandy roadway and more pines and more palmettos and more oak. Once, he thought he saw someone, a dark figure behind a tall growth of bear grass, but he couldn't have been certain. And he hadn't cared really. All he had wanted to do at that point was get out of there, get back to the road, get on his way back home so that he could wash and dress to meet up with Dodd back in Orlando.

When he had come out of the woods and onto the asphalt, he had left a good hunk of rubber there, heading out.

At home he had checked his mail and his answering machine. Nothing but a few bills in the former, and, at last, a message from Kate on the latter.

"Ron. This is Kate," the machine said, accentuating her husky voice. Ron smiled. "Since I guess you're out chasing gators or teaching kids, I'll just leave a message. We'll be busy here today, so I won't have time to get up with you, but maybe this evening. Why don't you give me a call? I'm going to give you my number, so write it down and call me back later." He had scrambled through the mild jumble that was his house, and had found a pad and pen and soon had her number jotted down for posterity.

And that was why he had called her shortly before leaving for Dodd's new temporary abode on International

Boulevard. Luck being still with him, she picked up on the first ring. No answering machine.

"Kate. This is Ron Riggs."

"Hello, Ron. I'm glad you got my message." She sounded tired. There was a breathless catch in her throat. Her husky voice excited him, though. Yet again he felt himself aroused by her, as he had not been aroused since he'd ended his romantic relationship with Mary.

"You sound pooped," he told her.

"I am. Hard time today. We've been all over Creation."

"Creation?"

"Well, the back country. I went with Vance and a crew out into the wilderness today. We had some work to do. Some population studies. We were gone most of the day."

"Well, that explains why I couldn't get a rise out of any of you today."

"What?"

"I went down to the Eyesore. To see you. But no one was there."

"You went down there today?"

"Yes." He could tell that she sounded annoyed, for some reason. "I figured I might be able to see you. I didn't have much to do in Salutations today, and we figured our job was over there, anyway. So I had some time to kill." Ron was nervous, now, and trying to hide it.

"You came down to the compound, though? And no one was there? How do you know no one was in?"

"Well, I thought someone would be at the gate. They weren't. I called out. Pretty loud. For Adam. For you. Even hollered for Vance Holcomb, which I guess he's probably not used to."

"You'd be surprised," she told him. He could hear a chuckle in her voice, which reassured him.

"And then I honked the horn a time or two. No one came out. I guess they were too busy. That is . . . if there was anyone there."

Kate said nothing to that. Neither denying nor confirming. Finally, she spoke. "Why'd you finish up early in Salutations? Catch any big pythons?"

"No. Not at all," he told her. There was no reason she shouldn't know what he and Mary had discovered. And maybe if he were frank with her, she'd warm up to him. She was playing a bit too hard to get, and he didn't really care for too difficult a chase where women were concerned. "Mary Niccols—a woman I work with sometimes—I took her with me to talk to a gentleman who lost a dog, and he showed us something he'd found."

"What was it?" Her voice sounded tense again.

"Well, it was kind of gruesome, really. But it was his dog's paw."

"Its *paw?*"

"Yes. Just the paw. And part of its leash," he added.

"Part of its leash?"

"Yeah. The really nasty thing was that the paw, and the leash, had been cut with some kind of tool."

"A tool? What do you mean? What kind of tool?" She sounded really very interested now, and Ron imagined her sitting on the edge of her chair, leaning into the receiver, hanging on his words.

"Yes. We took a close look, and the cut was too clean and too smooth to have been made by anything other than some kind of blade or clamp. Even the metal links in the leash had virtually no scoring on the chopped ends. Whatever the guy used, it went through bone and metal like cutting rubber with a razor blade."

"Good grief."

"Yeah. That's what we thought. In a way, I was kind of relieved. I don't like having to have animals trapped and euthanized, even if they do pose some vague threat to people. It was nice that it wasn't a snake."

"I know what you mean," Kate told him. "Did you find anything else?"

"No," Ron said. "We didn't really look around much, to tell you the truth. Not after that. We turned the evidence over to Bill Tatum, head of security out at Salutations. He didn't look too pleased to be handed a severed dog's paw, I can tell you. And I think he'd have been happy if it *had* been a snake. Dodd's *Jurassic Park* stories were starting to wind down, and they'd be easier to take than would some dog mutilator stalking his perfect little town. That kind of thing just isn't supposed to take place in a planned community, you know."

"You gave it to Tatum? Damn. I'd like to have examined it."

"What for? I told you something metal cut it. What interest do you guys have in a dognaper?" Ron was confused, a bit. Could the perpetrator be someone from the Eyesore? He thought of Levin carving at the tubful of buzzard guts.

"Ah, no reason," she said. "I'm always tinkering."

"Tinkering? With a dog paw?"

She utterly surprised him, then. By asking him out. "What are you doing tonight?"

"Well . . . when?"

He thought of her looking at a clock, to get the time. "How about eight o'clock? I could meet you somewhere. How about St. Cloud? I know a really good Cajun restaurant there."

"Damn."

"What? Don't like Cajun?"

158

"No. I mean, yes, I like Cajun food just fine. But, I have to meet someone in Orlando at seven. I'd have to drive from Orlando down to St. Cloud after that, and there's just no way I could make it by eight." He thought, trying to figure a way. "Can you meet me in Orlando?"

"God, no. I *hate* that place. Stay away from there as much as possible," she told him. "Who are you meeting, anyway? Another lady?"

That sounded almost like jealousy. That was a good sign. "No. Nothing like that. At all. I have to meet that reporter, Tim Dodd. Funny little guy."

"Dodd? I know who you're talking about. The one who wrote all of those funny stories in the *Inquirer*. Why meet him out there? Isn't he in Salutations?"

"No. He pulled out of there today. In a hurry, too."

"A hurry?"

"Yeah. He was really very upset. Said something strange had happened to him and he needed my input."

"Strange? In what way?"

"I couldn't say. He was all scratched and bruised. Said he'd gotten lost in the woods. Wanted to talk to me about something, and said he had to check out of the hotel and get a room in Orlando."

"Oooo. Sounds mysterious," she said.

"I don't know about that. But I'm to meet him at the Penta on International Boulevard. In fact, I'll have to be leaving soon if I'm going to make the meeting."

"Well, I'll let you go, then."

"I wish I hadn't promised to meet him out there," Ron admitted. "I'd rather spend some time with you. Get to know you better."

There was some uncomfortable silence from the other end. Ron even fidgeted. Finally, Kate spoke. "That's flattering, Ron. I enjoyed your company, too. We need to get together to talk at length."

"No problem to that," he said, blushing invisibly to her. "You're a unique woman."

"We can talk about it. Tomorrow? You call me tomorrow."

"I will," he said.

"Well. Bye."

"Goodbye."

He sat there for a while, thinking of Kate, wishing he hadn't promised Dodd to meet him. And then he remembered the way Dodd had passed the object to him as he'd left. As good as his word, Ron hadn't so much as looked at whatever it was. It was still in the pocket of the shirt he'd been wearing earlier. He had to get it.

Ron went to the clothes hamper and found the shirt lying on the very top. He dug into the left pocket, recalling that Dodd had been left-handed and the thing had ended up in the *wrong* pocket. He took it out and looked at it. Yes. It was as he'd thought. A computer disk. But not a CD, and not a 3.5" floppy. This was something else. It looked like one of those digital disks he'd seen at a technology demonstration at the office a few months before. In fact, he was fairly certain it was for a digital camera. Well, it wasn't Ron's business. He'd give it back to the guy as soon as he saw him.

He put it in the pocket of the short-sleeved shirt he was wearing and tried not think of it. For all he knew, it contained some incriminating evidence against some executive from Berg Brothers. Yes, best to give it back to Dodd as soon as possible.

Quickly, he had locked up the house, climbed into the little Toyota Corolla he owned, five years old and going to have to serve for five more before he bought another one: Fish & Wildlife did not pay as well as Ron had hoped. He headed toward Orlando.

In less time than he would have thought, he had pulled off the interstate, on to the big boulevard that paralleled it, and was in the parking lot of the Penta. It was a very nice hotel. Four stars, and very plush. He had stayed there with Mary once, doing the tourist stuff when they weren't having sex, which was only about half the time. She had almost been the one for him. Maybe Kate would be the real thing. He thought of the rest of his life with a woman half a foot taller than he was. Well, they'd turn a lot of heads.

But not as many heads as yours and Mary's dark-skinned children would, eh, you jerk? Ron shook the subversive thought from his mind and tried to pretend it had never been there.

The evening was dark, no moon, but you'd never have known it. Orlando was, as usual, lit up like the all night party it was. There were people everywhere, going to restaurants, to clubs, to parks, to money traps, to everything one could imagine. He doubted any of them were headed home.

Soon, he was in the lobby of the hotel. If the façade was false marble, and not the real thing, then it was an excellent imitation. The place was all pink and white; carpet and what appeared to be polished stone. Very nice. Again, if you liked that kind of thing. Ron was one of those people who did like it, from time to time. He'd never be able to take a steady diet of it, though. It was good for a laugh, now and again.

He got in a short line at the front desk, waiting his turn. Finally, a lean, dark-headed and cleanly pressed young man indicated with a friendly wave that he could step forward.

"May I help you?" the young man asked.

"Yes," Ron said. "I'm meeting someone here. Someone who's supposed to have checked in today. Could you ring his room for me? I don't know the room number."

"Certainly," the man said, picking up a receiver, his manicured fingers poised above a bright yellow keyboard. "What is the guest's name?"

"Dodd. Tim Dodd."

The young man's fingers played quickly and expertly over the keyboard, flitting with practiced speed. There was a short pause. Then, "I'm sorry. We don't have anyone by that name registered. Not even a Dodd," he added.

"Huh," Ron grunted. "Hmm. How about his company? Maybe he's registered under the company name. He works for the *National Inquirer*."

The young man's eyebrows perked up at that. "That's interesting," he said, his fingers already jotting away. And then, "No. Nothing registered to them, either. I'm sorry, but your friend doesn't seem to have checked in yet."

"Were you guys full today? He was going to come in early this afternoon. Maybe you had no vacancies."

"No, sir. We've had vacancies all week. This isn't our peak season, you know." The young man was still smiling, but Ron could tell he wanted to be done with this so that he could deal with paying customers.

"Okay, then. Maybe he just hasn't had time to check in. I'll have a drink at the bar and then come back and see if he comes in."

"You do that," he said, already motioning for the next person in line to come forward.

Ron faded away, and found himself on a stool in one of the Penta's less expensive bars. The place had four clubs and three restaurants, all part of a mini-mall attached to the hotel. So, for an hour Ron nursed a couple of beers from chilly to warm as he slowly sipped them, waiting for Dodd.

At last, he went back to the front desk and once more asked the nice young man the same questions. And once more he received a negative reply.

Damn and hell. He could have spent the evening with Kate. He was really looking forward to getting to know her. To kissing her, in fact. He really wanted to kiss her. "Screw you, Dodd," he muttered.

And within another hour he was back at home, ready to crash. He was asleep about as soon as his head hit the pillow. He'd even forgotten about the disk, and it sat in the pocket of the shirt, which lay in a heap of sea green cotton fabric on the floor. He dreamed. In his dream, instead of Kate, there was Dodd, muttering to him. "I've got something to tell you," the scabby-faced dream image was saying.

That was when the phone awakened him.

Fumbling out of bed, he looked at the red light digits on his clock. "Seven ay emm," he groaned. "This is my day off. Who the *hell* is calling me on my day off? This better be good."

"Hello," he could not hide the drowsiness in his voice.

"Ron."

"Kate?" He was perking up already.

"Yeah. Listen. You were supposed to meet Tim Dodd, right?"

"Right."

"Well, he's dead."

"What? What?"

"Some Osceola County Mounty stopped a car late last

night. Pulled them over for something. Speeding, I think. Something wonky was going on with the license of the guy driving the car, and he tried to make a break for it. Wrong cop. Big chase. He ended up pushing the guy off the road. Somewhere off of twenty-seven, I think. Into a drainage ditch full of water and lily pads. Don't ask me how, but the driver got away. Something about a third car and another suspect. But when they pulled the car out of the ditch and looked in the trunk . . ."

"Dodd?"

"Dodd." Silence. "He'd been shot. Once. In the head."

"Jesus."

"I think you might want to talk to the cops," Kate said.

"Grief." He rubbed the sleep out of his eyes, stared at nothing. "Thanks for calling, Kate. But . . . I'd better go. You're right. I'd better call the cops."

And now. Now, he thought seriously about the small disk that Dodd had given him. He gazed down at the heap of cotton fabric that was the shirt, and was almost afraid to reach down and retrieve it.

But, finally, he did.

CHAPTER
TWENTY-ONE

Kate Kwitney was sitting in Vance Holcomb's huge office. The doors were closed tight, the big windows were shuttered, and she knew without having to be told that he'd activated and rechecked all of his safeguards against electronic surveillance. The room was cool, silent, relatively comfortable, and disturbingly silent. She waited for Holcomb to speak.

"What do you make of this?" he asked.

"I couldn't really say," she told him. "I only know what I've told you so far. Who do you think killed him?"

"I could conjecture, but I'd only be guessing."

"The studio. It was the studio, wasn't it?" She shrugged. "I can't think that they would be so upset over his little articles, which his editors were probably about to stop running, anyway. I really don't think anyone would kill him over that."

Holcomb snorted. "Do you have any idea how much money is involved in Salutations USA? Do you?" There was a razor-like anger in his voice.

"No, sir. A lot, I know."

"We're talking profits in the *billions* of dollars. Long term, in the *many* billions of dollars. These are just the profits, Kate. Not gross."

"I understand," she said.

"No. I don't think that you *do* understand." He moved from his post behind his desk. "Listen. I grew up with these people. My father was one of them. He earned hundreds of millions of dollars doing whatever it took to earn it." Vance looked over at Kate, his face all but in shadow. "Do you hear me? *Whatever it took*.

"These kinds of men put no value on a human life. A man like Dodd is a minor detail. An extra decimal point misplaced on a page, and to be done away with. Erased. Whited out.

"Do you understand?" He pointed at her.

"Yes. I understand. But what kind of danger would he have posed?"

"I think he saw something," Holcomb said.

"What do you think he saw?"

"I think he's seen what *we've* seen."

"How? I don't believe it. There's just no way. No way, at all."

Holcomb turned his back on her. "What about the dogs missing from Salutations? I think there's something to that. I think what your Mr. Riggs told you confirms it." He sighed. "Damn. I wish we'd been able to have a look at that dog's foot."

"I don't know if that's enough evidence that they're coming into the city, Vance."

"I think so. The red one. The scarlet one. It isn't with the rest, anymore. It's so big, maybe they chased it out of the group."

"God. I hope not. He's so *huge*. He could be spotted too easily."

Holcomb moved from behind his desk and walked slowly toward Kate. Finally, he stopped just in front of her. "I think Dodd saw one of them. Maybe the red one. I think he may have taken photographs."

"Why would you say that?"

"Because of the bullet in his head. I think they killed him because he had *proof* of something out there. I think they killed him to *keep* him from being *able* to prove it." He remained where he was and continued to stare down at Kate.

"Then . . ." Her hands moved up to her chest. She could feel her heart suddenly pounding at her ribs.

"Then, if they'd kill Tim Dodd, they might as well kill us, too," he finished for her.

"Do you think they know? I mean, that we're aware of what's living in this wilderness?"

"That would depend on whether or not Dodd had any proof, and whether or not they recovered it from him. And I think the answers to both of those questions are *yes*. Just taking the images from him would not have prevented him from telling anyone, nor would it have prevented him from coming back, with help, to get more proof.

"That's why the bullet in the head."

"Jesus." Kate swallowed. The idea of being shot or even the *chance* of it happening was not something she thought that she could deal with. "What should we do?"

"I think . . ." He stopped short. "I'm not sure, just now. But it might almost be time for us to go public."

Kate came out of her chair, standing up to face her employer. She was almost as tall as he was. "No. You know what will happen. This place will be crawling with people. We can't have that. Not now. Who knows how they'll react to other humans in their habitat? I mean . . . the only reason they haven't reacted to us is that our studies have no impact on their lives."

CHAPTER
TWENTY-TWO

"Geez-o-Pete," Ron muttered. It was a mild exclamation he'd picked up from an old girlfriend. He had pulled at his hair until it spiked up on his head like that of some punk or Goth, as he had tried to decide his course of action. "What the hell am I supposed to do?" he whispered to himself.

For a long time he had simply sat on the edge of his bed and had gazed down at the green shirt he'd shed the night before. It lay there harmlessly, the disk in its pocket, looking to Ron like some deadly viper waiting to strike at him. He had no doubt but that Dodd had been killed for the contents of that disk.

Ron didn't know if he'd be suspected of having killed Dodd. He could account for most of his whereabouts the previous morning. But of course part of that had been in the company of the murdered man, so what did that get him? And he had told two people that Dodd wanted to meet with him before he'd actually left to do just that. Mary knew him well enough to know he wasn't a murderer, but Kate was barely familiar with him beyond his name and occupation, and knowing that he wanted to date her. And if Dodd had been murdered after Ron had left the hotel, then he had no way of confirming where he'd been or what he'd been doing. It didn't look good.

With a groan, Ron had stood, gripping the disk in his

right hand, examining it. Maybe if he looked at what was on the disk *first*, he'd have some idea of what was going on. Cops loved to close the books on a murder, as fast as they could; if they could nail Ron as a prime suspect, then they'd certainly do it. He knew that much about police work. They hated not being able to close a murder case, and they dearly sought after anyone on whom to nail a felony. "What the hell *are* you?" he asked the disk, holding it between thumb and forefinger.

Where could he take it? He knew he only had a couple of hours. Kate had already made the connection between himself and Dodd, so if she was questioned, he'd have to admit that he didn't go to the cops for a while. Well, he wasn't guilty, so maybe he just cleaned up and ate some breakfast. And maybe they'd never get around to asking Kate, anyway. There was no reason for them to, unless she volunteered the information. He'd chance it, if he could decide where to go to have a look at the contents of the disk.

The office was out. He was on a rotating schedule and it was his day off, and he never went there when he was off. His coworkers would be suspicious. At any rate, he'd have to show it to someone there, to see if they had the hardware to download it, and then he'd have to ask someone in the office for help if it proved to be too technical for him. He had a couple of hacker pals, but Ron didn't really want to implicate them. Where, then?

"Kate," he said. He could take it out to Holcomb's compound. He knew he had seen some impressive computer equipment there. In Levin's lab and in a room he'd passed on his way to Holcomb's office. Surely Kate would give him a hand if he told her what was going on. He'd do it.

Ron went to his desk, where his own computer sat, an ancient 486 that had become obsolete years ago, and of no use for downloading this type of software. But he found a small envelope of thick paper that accommodated the bare disk, and he dropped it in and sealed it shut. He took a pen and scribbled a *D* on it, and dropped it in the top drawer.

After securing the disk, he went back to his bedroom and began to assemble his clothes for the day. He picked out some denims and a white cotton shirt. It would be sufficient if he were going back out to Holcomb's compound. He thought of the place sitting there, so close to Salutations, but so isolated from everything, all of that wilderness looming just beyond. Thinking of that, he got a pair of lightweight hiking boots out of the closet and drew some good thick socks out of the drawer. That would do it.

Quickly, he went to his bathroom and took a hot shower. He didn't linger, as he normally would on a Saturday morning, enjoying the warm water as it washed away the sweat and dirt of the previous hours. For now, all he wanted was to get clean and get out of the house and over to see Kate. In a few minutes he was done, had draped a towel around his hard waist, and was headed back to his bedroom.

And, intent merely on getting out of the house, he did not see the men hiding just beyond the doorway, waiting for him to emerge. Ron walked out, turned toward the bedroom, and was knocked instantly to the floor by the power of a strong sap-carrying right at the base of his skull. He went down, the towel still tight around his waist, his cheek meeting with the hardwood floor. The breath whooshed out of his lungs in a prolonged *oof*.

Before he could do much more than acknowledge that he'd been struck, Ron felt rough hands grip his wrists and peel him from the floor as two men stood him up, slamming him against the wall. Almost immediately, a fist plowed a vertical furrow into his stomach and he doubled, going down again, this time to his knees. He felt a couple of woody splinters driving into the flesh just at the top of his shins. "Oog," he said.

The men grasped him by the hair and pulled him up that way. His scalp screamed in agony. He almost forgot the pain in the back of his head, in his gut, and in his knees. And he did forget when one of his so far unseen assailants slapped him expertly across the front on his face, splitting both of his lips. Wincing, Ron could taste blood.

"Don't look at us, boy. Keep your eyes shut."

Ron did not have to be told again. He could feel what might have been a gun barrel stuck in the base of his throat.

"Now, where is it?" The voice was calm, smooth.

Ron swallowed. "Where is *what?*"

The same hand slapped him across the lips again, and Ron tasted a new trickle of copper as the blood burst through his clenched teeth and onto his tongue. "We're not here to play games, son. Just tell us where it is—keep your *fucking* eyes shut!—and you'll live through this. Now," a fist smashed against his right ear. "Where the *fuck* is it?"

"I—" was all Ron said before he heard the intense *crack* of something wooden against what sounded to be something harder. He heard one of his attackers go down as the second released him, the object at his throat vanishing. He opened his eyes.

And he watched as Mary Niccols released the short section of two-by-four she was holding so that she could punch a strange man solidly in the face. The blond crewcut invader tried to dodge the blow, but Mary's work-hardened fist met him perfectly in the midst of his big nose and there was the unmistakable sound of cartilage snapping; Ron had heard it enough to know what it was. Broken-nose backpedaled, away from Mary, stumbling over his partner who was trying to rise, his brown-haired scalp ruddy with blood.

"Assholes," Mary screamed. Her right foot lashed out and caught the blond assailant full in the rectum. She knew that the man would be passing blood for at least a week. The guy finally did go down, but was up again, scrambling for the front door. His companion, who was a bit slower, due to having been bashed over the head with a two-by-four, found his own ass the target of a renewed and well-planted kick. He grunted once, fell forward and found himself outside as his companion led the way toward their automobile, a dark, late model sedan.

The pair at last made some speed toward the car and climbed inside. Mary latched the front door behind them, and watched as the two cleared out, tires spinning in the sandy soil as they left. Mary waited only to see that they were leaving before going back to assure herself that Ron was not seriously injured.

"You okay, Ron?" She reached out and put her hard hand on Riggs' left shoulder.

Ron ran his tongue across his front teeth. "Yeah. I guess." He shook his head, damp hair dangling into his eyes.

"You sure you're okay? Looks like they smacked you around pretty good before I stopped them." She patted Ron's shoulder, reassuring him. "Who were they, anyway?"

"Hell if I know." He looked up, into Mary's face for the first time. A feeling of guilt shuddered through him when he felt a surge of desire for her. "Did you get their tag?" he asked, doing a good job of ignoring the feeling.

Mary shook her head. "No, man. I was worried about you. Just made sure they were running, is all."

"Jesus. What the hell is going on here?" Ron reached down and picked up the towel, covering himself. He turned away from Mary and took an uncertain step toward his bedroom.

"Damn. There's going to be a nasty bruise at the base of your skull."

Ron's fingers traced over the lump there. "Bastards hit me with something when I came out of the bathroom. I didn't even *see* them. Didn't even hear them come in."

"Who were they?" Mary asked, following Ron. She watched her old boyfriend sit heavily on the side of his bed.

"How the hell should I know? Two jerks hunting for something. They kept asking me where something was."

"I know. I heard that much while I was sneaking up behind them. Dumb bastards. What were they after? You must have some idea."

Looking up at Mary, Ron blinked, shook his head to clear it, to assure himself that he was okay. "Yeah, I know what they were after. I don't know *why* they're after it, but I know what it is. At least, I *think* I know what it is." He paused, blinked again, and looked at Mary. "And what brought *you* here? You haven't been down here in months. Not since I . . ." He let the statement trail off.

"Well, if you didn't live so far out in the boonies, I'd come around more often. But to answer your question, I heard about that reporter, Dodd. He's dead, you know."

Sighing, Ron admitted it. "Yeah, I know."

"I tried to call you. About thirty minutes ago, but I couldn't get an answer. So I figured I'd drive out and see you. I had to come out this way, anyhow. See some people about a problem gator up near Lake Caloosa."

"Couldn't get an *answer?* I've been right here all morning." Ron stood up and stepped over to the phone. "It's dead," he said, staring at it. "They cut the *lines?*" It had to have happened just after he'd talked to Kate.

"What are you into, Ron? What do you know about this Dodd fellow getting killed?"

"I don't know *anything* about him getting killed. *Jesus.* All I did was take that disk from him. *Damn.*" He reached for a pair of briefs and put them on.

"Thanks," Mary said. "I was getting tired of looking at your bare ass."

"What the hell were you doing looking at my ass?"

"Hey! I just *saved* your ass."

"Doesn't give you the right to *look* at it." He went for the pants, next, and pulled them on. "How does my face look?"

"Looks like you been smoking firecrackers, is what it looks like."

Riggs felt at his lips, could tell that they were, indeed, swollen. "I guess I should feel lucky that's all I have to worry about." He looked Niccols in the eye. "Thanks, Mary. I owe you. You really kicked their butts."

"Don't mention it. For now, at least. I'll wait until I need a heavy-duty favor." Niccols stood and waited while Ron finished dressing. "So. What are you gonna do, now? Go to the cops?"

"Yeah, I am. But first I'm going to go see someone about what they were after."

"Who? Where?"

"Gonna go see who's home at the Vance Holcomb residence out past Salutations. See if I can't get a certain young lady out there to take a look at something."

"At what?" Mary asked.

Ron strode over to his work desk, opened the top drawer, and pulled out the white envelope marked with the scrawled *D*. "At this," he said.

"Mind if I ride along?"

"Hell, no," Ron told her. "Way things have been going, I might need you either for backup or as a material witness." He hiked up his jeans, wiped his lips with the damp towel. "You ready?"

"Ready Eddie, they calls me."

The pair walked out, locking the place behind them.

CHAPTER
TWENTY-THREE

Word had come by courier that William Davis Cauthen was on his way. It was important, it was big, and it was for Grisham's eyes only. That meant that there would be no bull on the table when Senator Cauthen got there.

Cauthen was a pal of Grisham's from way back. From before Vietnam, from before he was so much as a captain in the Marines. They had both attended the Virginia Military Institute together as young men, and before *that,* they had known one another. Even their families went back several generations; their great-great grandfathers had conducted business together. That was the mark of something that went deeper than friendship. That was the mark of two true-blooded American families. They were both steeped in the South and bathed in loyalty. Each knew that the other's word was steel. He looked forward to seeing Davis.

So, when his friend, the esteemed state senator from the panhandle of Florida called him to say that something big was in the works, Colonel Winston Grisham, U.S. Marines (retired) listened. He had told his wife to have the cooks prepare an early supper for his friend's arrival: a good, southern meal. Grisham was inspecting the kitchen, to see how things were going and what was being prepared. He stepped through the door that led from the parlor into the dining room, and the faint scents he had detected from the other side of the house were stronger.

Collards, he thought. How he loved a good mess of collard greens. He straightened his shirt, tucked it neatly into his pants, his stomach still as flat and hard as it had been as a teen, and pushed on the lockless door that led into the kitchen. Wonderful smells surrounded him, and he smiled, his big grin cracking his weathered face.

"I see you ladies are busy," he said, surveying the action.

"As long as you don't get in our way." It was his wife, and she was overseeing the activities, as usual. Mazie was still beautiful to him. Like the Colonel, she was lean and erect, only the crow's-feet around her eyes, the whiteness of her hair proving that she was older than her figure would indicate. She could still fit into her wedding dress. Grisham knew, because he'd seen her in it not two months before. She'd been in the upper room, the main guestroom where she stored it, trying it on when he'd walked in. *God, I'm a lucky man,* he'd told her. Indeed he was.

There were three other women with her, doing their best to attend to her instructions, and to keep up with her when she put her own hand to the task. All of the women were black, and all of them had been with the Grishams since they had bought the land and built the farm twenty years before. These women knew that the Colonel was called a racist by many. But he had never shown them anything but kindness, had even hired their young sons to work around his farm when he wasn't being visited by the groups of stone-faced men who came to the farm from time to time to act like soldiers and troop out into the bush. Of course, none of the women had ever read Grisham's mind. If so, then they would all surely leave at once and never return. His mask of kindness where they were concerned was merely that: a mask.

Grisham breathed deep, sucking in the aromas. "Let me see," he said, exhaling. "Collards, of course." He sucked in again. "And sweet potatoes." Again. "And okra, and squash. *Fried* squash." Grisham stood on tiptoe to peer over his wife's shoulder. "Fried chicken, of course," he noted, watching as Mazie moved breasts and thighs, drumsticks and wings about a truly huge cast iron skillet full of hot oil and frying chicken. The batter was turning a golden brown. "What's for dessert?"

"Shoo! You get out of here, now." Mazie had turned on him, handing the big two-tined fork over to Elaine, one of her cooks. The place usually needed all four of them at meal times, especially when Grisham was running one of his military camps or training sessions. Which he was doing more and more often of late. Even at that moment, the bunkhouses and the apartments over the barn were filled with the serious men who came to talk and prepare for a time when they thought they would be needed to save the nation. Mazie knew what was going on. "You'll see what's for dessert when it's served this afternoon." She prodded her muscular husband until he relented and backed out of the kitchen and returned to the dining room. "Now, *get*." He let the door close in his face and he chuckled.

That woman. How she can work those niggers.

Slowly, savoring what remained of the cooking smells that clung to him, he went out of the dining room, through the parlor, and into the foyer. There, he stood and looked around him, at the antiques he'd carried from his father's house to this one when he'd put up the farm more than two decades before. All of the furniture in that room had been in the Grisham family for generations. Some of it predated the War Between the States, in which his great grandfather had fought, in which his great uncles had all died, leaving

178

the Grisham lands to the line that had culminated in Winston Grisham and his two sons.

And then he frowned, his mood broken by the reminders.

Both of his sons had been lost to him. One, Ronald, had rejected military life on so-called *moral* grounds, had even refused to join the Marines, and had spent his two years as a conscientious objector in the *Coast Guard*, of all places. But the worst of the two had been John, who was dead to him, if not in reality. Of course, he couldn't know, for sure. He'd forbidden anyone in the house to ever speak John's name, and he knew that there was no one with guts enough to break that particular taboo. Sometimes, Grisham did think of John, but he tried not to do it around Mazie, for she could see through his masks, could see exactly what was going on in his mind, sometimes. She would know if his thoughts ever turned toward memories of that traitorous, homosexual beast. Grisham rubbed his eyes, and John was gone again.

Today, he was tired. He was tired because he'd spent most of the previous two weeks out in the country with his boys. This was a particularly gifted group. Most of them had been talented soldiers until they'd been discharged, all of them honorably, within the past few years. These were good, brave, focused men, who were not yet ready to retire their anger and their talents. Grisham gave such patriots a place to prepare for the coming struggle, which they all knew must come sooner or later. He hoped it would come soon, sometimes. For despite his daily workouts and the fact that he was in enviably fine condition for a man of his years, he was getting on and the day would arrive when he'd no longer be able to lead these young soldiers into the bush to train.

Thinking of that, Grisham went through the wide foyer and out of the polished oak doors that led out to a covered porch that wrapped around the big farmhouse. He had planned and overseen the construction of every square inch of that porch. It was twenty feet wide, the roof twelve feet overhead, with silently, slowly spinning fans wafting air every eight feet the length of the porch. And there were oak rocking chairs all along the walls, thirty of them. He picked one out and sat down to relax and to think. It had been a long time—six months or more—since he'd seen his friend, Davis. It would be good to see him.

In a moment, although he hadn't asked anyone, a tall glass of iced tea appeared on the little table next to his rocking chair. He hadn't even noticed exactly who had brought it, only that it had been one of the colored women. He picked up the glass, put it to his lips, and enjoyed the sweet taste and the cool drink as it trickled down his throat.

And he waited for Davis.

The Mercedes arrived just before three in the afternoon. Grisham had actually dozed as he'd sat and rocked, and had only noticed when the big, white car had pulled up to the split rail fence at the edge of the lawn, about fifty feet away. Quickly, he stood, rod straight, and marched down the red brick stairs to meet his friend. He grinned in genuine pleasure as Davis Cauthen emerged.

Cauthen was currently serving his fifth term of office in the Florida State Senate. For years he had fended off the badgering requests of hundreds of men, local fans to real shakers and movers, that he run for some national office. It wasn't his style, he had told them. He did things best in the more informal state house, where he could get things done, where he could still have time for his family and his friends.

Where he could still work the kinds of deals his father had worked, which his grandfather had worked, and at which even his great-great grandfather had already been adept those generations ago. His family had almost been original snakes in the grass. They were good at it.

Grisham, standing at the foot of the steps, greeted his old friend. They looked almost to have been stamped from the same mold. Tall, lean, weathered, both men were in better shape than they had a right to expect to be. But of course they expected nothing less than everything they ever wanted. And both usually got it.

"Davis, how are you doing?" The colonel's arm was extended and he took his old friend's hand and gripped it.

"I'm fine, Win. You know, I think you must have the only three-mile long driveway in the state of Florida. And I should know, because I've been down the ones at most of the really big estates. Can't recall another one quite this length, though." He smiled back at his old school chum and both men went up the steps to the porch.

"Well, you know how I feel about things. Same as you, only I can't tolerate the Yankees and the niggers the way you do."

"Just part of my job, old man. Part of the job."

For a moment, the two merely stood on the porch, out of the hot summer sun. Off in the distance, in the far pastures, cattle were slowly chewing their way along; some lying in the shade trees spaced here and there, some wading in the ponds. The politician sighed and took it all in. "Wonderful place you have here," he said. "I've been sorry to hear about your problems with those developers at your doorstep, but you know how things are."

Grisham put his hand on Cauthen's shoulder. "And I've appreciated your sympathy, and all the help you've given me." He followed Cauthen's gaze out toward the pastures and all of the cattle. "I assume this visit has something to do with that?"

"Winston, I'm not even here. I have a dozen witnesses who'll swear on a stack of Holy Bibles that I'm in my offices in Tallahassee right this minute. The waitress who serves me afternoon pie at my favorite diner will state that I was there an hour ago eating blueberry cobbler and had four cups of black coffee."

"I understand, Davis."

"Frankly, you're going to receive an offer of some import in a few minutes, but I don't know anything about it and won't until it becomes a matter of public record some months from now."

"I see." Grisham stood even straighter and taller now. "Should we sit here on the porch and discuss it? You know the only ears in this household are right here on my head."

"Well, I know that, Win. But let's go to your office so you can see what's in this briefcase you're about to get. And then, after that . . . well, even from way out here I can smell a good meal cooking. What's Mazie got for me this time?"

The soldier laughed, and slapped his friend on the back. "You'll just have to wait a bit longer. I'm not going to spoil Mazie's surprises. She'd have my hide, you know."

"Well, let's get this business over with as quick as possible. That cobbler just didn't hold me, for some reason."

The two men chuckled as they vanished into Grisham's offices.

Long after Cauthen had left, after returning to his viper's nest in the state capital, Grisham sat at his desk and reviewed the papers, the photographs (which he was instructed to destroy), and to muse over the offer. It was beyond tempting. It was a taker. It was almost a dream come true.

His fingers traced over the crown jewel in a heap of glittering finery. The Berg Brothers Studio, which had first refusal on roughly 100,000 acres of what would be real estate prime for development, had deeded over to him a 15,000 acre tract of that land that abutted his own acreage. It would serve as a true buffer between his holdings and those that would soon be homes and businesses and streets and parking lots and well-groomed parks. He would still have his privacy and he would still have plenty of room in which to flex his military muscle. Seventeen thousand total acres was more than enough room in which to continue to train and to prepare. So what if filthy Jews were handing over the land to him? It was still going to be his.

Added to that was that he wouldn't have to pay for it. Not a dime. The studio would *settle* his suits, out of court, by buying the land and signing it over to him. The title would be his.

And all for doing something for which he was uniquely prepared to do. Something which he would actually *enjoy* doing. "Lock and load, boys. Lock and load," he muttered, thinking of what was to come. Who would have thought that he'd be given everything he currently wanted, all for merely killing some big game and a few troublesome idiots?

He moved the land offer away; stacking the papers neatly in a pile to his left, and took out another set of papers. Grisham had been instructed to destroy them, also, but he wanted to linger over them, observe them. They were photographs of a most amazing sort. The pictures looked to have been taken in a hurry, and most of them were not well structured, and most of them were not very clear. But what they showed was something truly shocking.

Whoever had taken the pictures had come face-to-face with a creature stranger than anything Grisham had ever seen. And he had once killed a tiger in Vietnam, a tiger that had come into his camp one evening to drag away one of his junior officers. He'd killed the thing with a burst from his M-16. When they'd measured it, the thing had taped out at sixteen feet from nose tip to tail tip. He'd been told it would probably have been some kind of record, if he'd saved the skull and weighed the thing. But all he had to record it was a grainy photograph of himself and his men standing beside its hoisted corpse. But this . . . this was something else, entirely.

He pulled the best of the nine photographs to him and eyed it carefully. Almost, he chuckled. Whoever had taken the picture had done so on *Grisham's own property*. In the background, just behind the creature's big head, was a *posted* sign, and a tree with a length of barbed wire coiling skyward. That sign was his, marking his property line. That tree with the barbed wire on it was growing not more than two miles from his very house. He knew, because he'd been there just a few days before, when he'd stumbled upon the reporter, that Dodd fellow.

Well, he knew who had taken these pictures. And he knew who had been found shot through the head two nights ago, a corpse left behind by a stupid idiot of a mechanic who should himself be dead now if he had been working for Grisham.

Grisham continued to peruse the photo. This thing looked, at first glance, to be a dinosaur. But after studying the photograph for a while, Grisham could see that it was some kind of bird. A bird with arms instead of wings. A bird that stood, if he was measuring his reference points correctly, probably ten feet tall. A bird that size most likely weighed in at something around a thousand pounds. And all he had to do to take possession of 15,000 acres of land was kill it, destroy it, sponge its existence from this Earth.

Of course, where there was one, there were more. He had to eliminate them all to get what he wanted, what he needed. It wouldn't be difficult. He had a most impressive armory at his disposal, and he currently had some of the finest military men one could hope to gather staying right there on his farm. He would choose a team, arm them appropriately, and they would sweep the wilderness until they found and killed each and every one of these mad, glorious creatures.

And of course he'd had to agree to take care of those fool environmentalists who were causing so much trouble. That part also would not prove to be terribly difficult, since they would have inside help. He was never surprised to learn that those left-wing ideals could be bought with good, capitalist money.

Well, he had a job to do. He had to kill some people and exterminate an entire species.

It would be a pleasure.

CHAPTER
TWENTY-FOUR

This time, Ron did not have to wait in silence and frustration outside the gates of Holcomb's compound. As he and Mary arrived, the gates were opening to allow a pair of ATVs to leave. One of the small, yellow six-wheelers carried two passengers and Holcomb was alone on the other. Each pulled an even smaller trailer filled with closed nylon bags packed full of supplies and equipment of unknown variety. In the action and noise, Kate had tried to yell a request at Ron. It had been Mary who had understood and had retrieved a backpack from the tailgate of one of Holcomb's pickup trucks. Mary took a look at it, ran her hands across the fabric, and then handed it over to Kate who grabbed it without so much as a glance at Mary before rushing it over to the ATV being piloted by Vance Holcomb. Despite the fact that these people were moving about in full daylight, Ron was curious about their intentions, and was suspicious.

"Nice pack he's taking. Wonder where the hell they're going," Mary said to Ron as he pulled to the right to allow the squat vehicles to pass by them.

"Well, whatever it is they're doing, they're not paying *us* any attention. Look at 'em go."

In fact the ATVs were heading out at some speed and soon left the narrow road on which Ron and Mary had arrived, quickly vanishing into the forest. Both watched the trees swallow up the bright yellow vehicles. When they turned their attention back to the compound, Kwitney was standing at the entrance, appearing out of the clouds of sand and dust the all terrain vehicles had left in their wakes.

"That's Kate, eh," Mary said. "Can't be too many women around that damned tall." *Or, unfortunately, that good looking,* she thought. Despite her better judgment, she felt jealousy welling up.

"Oh, that's her, for sure. One of a kind, I assume." Ron walked away from his truck without another word and walked toward her. Just behind her was the Seminole she had pointed out to Ron the first time he'd been there. Billy, his name was. Riggs didn't know the man's last name, and again he felt the twinge of guilt he often got for knowing so little about that side of his heritage.

Before he had halved the thirty feet between them, Kate spoke. "You go straight to the cops?" There was a hard look in her eyes. Again, Ron was a bit disturbed at his inability to read her, but that was also part of the fascination he had for her.

"Well . . . no." He could see surprise flash for a second upon her face. "But that's what we're doing here unannounced." Ron indicated Mary, who was coming up behind him. "This is Mary Niccols. She's the trapper we refer for business."

"I've seen her work in the papers," Kate said, her voice flat and unemotional. "Thanks for grabbing Vance's pack for me."

"S'okay," Mary said.

By then, Ron was next to Kate, could smell her: a scent of soap and a mild perfume, and a bit of sweat. Her pleasant odor excited him. "I need a favor," he said.

"What kind of favor?" She stood her ground, unmoving,

watching Mary until she had joined them there at the gate. Behind her, Billy observed them soundlessly, no indication that the two Seminoles knew one another.

"I need to use some computer equipment, and I don't need anyone poking their noses into what I have to do. I figured this was the best place to come." He held his hands out, palms up.

"What kind of hardware?" she asked.

Reaching into his shirt pocket, Ron produced the envelope and quickly tore it open. He showed her the small disk. "I think this is from one of those digital cameras," he said. "Can you download the contents and show me what's on it?"

"Where'd it come from?"

He didn't answer her for a few moments. They were all quiet while he thought about what he was going to say. Finally, he just blurted it out. He never was any good at oblique strategies. "Tim Dodd gave it to me. Yesterday morning. I don't know what's on it, but I would guess it probably has something to do with his death."

"You sure?"

He could tell Kate wanted to take the disk from him. Her shoulders flexed for a brief second, as if she were going to reach for it. "I'm pretty sure. Two classic goons showed up some time after you called and tried to disconnect my head from my shoulders." He jutted a thumb at Mary. "If she hadn't shown up, I would have given the disk to them and no telling what might have happened to me. They might not have believed that I didn't know what was on it. Obviously, they beat it out of Dodd that I had it, or they would never have known to show up at my house."

"Obviously," Kate said. Once again she eyed Mary, giving her a good look. Ron wondered if Mary was jealous.

He'd not considered the emotional tension of the two being together. Kate looked hard, unreadable again, and then she softened. "Come on in. Let's see what's on there."

"Thanks, Kate." As soon as she turned and headed for the near building, Ron and Mary fell in behind her. At their rear, Billy remained to close and lock the gate. As the three went through the door and inside, the Indian was still outside, securing the garage from which the ATVs had come. Ron turned and gave him a final look, and saw that Billy was looking directly at Mary, even as busy as his hands were with work. For a second or two their eyes locked. *They must know one another,* Ron mused. And then he was inside, leaving Billy out there.

"Holcomb coming back soon?" Ron asked. They were heading down the long, wide hallway toward the millionaire's great office. Cool air surrounded them; soft fluorescence lighted the way.

"No. He and the others are going to be out in the bush today."

"Research?"

"Of course," she said. "Wish I could have gone with them. But I had to stay behind." She was walking fast, and Ron could tell she was as anxious as he was to see the contents of that disk. "Lucky for you I was here."

"Lucky for me," Ron said, wanting to touch her hand.

They came to a locked door and Kate pulled a keyring out of her front pocket and soon had the door open. This was not the room Ron had noticed during his first visit, but it was home to an even more impressive array of computer hardware than the other one had been.

"We've got our mainframe in here," she told them. "But we won't need that for your little disk there. If it is digitized photographs, as you say, then all we'll need is this handy-dandy Mac over here. It's my favorite machine for graphics."

"Doesn't mean a thing to me," Mary admitted. "I've pretty much resisted the computer age, myself. My cousin does all of that stuff for me. Does the books, types the bills, handles the correspondence. He even built a website for the business."

"I didn't know you had a website," Ron said.

"Sure. Landed a couple dozen jobs from it last month."

Kate was soon seated before a computer and monitor at one of a dozen similarly equipped desks. The machine was already booted and warm as she tucked her long, shapely legs under it and made herself comfortable. "Give me the disk," she said, her hand waiting for the delivery.

Even though he was in a position of having to trust her, and even though he had no reason to distrust her, Ron felt a tug of reluctance as he transferred the item from his hand to hers. She took it so quickly from him that their flesh never even made contact. In a few seconds she had the disk inserted in a zip drive and was downloading the information it held.

"How long will this take?" Ron asked.

"Depends on what's on here," she said. "But even if it's some complicated graphics it'll only take a minute or so." While the machine whirred and purred, Kate turned in her swivel chair and looked up at Ron. There was an expression of concern on her face. She reached up and gently brushed his chin with the tips of her fingers. "Are you okay?"

Ron rubbed his lips and drew his hand away. "Oh, sure. One of the guys slapped me a couple of times. Once to get my attention after one of them suckered me with the pro-verbial blunt instrument." He reached back and touched the swollen flesh on the back of his neck. Kate winced as he did so. "And again when I didn't react to his question fast enough."

"But don't let that fool you," Mary said. "He was getting ready to sing."

"*The Barber of Seville*, if he'd asked me to," Ron admitted.

Kate smiled and chuckled lightly. "You guys are a couple of jokers. Been pals a long time, have you?"

"Entirely too long," Mary said. Which made Kate laugh aloud, and Ron wince.

"Just pals?" Kate added the question; it exploded like a landmine underfoot.

Before Mary could react, Ron said, "Just pals." Mary said nothing, but Ron could see the muscles of her jaws tensing.

"Well," Kate said. The computer had ceased to purr and hum, and had beeped at them briefly, getting their attention even over their shared unease. "Looks like the files are all downloaded." Her hands played over the keyboard, and soon she was pointing the mouse hither, thither, and yon.

"What is it?" Mary asked.

"Well, it's just as Ron thought. Photographs. These are the contents of a digital camera. Good one. Fast, with lots of memory."

"Much there?"

"Sixteen files, Ron." She was poking the little arrow and clicking.

"Can we see them? I want to see what got Dodd killed," Ron said.

"So do I. So," she pointed and clicked again. "Let's see what we shall see."

The screen then began to slowly fill with an image, line

191

by line. The photo grew smoothly, in grainy colors, as the file uploaded to the video terminal. Soon, they were seeing the green in the center of Salutations, what appeared to be a turtle crossing the sidewalk and moving toward the classically constructed bandstand. "What the hell," Mary uttered. "A tortoise?"

"Good eye," Kate admitted. "Gopher tortoise. A big one, too. Probably pushed out of its home by someone building a house over its burrowing ground. Salutations is displacing all kinds of animal populations. You'd be surprised at the things we're documenting."

"What do you mean?" Mary asked. "Most of that place was a military base for sixty years or more."

"Longer than that," she said, bringing up the next image, this one an alligator in a drainage ditch. "But the base was pretty compact. Most of the construction was very limited. Not much of a human population was here after about 1950, and before that it wasn't much to talk about and they were packed in here in some old Quonset type barracks. But now the studio boys are really creating some urban sprawl out here. They shouldn't be allowed to, but they are. Government's working hand in hand with them," she added. Once more Ron did an inward wince.

"Look," Mary offered. "Why don't you skip ahead a few pictures? Whatever got him in trouble was probably later on."

"Good thinking," Ron admitted. "Try that, Kate. Let's see what's on the ninth or tenth shot."

"Will do," she said. And soon they were looking at what appeared to be a hastily taken shot of bear grass and palmettos.

"Nothing there," Kate said.

But Mary's dark index finger was jotting at the screen,

actually touching it. The terminal shivered each time she poked. "No. Look there. What's that? At the bottom. *There.*"

"What the hell," Ron said.

Kate froze. And even Mary, who was not watching her every move, as Ron was, noticed.

"Seen that before?" Mary asked.

Kate was silent. All three of them peered close, leaning into the screen, looking at what appeared to be a scaly, three-toed foot of reptilian origin. "What the hell is it?" Ron asked.

"Look. Let's see the next one," Mary insisted. Kate just continued to stare at the screen, and only slowly complied with the command. Once again they were waiting as the terminal filled with image, line by line.

This time, they were all stunned by what they were seeing. Ron's mouth opened in amazement. Mary squinted, not believing what she was seeing. Kate sat stony-faced, quiet, almost in a kind of silent anger.

"It's a trick," Mary said.

"It's a dinosaur," Ron said. Then, his mind locked on the same track: "It's a *dinosaur.*"

"Can't *be,*" Niccols again insisted. "It's some kind of computer graphics, I'm telling you."

Finally, Kate stirred. She shoved back violently, pushing both Mary and Ron out of her way. They parted for her as she rolled to a halt beyond them, her eyes fiery with anger. Despite what was on the screen, they turned to look at the woman, her attractive face a bit frightening with the rage seething just beneath the surface.

"It's no trick," she said hoarsely. "It's the real thing."

Ron and Mary looked at one another, back at the screen, back to Kate.

"You knew about this?" they asked, almost in unison.

"We knew about it," she said. "And now those bastards at Berg Brothers know, too. And apparently they're willing to kill over it."

"Grief," Mary said.

"Grief says it pretty well, indeed." Kate was nodding solemnly.

CHAPTER
TWENTY-FIVE

Out in the shelter of the trees and the savanna, the Flock was bedding down for the day. Only the youngsters and the smallest chicks still stirred in the growing light. Soon, even those would have to cease their youthful fidgeting. It couldn't be allowed, especially on a day with a cloudless sky. The huge golden eye would be staring down at them for a long stretch, and they all knew what could happen if it spied upon you. The Flock had learned well over the generations. There were none in the forests as adept at hiding as they. There were things they could do that were unimaginable to the Man from whom they hid. They had quite a collection of tricks.

Soon, all movement ceased. Even respiration went into a lower gear. The Flock rested, a few remaining alert to taste the wind, eyes wide to watch for even the slightest sign of danger.

Walks Backward had chosen his mate. The female would be his, would bear *his* clutch after he had gained control of the unit. Indeed, he had already stolen a secret moment and begun a courting dance with her. She would not sing of it. Not until the battle between himself and Egg Father had been fought and he had emerged victorious. And even if he lost, she must sing a tune of lamentation, for which she would be killed, of course. But Walks Backward would not lose.

What had set him off was the latest appearance of the Scarlet. The rogue had come into the meal circle after the latest hunt and had stolen a great deal of flesh, taking it for himself. Nothing had been done to prevent it, and nothing had been done after the thievery. And then, some hours later, during the bedding in the early glow of dawn, once more the foolish one had rushed among them; he had tried to cull out one of the young females—one not yet even old enough to lay. It was obvious what he was doing, to all and to himself. Only the intervention of the Egg Mother had prevented the huge rebel from taking the female away with him.

She had rushed at him, and the Scarlet, confused at the belligerency of his own mother, had turned and run back into the forests. And his voice had been raised high enough for any creature to hear. Even men.

After that, the Flock had hunkered down for the day, letting sedges and branches and leaves cover them, their own silence and camouflaging doing the rest. It was after that moment that Walks Backward had come to the conclusion he had known he must reach. The Flock would soon become his complete responsibility. There would be a new Walks Backward to watch the rear and hide the sign. And he would take over as Egg Father. His name would change. He wanted to sing his new name, but realized that must wait. When night came, after they had rested hidden all the day, he would sing his song of challenge.

And, later, he would sing another song. One that would doom the Scarlet and save them all. He only hoped there was time.

CHAPTER
TWENTY-SIX

Levin was furious. Not at being called suddenly back from what he had hoped was going to be a rewarding stay in the bush, but at the outside discovery of their carefully guarded secrets. He was dangerously close to losing control of his emotions.

"This is crazy, Kate. Why the *hell* did you let them know?" On a hunch, after he and his companion had parted company with Holcomb, he'd radioed back to the compound. Kate had told him to come back, to bring Vance, if possible. But Vance was long gone and maintaining radio silence, as he almost always did in the backcountry.

Ron and Mary were there, standing quietly while the biologist pointed at them from across the lab, where they had all gathered. Mary was not amused at Levin's anger and was not going to sit still and be docile for long. Ron, by contrast, remained stunned by what they had so far discovered, and was confused as to how he should act or where he should next proceed. In addition to finding that the wilderness that had formerly been a bombing range was the last redoubt for a species of predatory ground birds, he was also concerned over any laws he had broken concerning his contact with the dead reporter. In fact, he was only barely aware of the screaming tech.

"*I* didn't *let* them find out *anything*. They found it out independently of *me*, you sanctimonious *bastard*." Kate was easily as angry as her fellow employee and her color was rising, her face flushed with anger and her eyes like frozen jots of ice. "What was I supposed to do? *Kill them?*"

That seemed to stun Levin for a second, and it looked to Riggs as if the man was actually considering it as a viable alternative. He did respond, though. "But you didn't have to *confirm* what they were seeing. Those photos could have been *faked*, for God's sake. That's all they had to know." In fact, Levin was almost in tears. His chest hitched with every other breath, and Ron had figured it was only his anger that had so far kept the man from breaking down and crying like a heartbroken fool.

"It's too late for that kind of thing, Adam. We can't keep it a secret any more. Ron and Niccols know about the Flock, now. Dodd apparently knew about it, and I strongly, strongly suspect that Berg Brothers know about them, too."

Mary, listening, spoke up. "Did you say *flock?* There are more than one of these things?"

Levin stared at him, his face blank with what remained of his rage, the panic and shock just beginning to rise. Kate rubbed a thin-fingered hand across her brow, wiping sweat and her auburn hair out of the way.

"Yes," Kate admitted. "There's a flock of them out there. We're not sure just how many. But maybe twenty or so. That we know of. Could be more."

"More?" Ron squeaked.

"Holcomb even thinks there are more than one flock. At least two, he thinks. Again . . . maybe more. There's almost half a million untouched acres of woods, swamps, and savanna out there." She waved a long arm in the general direction of the wilderness.

"Jesus," Ron swore. "How . . . how can things like this

exist with no one knowing abou

Levin backed up a few ste
wheeled office chair that he seeme
him with some sort of radar. He w
shirt, jeans, boots. He'd been ou
had contacted him via radio. E
equipped with the communications s,
cies. This, Kate had deemed a dire eme
his fellow crewmember, a very quiet Jap tholo
introduced to them merely as Kamagu returne
quickly. So far, there was still no sign of . Apparently, Holcomb and the four employees the compound were the only people who were in o covery.

Kate walked over to a desk and grabber for herself and sat back, relaxing. Briefly, she b r face in
her hands, then looked toward Ron. He r the first
time, that she was already in tears. Moist eaked her
cheeks. "This place has been, for all intent urposes, a
wilderness area for the last seventy years, You know
that. These birds apparently have been livin all along,
hiding."

"Hiding," Mary yelled. Her strong arms up. "You
can't *hide* something that big. How big hat thing,
anyway?" She stood there, shoulders squa facing the
seated figures of Kate and Adam.

"That one was Big Red," Adam muttered We've esti-
mated he stands about ten feet. Weighs arou nine hundred, maybe a thousand pounds. But he's the ggest. Most
of the other adults are no more than eight fe tall, maybe
six hundred pounds. Chicks and young are m ch smaller,
but we don't know since we've only gotten a glmps or two
at the young."

"You can't *hide* anything that big. I kno what I'm

ou' Mary insisted. "Nothing that big can live in ood nd not be discovered by men. *Nothing*."

u'r rong," Kate told her. "In the past twenty s revealed the existence of a number of large m while back, an unidentified species of peccary mm South America. Just five years ago we discov- as f oe of deer living in the rain forests of Vietnam. ered it happens."

It's not talking about *South America*, and this isn' in forest in Vietnam," Mary yelled. "This is Flor of the most populous states in the east. Drive an h half north of here and you're in Orlando with abou ion people. This ain't the same thing!"

"en't listening to us," Kate said. There was a barely tible expression of arrogance tilting her lips. "I said t e *hiding*. You get me?"

Slo n stirred and retrieved a chair for himself. He rolled ss the tiled floor until he was sitting a few feet in fron evin and Kate. "What are you saying, Kate? That t hings can think?"

"Yes

Ron ed to look into Mary's face, and then he was talking t te again. "So. They've always lived here, since even bef his place became a military base, and they *hide* from us ou're saying they think. Plan." He paused. "Right?"

"Yes. at's exactly what I'm saying."

Ron lo ed Adam directly in the eye. "Are these things something olcomb bio-engineered? Because if they are, I want to kn w right this *minute*. At least one person has been *killed* o er his, and someone was going to put me six feet under be ause of it, and I want a straight answer. Right now, god ammit."

Levin drew in a breath and sat up. "No. They aren't *bio-engineered*. You've been reading too many science fiction books. That's just in the movies and the ess eff mags, pal."

Mary stepped up, finally grabbed a chair of her own and straddled it; pushing off and rolling up until she was level with Ron, facing the other two. She didn't know where the quiet Mr. Kamaguchi was, but she was beginning to be worried about it. "I've heard about this kind of thing. I once saw a show where that paleontologist . . . whatsisname . . . the one who wears a cowboy hat . . ."

"Bakker," Kate said. "Robert Bakker." She followed that with a definite sneer.

"Yeah. That's him. I saw him talk about how you could take the DNA of a hornbill and mess with it. Tell it to turn off the feathers, turn on teeth, make a tail. Then you'd have one of those raptor dinosaurs. Maybe you guys did something like that. Huh?" She was looking at Ron, for support.

"That kind of stuff is *fairy tales*," Adam screamed. He went rod straight in his seat. "These creatures have survived here on the last remaining expanse of savanna on the Gulf Coast. The last expanse of any importance, anyway. They *know* what they're doing. They hide from us. They've been doing it probably since the first Indians came down from the north fifteen thousand years ago."

"How can you know that?" Ron asked.

Kate rubbed her hands across her face, through her hair, as if taking all of the tension from herself and pushing it away. "We've been studying them," she said. "We've seen them *do* things. Things that only a sentient, thinking creature could do."

"Such as?" Ron asked.

"Such as detecting our video monitors and cutting the power supplies to them. Such as locating hidden cameras and *stealing* them. Things such as altering their hunting patterns and movements to avoid us. We've only logged maybe six hours of actual sightings in the last four years of intensive observations. They leave absolutely no sign of their passing. Apparently, the flock has at least one member whose *job* it is to hide all sign of their presence."

"Hide sign?" Mary looked at her, the question painting her face with a frown.

"We think he picks up feathers, bones, that kind of thing. We think he scratches out their tracks, covers fecal matter, and consumes leftover prey. Things like that."

"Give me a break," Ron said.

"It's true," Levin told him. "We've got tape of the flock moving through the edge of a savanna about four miles north of here. They move almost as a single unit. Adults in the front, along the periphery, with young in the center. And behind them is this large individual, *walking backwards* and scratching in the grass, running from one side to the next. We got about ten minutes that time, with a night vision camera. But the one who walks backward found it, found the camera. Tore right into it. Cut through the cables like they were made of butter."

Ron and Mary stared at one another.

"What? What?" Adam repeated. "You guys know something we should know?"

"Yeah," Ron told him. "One of the dogs missing from Salutations. We found some remains. A paw and a chain, just like I told Kate. The chain looked like it had been cut right through. Same with the dog's paw. We figured some kind of saw."

"Their beaks are adapted for slicing," Adam said. "They're very narrow. In place of slicing teeth, they've gone with large beaks that are slimmed down like a pair of razor knives, one sliding inside the other. We estimate a pressure of eight, maybe nine thousand pounds per square inch, all along a pair of edges maybe one hundredth of a millimeter wide on the surface area. You can imagine the cutting power."

"Why haven't they done this kind of thing before?" Mary asked. "If they've always been here in Florida, and they like to eat dogs, then why haven't we known about them?"

"We think one of them is a rogue," Kate told him. "We think the big one, the one in Dodd's photos, is a rogue. Disrupting the flock. It's the only explanation. In fact, it's been our latest project to trap it."

"*Trap* it," Ron repeated. "How were you going to do that?"

"I could think of a number of ways," Mary said.

"I'm sure," Kate said. "That's what I was doing out in the field when I first met you, Ron. We caught you on a video monitor and Vance radioed to me to 'stumble' upon you. Bring you back to the compound and figure out what the hell someone from Fish and Wildlife was doing out in the bush. He thought maybe you guys had suspected something. And, as you know, Vance doesn't trust your kind."

"I know," Ron said. "Why didn't I see your radio? Or hear it?"

"I turned it off," she said. "Stuck it back in my pack."

"Oh." He sighed. And he had thought it was his boyish charm that had attracted her.

"Don't look so offended," she told him. "We had to find out what you were doing there. Vance knows you guys are working hand in hand with the studio to enable them to buy up all of the acreage from the old military base, turn it into subdivisions and shopping centers like the rest of Florida. He's trying to stop that. He's trying to save these animals."

"Then why didn't he just go to the public about them?" Mary asked. "It doesn't make sense to keep it all a secret."

"He doesn't trust the public," Adam said. "He knows what happens when the destiny of wilderness is in the hands of our esteemed public. I do, too. It all gets gobbled up and destroyed. Nobody cares about it. Nobody's willing to pay to protect it. Vance was trying to buy it all up and give it to the Department of the Interior, and tell them what's living here. That's been his plan all along. The last thing he wants, and the rest of us included, is to let the public know about the flock, to have them try to come in here and disrupt their habitat."

"Well, it's a moot point, now," Ron said. "I can't stay quiet about it. I've got to go to the police and tell them what I know about Dodd's murder. And I'll have to show them the disk."

Levin sobbed, and Ron and Mary looked at him, shocked at the sudden burst of sadness. "Oh, hell," he muttered from between his fingers.

"I wish I could figure out something else," Ron told him. "But I don't have any other option. Someone killed Tim Dodd, and I have to tell the authorities what I know. I've *got* to."

"We understand, Ron." It was Kate. Her face was solemn, but there was no accusation there.

Mary stood up, arched her back. Everyone could hear her spine crackle as she bent backwards. Finished stretching, she looked at Kate. "What *are* these things, anyway? I've never seen anything like them. I mean, who ever heard of a bird with *arms* instead of wings?"

"They're Phorusrachids," she said.

"For-us-*what?*" Mary tried to pronounce it.

"For-us-RAY-kidz," Adam said, forming the phonetics for the word.

"I've heard of those," Ron told them. "They were a species of predatory ground birds that lived . . . what? Two, three million years ago?"

"Well, they're obviously not extinct," Kate said. "But most paleontologists thought they'd been gone for at least a million years, although back in '95 a guy found an ankle bone from a phorusrachid in a Blancan deposit in Texas, which would put it at about twelve thousand years. And a fossil dig in a spring here in Florida revealed that their wings had evolved into arms—that discovery came around 1994. It just wasn't big news," she added.

"Well, this is big news," Mary told them. "It's *huge* news."

"They're doomed, now," Adam wheezed.

"Screw that," Mary all but yelled. "As soon as the papers and the reporters get hold of this, the whole place will be protected. You'll see. You'll all see."

All eyes were on Mary, the single voice of enthusiasm in the room.

"I suppose we will all see," Kate admitted. "I don't think there's any other alternative, now." She sighed, and slumped in her chair.

Ron looked at Mary, at Levin and Kate. He knew how the wheels of government turned. And, for now, he felt like crying.

CHAPTER
TWENTY-SEVEN

"You want me to ride with you to talk with the police?" Mary was walking down the wide corridor with Ron.

"Yeah. I'd appreciate that. You can back me up on the fact that my house was broken into and that I was threatened over this." Ron held up the disk before he stuffed it back into his shirt pocket.

"I guess it's the least a pal can do, huh?" She didn't wait for a reply to her sarcasm. "What about that Kwitney chick? Think she made a copy of the photos?" She hitched a thumb back toward the opposite end of the corridor, where they had left Levin and Kate.

"I didn't see her do it. Did you?"

"Nah. But like I said, it's my cousin who's up on all that computer stuff. Not me. I hardly know how to turn one on, much less use it. My thang is trapping."

"I know what you mean. But I can't see where it would do them any good. If what they were saying is true, they must have plenty of photographic and video evidence of these big birds."

"Hate to meet up with one."

"I'd love to see one. Hope I get the chance. This is going to change everything as far as Salutations and the old bombing range is concerned." They were almost to the entrance foyer of the main building. Sunlight streamed through the big, tinted windows, and through the skylights above.

"I wonder how that reporter got that close to one and lived through it? The one in those pictures looked as if it was bearing down on the photographer."

"I'm sure I don't know. And it was only a temporary reprieve, as things turned out."

"Yeah. Too bad. He didn't seem like a bad sort the times I talked to him."

"He was just a guy making a living, is all. Same as us." They were at the foyer, and could see the truck parked outside, its hood up.

"What the hell," Mary said, pointing at the pickup.

Riggs ran to the door and pushed it open, a great draft of cool air following him out into the muggy day. Almost immediately he could feel moisture and heat clinging to him as he ran toward the truck. He brought himself to a halt with his forearms, leaning into the engine to see what was going on.

Mary was right behind him. "What's going on, Ron?"

But she didn't have to ask. Both of them peered down into the engine, seeing that the distributor cap had been torn free. And something blunt and obviously heavy had been used to thrash about in the general vicinity of the block and radiator. Various liquids oozed and dripped onto the sandy ground beneath the truck.

"Damn," Ron said.

"What'll we do?"

"This is bad. I was *wondering* where that Kamaguchi guy went. Let's just get the hell out of here while we can."

"You don't have a gun in there, do you?"

"Hell, no. I work for Fish and Wildlife, not ATF. Let's just hoof it while we can. I don't want to go back in there."

They went past the cab of the truck and looked inside, seeing that it had been plundered, the glove compartment open, papers strewn about the seat and onto the floorboard. "Let's go man," Mary was saying.

"You'll go nowhere but back inside." It was Kamaguchi. He was standing in the narrow roadway just inside the overhanging shade of a pair of slash pines that flanked the trailhead.

"Try to stop us," Mary said.

The first shot showered a spray of sand over her boots, and the second bored a neat hole in the taillight of the truck just to the left of her knee. "You're not going anywhere but back inside, I told you. Now," he stepped out of the shadows and they could see the .22 semi-automatic he was carrying rather easily, holding it with some familiarity, "you two get your asses back in the building before I blow holes in your heads. I'll do it, too."

"Crap. I had a bad feeling as soon as I saw he wasn't in there with us, with Kate and Levin," Mary said.

"You're breaking all kinds of laws, Mister. I work for a federal agency, and you can't threaten me with a firearm without screwing yourself big time. You understand what I'm saying? Know what it's like in a Federal prison? Think about it, Kamaguchi."

"It's *Kahm-ah-GOOCH*," the man with the gun screamed. "You idiots don't even know how to pronounce my name. *Damn,* that pisses me off." He fired another round at their feet, spraying them with sand again.

"We're going, we're going," Ron told him as they both turned and marched back to the building. As they did, they could see Levin and Billy Last-Name-Unknown standing in the doorway the two had so recently exited. Billy, too, was holding a firearm, a .357 Ron and Mary immediately recognized. Kate was nowhere to be seen.

As they got in close to Levin and the Seminole, Mary looked them both in the eyes and spat at them. "What do you guys think you're going to do with us? Kill us and all hell breaks loose. That, I can guarantee you."

"We're not going to shoot you unless you try to get away," Levin told them. "These birds are not going to be allowed to go extinct just because two idiots didn't know what they were doing. No way. None of that crap for me."

"You *idiots*," Ron exploded. "Don't you know we're not the only ones who know, now? Someone else obviously found out and was willing to kill Tim Dodd over it." Suddenly, the breath froze in Ron's lungs. He stared at Levin who looked back at him with a determined hardness to his gaze.

"You guys killed Dodd?" Mary asked what Ron was thinking.

"No. We didn't. But that doesn't mean we aren't willing to do what it takes to protect our interests." He pointed toward the door and indicated with a shrug that they should go through. Behind them, they could hear Kamaguchi coming close, but not close enough to grab.

"Then why are you doing something so stupid?" The two prisoners went through, back into the building. They were quickly flanked by Billy and Kamaguchi who both stayed wisely out of arm's reach to prevent a quick grab by either Ron or Mary, but close enough in to get a clear shot if the unexpected should occur.

"You're going to be our guests. Until Mr. Holcomb gets back," Levin told them.

"Does he know about this? Does he know what you're doing? This on his orders?" Ron glared back at Levin who stood just behind Billy.

"No. We haven't gotten in touch with him, yet. He hasn't responded to our calls. He hasn't called in, so we suppose his radio is still down."

"Maybe one of those birds got him," Mary said.

"No. They don't hunt men," he said with conviction. "He sometimes doesn't communicate when he's out in the field. That's all. At times, he turns off his radio and leaves it that way until he's ready to talk. He's had more luck in observing the flock than the rest of us combined, so we can't complain about it." They were halfway down the corridor, the room in which they had all so recently conversed just down the way.

Ron looked around. "Where's Kate?"

"She's around," Levin told him.

"Did she tell you idiots to do this? Huh?" Mary twisted and looked back at the two gunmen, and at Levin. Although she was shorter than any of them, Ron felt that his lady friend was more than their equal. If not for the guns. And Kamaguchi certainly knew how to use a gun. It wasn't worth the chance, and Ron knew that Mary wasn't stupid enough to try.

"Let's just say . . . she's not in a position to complain," Levin said. "Now open that door and go through."

Riggs reached out and turned the cool brass doorknob. The door clicked open and quickly Levin was at the door, pulling it out of Ron's grasp and swinging it wide to admit him. The room was small: ten feet square. Obviously some type of storage chamber, but cleared of all contents. In the center of the floor was Kate, laid out, her long hair fanned out on the tile, a bright purple knot on her forehead. But Ron could see that she was breathing, could see the gentle rise and fall of her chest, one hand covering her right breast, her legs bent neatly at the knees, almost as if posing.

"You *bastards*," Ron said as, for the second time that day, and in *precisely* the same spot, he took a blow from a blunt instrument to the back of his head. This time, the lights went out, and the last thing he saw before he met the floor was Mary looking down at him as the door was slammed shut.

CHAPTER
TWENTY-EIGHT

"Load light and tight, boys," Grisham told his men.

He looked down on them from the vantage point of his office in the loft of the "barn." Yes, he actually boarded four horses there, at the rear of the building; and, yes, there was actually a pair of tractors and various wagons lodged safely in the overhanging shed that was attached to the big structure. But most of this barn was an armory and an array of intelligence gathering offices, with a recording studio added on for good measure. This was where Grisham spent most of his days, where he taped his thrice weekly radio shows, where he plotted his war games, where he preached to his men, where he prepared to do his part in the coming civil war.

Grisham was standing on a wooden deck, almost an elevated porch. Behind him was a plate glass window that showed his own well-kept office. A wooden staircase led down to the floor of the barn, maps tacked to the walls all around the gathered fire team. The commander looked down from a height of roughly twelve feet, which made him appear as superior as he currently felt. He was better than the lot of them rolled into one, and they all knew it.

"I've explained to you fellows why I chose you. We're not only going to have to hit human targets today, but we're also going to be doing some big game hunting. I'd say we'd do the big game first, but the truth is that I know where the people are going to be, but I only have a rough idea of where to look for the game."

He felt the heft of the bundle of neat, manila folders under his left arm. There was one for each man, and as soon as he'd seen that each of them had read every syllable of each report and had consumed every square centimeter of each photograph, he'd see to it that all of the intelligence was properly disposed of. Slowly, he began to descend the staircase, continuing to address his soldiers.

"You fellows know how fortunate you are. There are thirty men outside this building stewing in their disappointment right now. Any of them would have been equal to the task, I'm sure. But each of you is more than that. Each of you is the *best* I have, right now. I'd say that each and every one of you are the equal of anything the United States Armed Forces could throw at us these days."

Some of the hard-faced men nodded solemnly at Grisham's words.

"But you also all have extensive experience hunting big game. Dangerous game. As our other team eliminates the people on our list, we're going to be doing something truly great. Something you'll be able to think about for the rest of your lives." He then stared out at the group of six, and although he was not actually smiling, it was as close to a psychic grin as anything any of them would ever see.

"We're going to cause the extinction of an entire race of creatures Mankind isn't even aware of. An animal that exists right here in our midst, and which will be snuffed out within the next few days. We're going to destroy a creature that has no right to be." He was at the bottom of the stairway, standing on the wooden floor, hard planks under his military boots. Slowly, deliberately, he began to dole out the folders. Stenciled in stark, black letters on each folder was the term: *Operation Terror Bird.*

"Open them up, men." In unison, the half dozen bent back the covers and saw the face of the animal they were going to drive to extinction. A couple of them could not suppress a short exclamation.

"Goddamn, indeed, gentlemen. This animal has no right to be seen by God or man. So we're going to do something about it. We're going to kill each and every one of them. We're going to shoot every one of the beasts we can find, until the forests are bare of them and none remain."

He pointed quickly at the man nearest to him, a blond, almost gracefully built soldier with clear green eyes and reddish complexion. "You. Jim Gant. You've shot Bengal tigers. Two of them that I know of. Faced the damned beasts from a few paces and put bullets into their hearts." The man nodded, barely.

He pointed to another, a man standing far to the left. "Wallace Joyner. You once killed an Alaskan brown bear with a .22 rifle. Dropped him with a single shot at twenty yards. Fine shooting."

"And you, Redmond." Grisham indicated a very tall man standing directly in front of him. "You sly bastard. You killed a damned Komodo dragon with a *crossbow.* How you got away with *that* particular deed, I don't even *want* to know." The retired colonel cracked a smile. "The point is that each of you knows how to not only kill a man with a single good shot, but you also know how to track the kind of creature we're going to be hunting. Make no mistake about it. These animals are predators, and efficient ones. I'm sure they're agile, and I can tell just from looking at a single photograph of one that they are fast."

He turned and walked over to the map wall at his right.

It was hung with a number of topographic quadrangle maps showing the lay of the land for over two hundred square miles. "We've only got a short time to act," he told them. "We have to *disappear* our human targets and then get right down to business. While we're out in the bush, we have other members of our group doing the wetwork elsewhere. There may be problems. We have to plan for such contingencies. I doubt any of our law enforcement officers will be poking about in the wilderness outside of Salutations. But just in case, I want to track these damned things down and be *done*," he roared the word, "with them in short order."

Once more he faced his men. "And, in case we encounter any of the stray human targets in the bush, you must be able to sanction them, too. Keep that in mind and don't hesitate to act while we're out there.

"Now. Before I let you sit down here to consume these intelligence reports, I'll field a few questions." He stepped back, as if ready to take a shot in his hard gut.

"Sir." It was Gant, the red-faced one. "How many of these things are there?"

"I don't know," he said. "My sources say maybe a dozen. But I don't know."

Redmond cleared his throat and spoke. "*What* are they?"

"What do they look like?" Grisham returned.

There were a few seconds of hesitation from tall Redmond. "Well . . . I hate to sound foolish . . . but this looks like a dinosaur. Some kind of dinosaur."

"Then that's what it is," Grisham said. His expression grew very hard, his brow knitting into a fleshy shelf. "Any other questions?" he yelled.

"What about human targets? Do you foresee any problems there? There's a lot of bush to whack out there."

"Ah. We have an ace in the hole," he told them.

"Someone on the inside has made it much easier for us to find our main target, if he's out there. He has a transmitter he doesn't even know about, and I have the frequency. Piece of cake.

"Anything else?"

There was silence.

"Then get busy reading. After that, give the folders back to me. Then prepare to go in-country."

"Where am I?" His head hurt. Someone was slowly pounding a hole in the base of his skull. And it was dark. The lights were out.

"You're with me," she said.

Ron immediately recognized Kate's husky voice. "Kate. Oh." So *that's* whose lap his head rested in. He was slowly getting his bearings. He was pretty sure where up was and that down was against his back.

"Are you going to be all right?" she asked.

"I think so. Yeah." It was very dark in the room. He couldn't see Kate's face, and although he knew his eyes were searching the room, he couldn't see any sign of a flaw beneath door and floor. Or any place that looked like there might even *be* a door. "I'm going to try and sit up," he told her. He groaned and fell back.

"Just lie still."

"No. No. I'll be okay. It was just that first try. I can do it." He made another attempt and succeeded this time, propping himself up with one arm while he twisted his torso until he was sitting with his back against the wall. His legs splayed out in front, he could feel his shoulder touching Kate's arm. "How about you? Are you okay? That was a nasty bruise you had, too."

"I'll be fine," she said.

"How long have I been out?"

"I couldn't say. I came to just when you and Niccols were brought here. But I was too woozy to do more than just lie here. I think I passed out again when the door was shut, but if I did I don't know for how long."

"Where's Mary? What did they do to Mary?"

"I don't know. They didn't leave her here. I wouldn't worry about her anyway; your pal looks like she could maybe just pound a door down if she was of a mind to do so."

"She might at that," Ron told her. "What the hell's going on? What're Levin and those others up to?" He shifted and pushed a bit closer to Kate. Not completely involuntarily.

"He thinks he's going to save the birds," she said. "I think he believes that when Vance comes back, all of his troubles will be over. Vance will have all of the answers and will save the day."

"He wouldn't have shot us, then." Ron reached back and gingerly touched at the bruised and swollen knot on the back of his head.

"I don't think so. But that guy's an Earth First-er if ever I met one. I think he'd exterminate all of Mankind if he had the chance."

"For real?"

"For real." She arched her back, and brought herself a little closer to Ron. At least it seemed to *him* that she was closer. More of her was making contact with more of him, at any rate. "He used to be into all kinds of terrorist dogma. Spiking trees, poisoning livestock, setting mantraps in old growth forests. Pleasant stuff like that."

"Jesus."

"He's not a bad sort, really. He's just sick of seeing

Mankind eating away at the natural world."

Ron said nothing. He didn't quite know what to say.

"Ron?" He could feel Kate turn toward him. One of her long arms reached over and she grasped his right hand in hers.

"What is it?" He swallowed hard. Ron was nervous. Grade school nervous. He was being stupid.

"Since we've got nothing better to do, why don't we have that talk we were going to have?"

He could feel her breath against the side of his face. "Sure. I'd like that, I guess. It'll help pass the time until Holcomb gets back and they let us out of here."

"Yes," she agreed.

"You were going to tell me about some things I needed to know about you," he said. "I can't imagine what it might be, but if you think it's important, go ahead and tell me. If you're Jewish, I can always convert."

She laughed. "I will tell you," she said. "But first I want to ask you something."

"Fire away."

"The other night, when I took you back to your truck. You wanted to kiss me, didn't you?"

"Well. Sure I did. Fact is, I've wanted to kiss you just about since you came across that field and found me sitting under the pines."

"Well. Kiss me then."

"You don't mind?"

"Kiss me, dammit."

In the darkness, Ron reached out and found her. His hand closed gently on her long neck, and he turned and lifted himself to a kneeling position, leaned toward her, and found her lips. Their mouths met warmly, softly. It was as he had hoped. The smell of her, the taste of her, the *feel* of her was good. His breath came quicker; his heart beat a little faster. They remained that way for a few seconds, soft lips caressing and tasting one another there in the darkness. Finally, their mouths parted. Ron edged back a bit, feeling an erection.

"That was nice," Ron told her.

"Yes," Kate said. And then, "You enjoyed it?"

"Very much," he admitted.

"You trust me?" she asked.

"What do you mean? Trust you concerning what?"

"Let me put it to you another way," she said. "We've both been zapped in the noggin and tossed here in what serves as the lockup, right?"

"Yes."

"So we're both pretty much in the same boat."

Ron nodded, remembered that there was no way for Kate to see the movement, then said, "Yes. We're both stuck here. We were both sapped on the skull. As far as your former friends are concerned, I guess I trust you as well as I would anyone. What are you getting at?"

"Well." She paused. "I know you're not going to want to hear this."

"Hear what?"

"I think Mary is in with the studio. I think she had something to do with Dodd getting aced."

Ron's breath caught in his chest. And although he wanted to, he found he couldn't so much as swallow.

William Tatum looked up from the papers on his desk to see a true horror enter his office. The building was quiet, and not a sound filtered into the room from the hallway outside: not so much as a whisper. Of course the figure standing in the doorway had shocked everyone and everything into complete silence. His presence was not unlike God's, Tatum often thought. Michael Irons closed the door behind him and looked down on the seated figure of a suddenly very small and very insignificant Bill Tatum.

Tatum wondered what Irons had said to keep his secretary from announcing his visitation. He wondered if he'd said nothing at all. He could see, in his mind's eye, the perfectly manicured index finger coming up to those rosy, almost cherubic lips, just the suggestion of a mischievous smile painted on. *Hush, little Miss. I'm here to suuuuuuuuurPRISE your boss.* And she had remained obediently still, like a good little scared rabbit.

The chairman stood easily inside the doorway, saying nothing. Calmly, he reached into his coat and withdrew a silver tube from which he produced a cigar. He lit it with a gold lighter produced from another pocket, tilting his head as he did so, peering down at Tatum. He puffed, obviously enjoying each inhalation. A strong and pleasant odor was soon wafting throughout the room, despite the fact that a truly superlative circulation system drew out and replaced the air in the building every few minutes. Cigar smoke seemed to make a nearly straight line toward the ceiling, where it vanished invisibly. With the cigar champed firmly in those shark-like teeth, Irons replaced the gleaming lighter.

"You look a bit *stunned* to see me. Surely you can't say my visit is completely unexpected." Irons was not smiling, was not frowning; he seemed neither pleased nor angry.

Tatum shuddered, visibly. "I thought that you would call me in," he said.

Irons removed the cigar and waved it with a great, exaggerated flourish worthy of any stage. His bio, which every employee was required to read, said that he'd been an actor as a youth, and had abandoned that career by his twenty-fourth year, when he'd worked his way into surer, more lucrative work in the film industry. "You thought that I'd *call you in*." He blew out a puff of smoke. "That's really amusing, Tatum. Truly it is."

The security chief sat motionlessly, afraid to move, afraid to stand, afraid to comment. He merely sat and breathed, and waited.

"I thought you were a professional. I thought that you knew how to get the job done, my friend." His face remained a stony, unreadable mask.

"The men I chose for the job were a poor choice. I admit it. I won't even try to lay the blame elsewhere. It was my fault," he admitted. And, really, it *was* his fault.

"Well, I'm happy to hear you claim that." Irons moved toward the desk, toward the frozen William Tatum, chief of security. As soon as he was at the desk, his thighs *just* touching the oaken platform, he brought his perfectly manicured fist down on the top of it with a great deal of force. "I *like* it when a man admits he has *completely* fucked up!"

Even though he had known something like that was coming, Tatum flinched. He knew deep down that the somewhat voluntary reaction was at least partially for Irons' benefit. It was best not to make him any angrier than he already was. This was, in fact, the only time Tatum had seen anything like a true, human emotion coming out of the man.

"Fortunately for you, no one has been able to trace the *idiots* you hired back to this company. God," he breathed out hoarsely. "I'd hate to think of the money I'd have to outlay to shut it all up."

His voice cracking, Tatum tried to squeak a further apology. "I'm sorry, Mr. Irons. These men have worked for

me in the past. Had done some exemplary work. Up until
. . . until the moment they were discovered with . . . with,"
Tatum was struggling with a way to say it without stating
the obvious. He could see himself trying to explain away his
words in a court of law.

"With Dodd's body, you mean?"

Tatum stared at the boss, the ultimate chief.

"They got away, though," Tatum said. "The police
didn't capture them, even though they recovered the . . .
the . . . his . . ."

"Dodd's body. Yes." Irons continued to stand and to silently puff away, examining Tatum as if he were some interesting but bothersome pest. "Did you know that they even
fouled up their little visit to that fellow from Fish and Wildlife? The one who had talked to Dodd?" He waited for
Tatum to answer, but got no reply.

"You won't have to worry about the police questioning
them. They weren't around to be questioned. They did that
much, at least. And even if they left a fingerprint, it won't
matter. Neither has a criminal record."

Michael Irons used the cigar to jot a decimal point in the
air. "Oh, we'll *never* have to worry about those particularly
inept *assholes*. I won't. You won't. The company won't.
Their families won't. No one will. No one will ever again
have to waste a moment's grief on either of them."

"What?" Tatum croaked.

"Well. To put it in plain terms, my fine, stupid friend: I
had them both aced. They're dead." He removed the cigar
from his lips, unclenching his jaws in what appeared to be
an almost painful manner. There was something akin to a
grimace upon his smooth, unblemished, too-young-for-a-
chairman face.

"And as for you, Mr. Head of Security . . ." He paused,

drew in a breath and released it almost silently. "You will sit here for a while and do nothing beyond see to it that nobody picks any pockets in the malls, or steals some tourist's rental car, or takes advantage of some dumb broad visiting one of our fine hotels. I've passed along the responsibility of taking care of our . . . eh, our *problems*. You will *not* interfere in any way with the Colonel or any of his actions. Do I make myself clear? Hmm?"

"Yes, sir. Very clear, sir." Tatum remained sitting rigidly in place, but risked a swallow.

"You know . . . it's not *right* for a man of my position to raise more than an eyebrow in a situation like this. A man such as myself needs to not have to worry about such trivialities. It's not *right* for me to pick up a phone and deal with such unpleasantness and be forced to make *outrageous* offers or spend ridiculous sums of money. It isn't right, damn it."

"I understand, sir. You should never have felt the need t . . ."

"Shut up, Tatum."

Tatum stopped. Did not finish the syllable. Looked up at his fate.

"You will stay here. Right here in Salutations and act like you're nothing more than small town police chief. You'll stick your nose in nothing more serious than a fender bender, because that is the absolute limit of unpleasantness that I want anyone to experience in the confines of my town for the next little while. Do I make myself clear?"

Tatum nodded.

"Good. I'm glad that you are aware of my position." He put the cigar back in his mouth and clamped down on it. Tatum could hear his teeth mashing the rolled leaves of tobacco. "And Tatum? Stay here. Go nowhere." He held his arms out to indicate Salutations. "This township will be the extent of your little world until I say otherwise."

With that, he turned and walked back to the door. Quietly, he opened it and stepped out into the hall, which remained just as silent as when he had entered Tatum's office. No face peered their way from down the hall, no head popped out of any adjoining room to see what had happened. Everyone in the building was currently doing his job at peak performance. The Shark was about, cruising, and it was best to lie low during such times.

Irons went out into the hallway, closing the door to Tatum's office as he left. Inside, Tatum put his head in his hands and actually contemplated suicide.

CHAPTER
TWENTY-NINE

In the dawning, Walks Backward was not entirely surprised to see that the heads of the Flock had decided to bed down in close proximity to his own position. There were plenty of reasons for such a move. The Scarlet was not adhering to the laws, was not acting in a rational way. It could be that they were there at precisely the one point that the rogue would be most likely to attack were he to do the unthinkable and pierce the carefully hidden daylight sanctuary they had chosen to rest out the sunlit hours. It could be that they merely wanted to be close to Walks Backward, who guarded the welfare of the Flock as no one but themselves, and who was sometimes to be rewarded for that service by the honor of their physical presence while he lightly slept.

Or, more likely, this pair of intelligent mates suspected that their faithful watchguard was preparing for mutiny. Perhaps they knew that he had already chosen a prospective mate and that even the embryonic moves toward a mating ritual had begun. It could be that these two, who had spent their lives guarding and watching over their fellows, were aware of what was going through the mind of Walks Backward, and they wanted to be as close as possible should he actually threaten their primacy.

Walks Backward lay in the temporary nest he had chosen for himself. It was clear of the bothersome ants, and the colors of the forest floor and the surrounding plants perfectly matched his mottled coloration. The shadows and patterns of light that played over his feathered body revealed nothing to any eye but that of another of his own kind. He was merely a bit of brown there between the branches; it an additional patch of darkness in the shadows. He crouched there, at rest, but his hugely powerful legs bunched lightly beneath his torso, those gigantic claws even then tentatively touching the loam, prepared to dig in to produce solid purchase in the softness of decaying plant matter.

His head was locked into a position low to the ground, but high enough above it to afford him maximum sight of the surrounding territory. By flicking his great head in the tiniest of movements, he could make a complete circuit of their defensive bubble. He could see in each direction of the compass, and clearly, and he could also watch the forest canopy for any suspicious motions. And he could observe the skies. Few creatures bothered to search the skies or the roof of the forest. Men did that. And the Flock did that. Walks Backward twitched his huge, menacing head and looked toward Egg Father.

The rival-to-be was looking directly at him. There was something new in that wide, unblinking gaze. And Walks Backward had to admit that Egg Father knew. His leader, his lawgiver, his *commander* was aware of the ideas that had been forming in his mind; the emotions at war with long held beliefs. Walks Backward met Egg Father's gaze, the two great eyes, each clearest blue rimmed in crimson, staring unflinchingly into the other.

I know what you are planning, that gaze said to the watcher.

You know also why I have to do this, was the reply.

226

For a long time the pair merely sat and stared. But even so, Walks Backward continued to do his job, as he was able. His opposite eye continued to make a circuit of the surrounding territory, taking it all in, viewing with an amazing clarity of peripheral vision impossible to imagine for any man, or any mammal. And his keen hearing caught the breaths of the Flock, the tiny murmurs of chicks and young, of their fellow forest denizens moving and twitching and living. All was well in their world, for this moment, except for the probable danger each huge and terrible predator posed against the other. There was, perhaps, no avoiding it, now.

For hours the pair continued to stare, communicating things in ways alien and efficient. In their ways, they debated what had happened and what was going to occur. Walks Backward did not wish things to be this way, did not *want* this terrible thing to happen. But he was to be given no other option. This was how it was going to be.

Slowly, painfully, the Sun arced overhead, having come from its nest in the dawn and inching toward the same nest on the other side of the world for its evening rest. Its own life was the mirror image of that of the Flock. They had once, long ago, led the life the Sun lived. But for many generations they had been forced to go in the other direction, to hunt and to *live* at night rather than in the daylight hours. All during those long, hot hours the two lay, their eyes locked in soundless conversation.

And then.

And then, night was coming. The Sun was going, fading toward the horizon, the trees beckoning to it, supplying it with a place to settle with its great, red wings. In time, the heat of the day gave way to the cool of the night, and the Flock began slowly to stir, their breath coming faster, quicker, more lively, until they were moving, stretching their small arms, pairs of claws on each hand inching up and down, preparing for the hunt. And in the grasses and from the brush and from out of the trees came the Flock. They were ready, but waiting only for the Egg Father and Egg Mother to speak, to help them make order from the night.

Walks Backward stood, slowly, stretching his stiff muscles, breathing deeply and letting out a long exhalation. He watched Egg Father do as he did. The battle was going to come. Clawed feet tensed, talons digging lightly into soil.

The Egg Father raised up his huge, beaked head. A sound came out of that razored mouth. The Flock waited to hear the command.

Walks Backward was prepared for indignant accusation, for a rage and an acceptance of the challenge he was ready to offer.

But something else came out of Egg Father's powerful throat. Out of his great, wise head. He was commanding the Flock. The command was not "hunt," but an alteration of that familiar order. The command was *kill*, it was *war*, it was *self-defense;* and it gave a target, a recipient of the results of that singular command.

The target was the Scarlet rogue. The Scarlet rogue would be this night's prey. The one who threatened their existences would now pay for his foolishness by being dead, by becoming food for the Flock. Egg Mother's beak opened wide, and the command was copied, reinforced.

And a third voice trilled the same message into the night air, into the ears of the Flock, into the minds of young and old, male and female. Walks Backward had lifted his own head into the night air, joining them, *with* them, as was right and proper.

Kill, the three guardians said. Again and again. In unison. *Make war,* they commanded. Together, as the unit they would always be.

CHAPTER
THIRTY

Something was amiss.

Holcomb was sure of it. All of his employees who knew the frequency of his radio also knew that he had forbidden it to be used. He had, in fact, informed them never to use it, even though he had given it out to four people. Kinji Kamaguchi had it, as did Adam Levin, Billy Crane, and Kate Kwitney.

When he had paused, as planned, to use his radio to get in touch with Kamaguchi and Levin, there had been a severe feedback. Initially, Holcomb assumed that there was something wrong with the set, but he soon knew better. The small handheld radios had a range of about six miles. More than enough for the work for which he intended of them; they were powerful for their size. But as soon as he switched his on, the feedback had been tremendous. It was something that should not have occurred, for he was using that specific frequency not utilized by anyone transmitting in the area.

Something was very wrong. This was more than just his careful paranoia at work.

Holcomb switched the radio off and waited, to make sure it wasn't just a temporary glitch. As soon as he tried it again, the air was alive with that same feedback, the radio squealing at a high pitch. Alone there in the forest, the

ATV's engine warm with gasoline fumes, he sat and thought. Gazing all around, he spotted nothing but the familiar sights of the wilderness. Even above, the sky was clear and the nearest plane was nothing more than a streak of white tens of thousands of feet overhead and many miles north.

The source of the competing signal was obviously either on his person or aboard the ATV. Slowly, methodically, he disrobed there in the forest, examining each piece of his clothing until he stood completely nude, the soles of his bare feet feeling the cool forest loam. And just as slowly, he climbed back into his clothes, checking each piece for the source of the signal. It was possible, if the device were very small, that it might be concealed in the fabric of what he was wearing, or in his boots. But he found nothing out of the ordinary.

Moving away from his vehicle, he switched the radio on again. The feedback was still there, still severe, but he discovered as he walked away from the ATV that the feedback grew less and less powerful. So, he knew where it was. Perhaps someone had merely stowed another radio onboard and had left it on by accident. Quickly, Holcomb returned to his ATV and looked into the storage area behind the driver's seat. Deciding to just start in the most obvious place, he reached in and pulled out the last item he had placed there. It was his backpack, which could have been touched by any, or all, of his trusted assistants. In fact, thinking back to the moment he had left, the place a din of motion and sound, he realized that Ron Riggs had even been present. Someone with Riggs had lifted the pack to hand off to Kate who had brought it to him.

Laying the pack on the seat, he put the radio beside it and turned it on. The squawk of radio noise was insane. As methodically as he had disrobed and dressed himself, he began to go through the pack. It was a good, internal frame pack—the only kind he used. By the time he had emptied the fourth outer pocket, he had found the planted transmitter.

Holding it in the palm of his hand, he took a close look. It was a fine bit of workmanship. Not much larger, and about the same dimensions, as a cigarette; it looked to have been cobbled together in someone's workshop. Breaking it open, he soon found the power source, a tiny disc-shaped battery, and disconnected it.

Holcomb felt a curse rising out of his throat, but he stanched the flow of words before they could begin. He had always made a habit of never speaking when he was out in the bush. Animals might forget the sound of an engine, once the machine was silent for long enough. And they might ignore the casual sounds of something, even a person, moving through their environment. But they would always be spooked by human speech, so he never raised his voice over a whisper when he was doing his scouting. Holcomb clenched his jaws tightly and said nothing. But he did allow himself the pleasure of shattering the ingenious bit of electronics under the heels of his boots. He stamped down on it again and again until it was just a ruined bit of metal and plastic.

Something serious was about to happen. He was sure of it.

With the transmitter in ruin, he went back to the ATV and tried his radio again. There was no feedback, at all. He set it to a band that should have raised Levin and he whispered into it. His biologist was under instructions to be near enough at this point to hear him. "This is Holcomb. Over." He waited, giving his employee some time. He tried again. There was no response.

Something was happening.

Holcomb switched to the band that had been agreed for the use of Kamaguchi. His voice was a whisper there in the vast forest. Bluejays called nearby. "Kamaguchi. This is Holcomb. Are you there? Over." Time passed. There was no answer.

Something had already happened.

He could think of no reason any of them would deviate from their plans when they *knew* he was attempting to make a visual contact with the flock of terror birds. Even if the compound were afire, they would have left the lines of communication open. There was only one thing that came to mind that would cause his careful team to abandon or forget their routine.

Someone must have discovered that something previously unknown was living on this land. And if that were true, he supposed that they were trying to deal with it as quickly and efficiently as possible. Or else one or more of them had done something to reveal the secret. Either way, something was very wrong.

He had pondered this in a somewhat paranoid manner since the day he had found the flock of phorusrachids. Vance Holcomb had learned a valuable lesson when his Filipino friend had vanished from his own home. A man such as Vasquez, wealthy beyond most human dreams, with fantastic resources at reach, had still found it impossible to survive when at war against his own: the wealthy who lived only to increase their profits.

Knowing this, Holcomb had of course taken certain security precautions. And he had gathered a small circle of professionals who seemed more interested in a solid cause than in treason. However, there was always a chink in that particular armor. Even a seemingly inspired person could be swayed by circumstances. How did the saying go? *Need and opportunity makes a thief of any man.* Holcomb actually trusted no one. He realized that there could always be a Brutus among his disciples.

Someone had been trying to make him easy to find. Someone who had thought he wouldn't discover the hidden transmitter until it had served its use and he was found. But by whom? And for what reason?

He didn't know exactly why, but the reason could not be an honest one. Something nasty was waiting for him back there. Of that he was completely certain. He wondered whom, among the four, was at the core of it. Again, it could be anyone he trusted, or any combination of them, or perhaps someone from the outside. That fellow Riggs. It could be *all* of them. It was because of this that he always chose to do his field research on his own.

None of them knew just where it was that he would sneak away to in order to see the flock in action, to steal those rare photographs and videotapes. None among them realized just how much he knew of the flock's habits and motivations. These birds were, he had decided, far beyond any animal he had ever encountered in sheer intelligence. They were, he had learned, on a par with humans.

Holcomb had discovered the plant while he was headed across the southern edge of the smallest of the savannas that the flock enjoyed hunting. Quickly, he disconnected his radio from its battery pack. He didn't want to chance it being used to triangulate his position. If they were going to find him, now, then they'd have to do it the old-fashioned way. Being an excellent tracker, he thought that he could throw off the best of them.

He took his ATV a few miles beyond the point where he

normally left it. He had driven it north-northwest of the savanna, to a point he usually would have considered uncomfortably close to property owned by that right wing madman, Winston Grisham. Still, he had to say one thing for Grisham: the man expected his private property to be respected, but he never violated another's property lines, either. To Holcomb's knowledge, the Colonel and his private army had always stayed on the Grisham side of the line. So, he took the chance and stashed the ATV at a place that was barely a hundred yards from the strands of barbed wire that encircled most of the old Marine's land.

Leaving the vehicle, Holcomb had concealed it both in its vinyl covering, and with a neat and seemingly haphazard array of forest trash. He was quite good at that type of camouflage, had learned it from a Nepalese Army officer years ago. Only a trained eye could find his ATV. Without another concern over it, he had strapped the heavy pack that his people had helped him prepare to his back, and set out for a place which no one other than himself had any knowledge.

For most of that day, using up all but a sliver of the daylight left to him, he had made double time. He'd crossed the southern savanna, pierced a dense stand of tupelos and red oaks that grew on a low ridge of sandstone, and had pushed on until he had made the western arm of the largest of the savannas lying within the wilderness. This wasn't where most of the flock's activities occurred, but it was where he had painstakingly erected a very special structure. Concealed in a stand of white pines, partially buried in the limestone cap was a hidden room that he'd built, panel by panel over the previous four years. Holcomb had carefully dropped in each section of the small building by use of a glider he owned.

Every time the rich man came to his private and unknown little fortress, he thought of the glider drops, of sliding dangerously low on the currents to release his small packages of building material and other supplies. It had been during one of his flights, on that unpowered vehicle, that he had first seen the flock. No one else, he assumed, had ever flown over those savannas using a glider. The flyer made no sound; any sound, *any sound at all,* would have alerted those foxy creatures and he never would have found them.

But he had. Flying in low one day, the tow plane having long since released him, he had sunk perilously low, maybe two hundred feet above the treetops. And he had seen the flock.

At first, they had seemed to be merely dark places nestled down in the tall grasses of the longleaf prairie he floated silently above. But then he had turned about, tilting the left wing and had circled like a gigantic owl, no sound betraying him, his shadow far out and away from the things that had attracted his eye. A second pass had revealed that the spots were, in fact, living things. So a third pass was risked. And then, in the lazy, reddish light of the afternoon, one of the animals had stood.

And Holcomb, long ridiculed for his fanciful quests to seek out the sea monster that lurked in Loch Ness, to find the *mkole mbembe* in the Congo, to locate living mammoths in Nepal, had seen something he never truly believed could exist on Earth. He had found dinosaurs stalking a forgotten wilderness in the most unlikely of places. And it was then that he knew that he had been chosen to save them. Any way he knew how.

Later, he had discovered that the creatures weren't, technically, dinosaurs. They were great, predatory birds that had evolved the extremely efficient body forms of their saurian forebears. For a year, he had watched them, alone, not daring to reveal what he had found. It was only when his own attempts to purchase the vast acreage held in an accidental wilderness state were challenged that he had deemed it necessary to bring others in. He had built his compound and he had hired a core of research scientists to help him and to keep the knowledge a secret until he decided the world should share in it.

But none of that crew knew of his secret outpost here in the midst of that wilderness.

And one or more of them was about to betray him. The fortunate discovery of the transmitter had told him that much.

In the waning light of afternoon, he had come to his secret place, his fortress invisible. There were devices inside it by which he could find out things of which he was currently ignorant. Spying worked both ways.

Coming to a tuft of tall, green sedges, he had knelt and pulled the stuff aside. There, hidden, was the shallow tunnel entrance to his dome. He had pushed the heavy backpack in ahead of him and had closed the entranceway behind, inching his way along until he came into the secret room. As the sun set, as the darkness fell, he had activated a bank of batteries, closed a number of fragile circuits, put on a set of headphones.

He could use these to sometimes hear what was being said within his compound, and soon Holcomb was listening to what was happening at the Eyesore.

His paranoia was not paranoia, at all. Merely reason. When he heard the first gunshots, he knew he'd been right. But he remained ignorant of an even tinier transmitter that had been placed cleverly in his backpack, a small device left permanently open and sending out a regular pulse that would make triangulating his current position a very easy prospect.

CHAPTER
THIRTY-ONE

Mary Niccols was sitting quietly in a very small and very dark room. Kamaguchi and Levin had tied some pretty good knots for college boys. They must have taken classes in that as electives, she figured. At any rate, the knots had been well tied, and it had taken Mary all of an hour to work her way free of them. Good rope the boys had, too. High quality nylon, similar to the stuff she used on the occasional bobcat she trapped and trussed from time to time. As soon as she was no longer a human pretzel, she slowly and carefully undid all of the kinks in the rope and rolled it into a neat bundle, passing it through and through her callused palms, trying to decide what to do next.

The room was small. In fact, it probably wasn't really a *room* at all. Probably some sort of storage bay, or perhaps a nook for an absent mainframe. There were some small grates in the walls that she had found with the tips of her fingers, but far too small to pull free and escape through. She doubted she could get her forearm through them, much less her body. The ceiling wasn't very high, either. She couldn't reach it by extending her arms full length, even while on the tips of her toes, but she had managed to touch it when she'd leaped up. Her vertical jump wasn't bad for a short person. But the hops had proved that the ceiling was a solid section; there was nothing there to shunt aside and creep through.

It looked as if the only way out was also the way she had come in. As soon as she had gotten free of the ropes, Mary had gone to the door and had put her ear to it. In fact, she had done so every couple of minutes since freeing herself. The idea of her captors suddenly reappearing to check on her did not seem appealing. If she surprised them, there was a chance she could deck them before they knew what was going on. But there was also a very good chance that if she surprised them they might shoot her full of little holes. She damned sure did not want that to happen.

After pressing her ear to the door for some time, and placing her ear at the sliver of a crack at the bottom of the door, she had decided that there was no one directly on the other side. They must have all been quite happy and confident of their knot-tying abilities, since it seemed they had left her alone in that small room. Having decided that there was no one outside to hear what she might do, she had simply put her hand on the doorknob and had tried it.

The door had opened right up, having not been locked.

Niccols cursed herself. Shaking her head in disbelief, she inched the door open to chance a peek outside.

She was at the end of a short, dimly lit hallway. Looking up, she could see the fluorescent lighting, creating diffuse and somewhat disorienting shades.

Carefully, she went down the hall. It was a very short one, and again gave the impression that all of this area was some kind of utilitarian space. She probably was not far off the mark (or perhaps right on the money) in thinking that the room in which she'd been imprisoned was meant for a mainframe computer or for some similar use.

This place was all new to her and she couldn't recall having come this way. One of her captors had stuck her in the arm with a needle soon after Ron and Kate had been forced into that other room, and she had gone immediately woozy. Her last memory before waking up in the total blackness of the tiny room was of pairs of hands on either of her arms, supporting her.

At the end of the hallway Mary stopped and looked down. There was a wider space between the bottom of the door and the tile floor than there had been in the room. She could actually see under it, a bit, and could even see that there was light brown carpeting covering the floor of whatever room lay just beyond. She froze and listened. There was nothing. She couldn't hear anyone talking or moving or breathing on the other side. It *seemed* as if she was alone, but you never could tell. There was always the possibility of some very resigned and silent person waiting in there. She thought of herself standing patiently along some lakeshore, watching the surface of the water, ready to catch a glance of an elusive gator surfacing, ready to see it and act. Many a gator had gone to that great leather store in the mall for such foolishness.

Instead of just trying the door, Mary slowly and silently went to all fours and inched her way to a prone position. Once lying flat, she bellied up close to the entrance and put her head directly on the tile. With her right eye, she peered through the crack between door and tile. She was looking for shadows, a flicker, any movement at all that would alert her to someone standing in there, or someone pacing by. But all she could see was a standard and somewhat brighter lighting in the other room.

She breathed silently out, letting go with a mild sigh. There was nothing else for it but to just stand up and try the door. Basically, these guys weren't really *villains*. They were just misguided tree-huggers, she figured. In fact, she could identify with them to an extent. Maybe she did make a living trapping displaced animals who were only trying to reestablish themselves in the homes they had been forced out of, but she was no less an environmentalist because of it. Mary understood the passion of Levin and the others in wanting to save these dino-birds or whatever they were. But she really did not want to get plugged over it. Those guys probably wouldn't shoot her, she figured.

And so she sucked in a breath, stood up and took the doorknob in her strong right hand. Slowly turning it, gripping the cool brass so that it did not slip and make a slight noise, she felt the bolt come free and the door pull quietly toward her. She opened the door a sliver and peered out.

It was another computer room. There was a bank of monitors and keyboards in cubbyhole-sized cubicles all along the eastern wall. Seeing no one, she pulled the door to her a bit more and stuck her head out. The room was definitely empty, and was rather dusty, in fact. None of the monitors appeared to have been used in some time, a thin sheen of dust coating them all. Each covered keyboard was similarly decorated with fine dust, and now she was pretty sure the room in which she'd been placed was going to be a mainframe for all of these monitors. Niccols wondered just what Holcomb was up to. Why was he going to need all of these cubicles, unless he intended to fill them with people tapping away all day on those keyboards?

Well, this was no time to ponder. What she needed to do was get the hell out of Dodge. If she could, she would try to find Ron and Kate along the way, but if not she was just going to get out. She didn't like being attacked and locked up. It went very much against her grain. There were things she wanted to see done to the ones who had put her in this position.

At that point, she was facing yet another closed door and

this was beginning to get on her nerves.

Steeling herself, she paced quickly across the floor to the door opposite. This one had a large pane of glazed glass in it, and the hallways outside looked darker than the room. That meant that if anyone had been standing out there looking in, they would definitely have seen her silhouette and they'd be waiting for her to come out. Thinking of that, thinking of Kamaguchi standing there with that rifle, she stood at the door for more than a minute, gathering up the nerve to open it. Finally, she did it.

There was a loud and, for her, tooth-jarring click as the bolt came free and the door swung inward. She stepped out into the hall and moving as fast as she could glanced right and then left down the long corridor before pulling herself back into the room. Once more, she allowed herself a sigh of relief. There had been no one in the hallway. All she had seen were some doors, all closed, and the corridor-turning north at either end. It was time to go on. She went out, decided to take the left side.

At the next bend in the hallway she stopped, as she had each time before, and quickly peered down it. At the end of the hall, where it ended in a pair of double doors, each standing wide, she'd seen something.

She ducked back, took a further step in the direction she'd come, and pressed her body to the wall. Her heart pounded against her ribs. At the edge of the door, near the floor, she'd seen something. The glance had been a quick one, and she was glad that she'd continued to be careful even though she'd been having an easy go of it. But what she thought she had seen was a shoe. It appeared that someone was standing, or perhaps sitting just at the end of the hallway, beyond those doors and out of sight.

Mary had made virtually no sound, though. She doubted

anyone had heard her, and the shoe had not moved. But it had been just a quick glance lasting a fraction of a second. Maybe it *had* moved, or maybe it wasn't a shoe, at all. It was possible it was something else. But in her present situation she couldn't be too careful. She'd have to take another look.

Carefully, Mary bent down and went to one knee, inching closer to the edge of the hallway. She hoped that she would present less of a visual target if her head were low to the floor. Slowly, she crept out and looked down the hall. The dark object was still there, and it was a shoe, as she had thought.

However, it was not the foot of a man standing, or even sitting in a chair and biding his time. The toe was pointed toward the ceiling. Mary could even see the ankle attached to that foot, black sock pulled down to show a smooth-skinned ankle. Whoever was in that shoe was lying on his back. She squinted, trying to see some movement, anything at all, but there was nothing. The foot was still, and she could see nothing casting a shadow onto the floor in there.

Mary retreated to a kneeling position in which she was not visible from those double doors. She crouched there and thought. Who was it? And why was he lying there like that, not moving?

She got up and calmly and carefully stepped into the other hallway and began to walk down it. The double doors grew and grew in her field of vision until they resembled something like the entrance to some gigantic coliseum, until that foot seemed like a boulder blocking her way out of a cave-in. A few seconds passed interminably, and Mary found herself there at the doorway. Without pausing, she went through it and looked down.

Kamaguchi. It was the Japanese biologist. And he was

lying there on the floor, a great fan of blood around the top of his skull. Tearing her eyes from the sight of the dead man, Mary looked at the wall against which Kamaguchi was lying, his arms splayed out dramatically, and she could see blood and bits of brain matter stuck there, drying like some kind of gory sauce. There was the rifle, partially propped against the dead man's torso. Whatever had happened, it had happened some minutes before. Blood and brain matter didn't just dry out on contact with the air. How long had she been trapped in that room? Mary wasn't sure, but suspected it had been at least two hours, probably more. That meant that it was late afternoon, evening perhaps.

And then, even though her gaze and attention were locked onto the face of dead Kamaguchi, Mary heard something. It was very slight, just the tiniest scuff of shoe sole against carpet. Someone was coming. Mary's eyes took in the dead man, took in the gun lying there within her reach. Niccols was a damned good shot with a rifle, and she wanted that firearm almost more than she wanted anything. But if she took it and retreated, whoever had done this would know she was there, would know she was free of the ropes, *would, perhaps, think that they had someone else to kill.* It was possible the sound was coming from the approach of someone who was there to help her. But Mary did not want to bet her life on it. Especially when she noticed that the sound was increasing, that it was coming directly her way, and that it was not the soles of one pair of shoes, but of several.

Quickly, she backed down the corridor, returning the way she had come, and she did not look back. As she retreated toward the place from which she had escaped, the footfalls kept coming her way.

CHAPTER
THIRTY-TWO

"What's wrong?"

There was a great gulf of darkness between them. Each stared across the blackness, seeing only that.

"How can you make that accusation against Mary? What evidence do you have?"

Kate didn't reply. Ron stood against a wall, and he wasn't sure any more where the door was. Kate sat precisely where she had been when she and Ron had embraced. Short embrace.

"Two minutes ago you were kissing me," Kate said. "Two minutes ago I was the object of your desire. You were enjoying it, so don't lie."

"I didn't say anything about not *enjoying* it," he told her. He repressed an impulse to draw his arm across his mouth. "It. It's just. Hell. I can't believe that about Mary. I've . . . We . . ."

"You know, I'll never be able to understand your kind. I tell you something that's obviously the truth, then you're scared and frightened and *angry* because you don't want to hear it." She shifted, let one of her long, long legs slide until it was flat against the tiled floor. Ron heard her booted heel squeaking along the way.

"Angry isn't what I'm feeling. I'm confused."

"Think about it."

"Why would she do that? That's not like her. What evidence do you have?"

"See? You *are* angry. I can hear it in your voice and I can hear it in the way you're talking. You're pissed off with yourself, for not realizing it, but you're taking it out on me. Now don't deny it, because I've seen it too many times to mention."

"Crap," he said. Finally, he too slumped to the floor, the wall at his back as he came to a sitting position. "I just want out of here."

"That's not what you were saying a few minutes ago. A few minutes ago you were probably hoping no one bothered us for an hour or so."

"Yeah. Well, maybe. But that was before you were accusing Mary of murder."

"*Think* about it, Ron! Who else was with you when Dodd passed you the disk? Who else knew about it?"

"But she didn't know what was going on there, what he passed on to me. She . . ."

"But she was there. You even told her you were going in to town to see Dodd. And he never made it, did he? You don't know what she saw when he gave you the disk. She's a sharp young woman. Maybe she knew what it was before you did.

"And you're going to tell me it was just a coincidence that she showed up at your place just in time to save you? And I'm willing to believe a woman can defend herself. But come *on*, Ron! She bested two professional killers? Give me a break!"

"I . . . I . . . can't believe it."

"You'd better start believing it. Or at least consider the possibility," she said.

There was a long pause. They sat there in the total

blackness, each hearing the other breathing. From time to time Ron lifted his hand and passed it before his eyes, saw nothing, blinked, repeated the process. It had been a long time since he'd seen darkness this complete.

"You okay?" she asked. "Your head, I mean. Where he hit you."

Ron reached back and felt the large but unpleasantly soft knot on the back of his skull. "I'll survive," he told her. "If we had any light, you could ask me how many fingers you were holding up."

Neither of them laughed.

"We'll be out of here soon," Kate said, as if she were certain of it and could have announced the precise moment if only she could read her watch.

"How do you know that? They haven't seemed too anxious to check up on us." He rolled his head on his neck, checking out the muscles there, and for any traces of dizziness.

"I know Adam, and I don't think he'll leave us here for too much longer. Even if Vance doesn't come right back in, I think he'll let us out. At least out of this room. Kamaguchi won't let him keep us cooped up in here. For a stoic Asian, he's got a soft heart, and he'll talk Adam into letting us out to use the facilities and get something to eat and drink."

"Well, you know 'em better than I do. Whatever they do, they're up the creek, I can tell you that. You can be damned sure I'm going to have the lot of them arrested for this stunt."

Again, an uncomfortable silence settled in. They sat apart, facing one another across the pitch-blackness, the soles of their shoes perhaps six feet from the other. Ron coughed. Kate sighed, cleared her throat.

"What?" he asked.

"I wasn't going to say anything. I just cleared my throat."

"Oh."

They blinked. Breathed. Rested. A few minutes creaked past.

"When they let us out, we have to tell them about Mary. About what we suspect of her," she said.

"But we don't know. Not for certain."

"Are you willing to risk your life on it? If she helped to deep-six Dodd, she can arrange for the rest of us to go, too. Think about it."

And even though he could not see her, could barely even hear her, Ron could feel a wave of anger emanating from where she sat. "But you still haven't given a reason why would Mary do such thing."

"Why does anyone do such a thing? Money, Ron. And the folks who offered it to her have very, very deep pockets. Take my word for it. Even Vance is nothing more than a bump in the road to them. She'd do it for the cash. I mean, the gator trapping business can't be *that* lucrative."

"But, Mary and I . . ."

"What? You had a thing going? You made love to her? It's sometimes not that big a deal, Ron. Not to someone who would cooperate in the murder of another human."

"That's hard to take," he told her.

"Well, start considering the possibility really fast. I doubt we have a lot of time left if she's able to get word out to whomever it is helped her take out Dodd. So stop being mad at *me* for bringing it to your attention."

"I'm sorry. I'm sorry I reacted that way. But there's nothing I can do about it. It's just natural for me to come to her defense. It would be cruel to believe that about her."

"And we have another possibility to worry about," Kate continued.

"And what would that be?" Ron asked.

"She may have already gotten in touch with the other side."

"Other side?"

"The bad guys."

And although he didn't like what he was hearing and the suspicions that were creeping into his mind, he couldn't deny that Kate was onto something. Mary had been there when Dodd had passed him the disk. She had become a familiar face in Salutations—at least in certain quarters. There had been the surprise that she and Tatum were acquainted. She'd even known Dodd.

It was possible.

He had decided that he would not say another word until their captors returned to release them, or someone appeared to rescue them. Ron would just sit there and keep his mouth shut. It would be best all around.

And that was when the first shot rang out.

CHAPTER
THIRTY-THREE

The fire team came down the approach road to the Eyesore as if they were merely a group of lost tourists. That was the way it had been planned, and that was the way it was supposed to have played out with the mole. They were in a plain white Astro van, four years old and completely untraceable. The tag was legit, but it would become invisible and lost for all time as soon as the job was done. The Colonel himself had taken care of most of the fine details, and what he had not accomplished himself he had left to men who were well versed in such misdirection. The last thing on the minds of the five assassins was whether their vehicle could be traced back to anyone who worked with Grisham.

Silently, they sat hunched in the van and all of them merely surveyed the new territory. Their mouths were closed. They had said everything that needed saying before they'd left Grisham's property. The lay of the land and the interior of Holcomb's compound were parts of an open book to them. The outside of the place had already been a faux target to them for months; the Colonel liked to use it in his games and drills and had never seriously thought of it as a legitimate mark. But the interior of the collection of buildings was another matter. One could conjecture, based on the exteriors, what lay inside. But of course they didn't have to guess, for a certain traitor was waiting to let them inside, and make things a little easier.

The sandy road leading down to the Eyesore had been deceptively long. Grisham had warned them that it would seem longer than its mile and a half due to the closeness of the vegetation. And because of the twists and turns it took due to Holcomb's reluctance to cut any of the larger trees that would have stood in the way of any sane man laying out a road. Again, they had been prepared for the illusion of remoteness that lay about this place. Logic told them that these buildings were visible from the center of Salutations, from the windows of any buildings there that were higher than the treetops around the Eyesore. But at ground level you would think you were in the midst of the wilderness. Trees and brush pressed in all around, which was a good thing. Because all of that vegetation would muffle the sounds of gunfire, of which they were all certain there would be.

Mel Waters was the head of the fire team. It was his job to direct his men and see to it that this job went as smoothly as possible. None of them really knew why they were being ordered to do this, but they all realized that there must certainly be a fine reason for it. There were supposed to be at least five people inside Holcomb's compound, and only one of them was marked to walk out of there alive. Again, aside from the fact that this person had delivered up the blueprints of the buildings to them, Waters didn't know why he was ordered to spare this one life. If he'd bothered to think about it, he would have thought it best to kill that one, too. But Waters wasn't in charge and so had wasted almost no time thinking about it. It was his job to be a killing machine, to be precise, and that was all. He was certain that the rest of his team thought the same, if they thought at all.

Coming out of the forest, they were surprised at the

sheer size of the compound. Of course they had heard that Holcomb was a very wealthy man, one of the wealthiest in the state of Florida, and that was saying something. Perhaps these buildings had been pocket change to him. Whatever it had cost Holcomb, Waters knew that it was costing Colonel Grisham some amount of concern: all the more reason to just put an end to Vance Holcomb's socialistic environmental crusade. He pulled the van up to the gated entrance of the Eyesore and stopped. As soon as he shut down the engine and turned off the air conditioner, the summer heat began to infiltrate the cab of the van. A line of sweat instantly appeared across his red, sunburnt forehead and began to advance down the slope of his brow.

He got out of the van and took two steps to the west of it. There was a truck parked outside, as he had been told to expect. It was a government vehicle, and it would be a pleasure for him to kill its driver. He hoped that he would receive the honor of putting a bullet through the Wildlife officer's stinking skull. A dragonfly whizzed past, an almost machinelike burr to the clacking of its amazing wings. It was a flash of blue and gray, a retreating sound vanishing into the shrubs.

Waters looked at the watch strapped firmly to his freckled wrist. The gates were supposed to be open. But he could plainly see that they were locked. This wasn't right. Something had obviously gone wrong with the plans, blame lying at the feet of the resident Benedict Arnold inside. Well, they had a backup plan. It wasn't finesse and it wasn't pretty, but it was a plan. They had a schedule to keep.

The soldier climbed back into the van and started the engine, revving it a couple of times. He knew the resumption of the air-conditioning was a welcome relief to the uncomplaining members of his team, but of course none of them said a thing; they just sat stoically and waited for the moment they'd be allowed to act. He put the van into gear. Stomped the gas pedal.

And rammed the ridiculous excuse for a gate, tearing one side of it completely off its hinges. The block of chain link bounced against the hood of the van, smashing the left headlight and pulled free of its moorings to go sailing over the roof of the vehicle. At the front door of the compound, Waters brought the van to a halt, scattering sand and fine dirt that clouded into the air and provided them with unexpected cover.

As a unit, the doors of the van opened wide and all five men poured out. The big glass doors of the compound were unlocked, as had been promised, and they merely trotted inside. Firearms had sprouted almost magically from the duffel bags that had lain at their feet as they'd driven in. Quickly, they fanned out, Waters heading down the main hallway with Whitcomb, while Rhodes, Graves, and Hinton faded left. So far, no one had come running to investigate the destruction, but he knew that there would be targets soon. They knew to whom they owed their easy entrance, and anything else that moved was toast. That was all there was to this simple plan.

Wordlessly, each team headed down the hallways. They moved quickly, stopping at each doorway they came to, checking for movement. No target presented itself. Waters was poised to use the radio buttoned to his shoulder to contact Rhodes, but he hesitated, not wishing to break the vocal silence. At that moment he came out into a large room, just as he had figured, and saw one of the men he was expecting. According to his briefing, this one was named Kinji Kamaguchi, a Japanese national working as a zoologist for Holcomb. Intelligence had stated that the man knew how to use a gun if the situation arose, and as the two faced one another across the wide space of the room, Waters immediately noted the rifle that Kamaguchi was carrying. Someone had warned them that they were coming; that was the only explanation.

"What," Kamaguchi shouted as Waters and Whitcomb appeared from the main hallway. "Who the hell are you?" he was asking as he began to bring the barrel of his weapon to train on Waters.

Well, perhaps they hadn't been warned precisely what to expect. In the instant before he brought his Browning to his shoulder and fired, Waters thought that it could be something else entirely that had alarmed the inhabitants of Holcomb's compound. As Kamaguchi's head exploded in a quick burst of red, Waters pointed toward the open doorway that the Oriental had been sitting in front of before they'd arrived. It almost looked as if the man had been guarding the door for some reason. They would check it out as soon as they swept the rest of the building. There were at least four others in there, and that meant that they had at least three more people to kill.

Adam Levin had been in one of labs near the back of the main building when he heard the crash of something smashing through the gate. "Damn," he had cursed himself for being lax. His first thought was that Riggs had somehow alerted the police, telling them that he had been kidnapped. It would be just like those government types to overreact and come in with guns blazing. Holstering the .357 he had been saddled with since deciding to hold Riggs and the others, Levin had started toward the source of the commotion.

He was out of the lab, where he had been sitting nervously for some minutes, wanting only to be somewhere he could think clearly and relax. His first thought was to go straight for the source of the noise, but he passed one of Holcomb's locked security rooms and instead stopped there and unlocked it. There was a video monitoring system inside, and he would be able to access most of the compound from there with a flip of a switch or two. He knew how to use it quickly and effectively. In fact, he could even look in on Riggs and Kwitney if he so wished.

Closing the door behind him, he sat down in front of a big video monitor. The system, at least in this part of the building, used a single screen that could be split into four sections or used to singly watch the reception of any of the cameras placed throughout the compound. You could even see outside, and Holcomb had once shown him the view from one of the savannas where he had hidden a camera before the terror birds had found and disabled it. Shoving all such thoughts from his mind, he activated the screen and began to look.

First, he got a view of the main gate. It had been broken completely in, half of the chain link section lying in the sand. He switched to the principal foyer and could see a damaged Astro van parked just outside the door, but could see no one there. Where was Billy? He had left Billy to see to the garage when he had gone off to sit and think, to be alone. Billy should have been the one closest to the invaders and should have already confronted them. But he couldn't see his Seminole friend anywhere.

Levin knew precisely where Kamaguchi was, though. He had told Kinji to sit and watch the hallway and make sure that Mary Niccols did not escape somehow. That friend of Riggs' was no weakling, and it wasn't out of the question that she could work her way free of the ropes. They'd tied her pretty well, but it was best to be safe rather than sorry.

Adam tried to remember which camera number was assigned to the room where he'd left Kamaguchi. It was the west wing, and those camera numbers were all prefixed with a *W*. He jotted one, saw an empty lab. "W-8," he muttered to himself. And was rewarded with a soundless vision of Kamaguchi standing to face two men who had, at that instant, burst into the room.

Adam Levin stared in frozen horror as the strange man who had first stepped into the room brought his rifle to his shoulder and fired a single shot into Kinji's brain. Kamaguchi fell lifelessly to the floor in stark blacks and grays, and Levin's eyes were locked on the dead man's form. The killers didn't even pause to check on the man they had shot. They were sure that they'd killed him. As Levin looked on, the one who had fired the shot gestured toward the hallway Kinji had been guarding and then they both passed through the room and into the main hallway. Sitting and staring for a few seconds, Levin slowly realized that they were headed directly toward him and that they would be outside the room in which he would be effectively trapped in about fifteen seconds.

He shut down the security monitors and got up.

"That was a gunshot," Ron said.

"I'm not deaf," Kate told him.

"What's going on? You don't think Levin and Kamaguchi shot Mary, do you?"

Kate had stood, as Ron had done, and after some groping about, both had found their way to the door where each had pressed an ear to it, trying to hear more. "No. I don't think they'd shoot Mary. I told you I don't think they want to shoot any of us. Right now, I'm more worried about Levin and the others. He thinks Mankind is going to destroy this planet, and I can see him getting itchy in this situation." She sighed. "But, that wasn't Adam."

"What do you mean? How do you know?"

"First of all, Adam's not a gun man. He hates the things. Yeah, he knows how to put the bullets in, and has fired them, I know; but he hates them. Also, that was a rifle shot. Adam had a pistol. A .357. Kinji has the rifle."

"Or he did when they both left here. Levin could have it now, for all we know."

"He could. And there's Billy. He was armed, too. But I just can't see Billy shooting anyone. Especially not Mary."

"Why not?"

"Because he's a Seminole, just like Mary is. And I think he likes and respects her, anyway. Billy used to make his living trapping gators when he was a kid. He and his dad, he told me. Shooting Mary would be too much like shooting someone he knows. He wouldn't do it. Hell, he probably knows her."

"But Billy *did* have a firearm."

"He has access to a number of guns here. He's handy with a shotgun, as I recall. But I *told* you. Billy wouldn't shoot her. But Billy and Mary . . . they could maybe shoot at us."

Ron exploded. He couldn't see Kate, but he could feel her body heat. "How do you *know* that? Huh? You don't know *what* these dumbasses are capable of. Hell, they kicked your ass in here with me and leveled a gun at you. You don't know *what* they might or might not do."

He could hear her breathing, her low, even breathing, and once again Ron found that he could not read Kate Kwitney's emotions. Perhaps she had spent so many years hiding her feelings that she had become uncannily adept at masking them. It was something he had found intriguing before, but now he saw it as truly creepy. "I know, just believe me. If we're in danger, then it won't be from Adam or Kinji."

"I hope you're right about them, because I know Mary isn't capable of what you're accusing her of," Ron told her, an edge in his voice that he could not cover. "So, all around, that would mean we'll get out of this alive." Once again, in the darkness, he and Kate were facing one another, unseeing. Some of the things she had mentioned concerning Mary seemed too logical to dispute. But as Kate had outlined her case against Mary, Ron had felt the old feelings for her coming to the surface. He felt like defending her and he couldn't help himself. He did, he realized, still have strong feelings for her.

They were standing, facing one another in opposition when a key was jammed suddenly into the door's lock and it flew open, flooding the room with soft but blinding light. Ron's pupils quickly contracted to pinpoints and the pain caused him to flinch back. He caught just the glimpse of a human figure, arm extended, gun in hand. It was, he saw as he recovered, Levin. The .357 was aimed right at him.

"Let's get out of here," Levin said.

Ron stepped toward the doorway, right behind Kate whose long legged strides had already taken her out of the room. The three of them stood in the hallway. Levin's face was ashen, and he kept glancing up and down the hall, as if expecting Satan himself to come flying down it on gigantic leather wings.

"What's going on, Adam? We heard a shot."

"You didn't shoot Mary, did you?"

Levin's pale face turned toward them. "Someone killed Kinji," he said. "I saw them on the security monitor. They shot him in the head. He's dead."

"Who did that, Adam? Who did you see?" Kate's hand had reached out to take Levin's shoulder, to support him. "You see, Ron? What did I tell you?" Her hand squeezed Levin's shoulder to accent her request. "Now, who did you see?"

"I don't know who they are. Two men. With guns. They came into the room where Kinji was and they just shot him. Just like that. They were coming right for me, but I unlocked the freezer in the west lab and came through it to this hallway. I tricked them," he said, a silly smile on his face. "I tricked them."

"Suck it up, Adam. I think you're in shock. I don't believe you're thinking straight."

"I saw them, I tell you." His face was grim and as white as paste.

Kate reached out and without hesitating, she took the pistol from him. He didn't resist. "Let me have the gun, Adam. You do as we say and we'll find out what's going on." She, too, looked down the hallway and up it, searching for anyone who might be coming their way. "What did they look like?"

"Just two men. Nothing special about them. But they didn't even think about it, shooting Kinji, I mean. The one in front just aimed his rifle and shot him right in the head."

She took a second to glare at Ron. "Wonder how they knew we'd all be here? How about it, Ron?"

Ron ignored the verbal barb and stepped up to put his own hand on Levin's back, at the base of his neck. The man was shivering, perhaps already suffering from clinical shock. Now Ron knew he needn't have worried about this pitiful fellow killing anyone. "How were they dressed? Were they cops? Maybe someone called in cops or something. Maybe they thought Kamaguchi was going to shoot at them and they reacted to that."

"No," Levin said. "They aren't cops. They're dressed in regular shirts, jeans. Not cops."

Ron leaned against the wall, closed his eyes. "It must be the same people who sent those two to my house. It *has* to be."

"What? Finally coming around, Ron?" Kate looked at him suspiciously, but with less of that I-told-you-so anger.

"Look. If they're desperate enough to kill Dodd, and if they're desperate enough to come to my house and try to shake me down, then there's obviously no doubt that they'll kill all of us."

Levin's eyes went wide. "We have to get out of here. We have to get out and, and, and we have to warn Vance. God, we can't leave Vance out there with these people ready to shoot us on sight."

"Vance doesn't *know*," Adam screeched, grabbing Kate by the shirt and pulling her to him. He was losing the tenuous grip he had on his panic.

Ron reached over and restrained Levin, making him release his grip on Kate. He shook the biologist and spoke to him. "Look, man. You saw them kill your friend. But what about Mary? What about Billy? Did you see them? And what did you guys do with Mary?"

"We. We tied Mary up and put her in the room where the mainframe's going. It's empty and we thought it would be a good place to put her. She's way down a corridor where even we hardly ever go, so I don't think anyone would think to look there.

"And. And Billy was supposed to be near the garage. Supposed to be watching the gate for Vance. See if Vance was coming back. But I never saw Billy on the monitor. Never saw him at all."

Ron looked up at Kate. "How do we get out of here?

How do we get out of here without those guys seeing us? Can we go back the way Adam came? Through that freezer, like he said?"

"No. Not that way," Levin blurted. "They were coming that way, and they'll find the freezer. They were right behind me. Not that way. We'd be cornered if we went that way. And they have rifles. All we have is that." He pointed to the pistol in Kate's hand.

"Damn," Ron muttered. He looked behind him, and noticed the big windows leading outside. "Why not there?" he asked, gesturing toward the glass panes. "We can just go through there."

"No. I don't think so," Kate said.

"Why not?" Ron asked.

"Because of him," she said.

Ron looked to where she was pointing, and turned just in time to see Billy Crane out in the grounds beyond the window. He was standing braced, aiming a shotgun right at them. It roared, and the glass shattered into a fine rain of glittering shards around them. They all brought up their arms to shield their eyes. Ron could hear Levin screaming something about Billy trying to kill them; but his own panic prevented him from understanding all of the words.

CHAPTER
THIRTY-FOUR

Although the receivers were very small and hidden high in the tops of several nearby longleaf pines, as were the transmitters placed at strategic points throughout the Eyesore, Holcomb was able to get a good handle on what was going on back at his compound. He was crouching there in his hideaway, a pair of extremely expensive headphones clamped over his ears. Sweat trickled down the sides of his face as three pairs of small ventilating fans whirred silently above him, taking out the hottest air and keeping the temperature inside at a reasonable eighty-eight degrees. Ingenious baffles and air pockets kept out even the most stubborn of insects, so the room/laboratory was comfortable despite the heat and humidity that surrounded it. From a distance of more than twenty yards, his little lab was invisible. But he knew he couldn't stay hidden there for long. Someone was going to come for him as soon as they had finished killing the people back at his compound. In fact, it could be that they were already on the way.

He had flipped through a number of low frequencies as soon as he'd settled into the place. Holcomb had spent a considerable amount of money buying the components, and had dedicated a lot of his valuable time installing the system. Often, he had used it to eavesdrop on the ones he left there while he went out into the forests and savanna to search for the birds. On a number of occasions he had gathered some truly juicy bits of gossip, generally concerning how his employees thought of him. Mainly, they had seemed a loyal and hardworking lot. But not now. He could not get over the feeling that someone had ratted them out, and he could not quite figure out just who was there now, doing the killing.

Cursing himself, he realized as he had heard the panicked voice of Adam Levin recounting the murder of Kamaguchi that he could do nothing for them from his hiding spot out in the bush. While he could listen in on what was happening there, the equipment he'd stashed was good only for receiving and was practically useless with which to transmit. He had the small radio with him, but that was no good, either. It had a specific range, and he was afraid that if he used it now, then it would most likely be used as a point to locate him. If an armed group was at the compound, there was more than likely another one headed his way. It would be a simple matter to triangulate his location if they locked onto his signal for even a minute or so. He stared at his pack, where the little radio was stashed, and shook his head.

As he'd listened to the remaining members of his crew, he had heard them as they had realized that Billy Crane was outside the window. One of them, he thought that it had been Kate, had yelled something about a gun, and then his hidden microphone had gone full of white noise. It had been a gunshot, of course, and he thought he'd heard the unmistakable racket of shattering glass. After that, the mike had gone to all static, an overload on the sensitive component. He had continued to listen for a minute or so, but had given up, soon trying one listening post after another, but had picked up nothing else. In a while, he had slowly removed the headphones.

He knew that he must assume the worst. They had probably all been killed. Except, it seemed, for Billy Crane. That was strange, really. Of the ones present at the Eyesore, he wouldn't have suspected Crane capable of selling them out. When he had taken the Indian on, the man had seemed truly sincere in his desire to do something to save such a wonderful piece of wild Florida. Sincere enough that the team had finally decided to let him in on the discovery of the terror birds. It seemed appropriate to Holcomb, and the rest of them, that Billy be a part of the ongoing research. It had probably been a trite bit of white man's guilt to do so.

Holcomb sighed, stood, and stepped over to a foam mattress lying on the flooring. His lab was lined with a very expensive material he had commissioned; a synthesis of Gore-Tex and Kevlar mesh. The stuff breathed well, let out moisture and allowed the free flow of air, but kept out even the most persistent dampness. He lay there, his right arm covering his face. Holcomb was very tired, having hiked double-time across the miles to this place. But he didn't know how long he would have before he would have to cut and run. Running was a foregone conclusion. They'd find him at his little laboratory. Once that happened, he was as good as dead if he remained there. He'd have to rest for a bit, then leave. Men with guns would soon be after him.

Holcomb wished he knew who had been there doing the shooting, other than Crane.

Shifting, he looked at his equipment in the fading light. In a few moments it would be dark, and if he wanted to be able to see in the room, he'd have to use one of the small, battery-powered lights positioned along the walls. He thought of his friends, of the possibility of trying to sneak back to the compound to see if he could help. But Vance Holcomb was all that stood between the flock of terror

263

birds and their eventual extermination. Of that, he was pos-
itively certain. For them, for this entire wilderness, he was
indispensable. To endanger himself was an act of selfish-
ness he could not risk.

He would have to leave his people to Fate, and *he* would
have to escape. It couldn't be helped. With a flip of a single
switch, he shut down the receiver, conserving battery
power. For now, he knew what he wanted to know. In the
dimness of twilight, he turned, assuming a more comfortable position. It was time to rest.

CHAPTER
THIRTY-FIVE

On the wind. The sign and the scent, and the *warning* were coming on the wind.

The Scarlet rogue aimed his beak toward the sky, opened his mouth to hold the scent in his mouth, to allow it to linger there and to *tell* him what was being carried upon it. Night had fallen and there was more information there than he could ever decipher, should he have chosen to attempt to read it all. But he had learned in his years to filter out the noise of that which was unimportant, and to read only what was of consequence for the moment. And what it was telling him now was both confusing, and even a little frightening.

In the cooling evening he was aware that the Flock was in movement. And not in a routine way that indicated a hunt was on, or that they were merely relocating to a more advantageous position to assure that they remained undiscovered for another day. This was different. The Flock was moving out in a strange pattern, all of the adults at the forefront, with the chicks left far back and the youths behind them and flanking them, in a guarding position. This was not something the Scarlet had ever been a part of, something which he read in the way the scent of the flock members came to him on the wind, and in the sounds he detected from time to time. In addition, although they were still a comfortable distance from him, they were heading his way. Obviously, they were following the sign he had inadvertently left during his daylight journey, for the wind was currently in his favor and he knew that they did not have his scent, or even know his exact location. But it was bothersome to know that they were coming toward him. Since he had taken leave of the Flock, the Egg Father had kept a distance between their numbers and the Scarlet. Something had changed.

There was prey on the wind, the warm and *satisfying* scent of meat on the hoof. But he had placed that secondary to the other things he knew.

The Man Who Watches was among them again. The Flock had known of him for some time. He had descended into their midst some cycles before, making a covered nest at the edge of the open grasslands they sometimes liked to hunt. This man had scattered strange things, the things the Flock knew men somehow constructed, the way a worm constructs a cocoon, or a spider makes its web. Man's ways were a mystery to them, but they were aware of many of the things men did and made. For a time, Egg Mother and Walks Backward had sought out the places where *The Man Who Watches* had left his constructs, and they had bitten them, tearing them and dropping the remains into the river as they did with things they wished to hide. And after a time the man had ceased to leave the things where they disturbed the Flock. And they had decided not to remove the things this man had left high in the trees, even though there were young among them who could make the climb, who were not too heavy to do so. Egg Father had decided not to risk it.

This particular man had returned to his sometimes-nest, and was there now, resting in it.

And there was a third, and also disturbing development. The Scarlet had detected a number of men moving into the wilderness from the west. They were coming from that place where the men grouped and pretended to hunt, as men had done on this place at intervals for many years until they had left. This was the first time the Scarlet could recall that these men had crossed the line and had come into the forests and grasslands that belonged to the Flock. Their scent told him many things: there were six of them; they were, for men, being very silent; and they were hunting. He could smell it. Could taste it. Could sense it on the breezes—an electric spark that leaped from their great brains and traveled on a plane the Scarlet could sense, could read, could understand.

And the men were there to hunt *him*. He could see himself in their thoughts. *Red*. They had seen him, somehow, although he had never seen them. But his image was there, crossing the night winds from their minds to his. *The Red Bird*, they were thinking. *Kill it*.

Well.

Well, then.

He would be ready for them. He would be ready for his parents and for Walks Backward.

The Scarlet was not going to make this an easy night for any of them.

The Flock had set out on the trail the Scarlet had left for them. Alone, with no one to walk his trace and remove his sign, he was visible to them. There were two dozen adults moving along a V-shaped line, each of the great birds spaced thirty meters apart. Behind them, a half-mile back, were the smallest of the chicks and thirty youths of sufficient age and ability to guard them. One youth was serving as the sweep, as the one who would become Walks Backward when the time came. It seemed a good, safe way to protect the young.

The point of the *V* was Egg Father. The eastward end of it was Egg Mother, and the western point was Walks Backward. It was their plan to continue on the trail the Scarlet rogue had left until the spoor became hot, became fresh. At that point each trailing end of the *V* would come forward, would arch up and around until the *V* became a circle and they would quickly surround the rogue. He would try to break free, of course, and he was certainly large enough to do so, but even he could not hope to take on so many of his own kind. Not when the command to *kill* had been given.

For now, the rogue was not merely prey for the Flock. He was more than that. He was not just the object of the hunt, but also a thing they rarely had faced in so many years. He was their *adversary*. It was not unknown for a member of the Flock to fall to another predator. The great alligators who lived and hunted the waters sometimes took a chick or a youth at the edge of the river. It was unfortunate, but part of the cycle of life. When they had been more numerous, the wolf packs and even the big cats had been known to kill and eat a lone member of their number, as had bears. But not since the Flock had formed this new society, and had hidden from Man were they more than rarely a victim to anything that lived. And so the Scarlet had become not only the object of this night's hunt, but also their enemy. He was a danger they had never faced and tonight was his last night.

Leaving the youths behind, the formation had set out, moving through the forests and into the edge of the grasslands with the tall pines interspersed throughout. If this were where he was, then the task would be easier. Yes, his stride was great and his speed formidable. But out on the savanna he would be completely visible and they would run him down as they did a deer or a fox. Egg Father hoped that the rogue had been foolish enough to try to hide out there in the grasses.

As they went through the great trees, Egg Father scented the wind and looked all around. His night vision was superb. He could see the entire panorama of the forest in stark, tinted shades of black and gray. Even with almost no moonlight to show the way, they could all make out the smallest detail in the night. Sedges swayed on the wind, branches bobbed, palmetto twitched. Beneath their feet, small animals crouched on the ground or huddled in burrows. Above them, birds sat high in safe perches and looked on, making no comment. Clawed feet rose and fell, taking them along at a distance eating pace.

Colonel Grisham and his fire team passed over onto the old military range at sunset. By then, he knew that his men would have already groomed Holcomb's compound and were now cleaning it up. Hopefully there would be no sign of a struggle. And if there were, the cleanup would be so thorough that no one would ever know. How the bodies would be disposed of he neither cared nor wished ever to know. That it was done and that there would never be any comebacks was enough for him.

And then it was *his* turn. This was the job he wanted for himself. More than likely, if Holcomb was not at the initial target, then it would be up to Grisham Company to take him down and dispose of his mortal remains. Also, there was the issue of the *terror bird*.

'Phorusrachids. They were a race of ground dwelling birds of prey that became extinct about a million years ago,' his encyclopedia had told him. Someone at Berg Brothers had done what research they could, and the mole inside Holcomb's team had filled in the rest. That was a bit of luck, making a turncoat out of one of the billionaire's own. But Grisham wasn't surprised. Everyone had their price. He had yet to meet a human being who couldn't be bought.

According to their source, there was a flock of about a dozen or two of the birds living out there. They mainly hunted in the open longleaf savanna at night, and bedded down during the day. At least, that's what the traitor had told them. In actuality, even Holcomb's team had been unable to locate the birds' hiding places during daylight hours. And they had only a slim bit of direct observation of them during lightless times, when the things apparently did all of their hunting and socializing. Despite the fact that the birds were large, and also appeared to be built for speed, Grisham didn't think that killing them all would prove to be much of a problem. He, for one, didn't have any doubts.

The colonel and his five men were all equipped with personal radio gear, compact boxes attached at the epaulet, right side. They would be as silent as possible, but it would be foolish to head out, armed to the teeth in the nighttime bush without being able to communicate effectively. Each man was carrying an AK-47 rifle. Grisham had chosen the weapons, keeping the complement of firearms uniform in case any man exhausted his ammunition and had to rely on another for spare cartridges. The guns were accurate, fired smoothly, and could go to automatic with the simple flick of a switch. And each of them carried the reliable 9mm Beretta, Grisham's sidearm of choice. There were pistols that packed a lot more power, but he enjoyed these weapons immensely and had handed them out to each of the members of his fire team. In addition to the guns and ammo, they of course carried emergency provisions to enable them to comfortably endure several days in the bush without returning to base to resupply. But it wasn't going to take that long. Within twelve hours, he felt certain that both Vance Holcomb and his giant dino-birds would be extinct.

They all moved eastward in a more or less even line, roughly fifty meters between each man. In this way they could cover a lot of ground and were likely to notice any evidence of either man or animal. Nothing would move or try to get away from them without being seen. And, likely, nothing trying to hide from them would escape their notice. Each gun was equipped with a night scope, and as they trolled along, they would periodically stop, raise the scope and look down it, seeing what the night could no longer conceal from them.

Grisham was so at rest, peering down the barrel of his rifle when he saw something out of place. It wasn't anything living, no movement or quick flash of panic from something forcing itself not to bolt in fear. What he saw was a pair of sumac limbs, the leaves partially wilted and pointing in the wrong direction for a growing bush. Patiently, he held the gun to his chest, looked down the sight and stared. Someone—someone who had practiced it well—had tried to hide something in the undergrowth. The colonel stood still, held his breath, and moved the barrel of his gun up a degree, and down, then swept it right to left a few inches. There was a tarp under the limbs and brush, and just at ground level he caught sight of a tire. *An ATV,* he thought, seeing.

"Watkins. Number one here. Out."

"This is Watkins," came the reply, bulling through a very slight mist of static.

"Fifty yards ahead of my position. Hidden vehicle.

Approach with caution," Grisham ordered. He waited, watching, and soon Watkins's form came into view. The soldier approached the hidden ATV and soon had pulled the camouflage free of it. The vehicle belonged, he knew, to Holcomb. So that meant that Vance Holcomb was either out there, hiding in the forest and waiting for them, or sitting out there, somewhere, thinking he was just doing a little bird watching. Little did the billionaire creep know that Colonel Winston Grisham was about to hunt him down and kill him. Along with his stinking birds.

"It's time that we find Vance Holcomb," he rasped into his epaulet. "You all know what he looks like. Kill him on sight."

CHAPTER
THIRTY-SIX

As he stood, shielding his eyes to make as certain as he could that no glass got into them, he tried to see where Billy Crane was and what he was doing now. He could hear the Seminole shouting at them. What the hell did he mean?

"Come out. Hurry," Crane was yelling. "You don't have much time."

Levin was still cowering on the floor, his arms covering his head, his hands and back coated in a glittering sheath of broken bits of safety glass. Kate was crouching just below the windowsill, where Crane could not see her. So far, only Ron had chanced a look outside. If Billy had seen him, he hadn't fired at the glimpse of head Riggs had offered.

"Where is he?" Kate whispered.

"He's about thirty, maybe forty feet straight out," Ron said. He pointed directly through the wall in front of them, against which they were both leaning, as if holding it up as a shield.

"What's he saying?" Kate asked. They could both tell that Billy's voice was fading slightly.

"Come out, you idiots," the Indian repeated. "Come out before they kill the lot of you."

"He's crazy," Levin muttered, head still down, still coated in broken crystal bits.

"No. I don't think he is," Ron told him. "I think he was

giving us a way *out* of here." He braced to stand, but Kate's hand on his shoulder held him in place, her grip every bit as strong as his own.

"What are you talking about? He just *shot* at us."

"No. I think he was shooting out the window to give us an escape route. I believe he knows that's the only way we're getting out of here without having to face those guys who killed Kinji. There's probably more than two of them. We have to go. Now." Ron did stand, and had to exert some effort to break free of the hold Kate had on him.

"Don't *do* it," Kate said, her voice loud, forceful. "Think about it. It makes even more sense now than before. Mary and Billy are both Seminole. They're in this together." Ron heard Levin whimper as he stood and looked out to see what Crane was doing.

The Seminole was moving away, toward the corner of the building, where two of the compound's structures made a kind of open yard between them. Ron saw Crane glance back and motion for him to follow. "Hurry up, you damned fool," Billy yelled, his voice growing just a bit more faint.

Without thinking about it again, Ron knelt and grasped Levin behind the elbows and forced him to stand. Adam actually screamed, believing that he would soon be shot when his former companion caught sight of him through the shattered window. His eyes were wide and crazy as he looked up to see Crane retreating toward the forest. "What? What's he doing?" Levin asked.

"He wants us to follow him," Ron said. "He shot out the window so that we could get out of here without getting killed. Now, come *on,* dammit. Let's haul some ass before those other guys *find* us." He looked toward Kate who was just standing there, seemingly at odds with herself. "Make up your mind, Kate. I'm getting out of here now, while we can."

"You don't know," she stammered. She used the pistol to point toward the now all but invisible figure of Crane disappearing into the gloomy forest.

"We don't have time to debate this." He cast a glance toward the direction Billy had vanished. "We're getting out of here. Now," he said. He put his hands on the windowsill, not worrying about being cut, and he quickly vaulted over. On the other side, he was surprised to find that ground level was a full two feet lower than the floor had been, and he stumbled as he fell and went to the grassy earth. Grunting, he peered up and looked to see Levin following him, tentatively testing the sill.

"Come on, Adam. Get your butt in gear. Give him a hand," he suggested to Kate who he could see was still just standing there, watching them.

Levin jumped stiffly off the sill and made an even clumsier landing than Ron had. Riggs, afraid that his panic-stricken companion would twist an ankle and be unable to run, stepped forward to keep him from falling, which Adam would have done if not for Riggs' support. Still holding Levin up, Ron turned his eyes toward Kate who was at the window, leaning out, squinting at both of them.

"You coming, Kate?" Even as Ron asked it, he could see that she was bringing the .357 up, toward himself and Levin. But seeing her doing that, it did not occur to him that she could be aiming the weapon at them.

The shot broke the air into a billion bits of sound. Ron saw a puff of smoke appear around the big pistol, enveloping Kate's right hand. He saw the recoil from the weapon force her long arm up almost half a foot, her shoulder back an inch or so. Adam Levin's chest exploded, the exit wound a fist-sized crater that erupted in a shower of hot, crimson wet, spattering Ron's face with a horrid warmth.

Levin was dead in an instant, and the silly look on his face seemed almost a kind of reflection of the complete, numbing shock that was burning through Riggs. He had been supporting Levin, his hands on the man's torso, almost beneath the armpits. Later, but not right then, he would wonder how the bullet had missed him, had gone completely through his former captor and had ricocheted off some bone, sparing him a similar fate. Adam Levin first stiffened, for a mere split second, and then slumped to the ground like an enormous but leaking water balloon, almost taking Riggs with him.

Letting the dead man fall, Ron looked up at Kate. The barrel of the .357 was coming down from the recoil, and she was bringing it to bear on him. "What," he started to say, just forming the word with his lips but unable to make any air come up from his throat.

"I can't let any of you get out of here," she said. "It's time for you to go." Once more the pistol roared in her fist and Ron squinted, trying to prepare for the impact, for death.

The blow did not come. *She had missed.* He dove to the ground, rolling to his left and toward the building, trying to put the wall between himself and her aim. It would save him for a second, maybe, but then all she would have to do was lean out and take aim again. He was looking for something to pick up and throw at her. He chanced a quick look her way.

And he saw why she had missed him.

Mary Niccols had hit her from behind. And now she was punching her again, Mary's fist meeting solidly with Kate's skull. The impact of the punch forced Kate into the window and partially out of it.

"Mary," Ron screamed. He ran forward, looked to see where the pistol was, but Kate no longer held it in her now open hands. Even through his fear, he was enraged and reached up, grasping Kwitney by the roots of her hair, dragging her through the shattered window. She fell at his feet and he delivered a kick to her rib cage. "*Damn* you." She grunted as he kicked her.

Before he could kick her again, Mary scrambled through the window. "Let's get out of here," she said. "There's at least three armed men behind me somewhere. I got past them by hiding up behind the ceiling tiles. But they're going to be on us any second," Niccols said, her voice a very harsh whisper.

Ron put his fingers in Kate's hair and jerked her to her feet. "All right," he said. "But what do we do with *this* one? Is she coming with us, you think?"

Mary's work-hardened hand also grabbed a handful of Kate's long brown hair and pulled her back as Ron started off. "Bad idea. They might not be so quick to shoot at us with one of their own along, but she's a deceitful bitch. No telling what she might do out there. More trouble than she's worth, right?"

"Right. Just leave her here," he said, turning. "This way," Ron grunted, heading out where he had seen Billy Crane running before the woods had swallowed him. Behind, Mary was still standing with Kate, and Ron now saw where the pistol had gone. He watched Mary raise the weapon.

"Don't do it," he said.

Niccols brought her muscular right arm up and suddenly sent it down. The butt of the pistol met the back of Kate's skull. Kwitney went to the grass, her lanky frame lying still there in the fading light. Ron, his knees buckling, reached out to support himself against a pin oak sapling. A moment later, Mary reached him.

"Let's get going. *Now*."

Riggs followed, feeling the underbrush slapping against his legs, keeping his eyes front and looking for some sign of Billy Crane. He hoped the other man was not too far ahead. They would probably need the protection of his shotgun. Although he was running as fast as he could to keep up with Mary, Ron spoke between breaths, feeling relatively fresh despite the stress.

"I thought you were going to kill her. I wasn't sure."

For a moment Mary didn't answer. There was only the slap of grasses and tough shrubs against their pant legs, their boots thumping against the earth as they raced away from the Eyesore. But after a few seconds, she did answer.

"I almost did, Ron. I almost blew her brains out. She was going to kill you just like she killed that poor jerk, Levin."

I know, Ron wanted to say. He kept it to himself and would not have voiced it even if the sound of gunfire had not suddenly erupted behind them.

Just as the forest offered them some cover, they heard the first shot come, listened to it whizzing in the underbrush as it sped through the vegetation.

"Keep going," Ron said between gasps. "Billy Crane came this way. I think he knows where he's going, and he's armed a lot better than we are."

"Sounds like a plan," Mary said, the two of them now side by side. They let the forest take them in.

CHAPTER
THIRTY-SEVEN

The Scarlet rogue was ahead of the Flock. They were moving in a manner not unlike that used during a typical hunt. It was something he recognized and had been a part of more times than he could count. *Spread out:* they had done that. *Give the prey no way to run but forward:* that had been achieved; behind him was the bottom of an inverted wedge, probably three deep with adults. To the left and right of him was a line of strong members moving forward to pace him and outrun him if he tired; they were working as a group and would feed off their collective energy and purpose. *Be careful, but relentless:* this was the aim of the party and they would not deviate from that path unless the safety of the entire Flock was at jeopardy.

And although the Scarlet was still relatively young, still not the planner his elders were, he knew that was the weakness of his family. They would break off the chase if the well-being of the group became an issue. And only one thing could cause this.

Man.

And Man was here, now, in the Flock's domain, and in numbers. The big rogue did not know just *why* the men were here, except that he could feel something emanating from their group that was not unlike the song the Flock would croon when the hunt was on. From behind him, too close for his own comfort, he could *feel* that song moving perfectly from one flock member to the next. He heard it from his own Egg Mother, and from that damned Walks Backward, who he knew had wanted his own death for a long time. If there was any single number among the Flock that he feared, it was that one, the guardian who swept the way clean of their sign and watched everything, those eyes seeing it all. The Scarlet hoped that it would be possible to kill him before the Sun rose.

He was being herded toward the southwest. That thought was maddening to him, that he could be moved and chased like something to eat, like one of the frightened deer that sustained them. The inverted wedge that kept him moving was coming from the northeast, where the extended family had been bedding and hunting in recent days. It was far from the new activities of the men, where they had built their wooden and stone nests and had brought their dogs on which the Scarlet had been feeding.

The Scarlet had felt the need to attempt to cull some of the young females, so that he could begin a new flock of his own in a way that would not threaten the one from which he had been spawned. He had not intended to cause the present situation. There was an urge in him to create his own young, to expand the numbers of his kind. Wasn't he healthy, larger even than his own father, heavier than the huge male who stood guard over them and watched for danger? It was his *place* to create strong, new young, to move into places that had long been denied to his race. Man, he was convinced, was not the threat the histories dictated. He had never seen a man deliver death from a distance, without touching: it was only a story. He had chased that lone man and would have feasted upon him if the others had not appeared.

And it was those others who were now invading the land that had protected and sustained the Flock for so long. He recognized the taste of them that was delivered in molecules floating on the night air. His great nasal cavity drew in the motes, the particles, the gasses, and he held them there, tasting and scenting and *examining* each indicator. Yes, he had scented these same men before. They were coming, and he would use them.

With a song of triumph barely concealed, the Scarlet felt his great heart push blood through his lungs. His wide, taloned feet pounded the grasses as he headed toward the wetlands that lay ahead, and toward the men.

Grisham and the others had examined the ATV before pushing on. Their intelligence had indicated that it was likely that Holcomb would use such a vehicle to take him to his camps in the bush. Without radio contact to the fire team sweeping through the billionaire's compound, he couldn't be absolutely certain that the man was dead. However, the presence of the ATV was all he needed to prove to him that one of their targets was nearby. There were items, technical instruments still in the covered bed of the little vehicle that also told them that Holcomb had perhaps left it in something of a hurry, that he might even know that there was the possibility of pursuit. Grisham was willing to work on that assumption until they had located the crazy tree-hugger and eliminated him.

Running point, following the occasional sign of Holcomb's passing, Grisham set his face in a grim mask and thought. He would never be able to understand a man such as Vance Holcomb. The spoiled cad had inherited great wealth, had expanded his wealth by virtue of utilizing the vast system of free enterprise that had been protected and defended and *expanded* by soldiers such as Winston Grisham and so many like him. How could a man who enjoyed such wealth even *consider* standing against a system of economic freedom that had sustained and enriched him? The old Colonel had encountered such men in the past, could not fathom the way their stunted minds reasoned, and it would be good to kill one of them.

Pushing on, moving relentlessly through the brush, the soldier enjoyed the images of Holcomb's death that flashed periodically through his mind. He almost wished that it were daylight so that he could watch the fan of crimson that would open up behind the doomed man's body or skull when the steel jacketed slugs tore through him. It would indeed be a pleasure to finally make his acquaintance.

"Sir," came the voice. It was Gant, who was scouting the line to the north. Gant was the one who would come to the wetlands first, would encounter the edge of the stream that led toward the low country down at the bottom of the ridge.

"What is it?" Grisham replied, whispering.

"Kilgo Creek dead ahead. I'm less than forty yards from the bank."

"Anything?"

"Nothing but some nesting egrets. Saw a gator's eyes off in the water a ways. That's about it."

A dozen types of crickets and four species of cicadas joined in a chorus, whirring, chirping, screaming into the night. Grisham slowed and breathed in the warm, moist air, tasting the richness of the southern winds. It was all in there: the soil, the pines, the moss, the collected blood of billions of living *things* cruising the darkness. God, he loved it. This would truly be a fine night to kill a troublesome enemy and to make history by exterminating the last of a species. Some day, it would be spoken. Maybe he would live to hear it or see it appear in print. But he didn't really care. It wasn't important for the stupid cattle-public to know, but it was going to be a great thing. He breathed deeply and smiled.

"Joyner," he said. "Respond, Wallace."

"Joyner here," came the reply. "Moving out. I'm closing in on the big fields you said we'd encounter. Definite sign of the target's passing." In the night, Wallace Joyner was looking down at the broken twigs and the trampled grass that had marked Holcomb's hurried passing. The man was as good a tracker as there was, and he was going to quickly discover just where the millionaire had bedded down for the night. There was no doubt about that particular fact.

"Keep your eyes open. You think you're near him?"

"Yes. Couldn't have passed this way more than two hours ago. Unless he's trying to hack through here in the dark, we're going to happen on him pretty damned soon. Instructions?"

"Hold your position." Grisham hissed into his radio. "Fire team. Joyner's position. Assemble now. Double time. Go." As one, they moved, becoming a single unit again.

Vance Holcomb gasped and snapped instantly awake.

He blinked, shook his head. For a second or two he couldn't remember where he was or why he was there.

Oh, he thought. *I'm here.*

He hadn't meant to sleep. He turned his head toward the face of a backlit digital readout that never faded, never went down. It was the timer on one of the monitors. 10:15, it read. God, he had been out for over two hours. Not good.

What woke me? He peered around, not moving from where he lay. A half dozen microphones fed him the sounds of the darkness. Billions of excited insects screamed lust at one another. Some night birds sang a few tunes, telling also of love, perhaps, or threatening to kill a rival if space were invaded. Hard to say, actually. Who knew, but the birds?

Sighing, he supposed he must just have awakened from the stress of the day getting to his subconscious. The interior of the little room was completely quiet. He could even hear the light push of his own lungs, and little else. But *had* something else brought him to? He sat up.

There were always the perimeter cameras through which he could spy. He had set up a number of them throughout the area, high in the tallest longleaf pines where he had finally supposed none of the members of the Flock could reach. Holcomb had never actually *seen* any of the birds take out one of the electronic eyes, but he knew they had done it. The remains, typically just the fiber optic cable, had always been sliced cleanly through. Those jaws were frightening in their power and dangerous cutting ability. On one four-second tape of action he had witnessed a fully-grown whitetail buck having its head severed with three quick slashing bites of a single terror bird. In the lab, he and Kamaguchi had slowed the tape down more and more, turning split seconds into minutes. Those birds moved faster than any man could move, faster than any human eye could see. The deer had gone to the ground with its head detached from its body. Both prey and hunter had been moving at perhaps forty miles an hour during the attack.

Holcomb grunted and stood, stretching, arching his back and bringing his arms out fully. Still thinking of the birds, he looked around the little room, letting his eyes become accustomed to the bare light given off by the few electronic readouts that he allowed to burn constantly. In otherwise total darkness, such illumination was reassuring. The terror bird was fast, he knew. He wasn't certain just how fast, but Kamaguchi, from examining the film and calculating length of stride and frequency of movements had come to the conclusion that some of them could run at speeds approaching fifty miles per hour. They were magnificent creatures. He would have to ask Kamaguchi . . .

The wealthy man groaned and sat back on the foam mat. He had forgotten. Levin had said that Kinji was dead, shot. "Two men," he had babbled. Now Vance wondered if Levin and the rest of them were still alive. Probably not, he figured. It was time for him to get moving himself. Crawling across to one of the video monitors, his hand rested upon it while he tried to decide whether or not to risk turning it on. What he needed to do was get out of there before he was located. What he needed to do was hit the north side of the old military base, move through what remained of the area of what was basically a no man's land of possibly unexploded ordnance and lost mine fields. He knew a way through it, had carefully mapped a way past the dangerous place. On the far side was the Kissimmee River. A quick swim would take him to the farms and campgrounds over in that direction. He doubted anyone would expect him to head that way, through the heart of the wilderness that Edmunds Military Site had accidentally protected for almost a hundred years.

"Throw caution to the wind," he whispered, and threw the switch. The monitor hummed to life.

The dark figure he could see on the screen was the same one who was at that moment speaking into the small radio on his right shoulder.

"Target positive," Joyner relayed to the others.

As Holcomb watched, five killers came out of the night to converge on the artificial shelter in which he thought he'd been hiding.

★ ★ ★ ★ ★

Both Ron and Mary paused for breath, kneeling in the tangle of a patch of young pines. Even if the men who were shooting at them had some kind of night vision scopes, they would have found them hard to hit in the tangle of limbs and brush and moss that were now affording them some cover. They crouched, gasped for breath, and listened intently for the sound of pursuit. So far, there was nothing. The sun had set completely beneath the line of trees, and stars had appeared in the clear sky. All around them the wildlife had geared up for the night shift. The whir of insect life alone was enough to drown out most other sounds.

"Think they're still on our trail?" Ron asked. He had one hand resting on his bent right knee, the left one touching down on the damp soil to support his weight.

"I don't think they intend to let us get away, if that's what you mean. But I don't think any of them are close enough to shoot as us. Otherwise the bullets would be flying right now." Mary was on all fours, her head slumping toward the earth. She was just a big dark shadow to Ron, one that shifted among the others.

"Wonder where Crane went," Ron whispered.

"Hell if I know. Without any way to see in the dark, I don't think we're going to find him. If he was smart, he hauled ass out of here and is halfway to Salutations by now." Mary's breath was coming easier. She went to a kneeling position, her head turning this way and that, straining to hear if anyone was trying to sneak up on them.

"We'd better not stay here," Ron said. "They'll be coming this way soon, I'd think."

Mary stood up. "How many do you think there are?"

"I don't know." Ron stood, too, ready to be off. "You saw, what, three of them?"

"Yes. And Levin encountered two. So let's go on the supposition that at least five men are going to be tracking us. I saw the van they came in on, and I doubt it could carry more than six without being conspicuously overcrowded. Let's say five."

"Okay. Five."

"And all of them are probably heavily armed. I think they were carrying rifles. Can't say what kind. Some kind of assault rifles, though. That last volley sounded like it, to me."

"I'll take your word for it," Ron told her. He wasn't particularly fond of guns.

"So. Here we are. Two of us. One gun. Four shots."

"Only four?"

"Yeah. I checked. Four shots. That's all."

"Damn."

"You got it."

Ron shook his head, rubbed the sweaty locks of hair out of his eyes. "So. Best we could do, optimum, is take out four of the five."

"Fat chance," Mary admitted. "I ain't that good with a pistol, tell you the truth. How 'bout you?"

"Don't even mention it. I probably couldn't even figure out how to throw the safety off unless you showed me."

"Christ. What kind of wildlife officers is the government training, any—" Mary went silent, put her hand out to warn Ron. Both froze. Mary put her head in close to Ron's ear and whispered, so lowly that Ron could barely hear her. "Think I heard something. To our right, behind a little."

Ron turned in that direction to look, but could see nothing save black lying thickly upon black.

"I'm going to move," Mary said. "Same direction we were going. Haul ass. On three. One. Two. Three," she said.

They both exploded out of the patch of saplings, moving as quickly as they dared, doing their best to avoid the larger oaks into which they had wandered. The bigger trees were revealed to them as merely slightly lighter shadows that seemed to reach for the sky. It was a clumsy way to move, but they had no alternative. They were running as fast as they could under the circumstances when something dropped down from the limbs above, blocking their way.

"Jesus," Ron yelled, panic gripping his heart in a vise.

Mary was bringing the .357 up to fire a quick shot in the direction of the shadow. But before she could discharge the weapon, the figure spoke.

"Took you dumbasses long enough to catch up," Billy Crane said.

A volley of shots slammed into the Kevlar mesh fabric that formed Holcomb's low dome. Inside it, he heard the staccato firing and felt the impacts of the slugs, not unlike drops of a particularly nasty rain. Although the material had stopped the bullets cold, he still fell to the floor, hugging it and bringing himself as close to it as he possibly could. It had been his first thought, but he was still a little ashamed of his reaction. Holcomb could smell his own fear in the close air of the room, and it bothered him. He'd come face to face with wild tigers, had stood unprotected when a bull elephant had charged him, all without losing his cool. But this was different. These were men, with guns, and he knew that standing his ground wasn't going to bluff them off as it had the wild animals he had known.

There was another tightly spaced volley. They were acting in unison, he realized as the slugs once more pattered across the Kevlar walls, the metal seeking his flesh. Carefully, he reached up and flicked the switch to the monitors and they went dead, dropping the room back into almost complete darkness. He supposed it had been the light from those monitors that they had seen, probably leaking out through the air vents. Even clever air baffles couldn't shield out all light in the night. He'd made a mistake, most likely, even if they had already seen the building. Now they knew for certain that he was inside.

Still, the men were coming in from the west-southwest. That was also where all of the shots were coming from. And that was where the tunnel entrance he had used was located. They'd find it within minutes, if they had not already located it. But he had another way out, a secondary entrance.

One more volley of shots sounded, and this time there was the unmistakable sound of fabric giving way. The stuff was tough, but not invulnerable. A few more such rounds and the bullets would start to come in. He had to act fast.

Grabbing only a small fanny pack that was attached by Velcro holds to his main pack, he crouched and edged toward a low bench in front of him, a bank of receivers positioned on it. The smaller pack contained the only weapon he had ever carried into the site, a single shot dart pistol and a half dozen darts, each loaded with enough tranquilizer to stop a large bear. He doubted it would do him any good against the assassins, but it was all he had. Ducking, he crawled beneath the bench and pushed hard, releasing the very small doorway there. It led into a tunnel similar to the one through which he had entered. Creeping on elbows and knees, he went in.

Even as he squirmed down the tight space, there was a new explosion of gunfire and some equipment shattered as this time bullets entered the dome. He was pushing his luck. He had to get out of the tunnel soon, before they surrounded the dome and saw him emerge to the northeast.

He scrambled faster, pulling the little pack with him, abrading his knees and elbows.

The tunnel was semi-buried in the earth, and completely hidden by the sedges and brush that had grown to cover it. If any of the men who were firing at him stepped directly on it, they would realize what it was. But if he were quick, they wouldn't locate it until he was out and on his way. The length of the shaft was precisely sixty feet. The bulk of the dome, and the longleaf pine trees around the exit point would offer him at least some cover, he hoped. He was almost at the end, and was surprised when he passed through a series of spider webs. The little buggers had found a way through the far seal, which surprised him since he'd been assured nothing could. The spiders had obviously not read the manuals.

As he pushed on the flap of artificial material at the end of the tunnel, he listened as the rifles continued to open up on his former shelter, and there was the sound of metal being sheared by metal. His equipment was all ruined, now, he knew. It was a very good thing that he'd crawled out when he had. He pushed hard and felt the flap give.

With a soft *pop,* the Kevlar/nylon mesh let go and he felt night air on his face. Holcomb did not pause at all, for it no longer mattered if they were watching for him, or not. This was the only way for him. He burst out of the tunnel like some obscenely huge afterbirth, went to his feet and began to run. This was the open savanna, and while it was not without its pitfalls and its varied barriers, it was relatively open country and he would chance an all out dash for salvation. On the other side of the shelter the bullets flew again, bringing sound of material catching some of them and allowing others through. None seemed to be aimed directly at him. He flew.

★ ★ ★ ★ ★

Grisham sent Watkins in. He was the smallest of the team, and the quickest, also. The tunnel was probably the most dangerous way in, if Holcomb had survived the fusillade, but it was also the quickest entrance. A soldier had to take chances. The four remaining members stood outside, positioned around the dome in a semi-circle and waited for word from Watkins. It came quickly.

"He's not here," Grisham was told.

"Where did he go?"

"There's another tunnel entrance. North by northeast. Looks like he went that way. I'll follow it."

"We'll meet you," Grisham told him, motioning his men forward. They trotted around the clever dome the billionaire had erected out here. It was almost invisible, the way it seemed to grow up like a low blister from amidst the grass and pines. From a distance anyone might have missed it if they hadn't been looking for it. But Grisham *had* been looking for it. The need-to-know pages informing him of the possibility of some kind of permanent structure had been fed to them via the studio had come from that six-foot frail who'd sold Holcomb out. The old colonel shook his head in disgust. His people were made of better stuff than that.

In a few seconds all five team members were together, Watkins crawling up and out of the tunnel exit. As a unit, they brought their scopes up and aimed them out and away, dragging them across the landscape and looking for any sign of movement.

"There." It was Gant. He had a damned good eye, that boy.

"Where?" Grisham asked.

"One o'clock."

Grisham sighted down the barrel. Sure enough. There

was Holcomb, vanishing into a line of trees on the far side of the open savanna. The boy had been smart and had headed for the nearest trees, disdaining the open landscape that would have meant easier running but would have offered Grisham and his men a clear shot. "Good going," he told Gant.

Starting off at an easy trot, Grisham went after his prey. His men fell in behind and began to slowly spread out, forming a skirmish line. Holcomb wouldn't last long.

"Where are we going?" Ron asked. He was behind Billy Crane, keeping an eye on the man's back and trying to pace him so that he didn't run into the dark form leading them to what he hoped was safety.

"Shut up," Crane replied. "Save your breath."

Ron frowned. He wanted not to like the Seminole, but he knew the guy had saved them when he'd alerted them and shot out the window so that they could escape. If not for Kate's deception, they probably would all have escaped. For the first time he considered Levin's fate, recalled the man's face after the shot had plowed through his torso, killing him. Ron knew the man had realized what had happened to him, if not actually who had fired the shot. And maybe even that, considering he had given up the gun to her without a struggle. Riggs shook his head to clear it of the image, choked back a sob.

Mary was right behind him. He could hear her labored breathing and had been surprised at it, since he'd thought that Niccols was in far better physical condition than he was. It was Mary who was always out in the bush, tracking wild animals, hunting and hiking and fishing for her hobbies, and wrestling gators for a living. But so far Ron had been able to outrun her. It was surprising. He hoped it didn't mean that he'd end up having to leave Mary behind if they had to sprint for safety. Ron wondered if he could do such a thing. Flying bullets could make a coward as quickly as they could make a hero, he supposed. He didn't want to know.

No sooner had that thought passed through his mind than he realized that Mary's footsteps had grown a bit fainter, and realized that she was falling behind. Crane had apparently noticed it, too, and came to a halt, turning to look back.

"You're sick, aren't you?" Billy asked Mary.

"Yuh-yeah," Mary gasped.

"What? What's wrong with you? I didn't know you were *sick*," Ron said.

"Nothing serious. Bronchitis until a week ago. I thought I was over it, but I'm having a hard time ru-running." She was a halved shadow in the night, bent double with her hands on legs bent slightly at the knees. It was obvious to the other two that Mary was all but out of it.

"What are we going to do, now?" Ron was looking to Crane, his head a very black spot.

The black spot didn't move for a moment. "They're right behind us," it finally muttered. "Maybe a couple hundred yards. That's all."

"But what are we going to do?" Ron insisted.

"I think they've got night scopes," Crane said matter-of-factly. "We'll be sitting ducks when they catch up to us."

"What do you *suggest?*" Ron hissed. He was losing what remained of his cool.

"There's a shallow ravine about a hundred feet ahead of us. I was hoping we'd just go through it and head toward the river. But now I don't think we can make it. We'll have to try to hide there, ambush them from cover." And then

Crane turned and strode off at the same pace as before.

"Wait up," Ron started to say, but Mary suddenly straightened and trotted past him. After all, they only had a short way to go. "Damn." He followed them.

As Crane had said, they came to a low, narrow furrow in the otherwise flat landscape. Pines and pin oaks grew out of it, leaning at crazy angles and making a strange maze-like apparition in the night. At a point where the wall of the ravine fell sharply off, Crane eased into it and then lay against the slope, snaking down until his head was just beneath the lip.

"Do the same," he said to Mary. "You just squat down behind us," he told the unarmed Riggs.

The three prepared themselves. "When I hear them coming, I'll hiss," Crane said. "Don't shoot until I do. The chances of you hitting anyone from more than a few feet away with that .357 are slim so don't bother until you hear someone coming right up. My twelve gauge will have to do until then."

And with that the Seminole clammed up. Mosquitoes and gnats soon found where they were crouching and took them to task. Hearing only the continuous hungry whine of bloodsuckers, they prepared themselves for the approach of human hunters.

CHAPTER
THIRTY-EIGHT

Kate woke up.

She was lying in the fescue where Mary Niccols had slugged her, knocking her unconscious. Reaching back, she put her hand over the enormous lump on the back of her head. Running her fingers over it, a disturbing rise of livid flesh that connected the base of her skull to her slim neck. She shuddered, feeling nausea rising. Mary had not pulled the punch, at all. In fact, she thought that she was probably lucky to be alive. The bitch had really been afraid she was going to see her male companion get blown away. *Ha*. Kate had known from the moment she saw Mary looking at Ron that the woman was madly in love with the idiot. She didn't know who was dumber: the doe-eyed female or the stupid male who didn't want to return the affection. She didn't know if it was that saccharine image or her injury that was making her sick.

Knowing that it was likely not wise to stand, she just lay there, and in a little while turned her head. The view she'd had was of the brick wall to her right, dim light spilling out of the compound to illuminate the lawn. As soon as she turned her face, she wished she hadn't. Adam's body was on the ground, less than a dozen feet from where she was. His face was even turned toward hers, his eyes wide in death. A great number of flies had already found him, and they were crawling all over his lips, into his nostrils, over the opaque glaze of his dead eyes.

She sobbed.

It wasn't supposed to have gone that way. By the time Grisham's men had arrived, she was to have been ready to leave. All she was originally to have done was let them in and thereafter retreat to let them do the wetwork. Holcomb was to have been taken out, along with the others, and she was going to just disappear with her reward: a breathtaking sum of cash assets that were already sitting in various accounts under her name in a number of banks.

But she had not reckoned with Adam and Kinji's desperation. She had also not reckoned with that monkey wrench situation concerning Ron and his resourceful sidekick, Mary. Squinting both in pain and to hide the view of Adam's dead face, Kate put her hands out and braced herself to rise. Going slowly to her knees she got her legs under her. And she promptly vomited.

In a while, she felt well enough to stand. She went over to the wall, to the shattered window, using the brick structure to support herself. It was murder, now. This hadn't been what she'd wanted. The betrayal hadn't bothered her that much. The money had just been far too much to resist, and the idea of living out her life in the kind of luxury she'd only dreamed about had been far too tempting. Everyone had a price. Actually, they had overbid, she mused. A low chuckle gargled up from her lungs.

Looking around, she was wondering where the gunmen had gone. In fact, Kate had never really seen them, and had no idea what they looked like. That was good. She didn't want to know. And she certainly didn't want to encounter them at this point. For all she knew, they might now be after her head, too. But she doubted it. She'd awakened, after all. If they had wanted her dead, then they would have done her in after Mary had all but crushed her skull.

She was fairly certain she was suffering from at least a mild concussion. The dizziness was there, and the nausea. Before she left Florida, she would need to see a doctor. It would be a crime to die before she could begin to enjoy her newly earned wealth.

She needed to get to the garage, find one of the trucks and drive out of there. The quickest way was to climb back through the window and then merely walk through the building. That would take more than she thought she might have left in her. She might pass out, or fall and injure herself. The other option was to walk around the compound to the front and then back into the entrance there. The door was probably still unlocked and she could get into the garage that way. But it was a long walk in the dark. She might faint again; it wasn't out of the question as fuzzy as she was feeling. Her head throbbed and she found it slightly difficult to focus her eyes now and again. Blinking, she considered her options.

"Hell with it," she muttered, and got a grip on the windowsill, being careful not to cut herself and leave any more DNA evidence around than she had in the puddle of vomit. The bugs would probably make off with the mess she had made before any forensic work could be conducted. At this point, she just wanted to vanish. Gripping the window frame, feeling the cool metal on the palm of her hand, she braced and went over. Dizziness gripped her as she vaulted the barrier, her stomach tightened into a huge knot of pain. She blacked out again.

She woke up on the floor, lying in a crystalline pile of shattered glass. Gingerly, she got to her feet, looking around to see if she were cut or leaving drops of evidence of her presence everywhere. She was a murderer, and needed to keep that in mind. To her surprise, she was uncut. *Thank goodness for small gifts.* Bracing herself against the wall, leaning on it as she went, she started off toward the front of the building. All she wanted at this point was a truck to get out of there.

The building was sighing around her, blowing cool air through the long hallways. She passed empty rooms and vacant labs as she went, thinking of Vance Holcomb's plans for the place. This was to have been the research center for the wilderness that he was going to administer in partnership with the University of Florida (*at Gainesville,* Levin would have said) and the Department of the Interior. Kate had seen his proposals, had seen all of his plans. She'd seen everything, had even shared his bed a time or two before he had told her that it just wasn't for him. But that rejection wasn't the reason she had betrayed him. It was just that she hadn't been able to refuse all of that money. No one could have resisted that offer, she felt.

When Kate had walked all the way to Adam's lab, where he dissected his dead turkey vultures and examined the samples of plant, insect, and animal life the others brought to him, she went in. She was feeling very faint again and knew that he kept all manner of beverages and bottled water in the refrigerator in there. Pushing the door open she went in and did not even turn on the light. The icebox was a blocky shadow that was easy to pick out in the dim light that spilled in through the door, which she had left open. Staggering a bit, she made her way across the room and opened the refrigerator.

Reaching for a bottle of spring water, she unscrewed the top and turned it up, taking a long draw. In a moment, she had all but drained the twenty-four ounces. Turning, the bottle still in her hand, the yellow light spilling from the refrigerator revealed the man standing just on the far side of one of Adam's lab tables.

"Where did you think you were going?" he said.

Kate did not have time to respond before the rifle roared and her left side exploded in pain. For her, the lights went out again.

One more job done, the gunman sat tight and waited for his friends to return from finishing the others.

CHAPTER
THIRTY-NINE

Grisham and his fire team were in hot pursuit of Holcomb. Time and again they would catch sight of him through the nightscopes, occasionally getting off a shot or two before he would vanish behind cover or duck out of sight. Despite the fact that he was alone and was being pursued by five armed men, the colonel did have to admit that their prey had a slight advantage on a couple of points. Most in his favor was that the billionaire was traveling light; he didn't seem to be carrying anything at all. Not even a pistol from the view Grisham had caught of him. That meant that he wasn't going to be shooting back at them, but it also meant that he could move more freely and perhaps even a touch faster than the colonel and his crack troops.

Also, despite their crash course in studying the quadrangle maps of the area, it was obvious that Holcomb knew the land far better than they did. He kept following small, shallow ravines at the oddest moments; moments during which sure shots would suddenly vanish as he descended into low places, leaving them with nothing to shoot. At such times they would catch a glimpse now and again of the top of his head, perhaps, or a flailing arm or leg as Holcomb pushed on.

Eventually, Grisham realized, Holcomb would tire and they would catch up to him. In fact, they didn't even have to get terribly close. All they needed was a couple hundred yards, a clear shot. And then the runner would be history.

Even so, Grisham had been growing impatient for the kill, and so he had sent the small, quick Jim Gant ahead. He had cut the man loose, so to speak. "Go get him, Jim. Take him out, if you can get a clear shot." Gant had smiled, his teeth white in the shadows. *"Git,"* the colonel had said, slapping the little man on the back. The young soldier had quickly passed the rest of the team, left them far behind, and he was closing the gap between himself and Holcomb. Grisham would be very happy to hear the shot ring out. Just one, if he knew his men well.

In the meantime, he spread out the skirmish line, just in case Holcomb decided to hunker down in an unseen spot, or tried to double back and pass them going north as he went south. These were things that a good woodsman could accomplish if he were very careful. But Grisham knew that the chances of that kind of success with this group of men were highly unlikely.

With Gant moving on ahead and leaving them behind, the remaining four members of the team formed a line that skewed at a thirty degree angle from south to north, Gant being an oblique point moving forward from them. In actual fact, Holcomb stood no chance at all.

At fifty-four years of age, Vance Holcomb was in extremely good condition. He exercised daily, a strict regimen of running and biking and stretching. In point of fact, he was in better shape than most men who were half his age. But he was fifty-four years old. And he was being pursued by men who were all in at least as good condition as he was. His great mistake had been in remaining in his hidden dome, thinking he could rest for a while before moving on.

His idea of making it to the Kissimmee and swimming across it to the houses and farms on the other side now seemed to be an impossible goal.

The assassins were getting close. A couple of the shots they had taken at him had come uncomfortably close. He realized that it was just a matter of time before they got in near enough to get a clear shot and take him out. At least, he hoped, his death would be quick and painless when (and if) it came. The idea of standing and allowing them a clean shot if things began to look hopeless was a gruesome possibility that kept occurring to him despite his revulsion of it. At least there would be no pain if he did that.

To Hell with that, he told himself. He could outrun these buggers. All he had to do was keep going and not let them slow him down or trip him up. He knew that his biggest advantage was his knowledge of the land. No one knew these forests, swamps, and grasslands better than Vance Holcomb knew them. Each and every hammock, each stream and lowland, each stand of trees were places he had been to and explored on a number of occasions. Of the four hundred plus square miles of wilderness that made up old Edmunds, this part of it was most familiar to him. This was where he had spent the lion's share of his time and where he had made the most contact with the huge birds that had brought him here.

Pausing at a stand of tupelo gums, Holcomb hugged the trunk of a particularly large tree and looked back. He controlled his breathing and was as quiet as possible. He listened.

Not far away, perhaps half a mile back, he could hear someone approaching. The runner was good, efficient, and relatively quiet. But even over the chirp and screams of the forest insects Holcomb could make out the occasional snap of dry twigs and the very faint thumping of booted feet. And he immediately knew that they had sent one of their numbers ahead, to try to catch him and bring him down. This would be a young man, Vance realized; someone who could outrun him and get close enough to get a clear shot.

They were going to a lot of trouble to kill him, Holcomb realized. This was no ordinary group of killers. These were men well trained in all aspects of soldiering. And he knew exactly who was after him. Well, he was surprised the studio had been able to negotiate a deal with Grisham, but not terribly so. He wondered what they had offered the crazy retired officer. It didn't particularly matter, he supposed, since whatever it was, its ultimate result would be his elimination.

Taking a few deep breaths, filling his lungs, Vance turned north again and pushed on with renewed energy. He knew that he would have to move faster and run harder just to keep the distance he had made between himself and his pursuers. The one now on his tail would more than likely catch up to him if he slowed even a step or two.

Not far ahead, there was a tributary of the wetland that led down to Lake Arbuckle. His plan had been to skirt the south side of that low place and make his way toward the Kissimmee. But now he realized that if he did that, he would have to push westward in a straight line, and that the others would come at him on an angle and overtake him before he could make the river.

However, he remembered something.

This area of the base had been subject to the dropping of explosive ordnance for a twenty-year stretch from 1965 through 1985. He also knew that there was a lot of unexploded material in the soft earth. In recent months he had scouted it out and had found a way through it, a way that he knew would be safe if he could negotiate it in the starlight. If the assassins moved behind him in a wide skirmish line (as he knew they must), then they would be treading over earth that more than likely hid some particularly nasty surprises. It was the only viable plan he currently had, and not likely to succeed. Still, he had no other choice.

A further problem for him was that he would have to cross another of the grassy savannas just before he found the bombing site. That would leave him an open, easy target for a distance of perhaps two hundred yards or so. But he had no choice, as he had already realized. He would have to do it.

Well, he hoped the man at his back was a crack shot, if it came down to that.

Jim Gant was not far behind his quarry. From time to time he caught a glimpse of Holcomb through the trees. But, as before, the man kept finding cover before he could aim and fire, or would literally just vanish right at the last moment, finding a low place or passing over a ridge to disappear beyond it. He was using his knowledge of the area to his fullest advantage, and Gant had to admire that. Still, despite that admiration, he was going to put a bullet through the rich man at the very earliest opportunity. He wanted the kill and did not want Watkins, Joyner, or Redmond to have the honor.

To tell the truth, he was still pissed off at having been the one chosen to crawl through that fabric dome they had found. Oh, he hadn't minded doing it for Colonel Grisham: it was just that Holcomb's escape at that point had angered him and he did not appreciate his need to put himself in harm's way to find the target. Holcomb would pay with a quick shot to the head if he found he could comfortably take aim. It was riskier than a heart shot, but infinitely more satisfying, he thought.

Gant had closed the distance between them to roughly the length of two football fields. In fact, he could even feel and hear the footfalls of Holcomb as the man raced ahead. For a mature individual, the rich man could really move. But Jim could run the mile in five minutes and he doubted that his target could stay ahead of him for very much longer. Very soon, he figured, he would find himself able to take him down. Grisham would be very happy, and that would be points for him in the organization. This was a very big deal for the Colonel.

Racing along, Gant was aware that the ground was beginning to give beneath his boots. The earth wasn't actually *muddy*, but there was a slight depression each time his feet met the forest floor. *So.* He knew that they were close to the swamp that bordered the river. He doubted Holcomb would go that way, realized immediately that he was going to turn east and head directly north. Gant sped up and also moved east, away from the wetland.

He could very nearly hear each and every footfall that Holcomb made as he ran. He doubted there was a hundred yards between them, now and managed to pick up the pace even further. He knew that he would catch up soon. In a matter of seconds he would stop and raise his rifle and take aim. He only had to pass through a tight growth of short pines that lay ahead of him. Running at almost full speed, he burst through the needled branches.

And he saw immediately that he had come upon another of the weird grasslands that made up vast areas of the bush in this place. It was alien in appearance to Gant, and he didn't quite like looking at it. But currently he was very happy to encounter such terrain. For right in the midst of it, running along like the big, fat target that he now resembled, was Vance Holcomb. The man was right out in the middle of the big field, tall pines to his right and left, but nothing at all but a few wispy strands of grass between him and Gant.

The hunter stopped, raised his rifle and peered through the night scope. There he was. Vance Holcomb's head was like a water balloon waiting to be pierced. Gant pulled the stock tight to his shoulder, breathed easily out, put the crosshairs on Holcomb's skull, and began to slowly *squeeze* the trigger.

But he didn't do it.

Because of the gigantic creature that had suddenly appeared from the forest in front of Holcomb.

The thing was huge. Gant even lost sight of Holcomb, lost all *thought* of him. It was as if Vance Holcomb no longer even existed for Gant. The picture he had been shown of the thing was nothing compared to the reality of seeing it. It was ten feet tall, at least, looming over the grasses, and all but flying along with a deceptively easy stride. *This isn't any bird,* he thought. No bird was that big. None. No bird had *arms* instead of wings. No bird had a head so large, a beak so hooked, legs so huge. Its tail was straightened out behind it, resembling a huge pointed barb that extended for perhaps eight to ten feet. And as Gant was standing there, his jaw actually gaping at the sight of the animal, he realized that it was making a direct approach on Holcomb.

Holcomb, too, had seen what was happening. That the beast was coming at him. To the millionaire, it must have seemed as if a chunk of the forest had just detached itself and come flying at him along the ground. Gant continued to watch as the creature closed the distance between itself and Holcomb in a couple of seconds.

Its gigantic right foot came up, and it seemed as if the thing *hopped,* just a bit, and then that talon came down with great force on Holcomb's chest. Gant saw the one he had been chasing go down as if he were a rabbit being squashed by a man. Holcomb disappeared beneath the monster as it paused for a second to make sure that the little thing had been flattened beneath its foot. And then it continued on, toward Gant.

The soldier then caught his breath. He could see that the animal was coming fast, very fast. He couldn't have known it, but it was doing better than fifty miles per hour and would have been merely a great blur to him if it had been moving in any direction other than directly toward him. Realizing that it had targeted him and that it would be on him very quickly, he found his nerve. Straightening his posture, he pulled the rifle tight once again, drew in a breath and slowly let it out. The thing was a huge target, filling his scope. It would at least be easy to hit and was still far enough away to get off three shots, minimum, before it was on him. He once more began to squeeze the trigger.

There was a strange noise in the air. Like the whir of insect wings, but very, very loud. He blinked.

The giant bird was gone. Gone.

The Scarlet had been losing ground to the Flock. They were slowly closing the gap and he had detected the ends of the attack line beginning to close in on him. He could hear the songs coming loud and with great power from the adults pursuing him. But they were so intent on finding and catching him that they had not detected the humans who were moving slowly their way. Although the Scarlet could scarcely believe it, the probability that they would not spot the humans until they were upon them was growing greater as they went.

Most of the chase had been taking place in the tall hardwood forest in which they had been living for some days. The hunting was not so easy in such a place, but it was not a difficult task to hide there, and it was something that the Flock did more and more often in the time since Man had begun building their huge nests beside the Flock's home. The Scarlet had run swiftly, dodging between the tall trunks and bounding over fallen logs, over brushy barriers that would have impeded a lesser creature. But still he was losing the chase. He could hear the calls of his former mates: *food,* they called him. *Kill,* they said. There was nothing to do but run.

Suddenly, the Scarlet had burst free of the trees. He was out on the open savanna and saw his chance to put some distance between himself and the Flock. And, better than that, he saw the first of the men as he sped across the grasses, leaving great, dark furrows in the earth wherever his talons met the ground and pushed his bulk along at breakneck speed.

Out on the savanna he saw the man. He immediately recognized the scent as belonging to *The Man Who Watches.* The human was small and slow, running in their plodding manner. The Scarlet realized that the man was also being pursued by his own kind. It was a situation not unlike that of the Scarlet. A trill of humor came up out of the great bird's beak as he turned directly toward the man, bearing down on him.

Men, the Scarlet decided, were nearly blind in the night. Their eyes must not be suited for seeing the starlight world in the stark contrasts that made everything obvious to those of the Flock. He looked at the small man as he lowered his head for speed, tucking his short, powerful arms in tight to his chest. This man would serve as something to help him. This man would soon be a heavy portion of meat sprawled on the grasses and waiting for the Flock to find it. At worst, it would delay their progress toward him as he continued on, into the midst of the other men who were chasing *The Man Who Watches*.

Too late the man realized what was coming toward him from the edge of the forest. At the last moment he tried to duck under the heavy slashing claws that the Scarlet was bringing down on him. There was nearly half a ton of weight behind those talons as they connected with the human and bore him down onto the ground. The smell of blood welled up, finding its way into the Scarlet's vast nasal cavities and tempting him with the thought of meat. But he didn't have time. Better that the downed human becomes a marker that would delay the others and allow *him* to press on.

The Scarlet left the prone figure behind him and took aim at the other human who had been chasing the first. He looked. The human was standing fast, and there was no fear coming from him. It had something in its long arms, was holding something not unlike a branch, pointing it at the Scarlet. The histories of the elders came to him. Histories of the first humans who had come down from the cold north and who had driven the old Flocks before them, killing them from a distance. Those histories had told of claws thrown from a long way, or teeth delivered from farther than any creature could possibly reach. The Scarlet saw that this human felt no fear, that it stood its ground and was preparing to *do something*. Sensing this, the Scarlet did the first thing that came to mind. He decided to hide in plain sight.

Hundreds of tiny muscles throughout his legs and torso suddenly shifted. His mottled, striped feathering *moved* on their hard shafts, edged in dozens of different angles, *blending* with the grassland surroundings. The Scarlet suddenly became virtually invisible. He sped on, toward the human, from which it could now detect emotions equivalent to confusion.

And just a spark, perhaps, of fear.

Gant spoke into his radio. He had disdained it until then, not wishing to alert Holcomb. But now he felt the need to contact the others, to let them know what was happening. He began to speak quickly.

"Gant here. One of those . . . *birds*. It got Holcomb."

The fuzzy rasp of Grisham's hard voice replied. "Make sure he's dead. Wait there for us."

"I lost the bird, though. It. It's really big, Colonel. Bigger than we thought."

"Where is it?" Grisham asked.

Gant wished the others were already there. He peered this way and that down the barrel of his rifle, looking through the scope at the greenish landscape, looking for movement, for the bird. "I don't *see* it," he yelled.

"Where did it go, Gant?"

Gant was aiming the barrel of his rifle left and then right, scanning the horizon for something, movement of any kind. He was completely surprised to feel his gun torn from his grasp, to see it go cartwheeling away from him as something big and very heavy smashed into him. It was only at the last that he realized his right arm was also spinning through the air, trailing a stream of blood after it.

On their way toward their fellow soldier, the others listened to the voice coming to them over the small radios.

"Jesus," Gant's voice was shrill. "Jesus Christ, it *killed me*."

And then the forest was silent again. But for the mad screaming of the insects.

CHAPTER
FORTY

"Hold our position *he*re," Grisham commanded. He could sense that his team did not like his decision. But they were good soldiers and would do what he told them to.

Redmond cleared his throat.

"Forget it," Grisham said. "We hold right here and wait."

The night was silent except for the constant background screech of the bugs. The crickets and cicadas nearby continued to chirp, which let them know that nothing was stalking them or creeping in on where they were hunkered down. They had formed a defensive circle, each man crouching low to the ground, allowing the sedges to offer cover and keep them from being good targets. Their scopes were up; each of them scanning his portion of the horizon for anything that might indicate an attack of any kind.

"You think he might be okay out there?" Redmond finally asked.

Damn, Grisham hated that kind of comment. It meant that Redmond was *weak*, that he was distracted. A distracted man was a very poor link in an otherwise sound chain. His first reaction was to turn and slap the utter pity out of him, but that could result in further disruptions. He bit down on his anger.

"We'll find out how Gant is just as soon as we ascertain

that there's not a direct danger to ourselves."

"What about the initial target? What if he's getting away?" It was Watkins speaking now.

The colonel did not appreciate all of this speculation. He was beginning to realize he'd made a poor choice. Better he had brought along some purer soldier types and not these game hunters. Well. Live and learn. "Gant said that Holcomb was down. Dead, probably. I trust Gant's judgment. We'll check it out as soon as I decide we can move in."

Something rustled in the grasses to the north. That was the direction where Gant had been. Grisham left his post, where he had been watching the west, and he sighted down the barrel, seeing the world in yellow-green contrasts. There was nothing. Just sedges shifting in the slight wind blowing from their backs. "See anything, boys?" he asked.

"Nothing," both Watkins and Redmond told him.

"Joyner? You see something?"

"I . . ." The man hesitated, lowered his head, blinked, then looked back into his scope. "I *thought* I saw something."

"What? What was it?" Grisham asked impatiently.

"I don't know. Like the grass went all . . . I don't know, kind of *misty* for a second. But not now. Must have been something in my eyes." He jammed the stock of his rifle tight to his shoulder and continued to scan the field.

There was a rustling off to the north again.

"Damn," Joyner said. "Thought I saw that again. That *blurry* patch. Right in front of us."

"Where?" But before Joyner could answer Grisham, they heard a voice.

From out of the grasses, from where the slight rustling had come, there was that shrill screech they'd heard moments before.

"Jesus," it said. "Oh, Jesus. It."

"Gant," Watkins yelled. "It's Jim. He's trying to crawl this way." They could see the grass weaving as the man attempted to come to them.

"Je. Zuz." Silence. Rustle. "Oh." Silence. Crackle of dry grass. "Oh. Jesus. It. *Killed*."

Watkins suddenly stood and stepped toward his wounded comrade who he could not yet see, but who was crawling closer and closer. "Wait there, Jim. I'll be right with you." Without waiting for Grisham to give the order, he strode toward the wounded soldier.

"*Oh. Oh, Jesus. Oh, JesusohJesusohJesusJesusJesus,*" said the Scarlet rogue, rearing to full height and cocking his gigantic talons for a killing slash. "*It killed me,*" the bird mimicked perfectly. "*It killed me.*" His claws came down, half a ton of impossibly muscled fiber powering the horny talons which went ripping through Watkins's chest, parting skin and tearing through bone and cartilage. Watkins was pinned to the earth, still standing, his thighbones jammed down into his shin bones and his entrails spilling out in a great warm gushing of blood and fluids. He wasn't dead in the split seconds as all of this took place, but when the Scarlet leaned in with a motion too quick to see, Watkins's head was snipped neatly off at the neck and he ceased to experience anything.

"Oh, Jesus," said the Scarlet rogue as he dashed in among the three men and kicked out at them before any could so much as move. Each went sailing through the air; rib cages protecting their guts, but small bones cracked and broken, muscles severely bruised. Guns went sailing away, scopes and all, leaving the three in the dark, which would have filled them with fear. But all of them fell to earth unconscious, a blackness filling their minds as they thudded to the ground fifteen, twenty feet from where they had stood.

"Jesus," said the Scarlet as he sprinted away, leaving these for the Flock, which was gaining fast. He could hear them coming out of the forest and on to the savanna. All of this blood would be too much for them to resist, he suspected.

In a second, he was gone.

CHAPTER
FORTY-ONE

Someone was coming. None of them said a thing. All three just lay where they were in the shallow gully and allowed themselves to be eaten by a few hundred gnats and mosquitoes. The urge to slap and to scratch was maddening, but to so much as twitch could mean detection, and that would also mean their deaths. So they just lay still and waited.

Ron could not tell how many were moving through the woods after them. One person, he figured, maybe two. No more than two, certainly.

Mary clutched the earth and put her ear to it. There were at least three men moving toward them. Possibly, there was a fourth.

Billy Crane gripped his twelve gauge but did not move. He lay next to it, the barrel extended out from him; he was ready to aim and fire it as soon as anyone came within range. There were only four men coming for them. And he realized that there should have been five. No fire team was complete without a fifth member. The other one must have stayed behind for some reason. To clear the buildings of evidence, he supposed. These guys were damned good, and he knew that they stood as much chance of surviving as three blind mice against a pack of wolves. But they would take a few with them. There was that, at least.

The way the other men were moving, it was obvious

both to Niccols and to Crane that they possessed some kind of night vision capabilities. If they were wearing goggles, then they would be moving freely but they wouldn't be able to aim and fire as well. If they were sighting with scopes and moving that way, then their fire would be more accurate, but their mobility would not be quite as fine. Either way, the three were in a lot of trouble. With nothing to guide them but their own two eyes and the slight sounds of subtle pursuit, they would have to guess where to shoot. In the case of Crane's shotgun, that wasn't too bad. He could get a shot off in the general vicinity of a target and still hit it. But the pistol was going to be useless unless Mary got very lucky and hit something while basically aiming blind.

Less than thirty feet away someone stepped on a dry twig. It cracked, going off like a rifle shot in the night. Ron bit his lip and did not move, despite rabbit fear welling up in him. Mary wanted to shift, to get into a better position to fire, but resisted the urge.

Billy Crane rose up and aimed, firing and immediately falling back down into the gully. A rifle shot had come simultaneously with the roar of the shotgun, but the scattergun's blast had all but drowned it out. Mary had detected it, but Ron had not. And only Billy realized why he had suddenly lost all strength in his legs and had toppled backward, landing in a loose heap near the bottom of the small ravine, his back lying painfully against a devil's walking stick, the thorns jutting into his flesh. Still, it was a small pain compared to the lethal wound the steel-jacketed slug had drilled through his chest. The man Crane had shot full of buckshot was screaming, and the yells hid Billy's own muffled groans.

Ron scrambled over to where the Seminole was lying. He was surprised to be crawling through a great, warm puddle to get to him. The metallic smell of blood was everywhere. The gnats were swarming crazily.

"T-take the shotgun." Crane made an effort to thrust a canvas bag at Ron. It was wet with his blood, but heavy with shells. "Take these, too."

Without saying anything, Ron grabbed the shotgun and hung the canvas bag around his neck. Reaching out to find Crane's head, to prop it up, he heard a long, wet breath throttling out of the Indian's lungs. Death rattle. He'd heard it a few times when he had worked in a hostel as a college student. Scrambling away from Crane's body, he said nothing and began to move away from the spot, throwing himself into the tightly packed undergrowth at the bottom of the gully. He was afraid to call out to Mary, and the man Billy had shot was now screaming.

Someone was coming up to the lip of the shallow ravine. Mary took a chance and rolled onto her back, knowing that the screaming man would hide the small sound she'd made rolling over. She just lay there, the .357 held tightly to her chest. Mary looked skyward, at the pattern of stars overhead: too many stars to count, a patchwork of brilliant little green lights against a tar-black heaven. Suddenly a shape like that of a human torso blotted out some of those stars. Mary extended her arms and fired, hearing the surprised exclamation of the man who had stepped up to take a chance. "Oh, damn," the man had said before the slug took off the top of his skull, sending a fountain of brain matter toward those numberless stars. They'd never make it, though.

Crappy last words, Mary thought. She followed in Ron's kneeprints. The wounded man continued to scream, and Mary wondered where Billy had nailed him.

Mary could hear Ron scrambling ahead of her. Thorns and sharp twigs ripped at her arms and scratched her face in dozens of places. But she pushed on, knowing that if she slowed down long enough to give anyone a good target then she was dead for sure. There was the crack of a rifle shot and the bullet whizzed through the brush, slammed into a tree trunk six feet to her right. That told her that they couldn't see her, at least. She was catching up to Ron and could see what looked like the soles of her friend's boots pistoning as the man crawled as fast as most people chose to run on a brisk morning jog. She would have laughed if her life hadn't been in such danger.

Suddenly they were free of the brambles and undergrowth. She watched Ron stand and begin to run. *Hell with it.* She did the same. They were at the far end of the gully and it played out on a low ridge of oaks that were widely spaced, forming a canopy of limbs overhead that blocked out the sun in the day and hid the stars at night. It was very damned dark. There was another shot, and a tree less than ten feet away took a bullet meant for them; brave soul. The wounded man's screams were growing fainter, but because of distance or because he was running out of life, neither Ron nor Mary could tell.

Mary was looking at the blotch of shadow that was moving in front of her, the one she took to be Ron. She heard Riggs' *oof* of surprise, wondered what was going on, and soon discovered as the ground suddenly opened up beneath their feet. They fell. And fell. Bounced once against a fortunately soft bank of earth, and then found themselves treading water at the bottom of a very deep sinkhole.

Ron choked, spat water. "What the *heck*."

"Sinkhole. You know what they are."

"Jesus. Now we're screwed."

"Maybe not. You got the shotgun?"

"Yeah," Ron told her as his boots finally found solid

purchase and he pulled himself to the almost perpendicular bank. A big chunk of limestone jutted out at them, and they both forced their bodies against it. Swimming while clenching guns had proven almost impossible.

Mary reached out and took the shotgun. "Take this," she said, handing the pistol to Ron. "He gave you shells, right?"

Ron reached into the canvas bag, turning back the flap, and shoved a couple of shells her way. "Yeah. Poor Billy. He nailed that one bastard, though."

"Look," Mary whispered. "In a second or two they're going to be looking down at us. Do what I did earlier when I shot one of them."

"You *got* one of them?"

"Yeah. Just look toward the stars. As soon as you see something get in the way of some stars, shoot at it. I got lucky, close range and all. But this shotgun will do the job. I think there might only be one of them left, anyway."

"You think the guns will still fire? Wet?"

"Only way to find out is to try them," she replied. "You look south, I'll look north. Just watch for *anything* that blocks the stars."

Clutching the rough, pocked surface of the rib of Florida limestone jutting out of the sinkhole, they scanned the edge of the collapsed cavern above them, seeing the silhouette of trees and earth below the bowl of brilliant stars twinkling in the sky. They waited.

In a while, they began to hear something. At first, both thought that it was just their imaginations. It seemed to be coming from a distance, as if something were *moving* very quickly through the forest. Neither said a thing to the other. They were afraid to move, almost to breathe for fear of giving away their position to some sniper waiting just beyond the lip of the sinkhole.

But after a few minutes the sound began to increase. They could definitely hear something, or some*things* moving through the forest, sliding amidst the trees and brush. Whatever it was it was coming in their direction, as if led there somehow. And finally they could actually feel the approach of whatever it was in the earth, which they clutched in their hands and on which they lay. And it was then that they realized it wasn't a single thing coming their way, but perhaps a herd of . . .

"Horses," Mary whispered. The sky was growing lighter and they could see the sun beginning to tint the dome of black above them.

"I don't think so," Ron said. "I think it might be something else."

"What?" Mary asked.

From the forest to the south they heard a pair of voices. First one and then the other, and they realized that the men stalking them had just been waiting for light so that they could finish them off. But something else had their attention just now.

"Shoot it," one voice yelled.

"I *can't*. It's moving too fast!"

"Look out! Look out! There are more of them! Look ou—"

"Oh, God."

Someone screamed. There was a strange but quick and disturbingly liquid sound from above. Ron was staring up, and he suddenly looked to where Mary was pointing her outstretched finger. For a moment, for just a second, the enormous and blood spattered head of a gigantic predatory ground bird appeared at the edge of the sinkhole. It gazed down at them with a wide, unblinking eye, and for a frozen instant they both thought that it was considering coming down after them. But as quickly as it appeared, it was gone, and soon after the forest was alive as the great flock of the creatures was stomping through the oaks.

Within a few minutes the forest was silent again.

The sun continued to light the sky. Slowly, the two found that they could tear their gaze from the top of the sinkhole. They looked at one another.

"What the heck was *that* all about?" Mary asked.

"I guess we're going to have to wait until we climb out of here to find out." And in a while they began to pick their way up the slope, clinging to roots and bits of limestone jutting from the black, sandy earth.

CHAPTER
FORTY-TWO

The first thing that surprised Vance Holcomb was that he was still around to *be* surprised. He sat up and the contusions on his chest sent an explosion of pain through his torso. "Cripes, that hurts," he said to no one in particular. He peeled away what remained of his shirt, torn into ribbons by the claws of *Titanis walleri*. He could scarcely believe he had survived the experience. Carefully, he undid the Velcroed straps of the flak jacket he'd been wearing. He'd put it on to protect himself from bullets, never thinking he'd be kicked in the guts by a gigantic bird. Looking down, he saw that his chest was a mass of bruised flesh. It was a miracle he had suffered no internal injuries, but he felt certain that he had not.

He wondered why the Scarlet rogue had not killed him. Vance had realized when the terror bird appeared out of the forest that it was the rogue, for none of the others was so large. The first light of dawn was pinking the sky, and he could see the forest as a line of darkness about a hundred yards to the north. That was where the Scarlet had appeared. He turned around and looked back the way he had come. What had happened, he wondered? Why hadn't the assassins come in and finished him off? The rogue must have attacked them. But had it been able to chase off a party of armed men? Holcomb considered that, and once again was led to conclude that these birds were possessed of an intelligence that might match that of humans.

With a few tentative steps, he retraced the way he had run. In point of fact, he was happy he had not had to negotiate the field of possibly unexploded ordnance that he knew lay just beyond the point where he'd been stopped. His chest burned with pain, but the soreness was slowly working its way out as he forced himself along.

Within the next twenty paces, he came upon the remains of Jim Gant. The small man lay in a pool of blood, a huge semi-circle of tacky black cooling around him. Flies and beetles crawled in it and were already working his body in the morning warmth. The man's right arm had been neatly severed at the shoulder and his dead eyes stared into a cloudless sky. Kneeling, Vance reached down, avoiding the pool of gore, and he removed the 9mm pistol that was still holstered at the dead man's hip. He stood and held it in his right hand. It made him feel better, safer.

He looked across the savanna. No one was waiting for him. No one had fired a shot at him. Either the terror bird had frightened them off, or maybe it had killed them all. He strode through the tall grass, his legs becoming wet with the morning dew clinging to the blades. Something dark lay in the field to his right, perhaps twenty feet ahead. He paced up to it and looked down. It was Winston Grisham, the retired soldier who had been legally battling both Holcomb and the Berg Brothers over the fate of this wilderness. Immediately, he knew that a partnership had somehow been formed between his two foes.

He saw that Grisham was still breathing. Vance chambered a round and aimed the gun at the colonel's head. Where his attempted assassin was concerned, he was not going to be squeamish or indecisive. His finger tightened on the trigger.

"Drop the gun," the voice told him.

Holcomb looked up to see another man in camouflage fatigues standing in the grass no more than thirty feet away. The man was aiming a pistol at him, but he was not standing solidly and did not seem to be in the best of health. In fact, it looked as if he might pass out at any second. The man squinted and tried to look determined.

"You drop your pistol or I swear I'll blow your colonel's head off."

The soldier continued to weave unsteadily. His chest was bleeding profusely, blood soaking through the military issue fabric. He'd obviously not had the protection Holcomb had enjoyed when the terror bird had drop kicked him like a leather ball. In a second, the wounded man dropped his pistol and then went to his knees.

"That's a good little Fascist," Holcomb said. He knelt and found the pistol on Grisham's body. Taking it, he threw it as far toward the north as he could. The pistol landed somewhere out in the grasses with all of the other unfound weapons from years gone by. Taking a good look at the colonel's still form, Vance started toward the other wounded man and only stopped short when he encountered the man's pistol, which he tossed in the general direction of the other.

"Are your wounds terminal?" he asked the man. His injuries appeared to be very bad, and if the blood continued to flow he was not going to last very long.

"Screw you," the man muttered.

Holcomb kicked him in the ribs. Just as he was turning from the soldier who was lying limp and useless there in the grass, he heard yet another voice.

"Grief, but you've been a lot of trouble to kill." Watkins, rising up from the grass, had retrieved his rifle. The scope had been somewhat skewed, but he didn't need it at this range. He had every intention of sending Holcomb straight to Hell when a fearfully familiar sound came to him.

The nearby air was filled with a strange *fluttering,* again similar to the whirring of many insect wings. The Flock was suddenly there, appearing as by magic from the surrounding grasses. They readjusted the positioning of their striped and mottled feathers so that they no longer blended neatly with the savanna around them. Egg Father had left these three adults behind, to monitor the humans, to see what they did. *Act only if you feel threatened,* he had told them. They felt threatened.

The terror bird nearest the still unconscious Grisham made a sudden movement in the direction of the colonel. Watkins aimed as best he could and fired at it. The shot went slightly right and above where he had intended it to, but the bullet still struck the bird, passing through the fleshy muscle tissue along his left side. A small gout of blood showered out, and the bird, an adult female, quickly learned that *the histories were true.* Men could kill from a distance. She screamed this fact to the others, who all turned toward the armed man.

As the birds focused their attention on Watkins, Holcomb ran. He faced in the direction from which he had first come and he went, pumping his legs as fast and with as much energy as he could muster. Behind him, he heard the gun crack again, three times. The earth shuddered a bit under the tread of the huge animals. When Watkins screamed Holcomb did not turn to see what was going on, what they were doing. But he did hear a sound he never wanted to hear again. He supposed it was the sound of flesh being cut.

The pines swallowed him up, as behind he heard yet another volley of shots followed by a very short scream. He wondered if that had been the wounded man he'd kicked, or the awakening Grisham. Vance doubted he'd ever know as he once more began to run as fast as he could, realizing that it probably would not be enough. He pushed on, waiting for the sound of pursuit. The birds' tread actually shook the ground when they bore down on you. He'd know when they got close.

As he continued, he kept expecting to hear the approach of the huge birds. Fifty yards, a hundred. They still were not on him. At the place where the forest met the savanna he did not turn to see what was happening, but heard yet another explosion of firearms. This time it seemed to be a pair of weapons. But by then he was determined not to look back, not to stop running. Holcomb was tired, sore, and verging on clinical dehydration. He knew that even if nothing ran him down, he was still not going to make it very far without something to drink and a moment to rest.

He was tempted to slow down, and he recalled the sight of the Scarlet rogue bearing down on him, remembered how it felt when its foot—the toes splayed as wide as his chest—crashed down on him. Vance Holcomb ran faster and did not stop until he had reached the punctured ruin of his dome where he had left his backpack and roughly a gallon of fresh water.

Crawling into the dome he found his pack amid the wreckage of his equipment. He drank his fill and, recalling his previous mistake of remaining there too long, crawled back through the tunnel. He'd left his ATV only a few miles away. It was his last, best chance.

Jogging briskly, but conserving his strength, he went toward the place where he had stashed the tough little vehicle. Along the way, he chanced a glance back now and again. He saw nothing, heard nothing. Vance Holcomb seemed to be alone again.

CHAPTER
FORTY-THREE

The first sight that greeted them at the top of the sinkhole was what remained of a pair of men. They'd had guns, very good rifles in fact, but neither of them apparently had been able to get a shot off when they'd been attacked. Each of the men seemed to have been cut neatly in half. The sight was quite hideous, and both Riggs and Niccols wanted to get past them. It was only at Mary's insistence that they paused long enough to retrieve the pair of rifles.

"I think our guns are probably full of water and mud, anyway," she'd told Ron, who quickly dropped Crane's shotgun and shed the bag of shells at her feet. "Why didn't they shoot? Got any idea?"

"I can't imagine," Ron said. "The one we saw was certainly big enough to hit without much trouble." Ron shivered. "Damn. I didn't think they would be that *big*. Christ."

"What do you think's going to happen, now?" There was a definite rattle in Mary's lungs, now. The hours spent crouching in the water had done her bronchitis no good.

"I honestly couldn't tell you. I do know that this place will be shut down and probably by God fenced off as soon as word gets out." They pushed through the forest. Occasionally, they would spot an enormous three-toed track in the soft earth and one or the other would point it out as if making a great discovery.

"What's going to happen to that bitch, Kate?"

"If she's still around, which I doubt, I personally want to see to it that she's put away forever." Ron didn't want to tell Mary that Kate almost had him suspecting her of complicity in Dodd's murder. She might never forgive him if he told her.

"What the hell was she up to? I mean, who did all this?"

"I'm not sure," Ron admitted. "I've got my suspicions. But basically we need to be about as careful as we can be. In fact, I suspect we should avoid the Eyesore entirely and just get the hell out of here. Make for Salutations and forget about Holcomb and his compound. Best case, it's empty and there are only a few dead bodies. Worst case, someone's going to be waiting to pop us and add us to the list."

"Screw that," Mary said.

"My sentiments, too."

Ron stood there for a moment, just looking at Mary. Her own gaze was focused on the forest, as she searched for the likeliest route out of the stand of trees in which they stood. Her face was covered in grime, her hair tacked with sticks and leaves and dots of mud. But she had saved his life. She had put herself in danger, had stayed with him every step of the way. As if suddenly seeing the sun for the first time, Ron was hit with a rush of emotion he'd never really experienced. Suddenly Mary was the most important person in the world to him. He'd realized he had been such a fool.

Without saying anything, without asking for permission, Ron dropped the rifle and grasped Mary by the shoulder. He turned her to him and planted his lips firmly on hers. He kissed her long and hard, and his heart raced as he realized that she was returning the kiss with all of the passion he now felt flooding out of him. After a few seconds, he took his mouth from hers and looked into her face.

"Mary. I've been a damned fool," he told her. "I'm sorry I treated you the way that I did. Sometimes a man doesn't realize what he has. I've been an idiot."

"Well," Mary said, "that's what I've been trying to tell you for months." She bent and retrieved the rifle he'd dropped. "Learn to respect a weapon, son. We might need it."

"Yes," Ron said. "You're right. Let's get out of here."

Mary knew that by all rights she should have stopped caring for Ron when he'd rejected her. She knew his reasons. Not fear of commitment, not afraid that they'd moved too far, too fast. He'd been a snob. But she couldn't help herself. They'd had so many things in common, similar feelings and interests. And there had been the physical attraction. You couldn't help that, sometimes. And who the hell knew what love was, or how to control it? Mary certainly didn't. She had been stuck on Ron almost as soon as she'd met him, and she remained so.

There was a moment of silence as they plodded along; both were tired beyond words. Finally, Mary brought it up. "What about Billy? We going to check on him? He can't be far away. You never said . . ."

"Oh, yes. He's dead. No doubt about it." He recalled the feeling of the awful exit wound as he'd placed his hand on Billy's stomach.

"Christ."

Neither spoke for a while as they continued to walk, veering southward and away from Holcomb's buildings and going wide of the spot where Crane had been shot.

"Best thing we can do for him is get some help and come back," Mary said, echoing what Ron was feeling.

Before Ron could reply, the sound of a motor began to

come toward them. It grew until they felt the need to hide, concealing themselves behind a clump of Spanish bayonet. They soon recognized the sound of one of the ATVs they had seen in the Eyesore's garage. In a while, the stubby little machine appeared, and they could see that Vance Holcomb was astride it, guiding it skillfully through the forest at a respectable rate of speed. Even from the distance, they could clearly see that Holcomb was disheveled; his shirt was in tatters, open to the waist to reveal flesh a very nasty shade of black and blue.

"Think we should flag him down?" Mary asked.

"How?"

"Fire one of these guns in the air?"

"Unless I'm mistaken, he's the main target these guys were after. We were just in the way. I think that if we fired a shot he'd soil himself and find a few more rpms in that engine. I think we'd best just let him go."

"You're probably right," Mary said. And soon the gas vehicle roared past them and became a slight burr in the distance.

The sun rose in the sky, the heat began to peel the sweat from their skin. Slowly, they ticked off the yards, knowing they had miles to go.

CHAPTER
FORTY-FOUR

"Thank God for your eye," Grisham told Redmond. "I knew I was making a wise choice to add you to the team."

Redmond said nothing as the pair hit the Colonel's property boundary, moving quickly for two people who had been kicked in the guts by a creature who stood ten feet tall and weighed roughly one thousand pounds. They were jogging, in fact, Grisham scanning 180 degrees to the fore, while Redmond watched their backs. If Walks Backward had seen them, he would have approved.

"Damned good shooting back there, too, son."

At that, Redmond spoke up. "I didn't hit a one of them." He was thinking of the way they could alter their coloration, in a way in which they blended almost perfectly with their surrounding. He would almost have thought them capable of changing color as a chameleon does, until he realized that they had been moving their *feathers* to achieve the effect. As he'd admitted, he had been unable to strike a single one of the birds, although Watkins had slightly wounded one of them. It must have been that one good shot from Watkins that had let them understand what the gunshots meant.

"But you held them off, son. You frightened them away." Grisham moved with determination, but there was something like fear in his eyes as he went. And he was glad that Redmond could not see his face. He'd faced enemy fire in Vietnam and half a dozen other places the American taxpayers would never know of. But this was the first time he'd actually been frightened of anything. When he'd come to and seen those *things* moving toward him, he thought that was going to be the end for him. Being eaten was not something for which he could prepare.

"I couldn't save Watkins," Redmond blurted. "Or poor Joyner." There was a catch in Redmond's voice, and his own ruddy features went a shade darker at the memory of the huge things slashing and tearing at his two comrades. Watkins had exploded like a balloon overfilled with crimson dye.

"That's the kind of price we pay, son. We're all of us expendable." Now that it didn't look probable that he would end up that way, Grisham could speak of such things. He shuddered, though. They weren't home, yet.

Redmond said nothing at that. He only wanted to be out of this place. He only wanted them to find their way back to Grisham's house and to the safety of four well-built walls. Even the idea of a bellyful of good cooking was beginning to appeal to him. The whole venture had been a debacle, though he didn't know that he could lay the blame at Grisham's feet. Who knew those creatures could do the things they had seen them do? Who could have known?

"We can still salvage this operation," the Colonel suddenly said. He stepped through a broken section of barbed wire that had parted long ago, one of his *posted* signs hanging by a rusted nail from a cedar tree.

At that, Redmond actually tore his bloodshot gaze from their rear and he stared at his commanding officer. But he said nothing.

"We can still find Holcomb. I'm not going to let him get away with this."

"Sir. He's most likely in a very safe place by this time. We both heard the motor of his ATV."

"That was our only real mistake," Grisham blustered. "We should have incapacitated that machine. But I'm not going to let this get the best of me. I can still pull a victory out of this. We can still get the job done. Part of it, at least."

"Part of it, sir?" They were now on familiar territory. Within minutes they would find themselves at one of the outer pastures. The farmhouse would even be visible if they were where Redmond thought they were.

"Yes. Those animals. Those creatures. Now that we know what they can do, we'll be ready for them. I made a vow that we'd exterminate them. I'm a man of my word."

"But sir. We lost three very good men. Watkins and Joyner and Gant. They all have families, sir. Is it wise to go back out there? Take more men out there?"

"We don't have much time, boy." Grisham turned his head and glared at Redmond without slowing down. His own stride was growing as they neared sanctuary. He was gaining confidence and strength the closer they got to his home. "If Holcomb gets away and word gets out, I doubt that we'll have much more than twenty-four hours to kill these things."

"But, sir. I don't think we should . . ."

Grisham did not let Redmond finish. "You'll do as you're ordered, son. You took a blood oath when you joined this militia. You will *not* foul this up. Do you understand?" Grisham had stopped and turned to deliver this final bit.

Redmond stared into Grisham's mad face. "I understand, Colonel. I understand."

They broke through the line of young slash pines at the

edge of the pasture and in the morning sun they could see Grisham's farmhouse and barn off in the distance. The Colonel was all but jogging as he strode through the green grass dotted all about with mounds of cow manure. "We can still get something done," he said.

Redmond followed at a distance, and continued to glance back, to make sure that nothing appeared from the forest to kill them.

CHAPTER
FORTY-FIVE

His plan had worked well, the Scarlet rogue thought.

The presence of the humans had frightened off the main body of the Flock for a time. Initially, when he'd run amidst the humans and had taken them down, he had wondered why the Flock had always been so frightened of them. With only a little surprise, they were indeed easy to incapacitate or kill. In fact, they moved so slowly that they were easier to kill than anything that the Scarlet had encountered for such heavy creatures.

But the men that the Scarlet had left behind him had frightened the Egg Father and the others. Even though none of the men seemed to be even awake, the Flock had held back. The Scarlet knew this because the sounds of pursuit had died down and eventually vanished. That gave him enough time to find water. He had gone down to the banks of one of the streams that fed into the river that bordered the west side of the Flock's domain. On the other side of that river were the humans, in large numbers. He had thought briefly of swimming the distance and retreating there. None from the Flock would dared have followed him in that direction.

Still, something held him back. He had never crossed that barrier. Not because he could not swim it, because swimming was something he could do and do well. It was just *strange country* to him, and he didn't want to risk it. Not yet.

So he had drunk his fill, had run down and devoured a couple of armadillos. Revitalized, the Scarlet had done his best to cover his spoor, wading to the center of the stream, and swimming for a distance when it became too deep to walk. From that point he had come out and headed toward the huge rocky nest that belonged to *The Man Who Watches*. That area had been an old gathering space for the Flock before that man had invaded it. Once, they had used it as a wallow, playing in the pits of sand there and searching for the large tortoises that were so tasty. But the Flock had been forced to abandon it when the men had arrived, constructing the gigantic nests.

There were *always* men there, at this space they had once known as their own. The Scarlet was counting on more men being there. Men enough to dissuade the Flock from further pursuit. They were after him, to kill him. He was certain of that, now, having heard this strange new song coming up from the flock members who pursued him so rabidly. They were referring to him as some kind of enemy, as something to be eaten. And it had become his plan to make them break away from this chase and leave him alone, at least for a while. He needed time to plan, to organize his thoughts and decide what he should do.

As he had come upon the place, the Scarlet had sensed that something was not right. It was empty of sound, of movement, of activity of any kind. The men were not there. He could scent the thousands of strange smells, the alien stench that welled out from it. But of men there was nothing. And this was not good, for he had once again sensed the Flock on his trail.

Going right up to the structure, the Scarlet rogue had

called out a challenge to any man that might wait inside. Nothing came out. Only the odd light spilled from the place. He even made his imitation human calls. "Jesus," he said. "It killed me," he called. There were no humans to answer him.

His last chance was the place where the humans had built nest upon nest. Where they lived in numbers far outweighing those of the Flock. It was where the Scarlet had explored in the night, moving around the perimeter, slaying and eating the dogs. If that was where he must go, then he would. And just as he had decided to head there, the wind altered direction. There *were* humans nearby, in the realm of the Flock. The scents were coming from a point north, off in the depth of the oak forest, from near the deep sinkhole that had appeared in the face of the earth some years before. So the Scarlet rogue had moved off in that direction, leading the Flock on. They had obliged him by following.

Along the way, the Scarlet rogue had slowed his pace. He wanted to let them get closer. They would be right on his tail, and his own scent would fill their nostrils. He even began to urinate as he raced atop the forest loam, kicking up the dirt and leaving a powerful pungent mix of urine and hormonal scents overloading the unmatched olfactory senses of his pursuers. If they did not sense the humans until it was too late, that would serve his purposes well.

Soon, with the night ending, the Scarlet took a chance and peered back. Despite the fact that he wanted them to be close, he was surprised to see Egg Mother and Walks Backward less than four body lengths behind him. Walks Backward was in an impudent mood, he saw, the beta male's great brown crest lifted high as if he were leading the Flock. How great that one's hatred was. Putting on a burst of speed, he lengthened his stride and gained a bit of ground. He was coming upon the site of the sinkhole, and the humans were there. The scent of them came to him as he sprayed a last volley of urine mist into the faces of those who were at his tail.

Going wide of the great hole that gaped in the earth, the Scarlet almost fell to the slashing blows of the Egg Father who had come up on his left. The huge terror bird leaped toward his disobedient son, but his talons missed the mark and he was left to gather his speed and give chase again. The Scarlet knew that others would be waiting to make similar feints at his position, and he knew that he would not be able to last long now that they had caught up to him. He only had one chance, now.

And it came.

The rogue suddenly came upon the sinkhole. He rushed past the lip of it and peered down into it, seeing two humans who were lying partially submerged in the clear waters. It would not do him any good at all if this is all there was. He looked ahead and plunged on, and saw the others. There were not as many men as before, but this time the Flock was so close on his tail, and he had covered their scent so well that as he ran amidst the confused humans and left them behind, the Flock found themselves face to face with the men.

He ran, leaving the scene of complete confusion behind him. There was an urge in him to caw with laughter, and he did, despite the situation if his plan failed. Behind him the Flock found themselves revealed to men. This had not happened in a very long time. The terror birds, who could sense in others the urge to fight and kill, suddenly sensed that the humans were ready to inflict damage upon them. Egg Mother reacted first. She lashed out at the nearest human, cutting him down and ending his garbled screams.

The other men also began to yell, to begin to make the motions that the guardians of the Flock knew could mean death for anything on the other end of that motion. Walks Backward leaped to the right, toward a man sitting high in the branches of a great live oak. The gnarled limbs allowed him easy purchase and he all but raced up the side of the huge tree, using his short forearms to tear at the bark and add stability to his movements. Reaching up with his razored beak, he grasped the man by the thigh and pulled him down before he could aim his gun. Falling to earth trailing a hot stream of jetting blood, other adult birds were on him. Egg Father found the third man who was attempting to fire at a young male and pounded him to the ground, dismembering him quickly.

Walks Backward detected two other humans down in the sinkhole, but felt no threat from them. No terror bird went to seek them out with no order from the leaders. For a very confused instant, the Flock milled about the bloodied killing ground. None of them fed on what had been killed.

With a cry mixed with rage and confusion and *fear*, Egg Mother and Egg Father commanded the Flock to retreat, to end the chase for now. The Sun was rising; the rogue had left them behind and had utterly fooled them. Following the Parents, the Flock quickly sped back toward the interior of their domain, into the inviting places that had for so long protected them. *Away from here*, Egg Father called. *Back to safety*, Egg Mother reinforced. And each of the flock members did just so.

But for one.

As the Flock headed north and east, he turned. He turned on his track and moved south and west. Toward the Scarlet rogue. Damn the humans. Walks Backward would kill the fool.

CHAPTER
FORTY-SIX

"Well, I have to admit I had my doubts when I asked where you were taking us," Mary said, wheezing. They were moving down a trail with which Ron was familiar. He had walked it before.

"I told you I've been here," Ron said. "This is the path I took when I thought a python was killing the dogs in Salutations. That's the substation where you met me the other day." Riggs was pointing at the neat square of crushed red brick atop which the substation sat, the whole thing surrounded by chain link. It was a very familiar and reassuring sight. "You saw it from the other side. All we have to do is go about fifty more yards and we'll be out on the street at the edge of Salutations, USA."

"God bless Berg Brothers Studio," Mary shouted. Gripping her rifle a bit more loosely, she began to jog ahead of Ron.

Together, the pair trotted past the substation and moved beyond it. The sun was up and the full afternoon heat was bearing down on them. The couple looked to have been chewed up and spit out by a very large and very nasty critter. They were covered in mud and a thin sheen of sandy muck made up of forest detritus and human sweat. Where they weren't dirty, they were bloodied, a wealth of minor scratches, abrasions, and insect bites covering their exposed arms. No one was going to open a door for them, of that both were certain. They were either going to have to march into downtown Salutations or, more likely, await the arrival of a security detail. Probably the latter, from what they knew of the artificial town.

Coming out to the street, they were surprised to see a number of cars moving a bit more rapidly than the authorities in Salutations generally allowed. Standing there, staring at the caravan of speeding BMWs, Cadillacs, and Volvos they were surprised when a sedan pulled over to the shoulder of the road. An electric motor hummed as a tinted window quickly levered down. A familiar face appeared as Mr. Brill, he of the severed dog foot, leaned across the seat to address them.

"Hey! You guys must be chasing those giant birds."

Ron and Mary just stood and looked at one another.

Mr. Brill looked a bit bothered by their confusion.

"You *are* after those dino-birds or whatever the hell they are. *Aren't you?*" His reddish face was sweating, even in the interior of his air-conditioned Cadillac.

"Yes," Mary blurted. "We've been chasing them for *miles*."

"Well you sure as damned hell aren't going to catch them on foot. Damned things are fast." He swept his hand along to indicate just how quick they were. "Need a ride?"

"Hell, yes," Riggs told him. He reached for the door handle and jumped in beside the old man. "Sorry about the upholstery," he said as he smeared his way across the seat.

"Don't worry about it, son. Just get in and I'll take you in the general direction of where they were headed." Brill waited while Mary hopped in and made a similar mess of his back seat. And then he peeled away from the shoulder of the road and was soon doing a good sixty-five. His passengers seemed to wilt, luxuriating in the cool air flowing over and around them. There was a moment in which he actually heard them sigh in pleasure.

"What happened to your truck?" Brill asked.

"Huh? Oh. My truck. Left it back at Vance Holcomb's compound."

"Holcomb, huh? I thought that crazy jillionaire probably had something to do with this. Wonder where he found those things?" Tires squealed as he took a turn a bit too sharply. People pointed from big picture windows in big houses. Some braver citizens stood on front steps to watch.

"How many? How many of these birds did you see?" Mary asked.

"Saw two of them. A red one being chased by a brown one. The red one's bigger, but the brown one is doing all the chasing." He grunted, gripped the steering wheel and took another turn. "Those things are what ate my dog? Aren't they? Huh?"

"Well, probably."

"You told me it was a *snake*. Isn't that just *like* the government? Hide things. Cover them up." He took half a second to scowl at Ron.

"Truthfully, sir. We didn't know it was a giant bird at the time. I really did think it was a python. I swear. We only found out later what was going on." Ron had his left hand raised as if taking an oath; his right hand was gripped firmly around the rifle rather than resting on a Bible.

"What *is* going on, anyway? What *are* they? Where'd they *come* from? They look like *dinosaurs* for God's sake. I thought they were some kind of allosaurus or something until I saw the feathers." They were coming in close to downtown Salutations.

"Well, they're phorusrachids," Ron said. "Big predatory

ground dwelling birds that we thought had been extinct for a long time. Either a million years or fifteen thousand years depending on which paleontologist you talk to."

"They don't *look* extinct."

"Obviously not. And apparently they've been here all along. Living here on what was the military base and bombing range. Kind of protected by the base, strangely enough."

Brill slowed the car, his big hands gripping the wheel. His faced looked sober and very serious. He had slowed the auto to a more sedate thirty miles per hour, still over the posted limit. "I'll be damned," he said. "You know . . . it kind of makes sense." Then he turned and stared directly at Riggs. "What's going to happen?"

"What do you mean?" Ron said.

"With these things here. There must be more than two of them. Right?"

"I'd say so, although we only actually saw one. But you say you saw two. Where there's two, there's probably more, I'd say."

"Right. Right. So, what's going to happen to this place, now? Isn't this some job for the EPA, or some agency like that?"

"Department of the Interior, most likely," Ron told him. "Some branch of it, anyway."

"Right. So, what's going to happen to us? What's going to happen to *Salutations?*"

And if Ron had had any doubts as to what had been going on for the previous two days, they were gone. Mr. Brill was no dope. He turned in his seat and looked back at Mary who had leaned forward. They nodded at one another.

"I'd think," Mary told Mr. Brill, "that the media will

gather in vast numbers here. Other than that, I couldn't tell you. I reckon we'll all find out."

Suddenly, the old man braked the car. Ron, who had not been buckled in, slipped forward and slammed against the dash, making a big black mark there. Brill was going to have to pay some bucks to clean his car, unfortunately. "Look," the driver said, pointing.

In front of them, at the next intersection, at least thirty cars clogged the streets. They were parked everywhere and in every conceivable angle. Most of the people who'd brought them there were still inside, locked safely behind a shield of safety glass and whatever currently passed for auto steel. A few, perhaps foolhardy, souls had gotten out to stand outside their cars and watch. The only clear area was the intersection itself, now a roughly circular spot of black asphalt and pale concrete sidewalks and curbing. In the center of that hard-surfaced ring, something like the ulti-mate cockfight was going on. Walks Backward had finally caught up to the Scarlet rogue. One of them was going to go down.

Walks Backward had not obeyed the orders of the Egg Parents. For the first time in his life he had failed to follow their dictates. It wasn't that he thought that he could con-tinue to keep the Flock a secret from Man. That was done and over. The Scarlet had ultimately and completely seen to that. No, what he wanted, what he *needed* at this point was to satisfy his hatred. He wanted and needed to kill the Scarlet rogue. Nothing less than that could satisfy him.

And so he had left the path of retreat the others had made. It had been his job to scour that path, to close it off to pursuit to any who tracked them. He hoped that another had now taken up the name he had lived with for so long.

But beyond that he had no concern other than to catch and kill the rogue who had put him in this position and who had possibly doomed the Flock.

Initially, the Scarlet had not detected that he was being followed. That was good for Walks Backward. If possible, he wanted to attack from a position of complete surprise. The rogue had proven wilier and a bit wiser than any of them had supposed. In the warning oaths communicated by his Flock elders, he had detected some perverse pride in the confusion the Scarlet had brought on them. But that pride was canceled by the danger he had created for them by allowing Man to discover their presence. Initially the Flock had suspected that the one man, the one they called The Watcher, had seen them, but later they had decided that he had not actually spotted them and only suspected their presence. Now there was no doubt. Man knew of them.

For some miles Walks Backward had trailed the rogue. The larger bird had moved closer and closer to the new abode Man had placed at the edge of their domain. The other was going to get as close as possible and bed down there at that dangerous place. That much he supposed. It had been his intention to wait until a time when the Scarlet would rest; then he'd strike. This surprise, coupled with his experience of longer years, would enable him to achieve the kill. It was what he hoped.

Almost, his plan had worked. As he'd thought, the rogue had worked closer and closer to the place where humans made their huge nests. On the very edge of the forest, where it gave way to the great paths on which the humans moved and to the short, grassy spaces that surrounded their nests, the Scarlet had found a sheltered patch of shade where he had stopped. There, he had settled down and actually rested his great head on the forest floor. At that instant, still undetected, Walks Backward had struck.

The smaller bird had sprinted in, covering the fifty-yard distance between them. He'd been happy that he had been able to creep that close without being seen, but the wind had been with him and the Scarlet had not been able to gather his scent. With the rogue still trying to rise to a defense posture, Walks Backward had kicked with his left leg, rising into the air to deliver a single downward slash with his right talon. The blow had been a good one, claws meeting solidly along the rogue's left side, tearing away a good swatch of those red-tinged feathers and leaving a deep furrow with his sturdy middle claw.

After that, the battle had not been so easy. The Scarlet had found his footing and had risen quickly to full height. Even though his adversary was the second largest member of the Flock, the rogue was considerably taller and roughly one hundred pounds heavier. From a standing posture he could look down on the feathered crown of Walks Backward. This gave him an attack advantage based on leverage, and the added weight meant that each blow he delivered would connect with that much more force. Screaming a return challenge, the rogue joined the battle. He did not intend to lose, despite having suffered the first wound.

Lashing out with his own great claws, he was able to force his attacker to back away. After that, he lowered his head and charged, meaning to get in close and bite at the other's deep, fleshy chest. The muscles there were large and thick and vulnerable to attack. Jaws wide, he lunged in and came close, retreating with a beakful of earthtone feathers.

But Walks Backward had expected such a move and had intentionally left that part of himself open to a feint. Waiting until the last possible instant, he had backed away, then kicked upward as the rogue drew back with his meager reward of chest feathers. His upward traveling foot smashed into the younger bird's head, snapping it back and up in a powerful and disorienting blow. The Scarlet rogue was stunned and at a sudden and overpowering disadvantage. His body reeled drunkenly and it even looked as if he would go down.

However, as the elder terror bird lunged to slash again with his right claw, the Scarlet was able to turn. Moving quickly the rogue found his feet steady beneath him, churning the loam and sending himself away from immediate danger. In seconds he had picked up a considerable speed and was heading directly for one of the human homes. There was only a stand of small pines and a low wooden barrier separating their battle site from the human nest. The Scarlet rogue rushed through those green limbs and bounded easily over the barrier.

Walks Backward hesitated only for a second and then followed the object of his hatred. It was too late to play the old games any longer. With a scream, he was after the larger bird.

Immediately the dogs of the humans began to emerge from small dens and from the nests of humans, barking and yapping and sending up a clamor of alarm that was not unfamiliar to any member of the Flock. They had heard the sounds many times from the packs of feral dogs who sometimes tried to insinuate themselves into the birds' domain. With the two sprinting across the grazed grassy patches that surrounded the human nests, men began to emerge from those nests, to see the two creatures who were moving at great speed and in plain sight. Now, if there had been any doubt, a long and successful era was ended for the Flock. With renewed hatred Walks Backward did his best to reduce the lead the Scarlet rogue had produced with his quick retreat and great stride.

The terror birds raced on and on through Salutations USA. The puny humans emerged time and again from their homes, chattering and screaming, chattering and screaming.

Ron got out of the car first. Gripping the rifle in his sweaty, bruised hands, he moved as fast as he was able past the parked vehicles and the people who were milling this way and that to get a good look at the battling monsters.

"What are they?" some woman asked him.

"They look like *dinosaurs*," someone answered.

"They ain't dinosaurs. All the dinosaurs are dead," a learned individual informed both.

"They're big birds," a young, blonde woman said, correcting them all.

"But birds ain't got *arms*," the dinosaur expert reminded her. And then, seeing Ron and Mary with the rifles they'd taken from the dead men, he addressed them. "You guys gone kill them animals, now?"

Shoving past the guy, Riggs and Niccols got in as close as they were able. Just on the other side of a ring of Caddys and Beemers the two terror birds were going at one another beak and claw. The street was covered in feathers torn free from flesh and spattered with bright red dollops of blood. Most of the blood and feathers seemed to be coming from the reddish bird, even though it was quite the larger of the two. The friends just stood in place for a moment, watching the fight and marveling at the wonderful creatures.

"How tall do you think the red one is, Mary?"

"Ten feet. Easy. Must weigh seven, eight hundred pounds, I'd say." The pavement vibrated for her as the thing came down from a leap and a slashing blow, as if to punctuate Niccols' estimation.

"God. They're beautiful," Ron said. He stared up at the things who towered over the small human beings watching the death fight. While he watched, the smaller, brown one got in a tremendous kick that sprayed blood over the hood of a car. This brought a cheer from some of the people watching.

"When you gonna *shoot* them?" the dinosaur genius screamed in Ron's ear from about six inches away. He'd not even heard the guy approach over the screeching of the birds.

"We're not going to shoot them, you jerk. Not if we can help it," Mary yelled at the expert, shoving the flabby man away. "Now get out of here before you get hurt."

At that point, a car belonging to the Salutations Security outfit came to a halt beyond the traffic jam, the sting of burning rubber gliding from opposite side of the intersection. Three men climbed out, rather in a hurry. All of them were armed with good hunting rifles. Ron and Mary watched in some horror as the three struggled in close to the two birds and took up positions that would enable them to get off clear shots. "Get out of the line of *fire*," one was screaming at the idiots on Ron's side of the battle.

"Damnation," Mary said. "They're going to kill them."

"They wouldn't," Ron stuttered.

"They by God would, too. They'll gun them both down right here and right now. You wait and see. And there's not a thing we can do about it, unless you want to be guilty of murdering those men."

Riggs watched, his throat tensing, his heart pounding as the security guards waited for the people to move away from out of their gunsights. They were slowly drawing beads on the gigantic animals who were still biting and clawing and slashing at one another. Two monsters who should have become extinct a long time ago were about to meet a delayed end. Ron could almost feel the fingers squeezing on those triggers. He waited to hear the reports.

"Stop," someone screamed. "Don't shoot them."

Ron looked across. It was Vance Holcomb. The rich man was literally climbing over cars to get to the three security guards. They all turned their heads slightly to see who was coming toward them, but none took their barrels away from the intended targets. Through it all, the two terror birds continued their battle, their screeching cries becoming more intense and louder as the fight became bloodier and more desperate. It was becoming obvious to everyone that the reddish one was losing.

"Get back, mister," one of the guards said to Holcomb as he came in close. But Holcomb did not get back. He dove right in and put his hand on the barrel of that rifle and forced it down.

"You shoot that bird and so help me God I'll kill you all," he growled at the trio. There was desperation and complete hatred in his dirty, tired, mad face.

The three private cops exchanged glances and the two who could once more aimed their guns.

"Wait a minute," Holcomb told them. "Let me try this, first." And, reaching into the nylon pouch around his waist, he drew out the dart pistol, the single item he had taken with him from his now destroyed lab. "It's loaded with tranq darts," he told them. "Let me try this first. That's all I ask."

The hired guns glanced again into one another's eyes, but said nothing.

"These animals are unique," Holcomb said. "You kill them and it's going to be bad news for you." This did not seem to melt their resolve. "And it'll be *big* bad news for

Berg Brothers," he added. They lowered their guns.

"Take your best shot," one of the guards said.

The Scarlet rogue and Walks Backward were still at it. Each seemed to be trying to avoid the other's slashing beak. And with good reason, for a claw slash was much less likely to deliver a killing wound that those razor-edged jaws. Up and down the two birds went, bouncing on massively muscled legs, the asphalt tremoring each time one came down.

Holcomb stepped up, drew a bead. The birds moved. First one was in his sights, then the other. Which one should he hit? The brown one was winning. If he hit the brown one, it was in the best shape to switch its attack to the people around it. But what if the brown one went down? The red bird might be desperate and also turn its rage on the people. He had already seen what the red one had done to Grisham's men. Making his decision, he aimed and fired. There was a quick report and the dart flew true, striking its intended target.

Both birds were aware of the short, quick explosion of sound.

Walks Backward felt a sudden, sharp pain in his side. It was just a prick. Like the times he had been stung by hornets—it was nothing serious. But almost immediately his legs felt weak and there seemed to be a cool numbness running through his muscles. He buckled and went down, seeing the great claws of the Scarlet rogue waiting just beyond his head, which now lay prone against the hard earth. With one eye he could see his adversary standing over him, and there was nothing he could do.

For a held breath, the Scarlet rogue realized something was wrong with his enemy. Walks Backward shuddered where he lay and he could not even kick out in defense. The rogue stood and peered in amazement. Death from a distance, just as the histories had said.

The Scarlet turned his head back, and he saw the human standing there. It was *The Man Who Watches,* and in his grasp was one of the things humans sometimes held. Other humans were standing with him, similarly armed. He drew his huge legs beneath him in a sudden moment of desperation and fear. Screaming one of the human sounds at them, he sprang forward, away from the man who had felled Walks Backward.

Ron and Mary and the dinosaur expert all ducked as the gigantic terror bird jumped and sailed over them in a long, fluid leap. It landed beyond them, impacting on the hood of a Caddy and leaving a cratered dimple there before it leaped again. In a second it had gained the yard beyond the car and it was sprinting, down the street, headed for the forest that beckoned down the way.

Looking toward Holcomb, Ron saw one of the security guards trying to draw a bead on the retreating bird. But even if there had been no one in his line of sight, it would have done him no good. For once again Holcomb was there to force the barrel toward the ground. Holcomb and the guard glared at one another.

And soon the bird was gone.

For a time, there was almost complete silence. Then, tentatively, first Holcomb, and then Ron and Mary crept up to the still form of the giant bird lying upon the dark pavement. And finally, the crowd held at bay by the guards and the others who were now arriving to back them up, the people began to mutter.

"Did you hear it?"

"I didn't imagine it."

"It talked. It *said* something."

"Did you hear what it *said?*"

CHAPTER
FORTY-SEVEN

Irons sat in his office atop the Berg Brothers tower in downtown Orlando. He was calm. He was cool. The news was pouring into him by the second. His fax machines whirred constantly and his e-mail was logjammed and his other lines rang incessantly.

But he was cool.

He had picked up the phone and he had made a phone call. One was all it would take. Now he would just have to wait. He sighed and buzzed his secretary.

A day later.

Davis Cauthen was there. He sat in Grisham's office, the two of them with Cauthen's own assistant, a willowy man named Morgan, and Redmond was there. They had things to talk about before Grisham went out once again to wipe out those damned birds.

"It's too late for this kind of action, Winston," Cauthen told him. "The word's out. Too many people *saw* them. The government is already down here like white on rice, and you know it. There's nothing you can *do,* now."

Colonel Grisham sat and steamed. His face was pale with rage. "Well, I'm not taking the fall for this bull. My men were supposed to clean Holcomb's place, mop it up, leave *nothing.* But those damned birds took my men *out.* All of them." He pinched the bridge of his nose and shook his military-cut head in disbelief.

"They're going to be here to question you, soon, Winston. And there are things you're going to have to say. You're going to have to take some of the heat for this. You know that." Senator Cauthen looked grimly at his old friend. His expression was not without some pity.

"No way. I'm not taking any heat for this. I have the proof of who ordered this action, how I was bribed and entrapped into it. And I'm going to cough it all up to the media. I won't play their stinking games. Do you *hear* me?" He smashed his hard fists down on the desk to punctuate his threat.

"I'm sorry you feel that way, Win. You don't really mean it, do you?"

"You're damned right I mean it. I'm not playing any games with these Yankee assholes. They don't know who I am or what I am. They know nothing of the things we deal with on a daily basis: our word, and the loyalty of our fellows. I've got the proposal they offered me, and I have the information they already had concerning the existence of these damned *monsters*."

"That's your final word then," Cauthen said.

"It is. You can take that back to them. We'll see how this ends up. You have my word on it. And I have my men. Men like Redmond here, who will always stand up for me."

"Well, then." Cauthen cleared his throat.

At that signal, Cauthen's assistant and Redmond were on Grisham in a flash. The younger men each rushed forward and held him down. The old colonel stared in complete shock at the two, then at his old friend. "What? What's the meaning, Davis? What are you do—"

But he never finished the question. For Cauthen produced and had jammed the barrel of a .44 magnum into Grisham's opened mouth and pulled the trigger. All three men were spattered with blood and tissue as the bullet emerged from the top of the colonel's skull and lodged in one of the old books on a shelf just behind his head.

"What happened here, Redmond?" Cauthen asked as he straightened.

"We *tried* to stop him. That's why he called you down here. To help him out of the jam he'd gotten himself into. He ordered the attack on Holcomb's compound, to try to get rid of the commie eco-freak. And while you were sitting here trying to talk him into turning himself in, he blew his brains out. We tried to stop him, but it was just no good. He was a determined man."

Wiping the pistol clean of his prints, the senator placed it in the hand of his old friend. "Very good, son. I'm sure you'll find your life enriched by your testimony. You keep mind of that each time you buy something nice for your kids or that new house for your wife."

"Don't give it another thought, sir."

No one did.

In Irons' office, a special line rang for him. Only three people had that number, and he *always* picked it up. On the other end a familiar voice spoke to him.

"It's taken care of," the voice said. "Grisham ordered it alone."

"Thanks for the news," Irons said. And he hung up.

CHAPTER
FORTY-EIGHT

Looking back on it, Ron had to be amused.

After the brown one went down and the red one ran off, the place had almost become the media-driven madhouse Mary had predicted. As if what had happened already had not been bad enough.

The first thing that happened was that Holcomb seemed to take command, despite the fact that most of the officials who showed up were employed by a company that thought of him as an implacable foe. It was rather funny, or would have been in a world in which true justice exits. A large truck with a large cage was needed, Holcomb had informed the security boys. And somehow, some way, just such a contraption was located. And before Big Bird woke up. It was all so comforting to see the truck arrive and the bird be locked safely behind iron bars just before it began to stir.

And that's when Holcomb noticed Ron and Mary. *Really* noticed them.

"What are you doing with those guns?" he asked, pointing at the rifles with the very fancy nightscopes mounted on.

Ron and Mary stammered for a bit, the hired cops looking upon them with suspicion now that the resident jillionaire had singled them out for questioning. Their cop brows went up in what amounted to curiosity behind their thick skulls. What came out of Ron and Mary was, basically, "We got them from dead guys." They were quickly disarmed and handcuffed.

But they were not formally arrested until the real police arrived from the county seat.

From there, things got interesting and it was only after long bouts of questioning and the hiring of lawyers and the arrival of further representation from Fish & Wildlife that first Ron, and then Mary were released. After a few days their story was finally believed and authorities took them at their word that they were not involved in the killings that had taken place at Holcomb's compound. It was roughly around the time that Holcomb appeared on their behalf with testimony from a witness to corroborate their tale.

"Kate Kwitney was there. She saw the whole sordid event unfold," Holcomb had told them. And sure enough, the wounded young woman had told her tale from her hospital bed. Her own story was pretty amazing, too, Ron and Mary thought. *The militia madmen had left the lady for dead,* and only when Holcomb had arrived with help was she discovered unconscious in the lab where she and her murdered coworkers had often worked.

In the days thereafter, Ron and Mary tried to convince everyone who would listen that Kate had provided the killers with aid, had even gunned down Adam Levin. But she said it had been an unfortunate accident; that she was aiming for one of the killers she saw in the forest. She would never touch a gun again as long as she lived, she pouted to one and all.

The newspapers and the video magazines had a field day with it. Grisham, extremist nut that he was, took the fall for everything. But Ron and Mary knew better. Not that the information meant anything. They had talked it over and had decided not to rock the boat. It wouldn't do either of them any good, and might even get them sued into oblivion, the only fate they knew of worse than death.

So they kept their mouths shut. "Sure," Mary had told the cops. "Come to think of it, I think maybe she *was* aiming at someone past Levin."

Case closed.

A week after things began to calm down, Ron was at Mary's for dinner. It was the first chance they'd had to really be alone together. They had sat and eaten Mary's good cooking. All kinds of offers for her exclusive interview were pouring in, and people were tossing very attractive money offers for the print rights to the story of her adventures in the land of the dino-birds. Several news shows were falling over themselves for exclusive rights to interview the quite photogenic young woman. *Playboy* had even sent an offer for a pictorial. She and Ron had laughed over it, and Mary was happy to note that the offer seemed to bother Ron more than a little.

For a while, Ron and Mary made small talk and tried to avoid the matter they were dancing around. "What's this about you signing on the register at the Seminole Nation, Ron?" Mary asked. "Why now?"

"I don't know," Ron said. He paused and thought about it, wondered whether he would tell anyone. "To tell you the truth, I still don't feel completely comfortable with it. But that's part of why I went ahead and did it. I've felt too uncomfortable about who—and what—I am for too long. And maybe I did it because of Billy Crane. And because of you. Just got me thinking, I guess."

And that seemed to weaken the barriers that Ron had erected between himself and his feelings for Mary. Some of the tension vanished.

"What about you, Ron? They *must* be calling you, too. The people with the money for your story, I mean," Mary said.

He looked into her pretty face, her black hair almost glowing like polished onyx. "Nah. I mean, I've had some offers, but not so much money that it would make a difference to me."

Mary looked at Ron, disbelief in her eyes.

"No. It's true. Really," he said.

"Well, you've obviously got the wrong agent," she told him.

"Agent? You're kidding."

"Do I have to do *everything* for you? I'll give you the phone number later."

With the dinner done and the dishes cleared away, they retreated to Mary's modest den to watch some television. Mary put a videotape in her player. "I wanted to make sure you saw this," she said. It was one of the recent fluff news pieces with Michael Irons' and Vance Holcomb's smiling faces showing as the two sat shoulder to shoulder at a press conference to announce the news.

"Berg Brothers has *always* been interested in preserving the natural world," Irons said through his shark's grin. "That's why Salutations USA was *already* a model of eco-sensitive development. But now, with the discovery of this priceless treasure of the existence of *Titanis walleri* living in our world, and *here*, why Berg Brothers could not stand idly by."

Holcomb chimed in on cue. "And that's why Berg Brothers, working with Holcomb Industries, is cooperating to lock up over four hundred thousand acres of pristine forest and lowland habitat as a wilderness to be administered by the Department of the Interior, with Holcomb and

Berg Brothers footing the bill for additional research. The studio will also, I'm happy to say, be sponsoring the redevelopment of Salutations USA as a combination educational center with continuing growth as a model of ecologically sensitive residential areas and entertainment complexes."

There was footage of the *Titanis* bird Holcomb had tranq'd being released at the edge of the forest. As the animal dashed from its cage, vanishing into the green, an appropriate selection of rather moving and dramatic music played in the background.

"What's going on with those birds, Ron? Are you hearing anything at work?" Mary asked, watching the footage of the bird dashing for freedom.

"I've heard a little. I talked to one of the big predator guys who came down from Alaska. He's been working with grizzlies for five years. I guess they figured he'd know *something* about how a *Titanis* might think. At any rate, he says that what they have been able to see is that the flock seems to be functioning as a unit. Except for the red one, the big one. He's off on his own, now. Has a couple of others with him. They say he's got two females, may be forming his own flock. Who knows?"

"Do you think they'll make it? I mean, now that Man knows about them? Now that we'll be messing around in their wilderness and tampering with them?"

"I don't think I even want to guess, Mary. Look. They've survived there for this long. And, if we're very careful and don't get in their ways and don't intrude . . . well, I'd like to believe that they will continue to thrive."

"Let's hope so," she said as she reached for the remote and shut the television off. "Can you believe that bullcrap with Holcomb, though? Berg Brothers tried to have him killed, and he *knows* it. How can he sit there with them like that?"

Ron sighed and slumped in the midst of the big couch. "Hell, I don't know. Maybe he's getting a vicious thrill out of them having to actually help him see his vision become a reality." He sighed again. "Damn."

Mary slid up close to Ron. She put her hand in his and motioned him to her. Ron was only too happy to cooperate and he soon had his arms around her, feeling her muscular form in his grasp. Their faces met, each breathing in the good scent of one another. They kissed, and kissed, kissed again. Ron was wondering how he had ever thought Mary had been anything less than the one for him.

After a moment, Mary disengaged and put her lips close to Ron's ear. "Beats smooching on that deceitful bitch, doesn't it?"

"Damn straight," he said.

Mary was laughing at him, her face pretty, her teeth showing brightly. She was beautiful to Ron.

"I've been such a fool," he told her. "I was afraid of falling in love with you. Of even admitting that I had fallen in love with you. A part of me—the part of me who's a fool—kept saying we didn't belong together. And . . . I can't explain it, and I know it doesn't make sense . . . but I didn't want to think of having a family with you. I kept telling myself we were too different. The fact is, we're so much alike. I know you must be sick of hearing me say it, but I'm sorry."

"It's ugly. That was self-loathing. I've seen it before, in others. But, I'm stuck on you, so I have to forgive you, don't I?"

They looked at one another, their eyes full of desire and growing love. Ron moved toward Mary again, to embrace her for another round of kissing that he hoped would lead them to the bedroom. But before they could begin, Mary pushed him away.

"Um." Mary cleared her throat. "I don't know if I should mention this, and I don't think you've heard, since one of the reporters I've been working with told me . . ." she trailed off.

"What?" Ron sat straight and looked at his host. "What is it?"

"That number, Kate Kwitney."

"What about her?" He blinked.

"She's going to be chief administrator at Holcomb's research center. Seems she knows more about these damned birds than anyone but Holcomb. So she's eminently qualified."

Ron covered his face. "God. Give me a break."

Mary reached over and gave him a playful punch in the shoulder. "Well, don't look too depressed," she said. "Look what came out today. Have you seen it, yet?" Mary reached beside the couch and produced a newspaper. Unfolding it, the paper rattling loudly, she presented it to Ron. "Ain't it a gas?"

Ron looked while Mary began to chuckle.

It was the *National Inquirer*. The front page was a grainy photo of the head of a *Titanis walleri*. *GIANT DINO-BIRD LIVES*, it said. *UTTERS THE NAME OF JESUS*.

Along with Mary, Ron found himself laughing.

"Now, then," Mary said. "Where were we?"

ABOUT THE AUTHOR

James Robert Smith lives with his wife, son, and two requisite cats near Charlotte, North Carolina. When he is not working for the United States Postal Service he can be found writing new stories or novels, or backpacking in various wilderness areas in the southern Appalachian high country.

He has made more than fifty short-story sales, and has had his comic scripts published by Marvel Comics, Kitchen Sink, Spyderbabies Grafix, and others. He was the coeditor of the Arkham House anthology *Evermore*. *The Flock* is his first novel.

To learn more, visit http://jamesrobertsmith.net/.